THE TIME OF
THE STRIPES

Amanda Bridgeman

Centralis Entertainment

Copyright

The Time of the Stripes

EPUB format: 9780995425972

Print format: 9780995425989

Cover design by Damonza

Edited by Stephanie Smith

Amanda is a Tin Duck Award winner, an Aurealis and Ditmar Awards finalist and author of several science fiction novels. Her works include the best-selling military SF/space opera AURORA series (previously published by Momentum Books/Pan Macmillan Australia), alien contact drama THE TIME OF THE STRIPES, and sci-fi crime thriller THE SUBJUGATE (published by Angry Robot Books, UK) which has been optioned for TV by an Oscar and Golden Globe nominated production company.

Born in the seaside/country town of Geraldton, Western Australia, she moved to Perth (Western Australia) to study film & television/creative writing at Murdoch University, earning her a BA in Communication Studies. Perth has been her home ever since, aside from a nineteen-month stint in London (England) where she dabbled in Film & TV 'Extra' work.

She was a finalist in the Universal AU/Screenwest Pitch competition (2019) and a finalist in the AACTA Regional Landscapes Pitch in partnership with Screenworks Pitch (2020).

She is a versatile writer who enjoys working across different genres and creative formats, be it novels, screenplays, short stories, etc, and creating both original and tie-in work.

More novels are on the way! Keep up to date with new releases here:

http://amandabridgeman.com.au/signup/

Also by Amanda Bridgeman

The Aurora Series:

#1 Aurora: Darwin

#2 Aurora: Pegasus

#3 Aurora: Meridian

#4 Aurora: Centralis

#5 Aurora: Eden

#6 Aurora: Decima

#7 Aurora: Aurizun

8# Aurora: Atlas

Aurora Box Set #1 (Books 1-4)

The Salvation Series:

#1 The Subjugate

#2 The Sensation

Pandemic Series (based on the popular boardgame):

#1 Pandemic: Patient Zero

To find out more, visit Amanda's website:

amandabridgeman.com.au

If you enjoy reading **The Time of The Stripes**, Amanda would appreciate if you could leave a rating or review wherever you can. It means a lot and really helps with making this book visible to others.

This book is set in an entirely fictional town, but it is perhaps a place far too real in the lives of many people throughout the globe.

Day Zero

Abbie Randell watched the strange patch of haze dancing in the distance. It seemed to float across the blue beyond, shifting and morphing, as though blown about by the wind on high. She rubbed her tired eyes and turned them toward the smokestacks of the Clivecorp plant on the outskirts of town. Gray plumes wafted upward from the tall cylinders, leaving a trail that eventually thinned and vaporized into the blue. She looked back to the unusual patch of haze, but it, too, had now vanished. She stared at the sky for a moment, wondering just how much of the air she breathed was fresh, and how much came from the plant's old smokestacks. It was a hot topic in the mouths of the townsfolk of late.

She yawned and stretched her body, reaching up toward the sun. It was an unusually warm start to autumn, which made it worth her while to be up this early. She put on her father's baseball cap and tugged her long, dark ponytail through the gap at the back. Up studying the night before, she'd been running late this morning and had accidentally grabbed his. But he wouldn't need it today; he had a big job interview this morning. She smiled and crossed her fingers for him. He'd been out of work for a while and really needed this job. The whole family did.

She reached into her bag, which lay on the grass by her towel, and pulled out a clipboard. She had two classes to teach today and first up were the toddlers. She checked her watch, then looked at the entrance of the Victoryville Aquatic Center. People were starting to arrive.

"Morning," Josh smiled, as he walked past toward the lifeguard chair.

"Morning," she smiled back. She'd officially met him yesterday in the VAC's cafe. Not only was he the new lifeguard, but he was also her new neighbor, having moved in across the street with his family a couple of weeks ago.

Candy, the other lifeguard on duty, a tall and slender blond, slowly walked past, saying quietly: "The view has suddenly improved around here, hasn't it?" Abbie glanced at her, amused. Turning back to the VAC's entrance she saw Deputy Cann's green SUV pull up and his wife Claire getting out. Abbie moved toward them, knowing that Claire would need a hand wrangling their two-year-old daughter and baby son.

"Morning!" Abbie greeted them.

"Morning, Abbie," Deputy Cann threw her a wave and a smile from the driver's seat, pulling his sunglasses up to sit atop his short dark hair.

"Morning," Claire beamed, as she unhooked Mickey's bassinet and handed it to Abbie. "Thank you."

"No problem," Abbie said, smiling down at the sleeping baby.

"I hear your father's team made it into the finals," the deputy said.

"Sure did," Abbie grinned. "They're going for back-to-back championships."

"Well, if they win, I'd say your father's a shoo-in for local

Little League Coach of the Year again."

"Fingers crossed," she said. "So today's the big Bateson Dermacell opening, right?"

"Yeah," he replied, "I'm heading into the station now."

"I heard talk of people protesting Clivecorp's involvement. You think there'll be any trouble?" she asked.

"Nah." The deputy shook his head. "I'm sure it'll be fine. The chief and I will be there anyhow."

"I hope it's peaceful," Claire said, unhooking her daughter's seat belt. "I think the research these Bateson Dermacell guys are doing is important. We need to know what the pollution is doing to us, and if they're willing to donate the lab to the schools when they're done, then who can complain? Let them study us."

Abbie nodded in agreement as Claire helped her daughter out of the car. Abbie smiled at the little girl's cute brown pigtails and green polka dot swimsuit. "Hi, Miss Lena! Are you ready for your swimming lesson today?"

Lena gave a big grin and nodded.

"You have fun, honey!" Deputy Cann said to his little girl, as he pulled his sunglasses back down. "I'll see you this afternoon, alright?"

"Say 'bye to daddy," Claire motioned for Lena to wave. Lena raised her chubby little arm and flung it about in the air, and they watched as Deputy Cann departed.

Abbie looked back at Lena and saw the girl's eyes were no longer on her father as he drove away, but instead were looking up into the sky.

"Sparkles!" Lena said, pointing into the air.

Both Abbie and Claire searched to see what Lena was pointing at.

"Sparkles? I can't see anything, honey," Claire said, holding her hand up to shade her eyes.

"Sparkles, momma!" Lena said again, grinning and pointing.

Claire lowered her hand and shrugged at Abbie as she took Mickey's bassinet. "Maybe you just saw a plane catching the sunlight, honey," she said to her daughter.

Abbie looked into the sky again, searching for the "sparkles" Lena had seen, wondering if it was the strange patch of haze she'd seen earlier. For a moment, she thought she saw something shifting across the blue, like a heat mirage or smoke. She blinked her tired eyes again to clear her vision, but whatever she thought she saw was gone. There was nothing but clear blue sky.

"Must just be this strange heat," she said to Claire, then turned back to Lena again. "What do you say, Lena, shall we get into the pool and cool down?"

Deputy Leo Cann entered the Victoryville police station and saw Chief Blackstone leaning on the front counter, engrossed in the morning's newspaper, mug of coffee beside him. Leo smiled to himself. The chief was old school, always saying how he couldn't stand reading things on cell phone screens. He looked up from the newspaper, smoothing down the thick, graying mustache that sat upon his dark-brown skin.

"Morning, Leo," he said in his deep, laid-back drawl.

"Morning, Earl."

"Grab yourself a coffee, then we'll make our way down."

"Sure thing." Leo moved over to grab himself a cup. "JT and Figgs already down there?"

"JT's over at the Clivecorp plant, keeping an eye on things, and Figgs is patrolling the area between there and the Bateson

Dermacell office," Blackstone answered, standing upright and folding the paper. "The other posts are on standby, but I don't think we'll need them. Josie's just gone off shift and Louise is over at Mrs. Morcombe's responding to a claim of theft."

"What is it this time?" Leo asked, amused, as he leaned back on the counter and sipped his coffee.

"Her cat."

"Her cat?" Leo nearly spat his coffee out. Normally, Mrs. Morcombe complained about stolen newspapers and pot plants.

"Mm-hmm," the chief nodded. "It didn't turn up for breakfast and apparently it *always* turns up for breakfast."

"Who would steal a cat?"

"If I was a betting man, I'd say it's under the tyres of some long-haul over on the highway," he said reaching for his Stetson. "Anyway, Louise will come back and man the fort while we manage the ceremony."

Leo nodded, taking another sip of his coffee. "How many are we expecting at the opening, you think?"

"A couple hundred maybe. The bigger the crowd, the happier the mayor will be."

Leo chuckled. "He does love to hold the attention of a crowd and tell everyone how good he is."

"I'll get the patrol car and meet you 'round front," Blackstone said suppressing a smile, then disappeared through a side door.

Chief Earl Blackstone pulled the patrol vehicle up in front of the new Bateson Dermacell office. Located just outside the town's center on the main road, it was a modest one-story building, though its white paneled walls and black-tinted windows gave it an expensive look. New, sleek, and years younger than many of the buildings nearby, it seemed to sparkle like a diamond in the rough: a hint of modernity among the years of faded history that surrounded it.

Blackstone and Leo exited their vehicle and glanced around. As they did, a black Lincoln, freshly washed and shined, pulled into the parking lot alongside theirs. It was the mayor.

"Go check the stage area 'round back," Blackstone ordered his deputy. "Check for possible entry points protestors could use." Leo gave a nod and disappeared around the side of the building.

Blackstone watched and waited as the mayor, Michael Russo, and his partner, Nicola, exited their vehicle.

"Chief!" Russo greeted him. "Lovely day for it."

Blackstone gave a nod and glanced up at the sky. "Indeed. Certainly a nice warm day ahead of us."

"Yes. It's a lovely day and a great step forward for the town of Victoryville," Russo grinned, adjusting his rimless glasses with one hand, while placing his other around Nicola's back. An ex-model from Miami, Nicola was normally half a head taller than Russo, but in heels, like she was today, she was a full head taller.

"It is," Blackstone agreed, tucking his thumbs into his belt.

"Are there any updates on the chance of protests?" Russo asked.

"Nope. I don't think there'll be any trouble."

"Word is, a reporter from New York is going to be here today?"

"Yeah, I heard that too."

"Well, if these protestors show they'd better not embarrass me or the folks from Bateson Dermacell in front of this reporter. Or Clivecorp! Not only are Clivecorp the major benefactors of this lab, but the jobs they provide at the plant help keep food on this town's table. The people better remember that."

"I'm sure they do," Blackstone nodded, although he personally thought the skepticism about Clivecorp's involvement was valid. A company previously fined for pollution suddenly investing in a research project into the effects of pollution? Some said it was merely a PR exercise. Some claimed it was a means of controlling the information released. "People in town don't have a problem with Bateson Dermacell or what they're doing," Blackstone said. "If anyone's going to protest they're likely to do it out at the Clivecorp plant not here."

"Well, if they turn up, just keep an eye on them," Russo said. "And keep them away from that reporter." The mayor straightened his suit jacket then turned to his partner. "How do I look?"

Nicola straightened his tie and gave a beaming smile. "Like a winner."

He smiled at her, threw Blackstone a glance, then ushered Nicola forward into the building.

Dr. Lysart Pellan stood alone in Lab-One of the brand new Bateson Dermacell project office, taking one last look at his new home before it became a hive of activity. He knew why he was here, why they'd handed him the reins to run things. They were trying to slowly pull him back in. He was one of their best scientists and they wanted him back working at full capacity, winning accolades and bringing in funding. But he'd been there and done that, and it had cost him his marriage. It wasn't him any more. Call it a midlife crisis, but he'd had to reassess things, and he realized there was more to life than working yourself to the bone. He loved being a scientist and working in the lab, but he didn't want all the other stuff. Not any more. The only reason he'd accepted this post was to get him out of Washington for a while. It gave him a chance to work away from the eyes of the board, and just do his own thing. Do what he loved to do.

The laboratory in which he stood was of moderate size, with four workstations set around the edges of the room, each with covered consoles and overhead shelves stacked with the necessary items they would require for their studies. Adjoining it, and visible through a large window in the shared wall, was Lab-Two. Although it was smaller, Lab-Two contained a Class II-A2 Biological Safety Cabinet with which they could examine the biological samples collected from the local population. For the parameters of this new project, the resources were quite adequate: the building and equipment was brand new, and they'd given him a team of seven to carry out the research over a two year period. It was their way of wooing him back he was sure of it.

As he stood looking into Lab-Two, he caught his reflection in the glass. He straightened the jacket of his dark suit, adjusted his tie, then glanced around again. Whether they were trying to woo him or not, the fact was, this was exactly what he wanted right now. To be left alone with science.

He moved over to the microscope beside the console he'd chosen as his, and brushed his light brown fingers over it as though touching the face of a newborn child. He suddenly remembered part of the reason why he'd come here, and reached into his jacket pocket and fished out a small framed picture. He studied the worn image within of the Hindu god, Ganesha—evoking memories of his mother—and smiled as he placed it on the bench.

The sound of footsteps caught his attention and he turned

to see Professor Meeks entering the lab. Dressed in an even sharper suit than Lysart's, Meeks carried a bottle of wine adorned with a gold ribbon.

"Dr. Pellan," Meeks said, "I thought I'd find you here."

Lysart smiled. "Just enjoying a quiet moment with my new home."

"And what a nice new home it is!" Meeks said, handing him the bottle. "A gift. For you. Consider it a lab-warming present."

Lysart studied the label. It was a very expensive red. "Harvey, you shouldn't have."

"Of course I should have. The board has faith in you, Lysart. And this," he motioned to the lab around them, "is the start of a beautiful new era for both Bateson Dermacell and you."

Lysart placed the bottle down beside the microscope. "I shall enjoy drinking this tonight."

"And you should. Are your daughters coming today?" Meeks asked.

"No. They've gone to Paris with their mother."

"That's a shame."

Lysart shrugged. "This town doesn't quite match the allure of Paris, Harvey."

"I guess not. Well, shall we go over the event one last time? There will be a reporter from New York here soon. Word is he's investigating Clivecorp, not us, but I want to make sure we present at our best for Bateson Dermacell."

"I'm sure you'll dazzle him," Lysart smiled. "That's your specialty, Harvey. Not mine. You do the talking and the fund-raising, I do the science."

"Come, Dr. Pellan," Meeks smiled back. "You know I have a scheduling conflict and need to return to Washington soon after the ceremony, which means I can't be here to dazzle him. You need to be the one networking with the locals at the gathering afterward. You're the face of this project office. You're the one who will be staying here in town for the next couple of years. You need to do this, not me." Meeks patted Lysart on the shoulder. "I know you won't let me down."

Lysart gave a small smile.

"Good," Meeks said. "Shall we?"

Richard Keene, CNN reporter, stood at the back of the ceremony, watching as the Victoryville mayor took to the stage to give his welcoming speech. There was a decent crowd gathered, some sitting in rows of chairs while the rest milled around in the yard behind the new Bateson Dermacell office where the ceremony was taking place. The local police chief and one of his deputies were present, positioned either side of the stage, but standing well back and casting their gaze about the crowd. There were floral decorations and streamers and balloons, and he could smell fresh coffee wafting out from inside the building.

With his leatherbound notebook in hand, he'd been scribbling down his observations of the people, of the town, of this new project office, but he paused when the mayor finally began to speak.

"Thank you. And welcome! As mayor of Victoryville, I am honoured to be standing here today and officially opening this new facility. This project office is a symbol of progress, in Victoryville, as we lay down some much needed fresh roots to replace the old. This town has a long history of fighting change, going right back to the days of the civil war. But for too long that attitude has caused the town to stagnate and it is at risk of dying, of fading into history and becoming a ghost town, if we do not stand up and embrace the future and run with it. We must work hard to progress every single day or we *will* be left behind. Many of our youth leave this town, never to return. I know this, because until several years ago I was one of them. And I left because, at the time, this town didn't offer me any reason to stay. This needs to change. And that's why this facility marks an important turning point for Victoryville. This facility sees us bringing fresh industry and new opportunities to our people. As mayor of Victoryville, I could not be happier to welcome Bateson Dermacell here, beginning what I hope will be a long and fruitful partnership." He beamed a broad smile at the crowd. "So, on that note, I will now hand over to Professor Meeks to speak on behalf of Bateson Dermacell."

As the mayor urged the professor onstage, Richard cast a glance at his cameraman, Benny, who was scanning over the crowd, recording their applause. Richard then looked at his producer, Lisa. Standing beside him, she looked like she was daydreaming, gazing up at the sky as she tucked her peroxide blond hair behind her ear. He suppressed a grin, then saw her eyes narrow and squint at something, raising a hand to shade her eyes. He turned his gaze upward, but saw nothing other than clear blue sky and sunshine. He tugged at the collar of his shirt, feeling the warmth, then fixed his eyes back on the stage as the mayor shook congratulatory hands with Professor Meeks and ushered him toward the microphone.

"Thank you, Mayor Russo. And thank you, people of Victoryville, for embracing our research project. At Bateson Dermacell our ideologies are very much aligned with the mayor's. Progress *is* key to the survival of any civilization. But we also believe that in today's world we simply cannot ignore the correlation between man's progress and its affect on the environment and on ourselves. At Bateson Dermacell we specialize in the study of the long-term effects our environment has upon us. That is the core mission of our research here. And there is no better location than Victoryville given the close proximity of the large coal plant to the local community. At this point I must thank Clivecorp, who run that nearby plant, for being our major benefactor. This proves to the people of Victoryville that Clivecorp care. That, right there, is a perfect example of a symbiotic relationship. Of progress, of stability, of care." The professor looked down at his notes. "Now, although I am giving this speech today on behalf of Bateson Dermacell, it is not I who will be the figurehead of this local office. The man in charge of the day-to-day running will be none other than Dr. Lysart Pellan. Lysart, if you would?"

The professor motioned to a man of Anglo-Indian descent in the crowd. Dr. Pellan stood, somewhat hesitantly, gave a slight wave and immediately sat down again.

"Dr. Pellan is a respected geneticist and has been an absolute credit to Bateson Dermacell in our Washington facility. We have no doubt that he will continue to do us proud here in Victoryville, unlocking the secrets of, and perhaps finding resolutions to, the effects of pollution on mankind." The professor glanced at his notes once again. "Now I think we've all talked enough, don't you? Let's call the mayor back on stage now to cut the ribbon and officially declare this facility open, so we may then indulge in the wonderful morning tea arranged for us by the Victoryville Chamber of Commerce."

The audience broke into applause again, the mayor took to the stage with a bounce in his step, and together they cut the ribbon to more cheers.

"Please," Mayor Russo said, leaning into the mic, "join us for coffee and cake inside, in the foyer."

Richard watched as the crowd began to move inside. Lisa pulled out her notes and skimmed them.

"Alright, we interviewed Professor Meeks before the ceremony and I've lined up interviews with the mayor, Dr. Pellan and the Clivecorp reps later today. So let's head inside and get some general reactions of the townsfolk."

"And eat some of that cake," Benny grinned, scratching his bearded chin.

"Always thinking of your stomach, you," Lisa chided.

"I'd just settle for some of that coffee," Richard grinned back, as they moved inside.

Dr Lysart Pellan stood with some of his colleagues: Dr. John Seevers, Mary Rodriguez and the young graduate, Cheung Liu. They stood in silence, drinking tea and nibbling on cake, watching those who had gathered for the morning tea.

Mary leaned in toward him. "Is that the CNN crew leaving?"

Lysart looked toward the front doors of the foyer, saw one of the departing males carrying a TV camera. "Looks like it."

"Why are they leaving? Aren't they supposed to be interviewing you?"

"I'm meeting with them later this afternoon. I told Harvey I was too busy this morning."

"Oh," Mary said, before the mayor's laughter rang out, snatching their attention. He stood in a group with Professor Meeks, who seemed to be regaling everyone with a fascinating tale. "I see Professor Meeks is entertaining the locals."

"Yes," Lysart said, "he's in his element."

"You should be over there, Lysart," Mary nudged him. "You're the one who'll be running this place. Don't let him steal your thunder."

"Harvey handles the people and raises the cash, Mary. That's the deal now. I handle the science and . . . keep to myself."

Mary chuckled, shaking her head as she folded her arms.

"You're not having any cake?" he asked her, noticing her hands were empty.

Mary slid her hand over her belly. "No. My medication makes me queasy."

Lysart's face softened with sympathy.

"How *is* the treatment going, Mary?" John asked her.

"It's early days. But I'm a fighter. I'll be damned if I'm going to let this cancer take me away from my kids."

Lysart smiled. "Good for you, Mary."

She smiled in return. "Moving out of the city for a while was a good thing, I think."

Lysart saw Professor Meeks excusing himself from the mayor's group and watched as he approached.

"Lysart, I must be going. I have to be back in Washington by three o'clock."

"It was a pleasure to have you here, Harvey."

"It was a pleasure to be here. Now, please, go and speak with the mayor. I need you to work the room."

"I'd prefer to work the microscope," he teased.

John stepped forward. "I'll go chat with them, professor."

"See!" Lysart grinned. "John has it all in hand." John moved off toward the mayor as Harvey shook his head, then checked his watch. "I'll call you tomorrow to debrief."

Lysart gave a nod and watched as he left the facility.

Richard Keene sat in the hire vehicle's passenger seat, his belly full of coffee and cake, as he, Benny and Lisa drove out of the Bateson Dermacell parking lot.

"I will say one thing for the town," Benny said with a smile, nursing his camera in his lap as he licked his fingers. "They do a damn good morning tea."

Richard smiled. "They sure do."

"The mayor was a little full of himself, don't you think?" Lisa said as she drove along the main road in town. "He was acting like some kind of rock star or something."

Richard shrugged. "I guess he's a big fish in a little town."

"I see these small town guys and laugh," Benny said, shaking his head. "They'd be eaten alive in New York."

"Hey, small towns aren't so bad," Richard said.

"Says the guy who moved to New York from Iowa the first chance he got," Benny quipped.

"Small towns have their faults," Richard nodded, watching as the streets of Victoryville went past his windows, some of the buildings old, some rundown, "but the big ones have their troubles too, you know."

"True," Lisa nodded. "You probably wouldn't get mugged in a town like this."

"Yeah, that's because most of them probably own guns," Benny pointed out, chuckling. "You try and mug them and you'll get your head blown off."

"I gotta say, I was disappointed there were no protests," Lisa said. "You think it was all hype just to get us here and give them free promo?"

"Maybe," Richard shrugged, "but it wouldn't surprise me if there is tension bubbling underneath the public front. I mean, you got half of those on the outskirts of town trying to grow crops, while the other half works at the plant that's pouring all kinds of stuff into the air. And now you've got this research group here to study the effects of that pollution, which sounds like a good thing, but it's being funded by the company doing the polluting. And not only that, it was the mayor's construction company that built the new Bateson Dermacell project office. Talk about symbiotic, everything's connected. Everyone's hands are in someone else's pockets. It's interesting once you scratch beneath the surface."

"You'll find a story in anything, won't you?" Benny said dryly.

Richard grinned. "If the facts support it."

"I don't think there's any story here," Lisa said. "It's just local politics, that's all. Besides, if the Clivecorp plant drags its feet any longer, the EPA will shut it down soon enough. They can only rely on 'grandfather-clause' type exemptions for so long. And if they can inject funds into a research office, then they can inject funds into upgrading their plant."

"Yeah, but the cost of the small project office versus the upgrade of an entire coal plant . . .?" Benny shrugged.

She shrugged back. "Regardless, for the size of the project office, that ceremony was just pomp and bullshit. I was bored."

Richard chuckled. "I know you were. I saw you staring off into the sky, daydreaming during the mayor's speech."

"Hey, I wasn't daydreaming! I thought I saw something weird up there, but I think I just need new contact lenses."

Richard turned to look out the window, into the blue sky overhead. "It certainly is a beautiful day."

By the time they arrived at their hotel and entered the modest, and somewhat dated, foyer, it was 11.30 a.m. A young African-American man gave them a smile and a nod from behind the reception counter as they did. Richard gave a smile and a nod back.

"All that lovely cake and I'm still hungry," Benny said, switching the heavy camera he held from one hand to the other. "How long until we head out to the Clivecorp facility for the interviews there?"

"We're lined up for 1.00 p.m.," Lisa told them, checking her notes.

"Let's go get a beer, then," Benny suggested.

"I thought you said you were hungry?"

"I am," Benny shrugged, "and beer goes good with food! Besides, what else are we going to do?"

"You know, I think you're onto something." Lisa slapped Benny's shoulder. "What do you say, Rick? You up for a drink?"

Richard shook his head. "Nah, I think I'm going to get some first impressions down while it's fresh in my mind."

"Rick . . ." Benny's slightly chubby, bearded face gave him a plain stare.

"I'll come meet you in a bit." He smiled and held up his notebook. "I just want to get a start on these notes."

"You're too serious, you know that?" Benny said. "You've just turned thirty. You're still young. Seize the day my friend! Smell the roses!"

"I am seizing the day," Richard said. "I'm going to head back to my room and seize this story while it's fresh in my mind."

Lisa chuckled and slapped Benny on the shoulder again. "C'mon Benny, let's leave Rick to do his thing." Benny scoffed as Lisa pushed him toward the bar that led off the hotel's reception.

Richard, still smiling at the pair, walked up the carpeted staircase to the first floor of the hotel. As he entered his room, he placed the security key card in its slot on the wall, and the lights automatically turned on. He walked over to the window and pulled the heavy curtains back to let in some daylight, then moved to the bed and threw his notes down. He fished the laptop out of his backpack, placed it on the desk against the window, and turned it on.

While his laptop fired up, he took a seat at the desk and gazed through the sheer curtain that remained across the window, studying the sky outside. The warmth reminded him of the summers back in his home town, reminded him of his parents. He would need to visit them soon. Between living in New York and traveling the world chasing stories, it had been a while since he'd been home.

The laptop beeped, stealing his attention. He checked the battery; it was at seventy percent. He began flicking through his notes, then started typing, capturing his initial thoughts on the ceremony he'd just attended, on the town, and on the Bateson Dermacell facility. When he finished noting down everything he could think of, he pulled up the internet, wanting to do another search on Clivecorp ahead of his visit that afternoon. He typed the company name into the search window and hit enter, but an error message appeared:

Unable to make a connection.

He double-checked his portable wireless device was plugged correctly into the back of the laptop, then tried again. Still no connection. He closed everything down and restarted, hoping that might clear the problem, but it still wouldn't connect. It was odd. Everything had worked fine last night. Still, he didn't have time to worry about it just now, so he moved to the telephone beside the bed and called reception.

"Good morning, Victoryville Holiday Hotel. How may I help you?" the cheerful hotel clerk said.

"Hi, it's Richard Keene in room 104. I'd like to use the hotel Wi-Fi, please. Can you tell me the password?" he said as he sat down on the bed.

"Certainly, sir," the man answered. Richard heard the clerk tapping away on his keyboard. He leaned back on the headboard of his bed and eyed the room's dated decor courtesy of orange and brown, and studied the artwork of sailing ships on the wall, which was weird given the ocean was a few hours' drive away.

"Sir, I'm sorry . . ." the man came back on the line, "but it would appear that our hotel Wi-Fi is down. I can't get on the internet at all. I think the whole system is offline."

"Oh," Richard said, "well, that explains why I can't access it from my personal device. Must be a glitch in the area."

"It must be, sir. I'll give you a call when it's back up."

"Thank you," Richard said, and hung up.

He stood, wondering whether he should join Benny and Lisa downstairs. He'd give it five minutes, he thought, stretching out his neck and rolling it from side to side. As he did, the room lights began to flicker. He paused and watched them curiously, wondering what kind of dump Lisa had booked them into. No internet, faulty lights . . .

Then the flickering stopped, and the lights cut out altogether.

So did his laptop.

His eyes flashed to the darkened screen. He moved over to the laptop, pressed the power button to restart, but nothing happened. It was completely dead.

"What the hell?" he said.

He looked over at the alarm clock beside the bed. It too had cut out. *Complete power failure then . . .* Although, that didn't explain why his laptop had died. The battery had shown a seventy percent charge.

His eyes were suddenly drawn to the window in front of him as a large shadow passed over the street outside, stealing the sun from the sky.

It was odd, just how dark it had turned, and how quickly.

He heard the sound of wind whipping up outside and wondered whether a tornado could be approaching.

Did they get tornadoes in Victoryville?

He leaned over the desk, and pulled back the sheer curtains to take a closer look.

But he never got the chance to see.

Day One

Stanley Barrick, Homeland Security, strode into the chaotic ops room. Specialists were spread across multiple desks, tables and consoles, some reading monitors and maps, some deep in intense discussions, some typing hurriedly on keyboards. He made his way to a table where the key advisors stood, ready to provide him with an update.

"What's the latest?"

"We're still trying to communicate with the town," Colonel Levin, United States military, answered. "The whole area is still a dead zone. We've been unable to make contact."

"Where the hell did that thing go?" Stanley asked.

"We don't know," Dr. Nancy Wattowski, NASA representative, answered. "We're trying to track it, but the technology . . . it's jamming our satellites, radars, everything. That's why we had no warning it was coming."

"So it could still be out there somewhere?" Stanley asked. He was trying hard to remain calm and focused, but found it difficult to shake the images that circled inside his mind. Images of the large alien aircraft that had hovered over the Virginian town for twenty-four hours. Obsidian-black in color, roughly oval in shape and utterly terrifying, it had then suddenly vanished into thin air.

"We don't know," Wattowski said. "Quite possibly."

"Still no other sightings globally?" he asked.

"None reported."

"Is the perimeter still secure?" He turned back to Levin.

"Yes," the colonel answered, "we've got a twenty mile exclusion zone around the town. It's guarded with everything we've got."

"No one's come or gone since?"

"No, we've had no physical visuals on any movement, and until our satellites come back online we can't get picture overhead."

"So what the hell are we dealing with here?" Stanley demanded.

Levin gave him a grave look. "Our forces couldn't get near it. It jammed our communications and other tech, and emitted some kind of pulse that made our planes fall out of the sky. I'd say it's the most sophisticated enemy we've ever seen."

"I'm not sure *enemy* is the right word to use here," Wattowski said, throwing her hand up in objection.

"No?" Levin countered. "Let's wait and see what's left inside that town, shall we?"

"The engines died on those jets and yet they landed softly on the ground," Wattowski said. "These things, with *that* technology, could've probably killed every living soul on the Eastern Seaboard with great ease, and yet for some reason they guided your planes safely to the ground."

"They fried the engines. That's a hostile move."

"It was self-defense. Your planes approached armed with missiles."

"Trying to protect the people in that town!" Levin said,

stabbing an angry finger into the table.

"Enough!" Stanley barked. "We've got the entire world watching us and we need to respond. Fast. So what's the plan?"

Colonel Levin looked at him. "We continue trying to establish comms with the town, see if anyone is left alive. We keep the perimeter guarded. No one leaves that town. If they try, we shoot them."

"Absolutely not," Wattowski said. "If anyone is left alive we quarantine them. That town has just become the biggest research project in history."

"Sir!" a technician wearing a Metallica T-shirt called out. "The satellites are starting to come back online!"

"Bring them up!" Stanley ordered, turning back to the room. "Get them on the screen now!"

The technician went into action at his console and the largest screen in the room suddenly flicked to a satellite view over the town.

"Get us in close!" Stanley ordered, as the room fell silent and all eyes turned to watch.

It was blurry at first, but slowly the picture sharpened as they zoomed in on the main street. They saw a few cars positioned haphazardly in the middle of the road. Unmoving. Then they saw what looked like bodies lying on the sidewalk—

Someone gave a quiet gasp, expressing the shared fear of the room. The fear that they were looking at dead bodies.

But then one of the bodies moved.

Then another.

"Oh, my god," Wattowski said in awe. "They're still alive!"

"Get the comms back online, now!" Stanley barked. "I want to know everything about that town, and everyone in it! Find us someone we can speak to!"

Abbie Randell stirred from what felt like the best sleep of her life. A sensation of heaviness pulled her body down, but her mind began to lift like a balloon. She noticed a mechanical, grinding sound, grating on and off in the background. It was strange. Irregular.

She blinked as her mind awoke. Her vision cleared and she realized she was laying on the floor of Mona's Cafe at the VAC. Her chicken and gravy roll was splattered along the ground in front of her, among shards of broken white lunch plate.

Faint groans sounded in the background. She wasn't alone. She sensed movement beside her and saw Josh, the new lifeguard, lying beside her.

Why were they on the floor?

He stirred and they stared at each other blankly for a moment. He looked how she felt: as though she'd just woken from a long, deep sleep, her head cloudy, her throat dry.

She heard more groaning and looked around to see a few bodies beginning to stir on the floor. Which was strange. *Hadn't there been at least a dozen people in the cafe just a moment before?*

"What happened?" Josh rubbed the back of his head, his hand shaking his shaggy, dark-blond hair. "Where is everyone?"

Abbie noticed his chin and neck were red and scratched from the fall.

Candy, the other lifeguard, staggered to her feet, and beside her was Justin, a twelve-year-old boy from Abbie's second swimming class of the day. Austin, a personal trainer from the VAC's adjoining gym, was the last of the bodies to his feet. He stared around at everyone, his eyes a little accusatory as though they'd been the ones to put him on the ground. Abbie noticed he'd scratched his chin and neck too.

A groan behind the cafe's counter made them all spin around in fright. Mona, the cafe's namesake, rose up slowly, holding the counter to steady herself. She stared back at them with her plump face and rosy red cheeks. No one spoke. Groggily they migrated over to the windows to see if the missing customers had gone outside. The grounds were empty except for a few souls who were picking themselves up off the grass. Which was weird, Abbie thought, because on her way into the cafe before she had seen a whole track team out there.

She looked quizzically at the TV located on the wall. The screen was black, yet ripples of static rolled down it, and that strange mechanical noise seemed to be emanating from there. Mona suddenly moved into the kitchen. She picked up a small radio that sat by the sink, brought it back to the counter and began twisting the knobs, trying to pick up a station.

"Maybe we had an earthquake or something?" she finally said, sounding unsure. "That's why we were on the floor, right?" Mona couldn't find a station though. All they heard was that staticky, strange mechanical noise. The cafe owner cursed. "What the hell is going on?"

Candy brought a shaky hand up to her mouth; her pretty blue eyes welling with tears. "Do you think it's some kind of terrorist attack?"

Austin threw her a dark look then pulled out his phone and dialed a number, his bulky personal-trainer body pacing the room. Josh instantly took his phone out as well, and Abbie saw him bring up the number for his mom. She did the same, hands trembling as she called her home number. But it wouldn't connect. There was no service.

"I think maybe we should head home," Mona suggested, looking at them anxiously, her double chin bouncing up and down as she nodded to herself. "I'm closing up."

They all nodded, and Austin and Candy immediately departed, heading off in different directions. Abbie moved to Justin who still stood there, wide-eyed and wordless. Behind in his swim lessons, and not as strong as the others, she'd always given him special attention in class. "Are you okay, Justin?" she asked, placing her hand on his shoulder. His freckled face looked up at her, his body shaking a little. He nodded, but still no words came out of his mouth.

"Are you alright to get home?" she asked. "You want me to go with you?"

He shook his head and immediately headed for the door. Abbie followed him to where his bicycle rested outside the cafe. She watched him ride away, front wheel shaking in time with his body, eyes still wide with shock.

"Let's go," Josh's voice sounded behind her. She nodded and together they left the VAC.

As they headed for their homes, they grew more and more concerned with every step they took. Abbie quickly realized there were very few people around, and those that were seemed to be in a state of shock, panic or tears. They noticed the cars on the road were all stopped. Many of them sat empty, their drivers' nowhere to be seen. Others sat in their cars, seemingly dazed and confused about why they were there.

"The cars on the road, why . . . why are some of them empty?" Abbie asked, trying to fight the alarm building within. "Where did everyone go?"

Josh responded with a worried look and, as one, they wordlessly stepped up their pace and began to run.

Richard Keene splashed water over his face. He studied his green eyes carefully in the hotel room's bathroom mirror. He'd never fainted before. This was new. He wondered what had brought it on. Stress? The story he was working on had a tight deadline, but that had never made him faint before. This is what he did for a living: work from deadline to deadline, chasing story after story.

And he could hardly say that covering the launch of the Bateson Dermacell project office was stressful. Sure, there was controversy over the funding, but the stories he normally chased were a lot bigger than this. This story was an in-between job. Fly out from New York, cover the launch, interview a few people, fly back the next day and file the report. Simple.

So why the hell did he faint?

He let out a sigh and wiped his face. He headed for the minibar to get a water, combing his fingers through his curly brown hair as he went. Maybe he was coming down with a virus? He had just gotten back from a trip to Malaysia where he'd been working on a follow up to his palm oil story. Could be he'd caught something on the plane; or been bitten by a mosquito or other bug, picked up some tropical virus. Maybe he should take a break once this story was filed—he was probably overdue for one. He thought of his parents again, back in Iowa, and how long it had been since he'd seen them. Or even called them. He'd better do that once he returned to New York.

He took the water from the fridge and began to drink, but paused when he heard what sounded like a man screaming.

He instantly moved over to the window and looked down to the road below. There were a few cars stopped in the middle of the street. He scanned for the scene of a crash or a fight or something, but couldn't find any. Then his eyes found the screaming man. He was standing on his own down the road, beside a car, its door ajar as though he'd just exited. The man was looking around, distraught, and calling to no one in particular.

Then Richard finally made out what he was saying.

"Where are they? Where did everyone go? What the fuck is going on!"

Richard's brow furrowed as he studied the scene below. His hotel was in the main part of town and he realized the number of people on the street had thinned considerably from what he'd seen before. He noticed the few people who were on the street looked equally as shocked and distraught as the screaming man. Richard scanned up and down the street again, then pulled away from the window and turned toward his laptop.

It was coming back to him now. He recalled seeing the large shadow cross over his window. He'd wondered whether a tornado had been on approach, had gone to look, then . . .

Then he'd woken up on the floor.

He darted his eyes around the hotel room. The lights were back on, the alarm clock on the bedside table flashing. He'd thought maybe Lisa had booked them into a shitty hotel, but maybe it was something else? He pressed the power button on his laptop and it came to life. Whatever glitch had caused it to crash before, it now seemed okay. He immediately tried to pull up the CNN website, but the internet connection was still down.

More yelling sounded from the street.

Curious, and with his heart now thumping in his chest, he swiftly moved to the door.

Deputy Leo Cann jogged toward the young teen girl lying on the sidewalk with spilled shopping bags around her. He was confused. The last thing he remembered, he'd been on his way home from the Bateson Dermacell opening. Next thing he knew, he was in his car, right in the middle of the main intersection in town. The car was turned off and as he'd looked around he saw other cars had stopped too, and some of them were empty. The traffic lights had been green, he remembered. And as he looked about, dazed, that's when he'd noticed the teen girl lying on the sidewalk.

He'd quickly snapped awake, got out of his vehicle and raced over to her, panicking for a moment that maybe he'd blacked out and hit her with his car or something. But as he reached her, the girl sat up, her heavily-pregnant frame now visible to him, and she looked as dazed and confused as he.

"Are you alright?" he said, helping her to stand.

The girl nodded, brushing off her dress.

"You sure?" he said, eyeing her large belly, concerned. His wife had recently given birth to their second child, so he knew what kind of toll those last months took on a woman's body.

She nodded. "Y—yeah, I think so. Did I faint?"

Leo looked around the streets. Slowly but surely an awful feeling sank into his bones. He eyed the empty cars in the middle of the road, saw a few people helping themselves up off the ground.

Why the hell was everyone on the ground?

He looked back at the pregnant teen. "You sure you're alright?"

"Yeah, I'm fine," she nodded again, looking more terrified now, as though the situation was slowly sinking in.

"You want me to call someone for you?" Leo asked.

"Mom's out of town."

"You're on your own? You live close by? You need a ride?" he asked her.

"I'm just over there in the block." She pointed to the only

six-story building in Victoryville. "I can walk."

"You sure?"

She nodded.

"Alright, just call the station if you need anything. Okay?"

She nodded again, pushed her long reddish-brown hair away from her pale skin, and began to waddle back toward her apartment block with her shopping bags.

Leo watched her for a moment, making sure she walked steadily, then turned his eyes back to the streets. He saw the dazed, vacant stares of a couple of teenagers looking back at him. They both had these strange, long red marks running down their chins and necks. He wondered briefly whether it was some new goth or emo fashion thing.

"Everybody head home," he called out, waving his arms. "Just head home, alright." Still somewhat dazed, he didn't really know why he said that, but it felt like the right thing to do. And as the words settled into his own bones, a thought suddenly struck him. He snapped a turn and raced back toward his car. He wasn't sure what the hell had just happened to put everyone on the ground, but he felt the urgent need to check on his own family.

He jumped in his car and slammed the door closed. As he did, he caught his reflection in the side mirror. And he paused at what he saw.

Running down his chin, was a single long red welt.

Abbie's pulse hammered in her throat as she saw her street ahead. They'd run the whole five blocks home from the VAC. As they reached their houses Abbie threw Josh a hopeful glance, then split off. She raced across the street from where he lived. She saw her mother's car parked in the driveway, and burst through her front door. She called for her mother, but there was no answer. Climbing the stairs to the second floor, she searched every room, but only an empty house awaited her.

And then it began . . . the tightening in her chest. The wheezing. The desperate need for air.

It was coming on quickly.

She closed her eyes and knelt down on the floor. She saw spots in her vision, but knew to stay calm. She'd had this condition since she was a child, and with patience and calm it was easily relieved. She fumbled through her bag for her Ventolin and inhaled long and deep, sucking the spray into her lungs. She tried to breathe, but it was still a wheezing struggle, so she sprayed and inhaled again.

She took a few moments, inhaling deeply, feeling the air force its way into each and every one of her alveoli. As soon as she regained control of her breathing, she stood and moved to the bathroom, heading straight for the basin. She splashed her face with water and, looking up, saw herself in the mirror. And then she noticed it.

The single red welt running from her lower lip down over her chin and neck.

She raised her hand to touch it. The red mark wasn't raised at all. Didn't hurt. It was almost like someone had just painted or drawn a stripe on her. Her fingers traced its path and pushed open the top of her shirt to see it end over her heart. She wondered whether she'd done it when she'd fallen to the floor, scratched herself on the broken plate? But it didn't hurt. There was no blood. She suddenly recalled the scratches she'd seen on Josh's face, and Austin's. They'd looked a lot like hers did. Except, they had more than one.

A shout in the distance caught her attention and she quickly moved into her bedroom to the window overlooking her street. Mrs. Robson, a couple of houses down the street, had collapsed on her lawn. She was in tears, calling out, *"Someone took my little girl!"*

Abbie's stomach pulled tight. She clutched the window frame to hold herself still and darted her eyes across the street to Josh's house. She saw him through his bedroom window, on the second floor, pacing with the phone to his ear. He threw it down, frustrated, then caught sight of her.

He leaned out his window. "I can't get through to anyone," he called. "You?"

She shook her head and he paused, face falling a little.

"Maybe they went looking for us?" he said hopefully.

Abbie stared back, numb, as thoughts of those empty cars surfaced inside her mind. Even from the across the street she saw the look on his face, and couldn't bear the truth it told.

Just like her, deep down, he knew that something was horribly, horribly wrong.

Chief Earl Blackstone drove the streets of Victoryville not sure what to do. When he'd woken up on the floor of Betty's Bagels, he immediately knew something was very wrong. Everyone was on the floor for a start. And some had vanished entirely, including the cashier, who, according to his last memory, had been handing him change. He had stumbled out into the street and soon realized that, whatever had happened, the whole town was affected. He saw people pulling themselves off the ground. Saw Roy Kenny from Roy's Hardware on his hands and knees. He'd rushed to help him up, and saw Roy had injured his face in the fall by the looks of the four long red scratches running down his chin.

He headed straight back to the station then, calling his officers as he did, trying the other posts in town, but static had been his only reply. He'd found the station open, but Louise

Kempton, the officer on duty, was gone, leaving a half-eaten apple and a cup of coffee on her desk. At first he thought she must've headed out into the streets to see what was going on, but he knew she was thoroughly professional and wouldn't have left the station open; she would've locked it up. He remembered looking back at the apple and the coffee and realizing that something was not right: a skin had formed over the stone-cold coffee and the apple was so brown it looked like it had been sitting there overnight, but Louise had been on shift barely two hours. He'd been in earlier that morning and her desk had been clear.

Still unable to raise any of his officers, even the ones currently off-duty, he immediately tried to call for outside back-up, but the lines were down. It was then he'd noticed the strange noise coming from the radio on Louise's desk. It was a grinding sound, industrial, like some machine trying to get itself in motion, but failing. He moved to it, listening. Something about it sent a shiver down his spine. He'd reached out and snapped it off, sending the empty station into silence.

Not knowing what else to do, he got back in his car and hit the streets again. And that was when he had really known something was wrong; that's when he realized the number of people in the streets had thinned considerably from the moment he'd entered Betty's Bagels. Of those who were in the streets, most were shocked, crying. And some of them had red marks on their faces . . . just like Roy Kenny had.

With no comms and lost for options, he started driving to all his officer's houses. He got no answer at Mark's house or Samuel's. When he arrived at Carmine's, his shocked wife reported that he was missing; that he'd been asleep in his bed and now he was gone.

Next, he drove to Leo's house. He saw his car out front, so he pulled over and knocked on the door. No one answered, but he heard voices inside, so he entered. He found Leo on the floor of his son's bedroom, comforting his hysterical wife and daughter. His baby boy, Mickey, had vanished right out of his cot.

Blackstone's heart struck pain through him at the sight of Claire's wet, anguished face. Leo had just looked up at him, shocked and vacant, his face painted with one of those strange red welts, and he asked: "What the hell's going on, Earl?"

He'd told Leo to stay put with his family, and he had hit the streets again with an even greater sense of dread.

Now, after twenty minutes of driving around, his radio finally picked up a communication. He swerved over to the road's shoulder and snatched the receiver off its cradle.

"Chief Blackstone, Victoryville PD," he said. His usual drawl, hinting at his southern childhood, wasn't sounding quite as relaxed as it usually did. "Who is this?"

"Chief? This is Colonel Levin, US military."

"Military?"

"Chief, we're aware of your situation and we're going to do what we can. Now tell us, what is the status of your town?"

"What is the status?" Blackstone asked, not sure what he'd meant.

"What is your status? Have there been any casualties? How many civilians are left alive?"

"Left alive?" Blackstone felt as though his blood had just rushed out of him.

There was a pause before the colonel responded. "Chief, are you aware of what happened to your town?"

"Er . . ." Blackstone tried to fight the blur in his mind. He scratched his forehead, wondering how the military already knew something had happened. "I—I don't know exactly. Something's happened . . . people blacked out . . . I—I think some are missing."

"And are you aware of what caused this?" the colonel asked carefully. "Are you aware of how long you were blacked out for?"

A thousand thoughts rushed through Blackstone's mind.

Why was the military asking him this? Had they done something? Did they cause these blackouts?

"I—I don't know," he answered. "I think it was just a second or two."

Again there was a silence.

"Chief," the colonel said, and from the tone of his voice Blackstone knew that what he was about to be told was not going to be good. "You need to listen to me carefully. You've been out for approximately twenty-four hours."

Blackstone stared at the street before him. For a brief moment, it felt as though time stood still. Nothing moved, he wasn't even sure he was breathing. Then he saw a gentle breeze lift the first of the fall leaves around in the air. One landed gently on the hood of his patrol car.

"Say again," he said.

"An unidentified aircraft positioned itself in Victoryville airspace. It was there for twenty-four hours. We have no idea what it did to you and the town during those twenty-four hours. Do you understand this?"

"I'm sorry, *what*?" Blackstone said, glancing around at the near-empty streets. He noticed a couple of the teenagers from Roy's Hardware standing on the street corner looking at him. Their faces held those strange red marks. "Say again."

Silence was his only response.

"I said, say again!" he said more firmly.

"An unidentified aircraft positioned itself in Victoryville airspace. It was there for twenty-four hours. We have no idea what it has done to you. Do you understand what I'm telling you?"

It was Blackstone's turn for silence.

"We're going to do everything we can to help you," the colonel said. "It's important that you understand this. But before we can help you, we need information. We need your help."

Again Blackstone was quiet, his mind mulling over what had happened: waking up on the floor of Betty's, his missing officers, Leo's missing baby, seeing people with those red marks down their faces. The colonel's words chased these images through his mind. *"An unidentified aircraft . . . Victoryville airspace . . . twenty-four hours . . . We have no idea what it has done to you . . ."*

"Chief," the colonel said firmly, "I repeat, we're going to do everything we can to help you, but in order to do that, we need your help. We need information. Do you understand this?"

Blackstone took a moment to focus his thoughts and get his mouth to move. "Er, yeah. Yeah, I understand."

"Good. Now what is the status of your town? How many are missing?"

"I—I don't know exactly," he responded, looking around the streets again, studying the empty cars. "I think . . . I think there might be a lot."

There was silence over the radio again for a moment.

"Is anyone hurt? Has anyone been killed? Anything unusual? Anyone acting strange? Anyone feeling ill?"

Blackstone looked at the teenagers again. He recognized one of them as Davey Ford's kid, Trent. He eyed the red mark running down the young man's chin. Noticed the boy next to him, Langdon Swann, had two welts.

"Well," he said, pausing to swallow, "some people . . ."

"Yes?"

"Some people have these red marks on their faces. These red welts. But they're different on each one. The number of 'em."

Again, there was a period of silence over the radio.

"Alright, you need to listen to me," the colonel said. "We're working on bringing up the last of comms. But right now, you need to get everyone inside and off the street. Do you understand? When these comms come back on, what they see, people are bound to panic."

"You got footage of the thing?"

"News crews filmed it the entire twenty-four hours. The footage is blurry because they had to film it from some distance away, but it has been airing all over the world."

"It was just us? No one else?"

"Just Victoryville."

"A—and it was here for twenty-four hours?" Blackstone furrowed his brow, still struggling to believe it. "But the clock. . ." He glanced at the digital display on the dash of his vehicle, then up at the midday sun. "What day is it?" he asked, confused.

"It's Thursday. Trust me, that thing was over your town for a whole day."

"Holy hell . . ." Blackstone muttered.

"I understand this is hard, chief, but you need to hold it together and keep the people calm, alright. Can you do that for us?"

Blackstone took another moment to clear his thoughts. "I'm going to need back-up. I think some of my officers are missing." He paused, then rephrased the statement. "I think a *lot* of my officers are missing."

"We'll need to assess the risk of infection before we can send anyone in. If it's feasible, we'll send in bio-units to assist, but we need to assess the risk first. We're trying to find someone on the ground who can help us. We need you to check the hospital, the local doctors, and see who's left. Or anyone else who might be able to help us."

Blackstone ran his hand over his face, trying to wipe away the shock that was trying to force its way into his body.

"Chief, there're still plenty of people left alive, right?" the colonel said. "We need someone of medical or scientific background. Someone who can run some initial tests for us. The sooner we do this, the sooner we can send help in. Do you understand?"

Blackstone nodded to himself. "Yeah, okay." He looked around the streets again, trying to force his mind to think, the morning's events flooding through his mind.

"Try Bateson Dermacell," he said. "They just opened their new research office this morning, er, yesterday morning . . . whenever the hell it was. There might be someone there."

"Good, chief," the colonel said. "I want you to head there now, but put any officers you have out on those streets and get people indoors."

Blackstone lowered his face into his hand, trying to wipe away the remnants of shock.

"Yeah, okay," he said softly, picturing Leo holding his distraught wife.

"Chief? One last thing."

"Yeah?"

"Are you marked? Do you have these welts?"

Blackstone glanced at his reflection in the rearview mirror, eyed his dark skin. "No. I'm clean."

"Good," the colonel said. "Stay by the radio. We'll be in touch."

Richard Keene crossed the deserted lobby of his hotel and entered the bar. Searching for Benny and Lisa to see if they knew what had happened, he spotted Benny's camera resting on an empty chair, but neither of his colleagues were there.

In fact, the bar was empty.

Richard's skin prickled . . . Benny *never* left his camera unattended. He would get his butt kicked by the network if it got stolen. *Maybe they just stepped out into the street to see what was going on?*

He made his way to the door, but stopped as he heard a whimpering sound. He scanned the room and saw a distraught waitress crouching down, peering around the corner of the bar at him.

"Wh—what's going on?" she said, looking at him, terrified.

He moved toward her, took her by her arms and helped her to stand. "It's okay. You're alright. What happened?"

"I don't know." She started crying. "I—I think I passed out. I woke up on the floor and everyone was gone."

His grip tightened on her arms. "You what? You . . . passed out?"

She nodded. "And everyone was gone. They just disappeared!"

Richard felt the hairs on the back of his neck stand on end.

She passed out. She woke up on the floor . . .

Just like he did.

He glanced around the bar. "There was a man and a woman here. He has dark hair, chubby, with a beard. She's petite and blond. Did you see them?"

The woman started crying.

"Did you see them? A man and a woman?" he asked again. "They were sitting with that camera." He pointed to it.

She nodded, her body rattling in his grip. "They were all gone when I woke up."

Richard's heart kicked up a notch. He looked around again, unsure what to do. He moved the woman to a chair and sat her down, then walked out to the street to see what was going on. For a town of over 15,000 people, it sure was deserted.

Where the hell did Benny and Lisa go?

He was walking back into the bar toward the woman when the TV on the wall suddenly came to life, startling them both. They turned to focus on it.

It was set on the Sky News channel and what he saw made him pause.

There, filling up the entire screen, was a blurry, shaky image that looked like it had been shot from some distance and zoomed in on. As best he could make out, it was a large, dark, disklike structure hovering over a town. He read the caption on the image: *Victoryville, Virginia, United States.* His eyes widened, then jumped to the text scrolling at the bottom of the screen.

The unidentified aircraft positioned over the town of Victoryville for the past twenty-four hours has now vanished . . . Military remain on high alert and an exclusion zone around the town remains in force . . . Communications are being restored to the town . . . It is unknown yet if there are any survivors . . .

"U—unidentified aircraft?" the waitress said, staring at the screen. "There was a spaceship?"

"Twenty-four hours!" the young hotel clerk exclaimed as he stepped into the room. "Twenty-four hours have passed?"

Richard stood as still as a statue, unable to do anything other than stare at the screen, at the footage of the large black spaceship that had apparently been hovering over the very town in which he now stood. He saw something shimmer over the black shape, like liquid metal: silver, mirrorlike.

Camouflage. Then the ship slowly rose into the atmosphere, barely visible in the way that heat waves roll off a desert highway, and vanished.

It wasn't often Richard was left short of words, but this sure as hell seemed to do it.

He swallowed hard.

"Holy shit," he eventually whispered. "Looks like I just got a new story."

Dr. Lysart Pellan sat in Lab-One, studying the magnified skin sample on the screen before him. The image was being piped through from the adjoining lab where, inside, Dr. John Seevers sat at the Biological Safety Cabinet. Arms beneath the glass frontage, Dr. Seevers was studying the physical sample that he'd scraped off the red welt on his own chin.

"Dr. Pellan!" the young graduate, Cheung, said hopefully.

Lysart looked around at his only companion in Lab-One. Cheung stepped up and pointed to the bars on the cell phone he held. "Communications must be restored."

Lysart looked up at the young man's hopeful face, then at Dr. Seevers and the other two colleagues who peered back through the window of Lab-Two, all wearing their safety glasses, face masks, and caps.

"I'll call Professor Meeks," Lysart said to Cheung, as he moved to the wash station in a corner of the room. "I'll see if I can find out what's going on." He carefully removed his gloves and threw them in the waste container, then washed his hands thoroughly. Once dried, he pulled down the surgical mask he wore, grabbed his cell and made the call.

"Lysart," Meeks answered, "thank god you're alright! Are you? Alright, I mean. I arrived in Washington and couldn't believe it when I heard the news."

"Harvey," he breathed with relief, closing his eyes briefly. "Yes, I'm fine."

"I can't believe it! I mean, I was just there that morning. I must've gotten out just in the nick of time."

"Yes," Lysart said solemnly, "you must have."

"I'm sorry, Lysart. Listen to me. Is everyone else alright?"

Lysart glanced at his colleagues and could see they were hanging on his every word. He turned away from their expectant eyes and walked into the corridor.

"Harvey . . . people are missing," he said as he closed the door behind him.

"I know. I heard. The military have been in contact with me."

"The military?"

"Yes. How many are left, Lysart? In the lab."

Lysart felt the seriousness of the events around him suddenly intensify. It was one thing to have woken up on the floor of the lab, to have noted two of his colleagues had disappeared, and another thing to have seen that alien craft on the TV. Now, Meeks was talking of the military. "Five. Why?"

"Five from seven. Right. How many of the five have these marks?"

Lysart paused. "How do you know about the marks?"

"Like I said, the military have been in contact. They're bringing in the CDC to help. How many in the lab are marked?"

"Three."

"And you?"

"No. I'm fine." Lysart began to walk down the corridor toward the facility's entrance. He was craving daylight, needing to feel the natural sunlight of the world outside, despite the thought that the ship might be out there somewhere. He needed an escape from the past couple of hours since he'd woken up; since some of his colleagues had disappeared into thin air; since some had awoken with those strange red marks on their faces. He needed the movement to get the blood flowing through his brain so he could think.

Meeks exhaled lightly down the phone. "That's a relief. Lysart, you need to enact protocol immediately and separate yourself—"

"We've already taken precautions," Lysart told him. "We acknowledged the marks immediately upon waking, put on our protective gear and separated into different labs."

"Good. Good. So who is left?"

"John, Mary, Grant, and Cheung."

"And who else besides yourself is unmarked?"

"Just Cheung."

"Lysart, the CDC are going to need our help. The local Victoryville hospitals, as you can imagine, are suddenly understaffed and inundated with people panicking about what's happened and what those marks are. They don't have the capacity or the equipment to assist the CDC with their needs. I've assured them that Bateson Dermacell will do what we can to help."

"We don't have the equipment either, Harvey. Our lab is designed for BSL-2 containment. This . . . this is going to need a biosafety level 4. I've collected samples already from the surviving staff, but we're going to need to send them to someone on the Laboratory Response Network—"

"No, Lysart, you can't do that."

"No?"

"No. Nothing can leave the town. You . . . you saw what did this, right?"

Lysart paused, images flashing through his mind from what he'd seen on the TV in the break room, the alien ship hovering over the town. "Yes," he said quietly.

"Then you know why the samples can't leave. The whole town has been quarantined. Whatever caused those welts, it's alien to this planet. It *cannot* get out. You've already been exposed to it. Your team is best placed locally to help the CDC. I've assured them Bateson Dermacell will do what we can to assist."

"And that is?" Lysart asked, as he stepped into the sleek, minimalist foyer of the building. He pulled up suddenly when he saw a figure standing at the front door: a tall, bulky African-American man with a thick, graying mustache. Lysart recognized him from the opening ceremony. It was the Chief of Police.

"They want us to run initial tests on the survivors and figure out what those welts mean," Meeks said. "They need us to advise if it's contagious and how to combat it. I know this isn't your specialty area, Lysart, but you can do this. The local chief is on his way to you now to make contact."

"Yes, he just got here," Lysart said, as the chief stepped through the front door and removed his hat.

"Good," Meeks said. "I've offered them our full assistance."

"I understand," Lysart said quietly, as he and the chief eyed each other. "We've already started an analysis. We didn't know what else to do."

"Good. I'll be in touch again soon. Let's help them get to the bottom of this, Lysart." Meeks seemed to pause before adding with an air of excitement, "This could put Bateson Dermacell on the map!" Meeks hung up, and Lysart couldn't help but stare at the cell for a moment, thinking how strange a closing statement that was to make, given the circumstances.

"Dr. Pellan?" The chief pulled him from his thoughts with a

deep drawl.

Lysart looked up at the big man as he stepped toward him.

"We need your help," the chief said.

Lysart nodded. "Yes. I believe you do."

Abbie Randell waited and waited, the minutes turning into hours, but her family did not return. Not her mother, not her father, not her younger sister. She'd tried their cell phones, and when she had finally gotten through, she'd heard her mother's ringing downstairs. Her heart nearly leapt out of her throat as she chased the sound to the ground floor, thinking her mother must be home. She found the cell sitting on the kitchen bench, buzzing and ringing with a solemn tune that bounced around the empty kitchen.

Her mother's car was parked in the driveway, her cell phone was here in the kitchen. Why would she leave without them?

She'd tried the cells of her father and sister again, but they too rang out. She left message after message, but they never called back. Most of her friends were away at university, but she'd tried to reach those still in town. Some didn't answer. Some were reported as missing.

Then she made the mistake of turning on the TV. The news hit her like a hard slap to the face. At first she thought it had to be a joke, but as the minutes ticked by, she realized it wasn't. She collapsed onto the couch in her living room and stared at the staticky footage before her. Just like the TV at Mona's Cafe, something was interfering with the reception, the screen jumping and that strange mechanical sound emanating from the speakers.

She watched the footage replaying before her, showing a massive black spaceship poised over her town. She saw the unmistakable image of the clock tower on the Victoryville Civic Hall. There was no doubt as to where this had taken place. She had lived in Victoryville all her life. She'd been to that Civic Hall many times, and that refurbished clock tower was the icon depicted on every one of the town's promotional flyers..

After seeing the footage, she had immediately peered out her front door, searching the sky, wondering if the spaceship was still there somewhere. She recalled little Lena pointing at something in the sky . . . had she seen something? Had Abbie herself seen something? That strange haze, the mirage in the sky before she'd blinked her vision clear. Had she missed something she should've warned people about?

Dusk was falling swiftly, casting the streets in a yellow-brown hue, but the sky overhead still looked clear. It just didn't seem real. It didn't seem possible that thing had been sitting over their town just hours before.

She moved back inside to the TV and saw footage of a military blockade twenty miles outside the town. The voiceover said that they had set up a perimeter, quarantining the town from the outside world. Abbie collapsed once more onto her couch, staring helplessly. The military looked armed to the teeth, like they were on guard in a Middle Eastern conflict zone. How could this be happening just outside of Victoryville?

She turned the TV off. She couldn't bear to watch any more. She picked up the baseball cap that sat on the couch beside her. It was her father's lucky cap. He wore it to every Little League game he coached. She turned it about in her hands, staring at it, wondering how his interview had gone that morning. Wondering if he'd got the job. Wondering why he hadn't come home yet. Maybe he was out celebrating with her mother. Maybe they didn't know what was going on.

But she knew that couldn't be true. Not after what had

happened. So why hadn't they come home to see if she was okay? To see if her sister Sarah was okay?

She got up and walked to the TV cabinet, picking up the framed photo perched atop that had been taken last Easter on their annual family holiday to the coast. Her father was wearing the very same baseball cap, her mother and sister wore the fashion outlet sunglasses they'd bought that trip, and Abbie was there with her hair wet and salty from the ocean. "The fish" her mother nicknamed her, for Abbie's love of the water and of swimming.

She remembered taking the picture, stretching her arm out as far as it would go to fit them all in. They were squished tightly together and managed to all get in frame, albeit in fits of laughter. She could almost feel the sun on her skin and the sand beneath her toes as she looked at it. She pressed the frame against her chest then moved back to the couch and continued to wait.

The town eventually grew dark and she began to pace the house, listening to the sounds of her neighbors and strangers walking along the roadside desperately calling out the names of their loved ones. Their *missing* loved ones. Abbie thought briefly about joining them, but didn't want to leave in case her family came home. So she sat there, listening, waiting. Holding that picture to her chest and rocking herself.

And still they didn't come home.

As each minute passed, Abbie's heart filled more and more with dread.

The flash of police car lights caught her attention and she moved to look out the window. She heard Deputy Cann's strained voice calling out to those on the street, telling them to head indoors. She wanted to run to him and report her family as missing, but she saw many others doing the same thing too. Hopelessly, she turned away and moved back to the couch.

Josh eventually knocked on her front door. When she opened it, the first thing she saw were his sad brown eyes, before her focus was drawn to the three red welts running down his chin.

"My parents came home, but . . . we can't find my kid brother," he said quietly.

She stared at him as tears suddenly rimmed her own eyes.

"They haven't shown?" he asked her. "Your family?"

She shook her head as a tear fell down her cheek. She wiped it away. Josh stared back at her for a moment as though unsure what to do. They'd only just met a day ago, standing in line at Mona's Cafe. Or maybe it was two days ago. She wasn't sure any more.

The thought caused more tears to course down her cheeks.

Josh reached forward somewhat awkwardly, and pulled her into a hug. She found herself clinging to him.

"What happened to us?" she whispered into his shoulder.

"I don't know," he whispered back.

Richard had been relieved when he'd finally gotten access to the outside world. His first call had been to Harry Dean, his editor at CNN.

"Harry Dean's office," the familiar voice of Kelly, his assistant, answered.

"Kelly, hi. It's Richard Keene."

"Richard!" she said anxiously. "Oh my God, are you alright? We've been so worried! Are you still in Victoryville?"

"Yeah, I'm fine. Is Harry about?"

"I'll put you straight through."

"Richard!" Harry answered abruptly, his voice suggesting

too many years of smoking cigarettes. "Where the hell are you?"

"Victoryville."

"Jesus Christ! Are you alright, kid?" Harry often called him "kid", but it didn't bother Richard. Harry had been his boss and mentor for a long time now.

"I'm fine. I'm okay," he said.

"Lisa and Benny, too?"

Richard paused a moment, clutching the phone tighter. "I can't find them, Harry."

"What do you mean? You think maybe they got out before it happened?"

"No." Richard tried hard to fight the awful feeling in his gut. "Harry . . . a lot of people seem to be missing."

"Missing?"

"Some of us woke up and . . . the rest were just gone."

"What do you mean you woke up?"

"We blacked out. Everyone left here in town, blacked out. And when we woke, everyone else was gone."

A moment of silence passed before Harry whispered, "Holy shit."

"I don't know what's going on. I saw on the news, the military has the town surrounded."

"Yeah. Look, don't worry. We'll get you out of there as soon as we can. Just sit tight and stay calm."

"Yeah. Okay."

"Listen, kid, I know you've just been through the wringer, but are you up to filing a report? Over the phone if need be. The world is going to want to hear what's going on in there."

Richard nodded to himself. He'd been expecting this. It's what he did for a living, after all. "Of course." He moved over to his laptop to check the internet connection. It was up and running again. "I have Benny's camera," he said, moving his eyes over to where it now lay on his bed. He paused a moment, swallowing the lump threatening to block his throat. "I'll send something through."

"Okay. Good. Just stay safe. We'll get you out of there."

"Yeah."

"You want me to call your folks? Let them know you're okay."

"No, I'll call them now. But, Benny and Lisa . . ."

He heard Harry sigh heavily down the phone. "I'll call their families. You just get me that report. Their families will want to know what's happening."

"I'll send something through soon."

"Thanks, kid. You hang in there, alright. And stay sharp! This is the biggest goddamn story there's ever been."

Stanley Barrick reentered the busy ops room with his aide, Colin, following close behind. With them, was Dr. Rita Hogarth, Epidemic Intelligence Service officer from the Centers for Disease Control and Prevention, brought in to help with the "stripe" situation. They joined the others at the briefing table and the necessary introductions were made.

"What's the latest?"

"It's strange," Wattowski said, shaking her head. "Even though our systems went down, even though we couldn't track or trace anything, *now* our systems are up and all the data is here." She motioned to the monitor in front of her.

"What do you mean?" Barrick asked, studying the display of graphs. "You've located the ship?"

"No. We've still got nothing on the ship. But it . . ." She held both hands up as though trying to explain the size of a fish that got away, "it blocked us from accessing anything while it was here, yet *somehow* our systems still recorded everything. It's like it froze our access, locked us out of our own systems, but it didn't hinder the actual systems from working. As soon as it was gone, it gave us that access back. It's all here. We have atmospheric readings, radar and heat signatures. We have an absolute wealth of data flowing through."

"On their ship?"

"Not the ship per se, but the effect of it on our environment. Which, in turn, we can use to gather some information on their ship. We have temperature spikes recorded, we have increased wind readings, we have metallic elements detected in air samples, all recorded from the nearest weather station, just outside of Victoryville."

"So what does that mean?"

"It means . . . well, I don't know what it means exactly. It will take us hours, days, to analyze this information, but it's fascinating. Whatever they are, they're not scared of us figuring out who they are. Otherwise, they wouldn't have allowed us to access this information."

"Maybe it was a flaw in their system?" Colonel Levin suggested. "They could block us temporarily, but not stop the systems recording or prevent our eventual access once they'd gone."

"No." The nearby technician in the Metallica T-shirt spoke up. "There's no flaw in their system." He tapped his screen. "I think they purposely let us gather data on them. They just didn't want us to have it while they were here," he shrugged, "in case we turned out to be as advanced as them and somehow used it against them. But I'll tell you something . . . during those twenty-four hours, we had a massive spike in data download, concentrated right there in the Victoryville area."

"What's your name?" Stanley asked.

"Er, it's Gavin Taylor, sir."

"So, what does that mean, Gavin?" Stanley asked.

The technician looked back at him. "They hooked into our systems, all of them. And they downloaded the data."

"What data?"

The technician looked back at his screen. "According to those figures, I'd say everything we had. Everything imaginable they could get their hands on. If they have hands, that is."

Wattowski nodded in thought. "They've gathered data on us too, then. They've given us a fair exchange."

"A fair exchange?" Levin seemed to disagree. "They have *everything* on us and we have, what? A temperature spike?"

Stanley stared at them all for a moment.

"Details," he told them, "I need details. Get analyzing now." He turned back to Dr. Hogarth. "Set yourself up at whatever desk you can find. Colin here," he pointed to his aide, "will get you whatever you need."

"Thank you," she said, then moved toward a table, trailing her roller suitcase behind her.

Abbie locked up her house, but left the lights on in hope. She walked across the road with Josh to his house, at his insistence. She was torn about leaving her home, but she didn't want to be alone either. The thought of that spaceship still being there somewhere . . . besides, it was only across the street, she told herself. Josh seemed friendly.

When Abbie entered the Chalmer home, she saw his parents look up expectantly, perhaps hoping it was their missing child returning. Josh's father had the marks on his face, but his mother's face was clear of them.

"Mom, Dad," Josh introduced them, motioning to each, "this is Abbie Randell."

His mother stepped forward, giving a sad, nervous smile. "Hi, Abbie. I'm Karen."

"Hi." Abbie managed a smile.

"Your parents? Sister?" she asked, looking over her shoulder at the doorway.

Abbie just shook her head, unable to get her mouth to move.

"Oh," Karen's shoulders slumped sadly. "I—I met your mother the other week. She was so lovely." She quickly caught herself. "*Is* lovely."

Josh's father threw Karen a glance at her slip-up, then gave Abbie a nod. "Nice to meet you, Abbie. I'm Peter. Do you have any other family in town?"

"No," she said quietly. "My parents moved out from California before I was born. They're all back there."

"Friends?"

"Most are away at university. The ones that were still here aren't answering my calls."

Peter eyed her sympathetically. Abbie managed a smile, trying to fight the pull to return to the comfort of her home.

"Have you heard anything new?" Karen asked with hopeful eyes. She motioned to the TV. "Reception is cutting in and out. There seems to be some sort of interference."

Abbie looked at the fuzzing, twitching screen. "I have the same problem at my house."

"There's talk that it might still be here somewhere," Karen said quietly. The silence sat thickly around them for a moment, before Peter touched his wife's arm and motioned for her to sit.

Josh motioned for Abbie to do the same, and they all sat down on the chairs in the living room.

"They don't seem to know what it was," Karen said, eyes shining with tears. "The ship. It froze everything, apparently. The satellites. The military planes crashed trying to get near it. They couldn't do anything, but watch. Those on the outside. They just sat there and watched."

"It's just us, too," Josh added, staring at the TV. "No one else in the world, just us. Why the hell would it choose this shitty town?"

"Josh," Peter scolded gently.

Karen looked at her husband, then at Abbie again, "No one seems to know what to do," she whispered. "They had to suspend trading on the stock market to avoid a crash. Everyone's panicking. Some people in nearby towns are packing up and running away from us. Meanwhile, we're trapped in here. They're not letting anyone out."

"How do people just disappear?" Josh asked, shaking his head. "There's gotta be hundreds, thousands of them."

"Some are saying this might be the end of the world," Karen said, staring at the TV blankly, before looking back at Abbie. "But if this is the end, why are some of us still here?"

An awful silence suffocated the room.

Victoryville mayor, Michael Russo, sat in the office of his apartment and dialed into the conference call. He'd just spoken with the state's governor, and was now connecting to a crisis meeting of the Victoryville Council and the Police Department. Given the chaos that had been thrust upon them, everyone had, in the first several hours, been busy assessing their personal collateral damage. Now it was time to widen the scope and deal with the town's.

Like many, it would seem, Russo had suffered loss. His partner of eight years, Nicola, was among the missing. After the ceremony, he'd left her shopping while he headed back to his office to tidy up some loose ends. When she hadn't returned home after "the Occurrence", he'd tried to track her down but couldn't find her. The jeweler she worked for hadn't seen her, nor the salon she regularly attended. She simply disappeared during the blackout. Russo wasn't sure how to deal with that. He wasn't sure how to deal with any of it.

Aliens . . .

He squeezed his eyes closed as though trying to erase the image of that black ship hovering over the town; the memory of waking up slumped over his desk. Opening his eyes again, he glanced around his apartment's study. The words *fight or flight* raced through his mind as he tried to decide what to do. The truth was, he was doing a little of both. He was throwing himself into work in the hope of regaining some control over this craziness, but also to distract himself from thinking of Nicola.

Or what these *things* might have done to her.

Or worse still, what they might have done to him during the blackout.

He'd watched the disrupted telecasts, had checked the latest on the internet, saw the social media posts of politicians and celebrities from around the world praying for his town and asking for calm. He tried desperately to shake off the shock that threatened to take hold of him. He'd been mayor of Victoryville for barely six months. Now he was going to be the mayor that had to deal with this.

Again the words "fight or flight" raced through his mind. He tried to look on the bright side of things. Weren't great leaders forged in times of adversity? This could be his chance to prove himself. This could be his chance to stand up and be the leader he knew he could be; to be someone who left his mark in the annals of history.

He was glad of the excuse to hold this meeting with the council and Chief of Police by conference call, since everyone was scattered across the town at their homes, dealing with what was left of their families. Russo's skin was unmarked, and the truth of it was, the more the hours passed and the more he heard about these "stripes", the more he didn't want to go near anyone who had them. And his fellow councillors just might have them; if they were sick, he couldn't be. If he got sick, he would lose control of his town.

The recorded voice of the conference call service prompted him to say his name.

"Mayor Russo," he said, swinging around in his chair and staring out the window at the lights of Victoryville. His apartment wasn't far from the center of town and the council chambers. He and Nicola were professionals, childless by choice, and they liked to experience the pleasures this life had to offer: travel, dining out, whatever they liked really. When they chose this apartment, they had done so because it was near their favorite restaurant in town: Segal's. At least once a week they would stop by and visit their pal, Rory Segal, the owner, and then walk home arm in arm, their bellies full of pasta and their cheeks rosy from several glasses of red. They were trying to make the best of things here in Victoryville. They both wanted to be living back in Miami, Nicola especially, but after his father had died, and a stock market tumble had seen him lose more money than was comfortable, he'd had no choice but to move here and take over his father's business. It was only supposed to be temporary, until he won a couple of lucrative contracts to help sell the business, but before he knew it he'd been sucked back into the life of the town of his birth, entrenched deeper into his father's business, and seduced into life as mayor. He'd told Nicola it would only be for a little while. Just until he made the right connections to move up the ranks into state politics.

As he listened to the recorded voice linking him into the conference call, he stared out the window and saw the red Segal's sign in the near distance, alight against the black of the strange, strange night around it.

"Mayor." He heard the deep drawl of Chief Blackstone.

"Chief," Russo replied, "who else do we have?"

"Graeme," Councillor Graeme Shother announced, "and Patty, Jeff and Darryl."

"That's it?" Russo asked.

"I've called around," Graeme said. "Bert, Helen and Marlie are among the missing." Graeme's voice softened as he spoke their names and a solemn silence settled down the line.

"My god," Russo said, running his hand over his face.

"Have you spoken with the governor?" Chief Blackstone asked.

"Yes," Russo answered. "He wants us to encourage people to remain in their homes and stay calm while the authorities try to get to the bottom of what's happened."

"People are already packing up and trying to head out of town," Blackstone said.

"Yeah, and go where?" Russo said. "The military have our town surrounded. There's nowhere to go."

"I know," Blackstone said. "Doesn't stop them clogging the roads though, does it?"

"Did the governor give you any other information?" Councillor Darryl Callaghan asked. Darryl was a good guy. They played golf together occasionally.

"No, it's too early. He said the military and various health agencies are on it and we'll know more soon."

"We will," Blackstone agreed. "Our new residents at Bateson Dermacell have been tasked with doing the initial investigation, given they're here in ground zero."

Russo felt a satisfied smile cross his face. "Thank heavens we and Clivecorp supported their new facility being built here in town, hmm?"

No one responded. Perhaps it was crass of him to gloat at a time like this, but given some of the negative remarks he'd had in the run-up to their grand opening, he couldn't help but feel a little vindicated. After all, what would they be doing now if Bateson Dermacell hadn't come to Victoryville? What would they be doing if he hadn't supported the new business in this stagnant town?

"So what do we do?" Councillor Patty Duke asked. Patty ran a beauty parlor—not the one Nicola went to—and was heavily involved in the local Chamber of Commerce. Russo thought she was a ballbreaker and a pain in the ass, but her constituents loved her.

"For now we wait," he said. "We just stay in our homes, remain calm and wait."

"People are losing it, Mike," Councillor Jeff Williams said. "They're terrified! How do people just disappear like that?" Jeff was a longtime councillor, but he was old-fashioned, outmoded. He rarely agreed with Russo's progressive ideas, always wanting to keep the town just as it is. Scared of change. "I mean, we're talking aliens here!" Jeff said. "Invasion of the goddamn body snatchers!"

"The disappearances are one thing," Graeme said, "but what about these stripes? What the hell do they mean? We could all still be at risk."

"Who among you is marked?" Russo asked, glad Graeme had been the one to bring it up. "Who has these stripes?"

There was silence for a moment, before Blackstone answered.

"I'm clear," the chief said.

"Me too," Graeme answered.

"I . . . I . . ." Patty stuttered, not sounding as confident as she usually was. "I have them."

"Me too," Darryl said quietly. Russo's shoulders slumped a little at the news.

"Jeff?" Russo asked. "You?"

There was a pause before he answered. "Yes. I have them."

Again silence filled the line as everyone contemplated this news.

"Alright," Russo said confidently, nodding to himself at the realization that he needed to take charge now. Not only was he the mayor, but he was unmarked. He was in no immediate danger. He swung his chair around to face his desk again. "Given the situation, we'll continue to link by phone for updates until we know more. In order to move forward, with Bert missing, I'll need one of you to step in as Acting Deputy Mayor."

"I'd be happy to," Jeff said quickly. Russo suspected that Jeff was still a little bitter about his failure to be elected mayor even once, given his long time on the council. But even with half a council missing, Russo still didn't think he was the man for the job.

"Thanks, Jeff, but I think Graeme should do it," Russo said. Given the gravity of the situation, Russo may need to hold some face to face meetings, and he couldn't do that with someone marked until he was sure it was safe. Graeme, like himself, was unmarked.

There was an awkward silence over the line.

"Alright," Jeff finally said. Thankfully he didn't argue the point. Russo didn't want to have to spell it out for him.

"Graeme?" Russo said. "Is that alright with you?"

"Yes, Mayor Russo. I'd be happy to step in."

"Good. Chief?" Russo queried.

"Yeah?"

"How many officers do you have left?"

"Well, I've still got one of my deputies, but he's marked. I'm waiting to hear back from the others."

Silence poured down the line for a moment.

"If they were still here you would've heard from them," Russo said, trying to sound compassionate.

"Yeah," Blackstone said with a relenting sigh, "I know."

"Well, you and your deputy should continue to run patrols and encourage people to stay off the street."

"My deputy's on it. I'll rejoin him when we're done here. But we're going to need help. Leo lost his baby boy, he needs to be with his family."

"As does everyone, chief," Russo said. "Hopefully, we'll have more clarity on the situation soon. Until then ..." Russo thought for a moment, wanting to say something profound and inspirational, but what could he say that would make everything alright? Finally, he simply said, "Until then, stay safe," he said. "I'm sure Bateson Dermacell will provide us with answers soon."

Dr. Lysart Pellan stared at the screen showing the comparison samples.

"They look normal," said Cheung, who stood beside him. "How can they look normal?"

Lysart glanced up at the graduate's young face, sighing

heavily. He looked back at the screen again, searching and searching for some kind of irregularity. But he could not find one.

An incoming call sounded over the speakers in their lab. They'd lost count of how many there had been. They both sighed.

"Disconnect it," Lysart said.

"Yes?" Cheung asked.

"Yes. Harvey and the CDC have my cell phone. It's just the media calling on the office line. Disconnect it."

"Yes, Dr. Pellan."

He watched Cheung leave the lab, happy to have a respite from the graduate looking over his shoulder and waiting for Lysart to magically solve the problem.

Lysart slumped in his seat and ran his hands over his face.

"Okay," he told himself, "you can do this. Find the anomaly. Find it."

He straightened again and slid his chair over to a second screen. Just as he moved to look closely at the results displayed, his attention was caught by the light reflecting off a picture frame. He reached out for it and stared at the worn and prettily-faded picture of Ganesha within. With its magnificent elephant head, human body, and decorative dress, Ganesha was the patron of writers, travelers, students, commerce, and new projects. Ganesha was apparently also rather fond of sweets, and it was for this reason Lysart's mother had bought him the picture when he was a child. He'd been a smart boy with a sweet tooth, and his mother had told him that Ganesha was well suited to be his patron.

He'd kept the picture all these years to remind him of his mother: of her kindness, her sense of humor and her faith, but mostly of her pride in what he'd achieved through his studies and his work.

He smiled at the image, then placed the frame back into position leaning against the wall.

"I could use your help right now, Ganesha," he said quietly. "I have a very big problem that I need to resolve."

He eyed the image for a moment, before returning his attention to the screen.

Abbie felt as though the night moved incredibly slowly, lasting hours more than it should. Whether that was because she'd lost a day somewhere, she wasn't sure.

She had wanted to go home, feeling uncomfortable in the Chalmer house, people whom she barely knew, but in the end she decided to stay the night. The truth was, she was scared to be alone, wondering if that thing would come back.

They'd sat glued to the TV for hours, trying to watch through the static, but it was chaos and confusion and constant replays of the ship hovering over the town and then disappearing again. It was surreal to see a replay of a brief address the president had made to the world during the ship's visitation, while Abbie had been lying unconscious on the VAC's cafe floor.

Pandemonium had been spreading across the world, everyone panicking that their town might be next. There were people buying up groceries and preparing their cellars. Groups were gathering in the streets, some praying, some demanding those in authority do something about it. But what could they do? The spaceship was gone.

The questions crying out to be answered were flying around like a locust storm. They seemed to cram inside Abbie's skull along with that constant mechanical noise being emitted from the TV. What the hell had happened to everyone? How did that ship sneak up on the town without any of the experts knowing? What did the mark on her face mean?

Information had slowly filtered through to the news channels on the status of people within Victoryville. Abbie felt a sense of relief, in some ways, to see the exchange of information with the outside world; to hear reports that the military had been in contact with the Victoryville Chief of Police. The reporters on the outside spoke with such excitement when they announced that, yes, people were still alive in the town. But then they looked morose and concerned when reporting that many seemed to be missing, and that some of the survivors had been left with these long red marks, which only led to speculation as to whether the marks were a sign of an alien infection.

Was it? Abbie wondered. Had she been infected with something? Was she going to die?

Abbie studied the Chalmers carefully and thought about those she'd seen on the street earlier that day. The red stripes marked many of those who remained. This had to be important, because not everyone had them. Of those who did, they were just like Abbie's: smooth welts that traveled from under their mouths, down over their chins, to the middle of their chests. Yet, of those who were marked, each were different. Where Abbie had only one stripe, Josh had three, his father had two. Upon first mention of a contagion, Josh's father made his mother wear a scarf over her mouth and nose for protection, in case it was airborne, and gloves in case it was anything else. It was probably too late, but . . .

And as the news crisscrossed from here to there, from one speculating expert to the next, and people of authority called for calm, Abbie kept looking out the window, over the street, hoping to see her family. Hoping to see her mother, father and sister drive up into the garage as if they'd just come home from the movies or something.

Josh and his parents were doing the same: Karen desperately wondering where her youngest son was, her blue eyes filling with tears, her face almost constantly buried in her hands; a vision of shaking shoulders and short, caramel, wavy hair. His father Peter was more stoic, but Abbie could see the worry tightening his tall, slim frame.

She and Josh eventually escaped upstairs to his room, wanting to get away from his mother's intermittent sobbing. Abbie curled up on a big comfy chair, while Josh sat on his bed. At first they sat in silence, but they could still hear his mother crying, so Josh put on some music to blanket it out.

"I don't know what's worse," he said, shaking his head, as his troubled eyes roved around the room. "Missing only one member of your family, or missing all of them."

Abbie stared at him, then looked back at her house across the street, so empty, so eerily quiet. Her mind's eye pictured her sister, Sarah, talking on the phone to her friends, the music channel blaring on the TV in the background; her sister had been in her final year of high school, her whole life ahead of her. She pictured her mother sitting on the porch in the sun, sipping a glass of wine and reading some exotic paperback. She imagined her father in the kitchen, trying to make some fancy dish like those TV chefs did, trying to make himself useful while he was out of work. She pictured herself in her room trying to study for her university exams, trying not to let herself gaze through the window at the new guy who'd moved in with his family across the street.

Abbie's family were working class, and after her father had been laid off from his sales job, they couldn't afford to send her to live in the city to attend university any more. At first she'd been bummed not to be able to follow a lot of her classmates out of town, but she got used to it. Although seeing their Facebook posts from time to time cut her a little. She'd been studying by correspondence part-time and working part-time ever since. She had one semester left before graduation. Just one semester until she could move on with the rest of her life, before she could get a full-time job and join her friends.

But now?

Now, sitting in Josh's middle-class bedroom, she stared at him and thought how weird it was to be here. They'd lived across the street from each other for the past couple weeks, had both worked part-time at the VAC, and they'd both lined up for lunch at Mona's Cafe. But other than the occasional nod hello, that was it. Friendly strangers. Until the day before, when he'd asked to sit at her table in the busy cafe and they'd talked.

They hadn't talked long, maybe thirty minutes, before she'd had to go teach another class. She'd discovered his family had come from Boston, he was twenty-one, a marketing graduate, and he was currently deciding what to do with his life; working a couple of part-time jobs and living with his folks while he figured it out. It turned out his father had grown up in these parts.

Still, it seemed odd to be suddenly sitting in Josh's room, his personal space, having barely said a word to him before yesterday. And just like that, because of lining up for that chicken and gravy roll lunch together, she was now here in his house being sheltered like some abandoned orphan.

Abbie stared at her empty house across the street again. She was grateful for the generosity of these strangers, but at the same time she felt she should be at home, and berated herself for not being more brave. She was supposed to be an adult, but right now she felt like a scared child.

A lump surfaced in her throat as she tried not to think about her family and what might have happened to them. Hoping upon hope that something bad *hadn't* happened to them. Because if it had, that meant she was now alone.

Richard Keene, after filing his report to Harry Dean, had sat glued to the TV, the internet and the phone throughout the afternoon, soaking up as much information as he could via the scattered and disrupted telecasts, taking notes on everything. Even as tiredness set in, and that mechanical noise emitting from the TV started to drive him as crazy as if it was a fly buzzing around his head, he couldn't stop watching or scrolling through the social media feeds.

It very quickly became known that Richard Keene from CNN was in "ground zero". Given his specialty was environmental issues and disasters, and that he was probably the only reporter in Victoryville right now, he had suddenly become hot property. He'd eventually turned his phone to silent, every station out there wanting a piece of him. Harry was working nonstop, trying to protect him from as much of it as he could, working out deals for access to Richard's footage. But that said, every reporter was on this phenomenon now. *Everyone.* How could they not be?

And Richard felt torn. This was the opportunity of a lifetime: he was the only one with direct access to the town in the midst of this crisis; he had prime position on the story of the century and everyone was looking to him for information. And yet, he was also a victim in this. So too, Benny and Lisa. This was more than just a story to him. This was potentially his life. To say he had a vested interest was a vast understatement.

At first, witnesses outside Victoryville told journalists and news anchors, they hadn't been sure of what was happening in the sky. Many reported seeing something unusual, like a heat mirage in the atmosphere, but simply mistook it for odd weather. It was only once the ship had disabled its camouflage that they, and the world, realized what was happening. NASA, the military, the government, and astronomers all over the world, had been shocked as to how this ship could have approached Earth without registering on any radars, sensors, or telescopes.

The US Air Force had immediately dispatched fighter jets to the scene, but as soon as they got close their electronics failed and the jets began to fall out of the sky. Next, the army rolled in with their tanks, but, again, as soon as they got close, their systems shut down. It seemed that the ship emitted some kind of signal, an electromagnetic field, that was causing everything around it to go haywire.

Just like the TV had gone haywire, he thought, hearing that strange buzz sounding on and off; watching the ripples of static roll down the screen.

With the ship supposedly gone and little known about it, the focus of the news had shifted to the survivors left inside Victoryville. They began to concentrate on what they *did* know, and the basic facts were these: many people were missing, and some of those who remained had been left with strange red marks on their faces. Richard was relieved that he wasn't one of them.

As a part of the report that he'd filed with Harry, Richard had submitted footage captured on Benny's camera of people in the hotel and on the street. Naturally, as part of that footage, he'd filmed some with the marks, giving the world professional footage, their first clear look at survivors that hadn't been captured on some shaky cell phone by a local resident and uploaded to social media sites.

The "Occurrence" was referred to as the Victoryville phenomenon, and the people with these marks became the central focus. Tuck Turner of Fox News soon dubbed them "Striped Ones" and the name quickly stuck. Those unmarked, like Richard himself, were soon dubbed "Clean Skins".

Reports filtered in on the various crisis meetings being

held by the government, the CDC and the WHO, and all media outlets were requested to broadcast messages asking for people to stay indoors and remain calm.

Naturally, fears were sparked that the Striped Ones may have been infected with something contagious, and measures were being taken to investigate. Richard almost couldn't believe his eyes when he saw Professor Harvey Meeks being interviewed on TV. He had just interviewed Meeks himself earlier that day, or rather, yesterday morning as he now knew, prior to the opening of the Bateson Dermacell facility. Richard sat glued to the screen listening to Meeks talk about his morning in Victoryville, his lucky escape, and how Bateson Dermacell were gladly offering assistance to the various agencies. Meeks had left town immediately after the ceremony, unable to stay for the morning tea due to commitments back in Washington.

Watching Meeks only made him think of Lisa and Benny again, and of the thousands of others who hadn't been so lucky …

And that's why he couldn't sleep.

He wanted answers. He wanted to find out what had happened to the missing. And he wanted to know what would happen to those left behind.

Day Two

Stanley Barrick sipped his coffee. He'd lost count of how many he'd had now. He glanced at his watch. Time was 1.00 a.m. He looked at the two people sitting on the other side of the desk in his makeshift office: Colonel Levin and Dr. Hogarth.

"So the people at Bateson Dermacell, the initial tests gave them cause for concern?" Stanley asked.

"No," Dr. Hogarth said, "they're still working on it, but we can't wait any longer. It's been over twelve hours since they awoke. If it is a contagion, they're probably already infected, but in the case of it having a long gestation period, we might stand a chance of saving the Clean Skins from infection if we do this. We need to mitigate the risk, and mitigate it now."

"It will take days to separate the survivors," he said. "They only have two cops left in the town."

"Yes, that's why we're proposing to send in a team of soldiers to assist them. They'll be equipped with the latest biohazard suits and instructed on the necessary precautions," she said, then shrugged. "We have no choice here. We estimate there're maybe 6,000 people left in the town."

"How many do you want to send in?"

"We'll send in three platoons," Levin answered. "They'll split the population, get the barrier up between the zones, then the bulk of them will pull back."

"The CDC will set up a small quarantine zone on the edge of the town," Hogarth added. "It will be used as a base for the soldiers, until we're sure they can rejoin the general population again."

"And," Levin said, "if there's trouble, being on the edge of the town enables the soldiers to respond much quicker than the units we have twenty miles back on the perimeter. Once the barrier is up between the zones, we'll post a skeleton crew along there as well, to make sure people stay where they should be."

"And you've got enough of the barrier to divide the whole town?"

"Yes," Levin said, "we've been shipping it in from surrounding areas since this happened. It's a modular design, so it's easy to handle and quick to lock in place."

Stanley nodded, darting his eyes between both of them. "You realize if you go in, then there's no guarantee we can let you back out again."

Hogarth nodded. "We know the risks. We go to war-torn countries and areas of outbreak all the time. We'll take every precaution."

"And my soldiers know the risks as well," Levin added. "If needed, they will give their life for their country. But if we're smart it won't come to that."

"When will you be ready to head in?" Stanley asked Levin.

"As soon as we're given the word, they'll be good to go."

Hogarth nodded. "We need to segregate the Striped Ones from the Clean Skins as soon as possible," she said. "That'll take a while, but if we start now, we should be able to have the people quarantined in their zones by midmorning."

Stanley looked at the colonel. "Send your soldiers in, divide the town and get that barrier up." The colonel nodded, stood and left the room.

Dr. Hogarth moved to follow, but Stanley stopped her. "Not you."

"Excuse me?" she said.

"We're dealing with an alien ship here. Going into that town is probably a one-way ticket."

"If there's a contagion, you need us to stop it."

"You can stop it from the outside."

"No, we need to be in ground zero—"

"We have people in ground zero, Dr. Hogarth. You direct the folks at Bateson Dermacell as you see fit, but they're the ones who collect the samples and do the physical study. They're already infected. There's no need for you to be too."

"And if they get sick and die?"

"Then you get your wish and can go in and take their place."

Richard Keene, despite a lack of sleep and the constant government-issued messages broadcast through the media to stay indoors, took to the town's streets, as did many others. It was dawn, the sun just a hint on the far horizon. There had been reports on TV of the military moving into the town, but he hadn't seen any soldiers yet. Wearing a bandana over his mouth and nose for protection from a possible airborne alien virus, he wanted to inspect things in the cold almost-light of day.

Day two of the phenomenon . . .

Aside from the reports of military movement, there had

been little in the way of updates overnight; and there was no news about whatever Bateson Dermacell had been doing since it happened. He was tempted to pay them a visit, but at the same time knew they'd have their hands full and didn't want to slow them down, so he stayed away.

Lots of debate was being held on the various social media channels: thousands were offering thoughts and prayers, hundreds wanted to help in some way, and some were recommending that Victoryville be wiped from the face of the earth taking the possible contagion along with it. It was the latter comment that worried Richard. Especially the ones who were offering to come and do it personally "if the military were too chickenshit to do it themselves."

It soon became apparent that the missing were still missing. The Victoryville Police Department, now consisting of just two cops, were doing their best to insist on the lockdown, yet people were escaping their homes and gathering along the main street, plastering walls and signposts with pictures of their missing, that said: "*Have you seen my son / daughter / mother / father / grandmother / grandfather / aunty / uncle / cousin / nephew / niece / friend?*"

Armed with his backpack and Benny's camera, Richard filmed the growing shrines, trying to steady his shaking hands, astounded at just how many seemed to be missing. It reminded him, hauntingly, of 9/11.

Looking at the faces in those pictures seemed to burn a hole in Richard's chest as he thought of Lisa and Benny . . . neither of them had returned any of his calls. He knew it was useless, knowing just how many were missing, but it was all he could do: keep calling them, keep hoping that they'd pick up. Keep hoping that maybe Benny was playing a trick on him and having a good laugh about it. But he knew it wasn't true.

Sympathy for their families flooded through him. He

closed his eyes a moment and recalled the sound of relief flushing through his mother's voice over the phone upon hearing that he was alive and unmarked. He'd heard his father's voice echo that relief in the background; his adoptive parents were so concerned they immediately spoke of flying out from Iowa to come to him. He'd told them to stay put, that he would visit them as soon as he could. It made him wonder if Benny and Lisa's families would ever get the chance to see them again.

He continued on filming with Benny's camera, but also used a compact hand-sized camera that he always carried in his backpack. Harry had drilled into him the importance of covering his ass. *"Always think ahead, kid, and always have a back-up plan."*

In the town center, some of the stores and apartments had boarded their windows, perhaps frightened by some of the reactions they'd seen on TV, from around the world, of people looting stores. Some people sat by the "missing" photos of their loved ones and cried. Some just walked around looking lost and shocked as though they were walking around the rubble of a bomb site. Others looked edgy, nervous, suspicious, and eyed everyone with mistrust.

He made sure to capture all their faces, paying particular attention to those with the welts, utterly fascinated. Only the Clean Skins wore facial coverings for protection. The Striped Ones obviously didn't see the point, as they were the ones who had been marked. The welts themselves looked the same on everyone in that they were uniformly straight lines, although blurred a little along the edges. The only thing different about them was the number. He passed a few ones, but also saw someone who had as many as four.

"May I?" he asked a Hispanic woman, who had two stripes running down her chin.

She looked at him, frightened, studying the yellow bandana that covered his mouth and nose. Richard motioned to the large camera in his hands.

"May I?" he asked again. "Film you."

She nodded cautiously and he zoomed in to capture the welts up close, then slowly pulled out again. When he saw the tears that had formed in her brown eyes, he lowered the camera again.

"What's going to happen to us?" she asked in a whisper of a voice, as her welted chin began to quiver.

Richard felt a sadness fill his body as he stared back at her. "I don't know."

Abbie and Josh awoke to sirens blaring. She looked at the clock; it was just after 6.00 a.m. Her neck sore, her eyes dry, she'd slept very little on the couch chair, insisting that Josh kept his bed last night. They both quickly got up and moved to his window. As they looked down their street, they saw soldiers in full biohazard suits entering the houses one by one and removing people.

She listened to the announcement blaring from the military transport's speakers: "I repeat, we ask for your assistance with this segregation. It is for your own safety. It is possible the Striped Ones have been infected with a virus. A quarantine zone will now be enforced and we must remove any Clean Skins from this area. We ask that all Clean Skins come with us willingly. If you do not come of your own accord, we will be forced to remove you. This is for your own wellbeing ..."

They learned the town was literally being divided in half: the southern side of Victoryville, where they both lived, was now declared a Striped Zone, and an exclusion zone for the

Clean Skins. The northern side had been declared the opposite: a safe haven for Clean Skins, an exclusion zone for the Striped Ones.

Abbie and Josh ran down the stairs and joined his parents at the front windows. Karen glanced at them worriedly. They watched as some residents moved out into the street willingly, bags packed, eager to leave, but Abbie also saw some Clean Skins who did not want to leave their homes. Those who resisted were physically forced: one woman was dragged onto the bus shouting and crying, and another man, after a scuffle, was knocked unconscious and taken away.

All Abbie could think was if this is what they were doing to the Clean Skins, then what on earth would they do to the Striped Ones they thought were infected?

She stepped back from the window and raised her hand to the welt on her chin.

"What are we going to do?" Karen said nervously, eyeing the soldiers two houses away. "I don't want to leave."

Peter turned to look at her.

"Where will they take me?" she asked.

Peter's eyes fell to the floor, his mind turning over.

"They have to take you away from us," Josh told her quietly.

Karen's eyes glistened as she stared back at him. "But I don't want to leave you."

"We don't have a choice, mom," Josh said.

"That ship . . . aliens did this! If this is the end, I want to spend it with you. Not them!" Karen motioned to the military.

Peter suddenly pulled Karen back from the window, startling her.

"I don't want you to leave either," Peter said. He hugged her tightly, then moved to the middle of the kitchen and tossed the floor rug aside. Underneath sat a hatch, which he opened.

Abbie saw stairs leading down into a dark, dank basement. Peter looked back at Karen.

"I won't leave you again," he said, eyes filled with emotion. He took hold of the tops of Karen's sleeved arms. "We stay together. No matter what."

"But... what?" Karen queried, face filled with concern. She glanced at the window. Abbie could hear the soldiers' voices now.

"They'll take you away," Peter said desperately. "This was our second chance!"

"They're right next door!" Josh called anxiously from the window.

"But we could be contagious," Abbie said to Peter.

"We'll take our chances," he said, then looked back at Karen. "Someone took our son, I'm not letting them take you too!"

Karen looked at the basement stairs, then back at her husband's pleading face. Her eyes shone with tears. He kissed her covered cheek firmly, then held her gloved hand as she moved down the steps and disappeared. Peter swiftly closed the hatch and threw the rug back over it. He ordered Josh to stand on top of it, and they waited nervously as the bio-suited military finally banged on the front door. Peter motioned for Abbie to answer it. She did. Three soldiers entered the house, weapons by their sides. Two quickly swept through each room, while the eyes of the one remaining by the door looked curiously over their striped faces.

Abbie tried hard to stay calm, but the tightness began across her chest. She started taking deep breaths, but the wheezing soon overcame her. She moved for her bag on the floor in the adjoining living room, but stopped suddenly as the muzzle of a soldier's weapon appeared in front of her face.

"Don't move!" the soldier barked.

She placed one hand up, pleading for calm, while the other clutched at her chest.

"Please!" she begged, struggling for breath. "Asthma! I have asthma!"

Josh threw her a concerned glance, but he didn't dare move from the rug covering the hatch. He shot his father a pleading look, and Peter quickly stepped up.

"Abbie? What is it?" He took her shoulders.

"Asthma ... Ventolin ... my s—spray ...?" and she pointed desperately at her bag.

Peter glanced at the bag, then the soldier. "Please?"

The soldier held his weapon firm, but motioned for Peter to go ahead. Josh's father fetched her bag and placed it on the floor in front of her heavily wheezing frame. His hands dived in and searched for her relief. When he found it, she snatched it off him and sucked with all her might to clear her airways. The seconds passed, while Josh, Peter and the soldier stared at her. By the time her breathing had eased, the other two soldiers had finished searching the house.

"Clear," one of them said.

"Where are you taking them?" Peter asked the soldier, as he watched Mrs. Robson being led toward a bus outside the window. "The Clean Skins."

"Somewhere safe," he replied. "When we're sure you Striped Ones aren't a health risk, we will return them."

"And what happens to us?" Peter queried, his thin, striped face looking gaunt with worry.

"Just stay calm, and stay put, and you'll be fine, sir," he replied, then signaled for his troops to move onto the next house.

And as quickly as they had come, they left.

Dr. Lysart Pellan studied the new samples of his colleague's skin, comparing it to the previous samples. He blinked his eyes to clear the blurriness, as his lack of sleep was beginning to get to him. He'd been working through the night, in constant consultation with the CDC, trying to discover what was behind the red stripes marking many of the survivors' faces.

The team had been sleeping in shifts, and both Mary and Grant were sleeping now. The Striped Ones had been predominantly confined to Lab-Two, using Dr. Seevers' office for sleep, and had been allocated the female toilets due to Mary Rodriguez being one of them. Lysart and Cheung, being Clean Skins, had free rein in the rest of the facility and used the male bathroom.

"Anything?" Dr. John Seevers asked, his colleague's voice sounding distant through the audio channel from the adjoining Lab-Two. Lysart looked up through the window between the labs as John pulled off his surgical mask.

"John!" Lysart called out sharply.

"I'm marked, Dr. Pellan," he said dejectedly. "What does it matter if the mask is on or off?"

Lysart stared at John's face, his eyes falling briefly to the stripe marking his colleague's chin. He sighed, feeling his breath fill the mask over his own face.

"Why can't we find any anomalies?" John asked.

"I don't know," Lysart said. "There's no evidence whatsoever of bacteria or virus."

"It is so unusual," Cheung said suddenly from beside him, having just returned from his sleep shift, "that we can't find any foreign material at all."

"It doesn't make sense," John said from the other lab. "I'm marked and you're not. There must be a reason for this? How can our blood samples both be fine? How can our skin samples both be fine? How can there have been no cellular changes these past hours?"

"Let me take another look at the skin sample from your welt," Lysart told him. "There may be a long gestation—"

"That ship was over the town for twenty-four hours," John countered. "After twenty-four hours we woke up with the welts and you didn't."

"Those of us unmarked may have some natural immunity to it," Cheung offered.

"It hasn't been twenty-four hours since we woke up," Lysart told him. "Let's not draw any conclusions just yet."

John stared at him, his face indicating he thought it was a long shot. And the truth was, Lysart was inclined to agree. But they weren't dealing with something of this world. They had no idea what parameters to set for *this* research project.

"Cheung's right. If we didn't wake up with the welts," Lysart placated him, "it could mean we have a natural immunity to whatever is causing those welts. We have to keep going until we find something to explain things."

John sighed and nodded. "I'm sorry, I'm just tired and frustrated."

"We all are, John."

"Have you eaten yet, Dr. Pellan?" Cheung asked, his young face looking aged from the events that had befallen them. "It's been a while."

"Thank you, I will eat soon. But, please, you should prepare some food for the others."

"I definitely need to eat," John said from the other side of the window, pulling off his surgical cap. "I'm starting to feel a little lightheaded."

John turned for the exit, but stopped as something behind

Lysart caught his eyes. Both Lysart and Cheung turned to see three soldiers entering Lab-One. They were dressed in dark hazmat suits, including black face masks—the only part of them visible, through two clear plastic circles, were their eyes.

"Can I help you?" Lysart asked them.

A soldier stepped forward, a woman he presumed from the shorter height and the body shape. She scanned both his and Cheung's faces, then moved to look through the window into Lab-Two. She saw John, then turned and motioned for the other two soldiers to move there. Lysart turned to see the soldiers enter the second lab and take Dr. Seevers by the arms.

"You need to come with us, sir!"

"Me?" John said.

"What is the meaning of this?" Lysart asked, watching them through the window.

"Are there any other Striped Ones here?" the female soldier asked, ignoring his question.

Lysart felt Cheung move closer to his side.

"Are there others?" she asked Lysart.

"Yes," he answered, "but what's going on?"

"Wait! What's happening?" John said, trying to pull back from the soldiers in the next lab.

"What is the meaning of this?" Lysart demanded.

"Sir, segregation is in force until more is known about these welts," the female soldier told him.

"But there's nothing wrong with me!" John said quickly. "I feel fine!"

"It may not be infectious!" Lysart held his hand out to them.

"I'm sorry, sir. Quarantine has been mandated and this is now a Clean Skin zone. The Striped Ones must be removed.

Government orders."

"But we're working for the government!" Lysart said. "We're trying to figure out these welts!"

"I'm sorry, sir." She turned to the soldiers and hiked her thumb, motioning for them to move it.

"No," John tried to argue, "I'm needed here." But the soldiers swiftly swept him from the room.

Lysart quickly stood and exited his lab, removing his face mask as he did. He followed them down the corridor, Cheung trailing behind, and witnessed Grant and Mary being swept from Dr. Seevers' office, where they'd been sleeping, by more soldiers.

"Dr. Pellan!" Mary called to him as she was being moved down the hall after John and Grant. "What's going on?"

Lysart shook his head. "I don't know."

"My kids!" she called over her shoulder, eyes flashing wide with fear.

"I'll see to them!" he called back, following his striped colleagues being marched down the corridor. As he entered reception, a soldier caught him by the shoulders and moved him back against the wall.

"You're a Clean Skin, sir. You stay here!"

Lysart watched, helpless, as his three marked staff members were marched out of the building. As soon as they were outside he swiftly moved over to the nearest window to see them being loaded into a bus. He saw John refusing to get on, arguing and struggling with the soldiers who had taken him.

"Dr. Pellan!" he yelled out frantically.

Lysart pressed his gloved hand against the windowpane to let his colleague know he was there. "John!" he called back.

He saw John trying to plead with those who held him, but

couldn't hear what was said.

"Please!" John said, then shouted, "*Dr. Pellan!*" He sounded frantic now.

It was then that Lysart saw John's head loll back and his body fall limp. The soldiers quickly caught him and laid him down on the ground. They slapped his face, trying to get him to come to.

"Oh, no!" Lysart's eyes went wide as he suddenly realized what was happening. He turned and raced past Cheung down the corridor into the break room and opened the fridge.

"What is it, Dr. Pellan? What's wrong?"

Lysart found what he needed, grabbed it, then raced back down the corridor toward the exit. As he burst through the front door, a soldier standing close at hand spun around, startled. The soldier saw what he was holding, caught him, then slammed him back against the wall, pinning his gloved hand.

"No, no!" Lysart shook his head.

"Drop it."

"It's not what you think."

"Drop the needle now, sir!"

"It's just a sugar solution! Please. For my colleague. He's diabetic." He showed the soldier his other gloved hand, which contained a vial.

The soldier looked around at John lying on the ground. He looked back at Lysart, made a quick assessment, then stepped back with his weapon targeted on him. "Slow movements, sir," the soldier warned, motioning for him to proceed.

Lysart held his hands up in a calming manner, then made his way over to John, kneeling by his side. He freed John from the protective gown he wore, then pulled up his shirt to expose his stomach and quickly administered the injection. They watched and waited in silence as John slowly came to. He blinked his eyes and focused them on Lysart.

"You're going to be alright, John," Lysart told him.

The soldiers grabbed Lysart and moved him back toward the door of the building again.

"Wait!" Lysart argued. "Here . . ." He pulled out another vial and handed it to the soldier. "He may need this. It's his insulin."

The soldier took it from him, then pushed Lysart back inside the front door of Bateson Dermacell and pulled it closed. Lysart once again placed a hand against the glass, while the other, holding the used syringe, lay limp at his side. He watched with concern as they loaded the groggy John Seevers onto the bus with his other striped colleagues, and drove them away to an unknown destination.

Richard Keene watched as a tank rolled down the street toward him, one of the many military vehicles now sweeping the streets.

"You!" A masked soldier standing on the back of a jeep called out to him. "You a Clean Skin?"

Richard nodded and raised the bandana to show his chin and neck.

"Then get on the bus, please, sir," the soldier said.

Richard looked to where he pointed, and saw other soldiers leading civilians onto the transport.

"Why?" Richard furrowed his brow.

"It's not a request, sir. It's an order. All Clean Skins onto the bus now! Move!"

"Where are you taking us?" Richard asked.

"Somewhere safe." The soldier jumped down from his vehicle and approached. He was tall and broad, and looked a little on edge although he wore a black, bulky, bio-mask. The Hispanic woman Richard had seen earlier that morning appeared beside him, but the soldier pulled the marked woman away from Richard. "Get on the bus, now, sir!"

"Wait, you can't order me—"

"Yes, I can, sir!"

"At least let me go back to my hotel room and get my stuff. It's just down a couple blocks."

"Everything down that way is now in the Striped Zone, sir. You cannot go there. You need to go to the Clean Zone."

"Clean Zone?" Richard questioned. "You're segregating the town?"

"Sir, you can get on that bus by yourself, or I can make you. Choice is yours." The soldier widened his broad shoulders and tightened his grip on his weapon.

"What about us?" the marked woman asked.

"You stay here," he told her, then called out to another Clean Skin couple. "You two on the bus now, please. Move!"

"Where is the bus going?" Richard asked again. "And what's going to happen to the Striped Ones?"

The soldier suddenly pointed his weapon at Richard. "Get on the bus now, sir!"

Richard held his hands up and backed up a couple of steps.

"YOU, TOO!" the soldier shouted at the Clean Skin couple.

Richard suddenly felt two soldiers grab him by the arms and escort him onto the bus along with the couple. He fell into a seat, clutching his backpack and Benny's camera, and craned his neck, and his small handheld camera, out the window to see what was going on. He saw the marked Hispanic woman reaching after the soldier in panic, following him down the street. She latched onto his arm, but he shrugged her off roughly, accidentally knocking her to the ground. Suddenly

Richard heard gunfire, and looked in the opposite direction to see a scuffle taking place between a man and two soldiers. The man was swiftly overcome and they dragged his unconscious frame onto the bus and dumped him in the aisle beside Richard.

He eyed the man's Clean Skin face, his closed eyes, his cut forehead, then turned back to stare out at the evolving madness.

"It's okay, we'll be safe," a man said from the seat in front of Richard, comforting the young boy who sat beside him. "They're going to take us away from these people."

"What's wrong with them?" the boy asked, eyes wide as he stared out the window.

"They're infected with something," the man said. "That's why we need to stay away from them. These soldiers are going to help us and take us somewhere safe."

Richard watched the man put his arm around the boy, then turned his eyes to the streets again.

Deputy Leo Cann eyed the line of cars queued up on the road out of town, and the new, closer, military post that was obstructing them. The cars were piled high with suitcases and furniture and food; people were trying to escape the nightmare. But they'd only managed to form a long car park that had seen them sleep there overnight. A few had tried to drive off-road, but the circling helicopters soon caught them in their spotlights and forced them to turn back. For most, the helicopter and the spotlight was enough deterrent. Some needed warning fire to convince them. God knows where they thought they were going. Hadn't they been watching the news? The military had Victoryville surrounded. There was no leaving. There was no escaping this. Everyone was trapped here.

He took off his hat, scratched his head, and rubbed his dry eyes. It had been a long night and he was exhausted. He wanted these people to go home. *He* wanted to go home. That's all he wanted to do, was get back to his family.

What was left of it . . .

He tried not to think of Mickey. Tried not to think how his baby boy had just disappeared from his cot. How *they* had taken him. He swallowed hard, fighting the lump in his throat and the heavy ache in his chest. The feeling of helplessness that he couldn't protect his son.

His heart burned at the recollection of bursting through his front door and Claire falling into his arms, hysterical, screaming that Mickey was gone. He'd felt so powerless. Frozen in shock. But somehow he knew his son hadn't been kidnapped. He'd seen everyone picking themselves up off the street. He'd seen some of their faces covered in those welts. He'd seen his own face . . . and he knew something bad had happened.

He'd stayed with Claire and Lena as long as he could, but then Earl had called, pleading for his help. They were the only badges left in town and people were freaking out. He'd had no choice but to leave Claire and Lena to go patrol the streets, trying to keep people calm and get them indoors. The last thing they needed was any further trouble breaking out. Not with everything else they had to deal with.

Now that the military was here and the division was in place, though, Leo found himself alone in the Striped Zone. Earl, a Clean Skin, was now tasked with policing the Clean Zone and, as both Claire and Lena were Clean Skins and their house was located in the Striped Zone, he'd had to say goodbye to his wife and daughter. They had been taken to the other side of town.

Part of him was glad. If he was infected with something then he wanted them far away, so they could be safe. He wanted to protect them. Something he'd been unable to do for his son.

He clenched his jaw and put his hat back on, fighting the tears for his missing son that threatened to swamp his dry, stinging eyes; fighting the burning in his heart to be with Claire and Lena again; fighting the fear of what these aliens had done to everyone. He exhaled loudly, trying to dismiss the emotion, and focused his attention on the military roadblock.

The soldiers were making their way down the line of cars in their black bio-suits, separating the last of the Clean Skins and Striped Ones. Some of the civilians yelled abuse at them and honked their horns, demanding to be let out of Victoryville; some broke down and cried. He heard one old man begging for his release, saying, "I don't want to die like this. Not like this! Not here!"

Others were attempting to bribe the soldiers. Leo saw a man trying to hand over a wad of cash; saw a young woman trying to offer herself as payment. Thankfully, the soldiers denied them. The thought of unleashing an alien virus on the world was enough for them to keep their priorities in order.

Then there were the ones who tried to fight their way out. One guy tried to make a run for it. He didn't get far before he was tackled to the ground. Another pulled a gun and fired a shot off. He hit nothing but air and didn't see the soldier approaching from behind. Leo was pretty sure the arm holding that gun was broken soon afterward.

Leo shook his head. The town and its people were in a right goddamn mess.

He sighed heavily and looked at his watch. It was just hitting 8.00 a.m.

Today was going to be another very long day.

Michael Russo walked toward his office in the local civic building. He had tried to get some sleep, but found it hard to lie in bed knowing that Nicola was not there beside him. Not knowing what had happened to her, not knowing if she was alive or dead. Wondering if that ship was coming back for those who remained. Wondering if this was the end.

He'd lain there most of the night, scrolling through his social media feeds, unable to stop himself from reading the mass of data flowing across the small screen of his cell phone. He saw wild rumors circulating, people on the outside discussing things they couldn't possibly know anything about; saw heated arguments between people living on the opposite side of the globe about what really happened and what the government and military should or shouldn't have done; saw declarations and prayers from all manner of public figures, from politicians on both sides of the fence, to Hollywood celebrities, to the Queen of England; saw one or two people reminiscing over the time they'd visited the town; saw others say they didn't even know it existed; saw others, albeit it only a few, making light of the situation in order to elicit cheap, easy laughs; and there were others who demanded the town be eradicated from existence. And there were more that subscribed to this way of thinking than he'd liked to have known about.

Despite the horrible situation he was in, he knew he was actually one of the lucky ones. He was unmarked and both his home and his office were located in the newly designated Clean Zone, which meant he hadn't been displaced like many of his remaining constituents. He almost felt a little guilty for the way things had turned out.

Eva, his secretary, met him at the office. He even still had her. Her Clean Skin face gave him a sad smile as she announced that Chief Blackstone was in his office. He gave her a nod and entered. The Clean Skin, Blackstone, rose from the chair in which he sat and shook Russo's hand.

"Chief," Russo said, eyeing the big man whose height seemed to cast a shadow over him. The hat the chief wore made him seem taller still, "how have you fared in all of this?"

"How have I fared?" Blackstone raised his eyebrows, the deepness of his voice accentuating that southern drawl.

"Are any of your family missing?"

Blackstone stared at him a moment. "Well, as you know, Erina died last year. I'm a widower."

"Yes, of course," Russo smiled sympathetically. "I meant your children, I know they visit you often."

Again Blackstone looked at him oddly. "No. My daughter's down in Louisiana and my son's in Illinois. I have no losses to speak of other than my officers."

"You're lucky, chief."

Blackstone pressed his lips together briefly, making his voluminous gray mustache move. "You?"

"Nicola. She's one of the missing."

Blackstone gave him a sympathetic look. "I'm sorry to hear that, mayor."

Russo exhaled loudly, and moved to sit behind his desk. "I guess things could be worse, though, right?"

Blackstone didn't respond, but his dark eyes studied him.

"I mean, at least we're Clean Skins," Russo clarified. "God knows what the hell those stripes mean."

Blackstone's eyes eased off, but his mouth still didn't respond.

"Now the segregation has taken place, I've noticed the soldiers have started lining up pieces of the barrier," Russo commented.

"Yeah," Blackstone said, "they pulled some of the soldiers back to the perimeter to guard the roads in secondary quarantine zones, though. They don't want them sticking around in town any longer than they have to. Just in case."

"Well, I guess it's quite fortunate that your deputy is striped. You can split the policing of the zones between you."

The chief stared back at him. "I'm not sure Leo would see it as fortunate. Being striped and all."

Russo leaned forward on his desk. "We have no choice but to work with what we've got, chief. We need to focus on keeping the zones in place and doing what we can to make sure the people stay calm. Has the exodus out of town slowed down?"

"Some," Blackstone shrugged. "The roadblocks the military have in place have stopped most of them. Well, that and the segregation. Some may have slipped past or hidden in the early hours before we could get a handle on things, though."

"Slipped past? How could they slip past the military perimeter?"

Blackstone shrugged. "If people really want out, they'll find a way."

"What other way could there be? You can see the choppers flying in the distance. They'll pick up anyone trying."

Blackstone nodded. "And that's why the attempted exodus has slowed. I'm just saying, never rule anything out. I have found, in life, that if there's a will there's a way. You threaten a man's life there's no telling to what lengths he'll go to survive." He eyed Russo with concern. "Cage a lot of people together against their will, there's no telling how things will pan out. People are scared. We've got to play this carefully."

"Agreed. That's why it's important we get out there and ease people's minds. Tell them they're safe if they stay put and that this will be over soon."

"Will it?" Blackstone asked. "Be over soon?"

Russo stared at him and shrugged. "I have faith in the external authorities, and so should you. The town is looking to us for leadership, chief. We need to assure them that this will pass. We want them to view Victoryville as a haven, not a hell."

Blackstone nodded in agreement. "I'm on my way to do another patrol now."

"Good. I'm going to head out myself soon, show my face, and talk to people. On the Clean Skin side, anyway. I'll see you out there."

Blackstone tipped his hat and headed for the door. Russo watched him leave, then took a deep breath and focused his mind on what words of comfort he would say to the people. With the eye of the world upon him, he had to make sure they were damn good.

Richard Keene stood inside the Victoryville Civic Hall on the northern side of town, with many other Clean Skins. More were being brought in by the hour. He demanded to speak with someone in charge, angry that Benny's camera had been confiscated by the soldiers as he stepped off the bus. They were patting everyone down to ensure no one carried weapons before being sent into the hall, and they had decided that Richard no longer needed his big TV camera, that they'd put it somewhere safe for him. They did leave him with his small handheld, though. And as soon as the bus had pulled up and he'd seen them patting people down, he'd slipped the pocketknife from his backpack into his shoe. He was told there was currently no one available to hear his complaints about

Benny's camera and he'd have to be patient.

He eyed the growing chaos of his surroundings, the people flooding in and the supplies being unloaded by the military, wondering just how long he was going to have to stay there. Volunteers were putting out coffee, tea and biscuits to placate the growing crowd, and a large screen was being erected to show cartoons for the children. Some of those gathered were teary with concern, some quiet with anxiety. Some people quite frankly looked relieved to be there. Of course, there were also others who were angry and debated among themselves over whether the phenomenon was real or a government hoax, and who got which of the camp and foldaway beds being placed in the main hall, the designated sleeping space for their immediate future.

He made his way to the nearest available bathroom for some peace and quiet. He dumped his pack on the floor and pulled out his phone. There was a message from Harry Dean. Richard returned the call and Kelly put it straight through.

"Richard, what's happening?" Harry answered. "Why'd the military move in?"

"I'm in the Civic Hall. They've segregated the town. They're rounding up the Clean Skins with nowhere else to go and bringing us here. My hotel is apparently now in the Striped Zone."

"They're worried about a contagion then. You feeling alright?"

"Yeah, I'm fine. Physically," Richard said as he tugged his hand through his curly hair. "At least, I think so. What the hell is going on, Harry?"

"You tell me. You got anything new?"

"Just some views and reactions on the street this morning. Plus I got a little as the military swept the streets too. I lost some of it because they confiscated Benny's camera, but I've got my little handheld in my backpack."

"You took back-up footage?"

"Of course," Richard said. "Isn't that what you always taught me, Harry? To cover my ass."

Harry laughed. "That's right! Always have a back-up and your trusty pack like you might not see the light of day for a while."

"Yeah! Thank god I took the pack with me this morning."

"Never leave home without it," Harry said. "You've got everything you need?"

"Yeah, chargers, batteries, some spare clothes, my pocketknife. I'll survive."

"Good. Can you send me through what footage you've still got?"

"Yeah. I'll record a report and send it over to you shortly."

"Good," Harry said, then began speaking with someone in the background. After a moment his attention came back to the phone. "Richard, we just got word that the White House is doing a live cross for another address by the president very soon. Let's see what he's got to say."

"Good. Let's hope they have answers for us."

"Let's hope." Harry hung up, and Richard put his phone back in his pocket. He reached into his pack and took out his handheld camera. It was time to file another report.

Abbie sat glued to the TV. She'd tried to distract herself with other things, but there really wasn't anything else she could do. The VAC was closed and swimming classes canceled until further notice, and she just couldn't fathom the idea of trying to study to take her mind off things. She'd called her swimming class families to check they were okay, and found that over half of the kids were missing. All those children, gone. Vanished into thin air. Or, worse, vanished into that alien ship.

Just like her family had.

The military had completed their sweep of Victoryville and most of the soldiers had withdrawn, while rumors spread that they were working on building a barrier between the zones. The few soldiers who remained had set up a guardhouse on the main intersection in town. The intersection was not only the central point of town, but also the central point of the new Clean Skin-Striped Zone border. The border that would soon run along the main street, west to east, virtually cutting the town in half.

An announcement had been made that an address by President Turner was imminent, and Abbie noticed that the streets had emptied. Karen emerged from the basement for the telecast, but the hatch was left ajar and the curtains kept drawn. Peter paced, and Josh bit his fingernails anxiously as they waited to hear what the President had to say.

Waited to hear their fate.

Finally, normal broadcasting was interrupted, the introduction made, and then the president appeared sitting in the Oval Office.

"Good afternoon. The past couple of days have seen us experience an event never seen before. An event that, due to its nature, will take us time to investigate fully. I come to you today with a message, one that I hope will provide you with comfort and assurance. A message to instill in you, the people of America, and everyone around the world, faith that we will work our hardest to investigate this phenomenon, to find the answers and to find a resolution for those in Victoryville.

"Please be assured that we have many people, the best of the best, working around the clock to try and understand what has taken place in Victoryville. The United States government and its many agencies have been gathering data on the missing, while the Centers for Disease Control and Prevention—along with the World Health Organization and its Global Outbreak Alert and Response Network—have been analyzing the results of initial tests on the survivors. They are working tirelessly to understand what is behind the marks left on some of the residents of Victoryville, what this could mean for those unmarked in the town, and for those of us throughout the rest of the world. Each and every one of these organizations is reporting to our government and we, in turn, will continue to report back to you, the people.

"Due to the scale of this phenomenon, it will take some time to complete the investigation, but please be assured that we will investigate all angles thoroughly until we have the answers we seek, until we know what the risks are, and until we locate the missing.

"In order to help us resolve this as swiftly as we can, we need the help of our people. So the first thing you must do is remain calm. We understand that everyone is feeling immense pressure, that you are feeling the absence of your loved ones, and you are feeling concern for the marked ones. But the best thing you can do for yourselves and for those around you is to remain calm. The United States military and NASA have assured us that there is no immediate threat to the people of America, or to anywhere else in the world. All available surveillance internationally is being actioned, and our forces are alert and ready to protect you should it be needed. But again I say, there is no immediate threat. You are safe.

"We have now stationed military personnel in the town of Victoryville and engaged the local police to assist us and ensure everyone continues to stay safe. Until we know more, we ask that the people of Victoryville remain indoors where possible. I repeat, this is for everyone's safety. I want you to know that the separation of those marked from those unmarked is merely a precaution and a risk mitigation measure. We don't know why some civilians have these marks, these welts, so until we do, and until we're sure there is no contagious disease involved, this separation has to take place. The town has, therefore, been divided into two areas: a safe zone for the Clean Skins, and a safe zone for the Striped Ones. Temporary barriers will be erected between the two, and these barriers are not to be crossed. Again this is for your own safety.

"I must stress that these barriers are only temporary, and will remain in place until we have resolved this issue. Please note that if your loved ones have been removed from you, they will be taken care of. The United States government will ensure adequate supplies are provided to the people of Victoryville. Those displaced from their home will be sheltered and fed by the many volunteers stepping up to help us in our hour of need. If you yourself would like to volunteer goods or services, please go online to the website you see listed below. If we require your services, you will be called to assist.

"Please also note the second website listed on the screen now. If you have not yet done so, please ensure you register any missing members of your family, or friends or colleagues. Many have been registered already, but we believe there are still many left to report. This is important information that may assist us in trying to uncover what has happened.

"Lastly, I would like to thank everyone for their patience so far. We will endeavor to bring you an update whenever we can until this situation is resolved. Until that time, please remain patient and calm, please report your missing loved ones, and please do not be concerned for any loved ones you have been separated from. They are being cared for and they will remain safe.

"Together we will work, and together we will get to the bottom of this situation. Thank you. And God bless America."

"Why the barriers?" Karen whispered, looking over at Peter. Her caramel hair was alight with the glow of the TV, and this, along with the scarf around her nose and mouth, gave her an odd appearance.

Peter stared back at her, but did not answer.

"Peter, maybe I should turn myself in? Go into the Clean Zone."

"No."

"But we saw what they did to those who resisted segregation. What do you think they'll do to those found hiding where they shouldn't be?"

"You'll be fine here, Karen. This will pass in a few days."

Josh looked at his father. "But what if we're contagious?"

"If we're contagious, then she's already been exposed. Removing her now will do nothing."

"But the president—" Karen began.

"Is covering his ass!" Peter said. "You'll be fine. This will pass."

She stared into his eyes. "Thousands are missing, Peter. Thousands. This won't go away in a few days."

"It will." Peter said. "They'll sort it out."

"That's what they thought about the Berlin Wall too, and how many years did that stand?"

"We've made our decision," Peter said firmly, his thin face accentuating his worry. "We stay together as a family."

Karen stared at him. Peter took her gloved hand in his and held it tight.

"We're in this together," he told her. "Forever." Karen's eyes glistened, and she slid her other hand over his.

Abbie noticed Josh staring at the two of them. The look on

his face showed a mixture of curiosity, sadness, anger, and maybe even resentment.

"We just need to stay calm. You heard the presid—" Peter's voice cut off at the sound of a low-flying helicopter. In panic, Josh grabbed his mother and pulled her to the floor. They lay still and held their breath, staring at each other until the sound of the chopper faded away.

When it did, they both slumped their bodies with relief. Karen brushed her hand over Josh's cheek, then quietly began to sob.

Abbie sat in Josh's room, staring sadly across the street at her house bathed in the afternoon sun. She desperately wanted to be back in her own room, but at the same time she was scared to enter the empty house. Scared to face the fact that her entire family was missing.

Still, she felt uncomfortable relying on the Chalmer family for support when clearly they had their own problems to resolve. They were grieving their missing son and hiding Karen, and she also sensed something else going on in their relationship, but didn't know what it was.

Josh watched her, looking across the street to her house. "That ship . . . they could come back," he said quietly.

Abbie looked at him. "I just . . . feel awkward," she said honestly. "I hardly know you. I feel like I'm intruding here."

"Yeah," Josh said quietly, looking down at his feet. "I know the feeling."

Abbie stared at him, wondering what he meant. Josh saw the look, hesitated, then spoke.

"We moved here, to Victoryville, to save the family," he said. "At least that's what my dad says." He began to play with a loose thread on the hem of his shirt. "We had to move here because he messed up. *He* messed up, and now he's trying to fix things. Me and my brother were dragged out here into the sticks, so he could suck up to mom."

Abbie stared at him, not knowing what to say. She watched him as he lay back on his bed and began throwing a football up in the air and catching it.

"That's why he didn't want to let her go?" she eventually asked.

Josh glanced at her, continuing to throw the football. "He should've thought of that before."

Abbie continued to watch him, waiting to see if he'd elaborate, not wanting to pry.

"He screwed a woman he worked with," Josh said, and Abbie heard the bitterness in his voice. "Mom found out. So he quit his job and moved us out here." Josh gave a laugh, but it had a harsh edge. "A new start!" he said sarcastically. "I wanted to stay in Boston, but my little brother begged me to move here with him. I told him I would, but only for a little bit, then I'm out." He gave another bitter laugh. "And now he's gone and I'm the one who's stuck here."

Abbie felt her shoulders soften in sympathy. She couldn't imagine how she'd feel if her family had gone through that. She could understand Josh's bitterness, but at the same time, she thought it was good that Peter was trying to make amends and save his family.

She sighed heavily. Perhaps too heavily, as it made her cough a little.

Josh stopped throwing the football and studied her a moment.

"Have you always had asthma?" he asked.

Abbie nodded. "Yeah. I was born with bad lungs," she

smiled. "But I've lived with it for so long I don't know any different."

He seemed to nod to himself. "I'm allergic to nuts," he said. "Same thing."

"Yeah?" she said.

He nodded, breaking into a smile. "And seafood. Makes my throat swell up."

"Really?" she chuckled, "That's bad luck."

He shrugged. "I never liked the taste anyway."

She smiled, but it soon fell away and a sad silence seemed to fill the air again. Still, in that brief moment, hearing about his allergies, he'd felt less of a stranger. They'd found something in common other than the phenomenon. And surprisingly, it felt good. It made her feel less alone.

They both turned their attention back to the small TV in his room. Another news report was airing. They saw scenes of Clean Skins being ushered and dragged onto busses from earlier that day, and images of the growing photo walls of the missing. All the while they listened to the voiceover of a reporter named Richard Keene, providing an update from the Victoryville Civic Hall in the Clean Zone. His voice was calm, but serious as he spoke words of concern for the events of the day; expressing his desire for answers and resolutions, but also imploring viewers for carefulness and kindness toward each other in these uncertain times.

The report ended on a still shot of a terrified, striped Hispanic woman. She was reaching desperately for an armed, bio-suited soldier, who was walking away from her. The image made Abbie pause. The woman's face, her eyes, were so lost and frightened; they expressed how Abbie herself felt deep inside.

And once again her eyes moved out the window to her house sitting across the street, and her heart sank heavily into the pit of her stomach.

Stanley Barrick stared at Dr. Hogarth.

"There has to be something, surely?" he asked.

"If we have nothing new by morning, we'll start taking samples from the wider group."

"But surely a stripe is a stripe. What does it matter who we get it from?"

"I agree, but so far Dr. Pellan has found nothing unusual in the samples he has. We, too, have gone over and over the results he sent us and found the same thing."

"Has he done the tests right?"

Hogarth held up her hand to stop him. "I assure you we've reviewed his procedures to ensure things were done correctly and they were. Admittedly, the Bateson Dermacell facility is a little substandard to what we would normally use in cases like these, but Dr. Pellan has a very good reputation and Professor Meeks speaks highly of him. Pellan's work has been impeccable."

Stanley sighed. "So what does this mean? We can't go out to the people with this. We need a definitive answer. If we tell them there's no contagion and then people start dropping like flies, we're done for. The whole goddamn country, the whole planet is at risk here."

"We've given Dr. Pellan until morning. That would make it approximately forty hours since they awoke. If he's found nothing new, then he will move into the Striped Zone to take a wider variety of samples." Hogarth studied him. "And if that does not net us any results, then I and my team will have to move in there."

Stanley stared back at Hogarth as his mind processed the

information. "I told you if you head in there, you may not come back out again."

Hogarth nodded. "I know. Three platoons of soldiers have already made that sacrifice. The CDC will do so as well."

Stanley gave a short, sharp nod. "Let's pick it up in the morning. I'll make a decision then."

Dr. Lysart Pellan, now situated in Lab-Two, his arms reaching through the gap of the BSC where Dr. Seevers had sat, carefully prepared the new samples. Given the time the Striped Ones had spent in this lab, not to mention the fact he was handling their samples—albeit with as much personal protective wear as he had available to him—meant he was at risk of contracting the contagion, should there be one, but he had no other choice. Desperate for answers, he'd already had several phone calls from Harvey, Chief Blackstone and Dr. Hogarth, all wanting updates, but he'd been unable to give them anything. He'd had to turn his cell to silent as the media had somehow got their hands on his number and were calling incessantly.

He'd gone over the skin samples from John Seevers, along with his own, again and again, but found nothing abnormal, nothing that wasn't within normal human parameters. He did observe that the stripes, the welts, sat beneath the skin; they actually lay in the reticular layer of the dermis. He established that the discoloration wasn't caused by an over-production of melanin, or by some other type of aggravated skin condition. Nor could he identify any foreign cells or tissue to account for it either. He simply had no idea what these marks were or how they got there, below the epidermis.

Failing to find answers with the skin samples, he had turned again to blood samples, saliva samples, hair samples, urine samples, feces samples, and again was left baffled.

The stripes were just . . . there. And no other change to human physiology could be detected.

Cheung had forced him to get a few hours sleep, but he'd been at it again for several hours now. He let out a weary sigh and rubbed his tired eyes. This had always been his problem. Whenever he was presented with a challenge, he worked at it until he overcame it. But it was also the reason he had been as successful as he had: he never gave up. He knew that every problem could be resolved. So why couldn't he resolve this one?

Was it the pressure? The world was relying on him to provide answers. The lives of the entire world might literally be in his hands; his own life potentially lay in his hands.

He felt his concern brewing for the marked survivors, but he also felt concern for those unmarked. Whatever had happened here, it had happened to *all* of them: marked or unmarked. This phenomenon had touched every single one of them, he was sure of it. But how to prove it?

His mind drifted to thoughts of his family. His ex-wife and daughters were on holiday in France. Based in Washington, they had not wanted to move to this Virginian town. Right now, he was grateful for the estrangement from them. He was relieved they had not come to Victoryville to celebrate the opening with him. Marissa, his youngest daughter, had called as soon as she'd been able to get through, to see if he was alright. That one phone call had touched him deeply and had given him the strength to carry on.

As he thought of his daughters, the guilt swamped him. He'd been working hard these past couple of years to rebuild his relationship with them. It had been a casualty of his problematic work ethic, his drive to resolve problems. He had achieved great things at work, but he had failed at home. He'd become an absent husband and father, a stranger in his own home.

Things were civil with his ex-wife, but they rarely spoke now. The damage had been done and any hope of a reconciliation had been long lost. He'd accepted that. When he realized what a mess he had made, he'd tried hard to reach out to his now-adult children, and save what he could of his family, but it was proving to be a long, slow process. Marissa, twenty-five, although hesitant, had been willing to give her father a second chance. Any contact he had with his family now was generally through her. Elizabeth, twenty-eight and a lot like her mother, had been harder to reach. But he felt that with a little more time she would warm to him once again.

If he ever got the chance to see any of them again.

Right now they were in Paris, and he was trapped in this town, separated by miles of ocean and this horrifying phenomenon.

He sighed and rubbed his eyes again. He needed to eat, needed some coffee. Anything to refuel his body.

He removed his protective gear, wanting to be free of it for a while, washed up and made his way to the staff room. He poured boiling water from the dual tap system into his plain, well-worn ceramic mug, staring at the gray cracks that adorned the outer shell as he rinsed the cup out. The mug probably should've been thrown out years ago, but it was his good luck charm. He placed it on the coffee machine's landing pad and made his selection, then opened the door of the fridge, found the milk and topped up his coffee. As he placed the milk back in the fridge, his eyes fell on the spare insulin that John had needed to keep on hand for personal emergencies, along with a vial of the sugar solution. It made Lysart pause as he recalled the soldiers taking John away.

He picked up an insulin vial and took a good look at it, rolling it between his fingers. There was something about it that bubbled in the background of his thoughts. Lysart hoped John would have enough insulin to tide him over wherever they were keeping him. Not only had John been taken away, this medical condition was an extra problem for him to deal with in exile.

He thought of Elizabeth, then, and of the terrible migraines his daughter suffered. He recalled seeing her in the emergency department once, being injected with strong painkillers. He pictured her in Paris with her mother and sister, and wondered whether she'd remembered to take her pain meds with her. He hoped she would not wind up in some Parisian emergency room, experiencing the nausea and vomiting that sometimes occurred with her migraines.

He was still staring at the insulin vial in his hands as his mind went back to the morning tea, the morning of the Occurrence. He recalled standing with John and Mary, and Mary telling him that she couldn't eat anything because the medication she was taking made her queasy.

He frowned as he thought of his colleagues, and how they had been taken away. He pictured the red welt that ran down Mary's chin, pictured the welt down John's as he'd spoken to him through the lab window. He thought of John lying on the ground, waiting for the sugar solution to kick in. Then he pictured Mary shaking her head at the cake and running a hand across her queasy belly.

And then the thought hit Lysart like a sledgehammer.

His eyes flew wide and he audibly gasped.

Suddenly wide awake, and with the insulin still in his hand, he spun around and raced back to the lab.

Day Three

Richard awoke from a restless, dream-filled sleep. As he rubbed his stubbled face and yawned, he recalled the dream he'd been having just as he awoke. It was a childhood memory of a holiday he'd taken with his parents and brother. The sun was warm, the grass was green, and the river was cool and flowing gently. He was young, they were happy, and he didn't want it to end. But it had.

He thought losing his parents and his brother—becoming an orphan—would be the worst thing he'd ever have to face in his life. But somehow, this seemed so much worse. At least death was a definite thing: it couldn't be argued. But this waiting, not knowing, this was something else. That an alien ship had hovered over the town for twenty-four hours and done something to him was . . . well, it was excruciating. It left such an uneasy feeling in the pit of his stomach, like a horrible cancer eating away at him slowly.

He wiped his eyes and looked around at the crowded Civic Hall, listening to babies crying, people coughing. A sense of fear and sorrow seemed to smother the atmosphere. He pulled himself up from the sleeping bag that had been his bed for the night on the floor of the main hall. There had only been so many beds to go around and preference had been given to those more needy. It didn't bother him. He'd slept in worse places.

He pulled his phone out of his pack and went straight to the online news. Although the President's address had made it clear what to expect, he was still shocked to see that, overnight, the temporary barrier between the Clean Zone and Striped Zone had been completed. The town was officially divided in two.

He grabbed his pack and made his way outside, wanting to take a look at it with his own eyes. The Civic Hall was a few blocks back from the main street where the barrier was located, and several blocks down from the main intersection of the town, where a small contingent of soldiers had set up a guard post. As soon as the barrier came into view he pulled out his small handheld camera. He saw a group of others had gathered, as curious as he. Bio-suited soldiers approached the group and waved them away. Richard was nervous, thinking they would try to take his camera, but they didn't. It fit in the palm of his hand and he held it close to his body, so perhaps they didn't see it. He moved obligingly to stand several meters back among the other bystanders and subtly panned along the gray makeshift wall in the early morning light.

The barricade itself looked to be made of a toughened gray plastic, in the shape of a traditional Jersey barrier, except a little larger. He wondered about its purpose: if this stripe thing was contagious, if it was airborne, what good would the barrier do?

"Looks like they're settling in, huh?" a voice came from beside him.

He saw an old man standing to his left, surveying the barrier with a suspicious shine to his eyes.

"It does," Richard agreed, as he continued to unobtrusively

film. "Although I'm not convinced that will stop a contagion."

The old man pursed his lips. "No, but I don't think that's what it's for, do you?" Richard glanced at him. The man's eyes seemed to narrow further in suspicion, a sharp glint within. "It's not enough to keep them out permanently, that's for sure. But it makes a great foundation to build a real wall atop it, don't you think?" The man's eyes caught Richard's. "If it comes to it, that is."

Richard studied the barrier again, then looked back at the man. "You think it will come to that?"

The man shrugged again. "I don't know. But they've gone to a lot of trouble to erect that. Wouldn't do something like that unless they planned for it to be there a while." The man nodded to himself. "Hell is on its way . . ." he said. "Well, hell has already been here, but . . ." he motioned to the barrier, "just in case it decides to come back."

"You think the ship will come back?" Richard asked.

The man studied him, the look in his eyes now bordering on skepticism. "There's something up with those Striped Ones. They've been marked for a reason . . . but there's also something up with the ones in here." He motioned over his shoulder into the Clean Zone.

"What makes you say that?"

The man looked over the barricade as though he were looking out at the ocean. "This," he said waving his finger between the two zones, "all happened in the blink of an eye. That ain't normal. Ain't ever seen anything like it. And those welts aren't normal. Nobody knows what's happened, nobody knows how to fix it. And people don't like things they don't understand. If they can't explain it, they don't like it. And if they don't like it . . ." he shrugged slowly. "Let's just say I'm sure as hell glad that I'm on this side of the wall, and not one of them over there."

Richard turned back to stare into the Striped Zone. As he did, he saw a man, a Striped One, approach one of the soldiers on the other side. He was holding up a photo and motioning over the barrier. The soldier shook his head and held his hand up to stop him.

"Steven! Steven!" A woman called frantically, a few meters away to Richard's left. "Steven!"

The man on the other side of the barricade waved back at her.

"Steven! Are you okay?" she called, reaching out as though she could grab him.

Richard didn't catch what the man said, but he saw a nod, and saw him blow the woman a kiss. The woman turned around and picked something up, then turned back with a small child in her arms.

"Look! There's daddy! There's daddy," she said to the young boy.

The man at the barricade waved frantically to catch his son's attention. In response the woman held the boy's hand up and forced a wave in return. Richard heard the woman's laughter but could tell it was tainted with sadness, as she stared at her partner in the distance, across the gray wall.

It was a moving scene, one that sent a shiver of emotion across Richard's skin. It seemed to capture the sentiment of what was happening to people throughout the town, of what was at stake for the residents of Victoryville.

And he captured the whole scene on film.

Abbie, despite the unknown horror that could still be out there, finally, nervously, ventured back across the street to her house. Despite her underlying reservations, she was actually glad to do it. After two nights at Josh's house, she needed a little space. The Chalmers were nice people, but they were still strangers to her and invading the privacy of a family caught up in this situation, with a missing child, with their own personal issues, and hiding a Clean Skin . . . it made Abbie uncomfortable. She felt like a third wheel that they really didn't need to be burdened with. Besides, she had her own situation to deal with. She needed the comfort of her own room, the sights of her own surroundings. She needed to be near the memories of her family. She couldn't avoid dealing with their absence any longer. Their loss. She had to face it sometime.

It had been alarming to wake up and see that Victoryville now had a barrier, making the town's division a physical reality. Groups of people walked past her house, making their way to view it. She decided to join them.

The gray barrier followed the east-west border, through the town center, along the main street. The Clean Zone was to the north, now officially separated from the Striped Zone to the south. The barrier wasn't overly tall; she could still see people on the other side. But it didn't feel right . . . to have had her family stolen from her, and to now be segregated from the rest of the town, made her uneasy. It very much felt like they were in a zoo and the Clean Skins weren't the ones being stared at.

The military, located at a makeshift gateway between the two zones in the dead center of Victoryville, didn't quite have the numbers to do much about the curious onlookers gathering to gawk at the barrier and the gate. They let people look, then verbally encouraged them to return home. After a while, Abbie did. But somehow that barrier came with her in her mind.

Two images kept circling her thoughts.

One was the appearance of the soldiers along the barrier near the gate, standing in their black bio-suits with large weapons by their sides, their masks giving them a terrifying look. Two circles of clear plastic revealed their eyes, and a bulky circular filter covered their mouths. More than that, Abbie noticed, they were very clearly standing on the Clean Skin side of the barrier, facing *out* into the Striped Zone.

Like the Clean Zone was the safe side.

Like the Striped Zone was somewhere to be wary of.

It was very much like they were guarding the Clean Zone *from* the Striped Zone.

The other image that stuck in her mind was the staring of the civilian Clean Skins, milling around at some distance behind the soldiers. And the faces of the Clean Skins said it all: they were part-scared, part-sympathetic, part-repulsed. It stood out most obviously when she saw someone that she knew. Candy, one of the lifeguards from the VAC who'd been in the cafe the day they'd awoken. The look the Clean Skin Candy gave Abbie stuck in her mind. The pretty blond had been looking curiously out over the barricade, her mouth and nose covered with a handkerchief. When her eyes fell upon Abbie, they paused briefly in recognition, before quickly looking away like she didn't know her. Like she hadn't worked with her. Like she hadn't gone to the same school, although a lower age grade. Abbie watched Candy as she walked away and she could see relief flood the girl's body. The relief that she was a Clean Skin. The relief that she was on the right side of that barricade.

Abbie's eyes moved to stare up at the apartment block that loomed over the barricade gateway on the Clean Skin side. It seemed a little out of place in Victoryville, which was predominantly a flat spread of suburbia, the only taller building in town being the Civic Hall's clock tower a few blocks down. Several people were out on their apartment balconies, many in face masks. They stared down at her like she was a freak. There were a few who didn't wear masks, though. Abbie looked at one couple, but they quickly, awkwardly moved back inside their apartment. Another older man simply stared back, either intrigued or defiant, she couldn't tell. Then her eyes fell on a young teen girl, with long reddish-brown hair and pale skin, who looked back at her with sympathy. The girl slid her hand over a heavily pregnant belly, then she, too, moved inside.

Abbie had looked around, then, at the few curious parties who milled about on the striped side of the barricade. She spotted Austin from the gym. He stood with a few other guys. Some of them worked at the local hardware store and she'd seen them down at the gym, lifting weights and taking boxing lessons from Austin. They stood bunched together talking quietly, eyeing the barricade and soldiers. She caught a look in their eyes that was as troubling as some of those she'd seen in the eyes of the Clean Skins on the other side. She sensed an uneasiness, a mistrust.

After her visit to the barricade, she'd walked back home feeling the weight of the stripe upon her skin. As she entered her house she felt the emptiness smack at her heavily. She headed straight upstairs for the bathroom, wanting to take a good look at herself away from the stares of the Clean Skins. As she looked into the mirror she couldn't help but see the freak that Candy and the other Clean Skins had seen. Abbie raised her hand to the welt that began underneath her bottom lip and traced it all the way down her neck. She tore off her shirt and traced it further to where it ended over her heart. It seemed so red, so angry a welt.

What was wrong with her? What did this horrible mark mean? Was she going to die?

Why wasn't she a Clean Skin like Candy?

She swallowed the ball of emotion wedged in her throat and ran her hand through her hair. As she did, her eyes caught on her sister's perfume, which was sitting beside the bathroom sink. It was a delicate bottle in the shape of a bouquet of flowers. She picked it up, studying the intricate detail of the glass, then pulled the cap off and held it to her nose. The scent immediately reminded her of Sarah, dressed up for her school ball, excited by the possibility that her date—Abbie couldn't remember his name now—might kiss her. How long ago had that been? Two months? Three?

And now Sarah was gone.

Why had she been taken? Why had Abbie been left behind?

She placed the bottle down on the bench as her vision blurred. She had managed to hold back her tears for the past day or so while at the Chalmer house, probably from shock more than anything, but it seemed her own personal barricade was about to finally crumble.

The vision of her red stripe, thoughts of her missing family, the emptiness of the house, all pushed her over her personal threshold. Before she knew it, the tears were flooding down her cheeks and her mouth was gasping sobs. She slowly sank into a heap on the bathroom floor, giving in to the emotion, and drowning herself within.

Dr. Pellan felt the tiredness press against him like a heavy chain mail suit. But, despite this, sleep was the last thing on his mind.

In the early hours of the morning he'd found a common denominator with the stripes. He'd woken Cheung at once and had the graduate double-check everything, just in case his exhausted brain had missed something. But he hadn't. Cheung agreed with his theory. There was more work to be done on the wider population, but based on the results from his small control group of Bateson Dermacell employees, he was sure he had made a vital discovery.

He sat there staring at the plush carpet of Bateson

Dermacell's small boardroom, awaiting his video conference. It had taken hours to get to this point. Professor Meeks had earlier granted Lysart access to the staff's personnel files to assist in gathering information. Once Cheung had confirmed his theory, he'd explained it to Meeks. The professor had then gone away to double-check the findings with other experts on the Bateson Dermacell board. Once they were convinced he was right, Meeks arranged a video conference with Dr. Hogarth. Three meetings and six hours from his discovery, Lysart was now about to present his findings directly to Dr. Hogarth.

The screen beeped and Meeks appeared.

"Dr. Pellan," he said formally. "No one else online yet?"

"No."

"You've done great work, Lysart," Meeks said. "Great work. The board are thrilled with your discovery."

Lysart gave a weak smile. He didn't feel quite as celebratory as his colleague. He may have found a common denominator, but there was still a lot of work to be done and many answers to be learned.

The screen beeped again and Dr. Hogarth appeared. Dressed in a plain blouse, her sandy-blond hair pulled tight into a bun, and wearing no makeup, she looked as exhausted as he.

"Dr. Hogarth," Meeks greeted her.

"Gentlemen," Hogarth gave a nod. "You've made a discovery?" she prompted them. Clearly there was little time for chitchat.

Meeks gave a nod. "Yes, I will let Dr. Pellan take the lead as this is his discovery."

Lysart stared at the split screen in front of him, at the eyes staring attentively back at him. He gave a little bow and cleared his throat. "Well, I believe I have discovered what the three groups mean."

"Three groups?" Hogarth asked quickly. Lysart couldn't help feeling as though he was the subject of an interrogation under her concentrated stare.

"Yes," Lysart nodded. "What happened, er, this phenomenon, I believe, has split the population of Victoryville into three distinct groups. There are those who are missing. They make up the first group. Then there are those who remain but were marked. This is the second group, the Striped Ones. Then there are those who remain, but are unmarked. This is the third group, the Clean Skins."

"Yes." She turned her face slightly, as though trying to hear more clearly, eyes still fixed firmly upon him.

"Well, I believe I have discovered what each group represents."

"And that is?"

"As you're aware, I did my analysis on a small test group of my Bateson Dermacell employees. I discovered, based on this group, that the population split relates to the state of everyone's health."

"Health?" Hogarth's brow furrowed in confusion. "Of course this is about our health. We're dealing with an alien contagion, right?"

Lysart shook his head confidently. "As you know, we've found no trace of a contagion. This doesn't appear to be a virus or a bacteria, or anything like that. There is nothing foreign present in any of the biological samples of the survivors. All I know, all I can find, is that we have simply become categorized."

"Categorized?" Hogarth did little to hide her skepticism. "What do you mean?"

Lysart glanced at Harvey, who looked wary, and perhaps a little alarmed, at the thought the CDC might think their time was being wasted.

"I'm talking about broad categories," Lysart explained. "Broad categories that group us genetically." He could see Hogarth was turning this over in her mind, so he carried on. "From what I can see, those who are missing were perfectly healthy. Those who remain and are marked, are sick in some way. And those who remain and are unmarked, are healthy except that we carry defective genes of some sort."

"Excuse me?"

"Dr. Pellan's findings have merit," Meeks chimed in. "I've reviewed his initial data and it stacks up."

Lysart decided to break it down in the simplest way he knew. "The missing were healthy. The Striped Ones are sick. The Clean Skins are carriers."

"Carriers of what?" Hogarth asked.

Lysart shrugged. "It depends on the individual. Based on the employees in my lab they varied. I, myself, although I am healthy in every other way, carry a gene for a predisposition to color blindness. My fellow Clean Skin, Cheung Liu, carries a gene that predisposes to celiac disease. We are otherwise healthy, but we may pass our defective genes to a child."

"And the Striped Ones?" she asked.

"Again, they vary. Those who became striped suffered from a range of illnesses. Where we carry defective genes, they have physical defects and they suffer from and display the symptoms associated with the conditions they've been afflicted with. My colleague, Dr. John Seevers, has diabetes. Another colleague, Mary Rodriguez, was recently diagnosed with breast cancer. Another colleague, Grant Cooper, suffered from eczema and has a lactose intolerance. From what I can tell, the number of welts corresponds to the number of illnesses they have. Where John and Mary had one welt each, Grant had two. Each individual is different, but as a whole we have been categorized according to our health and genetic profile."

Silence sat among them for a moment.

"Dr. Pellan has only tested this on a small group of subjects," Meeks said, holding up a placatory hand, "but we are confident that if we apply these findings to the wider population, they will fit."

"So you don't believe there is any alien contagion?" Hogarth asked.

"No," Lysart said confidently, "I don't believe there is."

Again silence filled the screens as Dr. Hogarth stared at them, her mind ticking over.

"Alright," she eventually said. "Let's say you're right. The people of Victoryville have been split into these three categories; the healthy, the sick, the carriers. Where, then, are the healthy? How does this explain the missing?"

Lysart shook his head. "I'm afraid I cannot answer that, Dr. Hogarth. It is beyond my expertise. All I know is what I have found. And that is, that somehow this phenomenon—" he paused, decided not to dress things up, "this ship, these aliens, have categorized us. For what reason, I don't know. But they have done something with the healthy and left the rest of us behind."

Hogarth was quiet as she processed the information. Lysart noted that she didn't look relieved by the news.

"Right, then," she said decisively. "Give me the evidence you have. We'll take a further look into it and get back to you. Until then, I would like you to remain on standby. You are to speak to no one of this. Do you understand? Until we are agreed on a way forward, this must remain classified. Ensure anyone you've spoken to knows this."

Lysart glanced over at Harvey's screen.

"This comes from Homeland Security," she added, "not the CDC. We've all been classified."

"Of course," Professor Meeks answered for them both.

Chief Blackstone walked toward the gate separating the zones of Victoryville. He'd noticed that the residents had calmed down a little, in part because the military-enforced road closures meant they couldn't leave, and in part because the barrier had been erected. It gave the Clean Skins, subconsciously at least, some reassurance that they weren't in any immediate danger from a possible striped contagion. It also meant that any ideas of escape were thwarted, because those who had loved ones stuck on the other side of the barrier couldn't connect to make plans.

He nodded to a soldier at the gate who eyed his approach curiously. The soldier gave him a nod back, then turned his bio-masked face back to scanning the Striped Zone. Blackstone himself only wore a cotton surgical mask from the first-aid kit in his vehicle. It felt a little odd to be wearing one, but he wasn't vain enough to risk illness or worry about not offending his deputy.

He came to a stop a few feet back from the gate. His colleague stood on the other side, a little closer to it.

"Leo, how you doing?"

His deputy gave a nod. Blackstone saw him studying the mask he wore.

"Just a precaution," he said.

Leo nodded again, then glanced about him. "Things seemed to have calmed down a little. I think the initial panic is over."

"Yeah," Blackstone said, eyeing the Striped Zone behind his deputy. "The shock and panic has passed. Right now people are waiting, probably feeling guilty for being left behind when their loved ones weren't." He shifted his eyes back to Leo, gave him a sympathetic look. "And scared about what happens next."

Leo clenched his jaw and his eyes darted away. "What does happen next, Earl?"

He stared at Leo. "I don't know. Possibly anger. Anger that this has happened. Anger that they aren't getting answers as quickly as they'd like. Fear. Fear that those things might come back. We need to keep an eye on that. Control it."

Leo stared at his boss, looking tired and alone. Earl studied the red stripe running down his chin.

"So there's still no word from Bateson Dermacell?" Leo asked.

"No," Blackstone said, "but they're working on it. The head scientist, Dr. Pellan, he's been working around the clock trying to find us an answer. They got separated too, though," Blackstone added. "The folks at Bateson Dermacell. There's just two of them left there, last I checked."

Leo didn't say anything, he just glanced down at his feet, his shoulders drooping, weighted down with worry and sadness and exhaustion.

"You spoken with your family?" Blackstone asked him.

Leo nodded. "Yeah."

"They doing alright?"

"As good as can be." He swallowed hard.

"I'll be sure to check on them, Leo," he told him. "Don't you worry about them, you hear? I'll make sure they're being taken care of."

Leo's face lightened a little. "Thanks, Earl."

Blackstone's eyes shifted to a group of people standing some distance behind his deputy on the striped side. The group was watching them both carefully. He recognized most of the faces, and a couple of them worried him a little. There in his wheelchair sat Magnus Bracks, local leader of the construction union. Alongside him was Roy Kenny, local hardware store owner, president of the local NRA, and a known conspiracy theorist. They stood surrounded by a group of young guys from the area: farmers' and laborers' sons. One of them was Austin Saller from the gym. Blackstone had had to question Austin just last week on reports he'd been selling steroids to his clients, but Austin denied the claims and he'd had no evidence to push any further. Although, via town gossip and chitchat, Blackstone had heard that Austin was pushing more than just steroids.

He returned his eyes to his deputy.

"There's a shipment of supplies, groceries and the like, coming in today. The government's shipping it into the Clean Zone and we'll arrange to pass half of it on."

Leo nodded, rubbing his hands over his tired face. "Just give me call when to expect it. I'll see the supplies get to the stores on this side."

"You take care of yourself over there," Blackstone told him. "I need you, Leo. I need you to stay sharp and keep your wits about you. Understand?"

Leo exhaled heavily. "I'll do my best, Earl."

"Go get a few hours' sleep," Blackstone told him. "I'll keep watch from here for a while."

Leo gave another nod. "I'll speak to you in a few hours."

Blackstone watched as his deputy turned and headed for his vehicle. All the while Magnus Bracks and the men surrounding him watched Leo as well.

Richard Keene, after taking a shower and putting on the last of the spare shirts from his backpack, began reviewing the footage he'd taken yesterday. After arriving at the Civic Hall, he'd spent a fair amount of time interviewing his fellow Clean Skins to find out their stories and capture their reactions. All of those he'd spoken with were local to town, and the majority had family and friends who were either missing, or over in the Striped Zone. He elicited a range of emotions from those he interviewed. Some were happy with the way the authorities handled things, some not. Many were scared and anxious as to what would happen next. Some had accepted what had already happened and just wanted to move on and get their lives back. Some talked of government conspiracies, some of military experiments gone wrong, and some suggested that footage of the ship was a hoax to cover up what *they* had done. Some thought Victoryville must be special to have been chosen, with many putting forward theories about why. Some had no ideas about why. Some brought religion into it, suggesting the town was being punished for something. While others thought the town had been chosen for a higher purpose.

Everyone told stories of where they were and what they were doing before the phenomenon occurred. Each story was interesting and unique, and no doubt fascinating to the outside world, but Richard found himself to be restless. He knew the real story wasn't here with the Clean Skins. He wanted to be in the other zone with the Striped Ones. They were the ones who were marked. The story here was them.

The stripes were quickly becoming the symbol of this phenomenon, and the cause of everyone's fear; TV stations across the world seemed to be utterly fixated on them. Expert after expert speculated on what the stripes could mean and whether there was any chance of this infection spreading. Richard had seen news reports showing more and more people from nearby towns packing up and moving on, wanting to get as far away from Victoryville—and the possible contagion—as they could. Some towns across the globe had succumbed to looting, with people panicking that the end of the world was nigh.

It almost seemed like people on the outside were taking things worse than those on the inside. Maybe it was because those left in Victoryville knew they didn't have any option but to wait things out. They were trapped in the eye of the storm until the authorities deigned to release them.

Despite underlying fears and concerns of contagion, Richard still wanted to get closer to the Striped Ones. Their story was clearly the bigger one. They were the ones who had woken up with these strange welts. They were the ones who didn't know whether they'd been infected with something, or why they had been chosen and others hadn't. He wanted to be the one to speak with them and hear their story, but unfortunately he was stuck here in the Clean Zone, unable to get anywhere near them. He, like other reporters, could interview people over the phone, but it just wasn't the same as being on the ground there. Experience had taught him that face-to-face interviews always ran deeper, always revealed more.

He noted that the temporary names given to things now seemed to have settled in as though permanent fixtures. There were, of course, the Clean Skins and the Striped Ones and their respective zones, and now the soldiers in their hazmat gear were being referred to as "Bio-guards" or "Bios" for short.

He was stunned when one of the Clean Skin civilians he interviewed referred, rather derogatorily, to the Striped Ones as "zebras".

The man had said: "It's a good thing they herded all those zebras. Don't want them running around wild now, infecting everything, do we?"

Another Clean Skin man had overheard this and given a chuckle.

Richard, upon hearing the comment and the chuckle, had paused a moment, staring at the two men. He couldn't help but say, "That's a little unfair, don't you think? Calling them that. They didn't ask for this to happen."

"It's a shame what's happened to 'em," the second man had said shrugging, "but it is what it is."

"They're infected," the first man agreed. "And the further they stay away from us, the better."

"You obviously don't have family in the Striped Zone, to be saying that," Richard said, a little bluntly. The men stared back at him. They didn't answer, but decided at that point to walk away from him.

From talking with the Clean Skins, watching other interviews on the news, and scrolling through the social media feeds, knowing what he did about human beings and their reactions to things, Richard detected certain mindsets, certain groups starting to emerge as a result of this phenomenon. First, were the Clean Skins who were obviously very happy to be segregated and very scared of what illness the Striped Ones could have, such as the men he'd spoken to. Second, were those Clean Skins who didn't want to be separated from their loved ones, people who wanted a solution and fast, like the couple he'd seen at the barrier with the child. Lastly, were the Striped Ones, but they didn't seem to be fracturing into any groups from what he could tell. They were just one big group of people who only wanted one thing: to know what had happened to them and how they could fix it.

When he tired of reviewing the interviews, he walked back to the barricade again, wondering if the afternoon sun would shed a different light on things. It didn't. The barrier was still there, the streets were nearly empty, aside from a curious party or two, and the bio-guards remained on alert. As the streetlights came on, Richard watched them carefully, listening to the buzzing and crackling that emanated; there still remained some kind of weird interference with electrical equipment that the experts hadn't been able to explain as yet. It was just there.

As he cast his eyes up to the sky, he wondered again whether the ship was still there somewhere. He scanned the horizon, but saw no sign of it. It seemed that they were alone . . . but that buzzing, what did it mean? Why would these things come here, take some people, leave some behind with stripes, and then up and leave? What did the stripes mean? Would that ship return for them? Return for everyone?

That thought alone worried him immensely.

If it came back, what would these beings do to those of them left?

He made his way back to the Civic Hall and sat down in front of the large screen, now allocated to the adults as the children had been given another room filled with toys and games. He caught up on what his colleagues were reporting on from the outside—many of them were using amateur footage sent to them by residents. He saw an interview with Democrat leader, Joe Calder, admonishing the Republicans for not reacting to the event quickly enough and segregating the people of Victoryville earlier. He likened the event to the disaster of Hurricane Katrina and the weak, delayed response. The Republicans reply consisted of highlighting irrelevant issues that the Democrats had caused.

After the news reports, the station went to yet another live debate via satellite between a series of experts. They discussed the barricade between the zones, and what would happen next. Apparently, the White House had just announced a press conference for the following day, so they attempted to preempt what would be said.

The panel then discussed where this alien presence might have come from and why they attacked. It became heated, however, when talk turned to whether or not this alien ship would return. Most on the panel agreed that it was a strong possibility. Some argued that their visit had been of a friendly nature because the fighter jets had not been destroyed, while others argued that it was an outright attack and the human race was facing extinction. And just as the host was calling for the panel to remain calm and not cause panic, the debate was suddenly cut off and a rerun of some 1980s sitcom began.

Richard's mind began to turn over, wondering whether the cut off had been accidental or intentional. He thought about the faces he'd filmed with their welts, wondering again what this alien life-form had done to them. Was it some kind of radiation sickness? But why had it only affected some people and not others?

He heard that mechanical noise, that staticky buzzing again, and looked up at the screen's speakers. He thought of the streetlights again. What was with this interference? Was it just an aftereffect of the ship's visit? His eyes glanced around the lights that were on in the room, remembered the lights and power going out in his hotel room the day of the Occurrence.

He sat there shaking his leg, both eager and worried.

And helpless.

He was sick of sitting here in this safe haven of Clean Skins and listening to people on the outside debating over the lives of those here in Victoryville. He wanted to do something. Three days in and the public had received very little information from the government. What were the scientists doing? What had they learned about the alien ship? How long did they plan to keep everyone prisoner in this town? Were they hiding something from the people?

The story was calling him. And he knew that when a story called, you answered it. Because if there was one thing he'd learned in his nine years as a journalist, it was that wherever there was smoke, there was generally fire.

And so he decided. It was time he became part of the external discussion. He had to call Harry and get access to that White House press conference.

The mayor watched Chief Blackstone enter his office.

"Mayor," the chief acknowledged. His hat was still on, shading his eyes. The man never seemed to take it off. Russo wondered if he even slept with the damn thing on.

"Chief," Russo nodded back. "What's the latest?"

"I had a call from your good friend," he said, tucking his thumbs behind his belt, accentuating the medium bulge of his stomach. "Magnus Bracks."

Russo scoffed a laugh. "That man is no friend of mine."

"Oh, I know," Blackstone said. "I enjoy watching the two of you every council meeting, like dogs fighting over a bone."

Russo ignored the comment, staring at the chief with his dry, sleep-deprived eyes.

"Anyway," Blackstone said, "Bracks wants to speak with you. Says he's tried calling, but you haven't returned his calls. He wants to know what's going on and how long the barricades will be in place."

"We'd all like the answer to that question, chief."

"Well, he wants it now. No, he *demands* it now."

"Magnus Bracks is good at demanding things, but he should know by now that I don't bow to his foot stamping."

"I'm well aware of it, and don't I just love being the messenger boy for you two. It's my favorite thing about this job."

Russo sighed, relaxing his shoulders as he sat back in his chair. "You're doing a good job, Earl. Unfortunately, our jobs require us to deal with zealots like him from time to time. It's important to ensure these zealots know their place."

"Bracks certainly isn't shy of spouting his opinion," the chief shrugged. "I'll give him that."

"Don't be fooled into sympathy by that wheelchair, chief. The man is cunning."

Blackstone looked back at him, his eyes twinkling a little despite the shade of his hat.

"What?" Russo enquired.

"As long as you're in office, he's going to target you. You know that, right?"

Russo's skin prickled a little. He nodded. "I know."

Again the chief eyed him, but said nothing.

"What?" Russo asked again, letting his annoyance escape.

Blackstone shrugged. "I gotta admit, I kinda understand his anger."

Russo sat forward again. "That is history and the courts have decided. I wasn't at fault that day. He needs to move on from that and drop this ridiculous grudge."

Blackstone shrugged again. "I know. Folks just tend to have a long memory when they feel they've been wronged, is all."

"Then I should hold a grudge against Bracks for every legal proceeding he's tried to tie me up in; dragging my name through the mud, trying to destroy my career. I've worked damn hard to get where I am, and he won't take that from me!"

Blackstone held out a placating hand. "Just so long as your issues with him don't get in the way of everything else we got going on here right now."

"Why would it?"

"Bracks is over in the Striped Zone. You and I are over here in the Clean Zone. I've been checking on the barricade in my patrols, speaking to my deputy over the wall, and I've seen Bracks milling about. Seen his mind ticking over. And he's talking to people over there, have no doubt. He didn't actually say anything when we spoke over the phone, but the tone of his voice spoke for him. I know what he's thinking. You're the mayor of Victoryville. He sees you as responsible for that wall. He sees you, and him, and that wall. The man's been looking for an excuse. If you're not careful, he's gonna use that wall against you."

Russo stared back at Blackstone for a moment, then gave a careful nod. "Thank you, chief, but Magnus Bracks will not intimidate me. I've handled him in the past, and I can handle him now if need be."

"You don't want to maybe return his call and smooth things over? Blow out the smoke before it becomes a fire."

Russo gave him a plain look. "Victoryville has just come under an unprecedented attack, chief. My partner is missing. Half the council is missing. The town is at risk of a potentially deadly contagion. I have other things to deal with here. Bracks isn't high on my list of priorities right now. He can wait his goddamn turn."

Blackstone's eyes surveyed him for a moment, before he gave a nod. "Alright, your call."

"If there's nothing else, I'm about to visit the hospital and say thanks to our medical professionals," Russo said, standing up.

Blackstone tipped his hat and moved for the door.

Abbie plunged her arm into the water, pulling it through before her opposite arm broke the surface, arced over and dived beneath the waves. She inhaled deeply, kicking her feet as she did. Stroke, stroke, stroke, breath. The water was cool, but invigorating. She swam the length of the pool, touched the wall, then turned and swam back down the length again. It felt peaceful. It centered her. She focused on her breathing, sucking the air into her lungs, thought of nothing but the stroke, her breathing, and the kicking of her feet.

It was so nice not to think about the alien ship.

Or the stripes. Or the barricade. Or her missing family.

She'd come down to the VAC to escape her house for a while. To escape everything really. She needed to feel normal again. To feel alive and free. To not feel marked.

She touched the wall of the pool and turned for yet another lap. She wasn't sure how many she'd done so far, but she wanted to keep going. Stroke, stroke, stroke, breath. Her arms and lungs were beginning to burn, but that was good. Her body was working, stretching itself, forcing the tension out.

She touched the wall and turned again. Catching sight of movement in her periphery, she abruptly pulled up and wiped her eyes. She thought she was alone. She had unlocked the gate to get in and had locked it behind her. Treading water, she studied the VAC's entrance. The gate looked closed. She saw movement again in her periphery and flicked her head in its direction. She caught the front door to the gym closing.

She watched it a moment, then swam back to the opposite side of the pool, deciding to get out. Her bubble of peace and isolation was disturbed. She dried off, keeping her eyes on the gym's door, expecting to see someone exit, but no one did. Maybe someone felt like her, needed a workout to take their mind off things? She was well aware of the looting that had occurred in some places around the world, though, and for a moment she wondered whether someone had picked the locks and was planning to do the same here.

Apprehensive as she was, she grabbed her things, and cautiously approached the gym. She moved her face up to the window, shading her eyes to take a look inside. The main gym floor looked empty as it sat in semi-darkness, the only light source being the window at which she stood. The various pieces of equipment within sat idle and unused. There was no one to be seen. But then she noticed a door ajar toward the back left-hand side. The lights within were on and someone inside cast a shadow onto the floor outside.

She glanced at her surroundings. No one else was around. Did she go for help, or did she venture in alone? She examined the lock on the front door; it didn't look as if it had been tampered with. Perhaps it was an employee then? She swallowed hard and turned the handle, deciding to be brave.

She slowed as she approached the open doorway, pausing at the edge to carefully peer inside. The room was a small office, and she saw Austin sitting on the desk, his back slightly to her, looking down into his lap.

"Hey," she said.

Austin jumped and flashed her a startled look as he yanked a syringe out of his thigh.

"Oh!" Abbie held her hand up in apology. "I'm sorry!"

"What are you doing here?" he demanded, standing up and swiftly throwing the syringe into the bin.

"I was swimming. I saw someone was in here. I thought maybe someone had broken in."

"I work here!" he said angrily.

"So do I," she said, her hand still held up in apology. "I didn't know it was you."

"What the hell are you doing sneaking up on people! We've

just had aliens here!"

"I'm sorry," she said, darting her eyes to a small box of vials that he quickly closed the lid on and shoved into his gym bag. "I was worried someone might be trying to loot the place."

"Well, it's just me!" he said, an angry furrow still present across his brow. "So get out!"

She nodded and left as quickly as she could.

Dr. Pellan found himself pacing the floor. It had been hours since his meeting with the CDC, and the lack of sleep, while threatening to envelop him, also seemed to wire him awake. That's why he was pacing: trying to force his body to stay awake, in tune with his mind. He wanted to know if they thought he was right.

And he wanted to know what they would do next.

Relief washed over him when he finally received word from Harvey that they were about to reconnect via video conference. This time Dr. Hogarth was joined by a balding man in a dark suit. His eyes looked steely, although just as tired as Lysart's, but he had an important air about him.

"Professor Meeks, Dr. Pellan," Hogarth greeted them. "This is Stanley Barrick of Homeland Security."

"Mr. Barrick," Meeks said, while Lysart acknowledged him with a nod.

"Was I right, Dr. Hogarth?" Lysart asked, eager to know.

"It's still very early, but we believe so, Dr. Pellan," she told him. "We're in the process of applying your theory across the rest of the town, but based on your sample findings, early indicators on the medical records we've accessed so far, seem to match."

Lysart sighed with relief. There wasn't a contagion. His

colleagues could return. Not only that, but he could see his daughters again soon.

"That's good news," he said, smiling. "This means the barricade can come down. Our colleagues and families can reunite."

"Unfortunately not, Dr. Pellan," Barrick said cautiously.

"No?" Lysart asked.

"Early indicators may have established that there is no contagion as such," Hogarth said, "but we still have a lot of unanswered questions. This needs further study. We can't risk dropping the segregation just yet."

"But there's nothing communicable?"

"It appears not, but—"

"No, Dr. Hogarth, there's not. The Striped Ones are sick, but what they have we can't catch."

"We understand that, Dr. Pellan," Barrick said. "However, we need to find out more before we can relax security. We are dealing with a major incident here, and we cannot take the lives of millions of Americans, billions of people around the world, lightly."

"Look, I know this involved an alien ship, but there is no contagion here—"

"Thousands of people are missing from the town, Dr. Pellan. Thousands, quite possibly murdered by these things. And they left many of you behind, marked. We must proceed with caution."

"I understand that, but—"

Barrick held up his hand. "We're only three days in, Dr. Pellan. We cannot rush things. We're still investigating, and we will continue to do so thoroughly."

"Investigating what?" Lysart asked. "The ship is gone and there is no contagion."

"Dr. Pellan, we have every resource available working on this," Barrick said. "Until we know more, the barricades and the segregation will stay in place. Your town must remain quarantined."

"But what about those with families? Surely the barricade within the town can come down at least? My colleague, Mary Rodriguez, is a single mother. She has children that she was separated from and no other family here in Victoryville."

"I'm sure they're in safe hands in one of the local centers for the time being," Barrick said. "We appreciate your concern, Dr. Pellan, and we appreciate what you have accomplished, but as a scientific professional you must understand the need for caution until further investigations are done."

"Yes, I do, but—"

"Will you be announcing this discovery?" Meeks asked. "Of Dr. Pellan's theory? Of Bateson Dermacell's involvement?"

"No," Barrick told him, "not yet. And that is why I'm meeting with you now. This is considered a matter of national security and the two of you, anyone else in your lab, or on the board, who is aware of your theory, have now been classified by the government of the United States of America. Do you understand?"

Lysart darted his eyes to Harvey's screen, then back at Barrick and Hogarth. Barrick held up a contract of some kind.

"You will both need to sign these agreements, which are being issued to you as we speak."

Lysart's brow furrowed.

"And the board?" Meeks asked.

"Yes. *Anyone* who has been made aware of your findings. I will need a complete list, Professor Meeks. This is an order issued at the highest level."

The professor gave a shocked nod. "Absolutely. Yes, of

course."

"People have the right to know," Lysart spoke up. "The Striped Ones have the right to know that they're not infectious."

"They will be told when we're absolutely sure there is no further threat," Barrick said firmly.

"But—"

"Dr. Pellan, everyone is on edge. *Globally*. We need to do what we have to, to keep order. That is paramount right now."

"How will you keep order by refusing to allow people to be with their loved ones? If they think they're sick, possibly dying—"

"Dr. Pellan, you have identified that our citizens have been categorized, but what we don't know is why. There could still be some kind of alien contagion lingering within them somehow, in those welts, that could possibly have a long gestation period. Something we know nothing about because it isn't of this world—"

"If there were any abnormalities your experts at the CDC would have identified them already."

"Not necessarily, Dr. Pellan. There is no precedence for what has happened here, and I will not be the one to lower that barricade and release a contagion that wipes out the town, the entire Eastern Seaboard of the United States and possibly further afield. Until we know for sure what we're dealing with, Victoryville and its zones will remain quarantined."

"We would've been able to isolate and identify anything that was abnormal to the human structure, and we did not," Lysart said, as immense worry consumed him. There was something about the way Barrick had said "Victoryville and its zones will remain quarantined." Something about the tone of his voice that struck fear down Lysart's spine. "You're using the contagion as an excuse," he said, his voice losing volume.

"That's not what you're worried about, is it? You're worried about the categorization. You're worried about why they did this. You're worried about what happens next . . . you think those things are going to come back for us, don't you? And you're going to leave us locked up in this town until they do."

"Dr. Pellan, you've been working very hard for us since this happened. You're tired, you're emotional and you're overreacting. This is simply about precaution and risk mitigation."

"This is about saving your neck and sacrificing ours."

"Dr. Pellan," Meeks cautioned.

"This discussion is over," Barrick said abruptly. "You will sign those agreements, you will keep this information to yourselves, and you will remain calm. Rest assured, once we have more information to hand, we will consider sharing this information with the general population. Until then you and your research are classified, do you understand? Public safety, security and stability are our primary objectives here." Barrick stared at them both firmly.

"But," Meeks spoke up, clearing his throat, "when you do release the information, Bateson Dermacell will get full credit, yes?"

"Yes, Professor Meeks," Hogarth said with a placating tone. "If and when the information is released, your lab will receive due credit."

Meeks gave a confident nod. "Send through the agreements."

"What if we don't sign?" Lysart asked, curious.

"There's no need to go down that path, doctor," Barrick told him. "This is just a temporary measure for the good of the people, for our national security and for international stability. That's all. In times of uncertainty, control is fundamental." He glanced at someone offscreen, then back at Lysart. "The agreements have now been sent to you. Please sign the document, Dr. Pellan."

Lysart noted the stare Barrick gave him. It wasn't one that gave him an option.

"We will sign it," Professor Meeks assured them. "You have our word."

Deputy Leo Cann held the phone tightly to his ear, as he leaned against the doorway of his kitchen.

"You're alright?" he asked gently.

Claire sniffed. "Yeah, we're okay. Donna's been real good putting us up like this."

"Lena's in bed already?"

"Yeah. She had a big day playing with Jacob and Carly. Ate too much candy."

Leo smiled, picturing his daughter with chocolate smeared across her mouth. His smile faded though. "And you?" he asked. "How are you doing?"

Claire didn't answer. He heard her sniffing, knew she was fighting her emotions. He felt his own eyes begin to sting and his throat tighten.

"I love you, Claire," he whispered. "I miss you."

She began crying then, and he closed his eyes, wanting desperately to be able to hold her.

"Why did they take him?" she managed, her voice high-pitched and strangled. "He was just a little baby . . ."

"I don't know," Leo said, shaking his head as she continued to cry. "I don't know, but you have to stay strong, Claire," he told her. "For Lena."

"What about you?" she cried. "You've got that stripe.

What's going to happen to you?"

"I'm okay," he reassured her. "I feel fine."

"But those things did that. What have they done to you?"

He was silent a moment. "I don't know," he said softly, "but I feel fine."

Claire continued to sob. Leo pulled the phone away from his ear, the sound killing him, burning a hole right through his chest. A tear escaped his eye and he wiped it away. He held the phone back up.

"Honey . . ." he said, trying to break through her tears. "I gotta go. I gotta go back on shift."

"I want you here with us," she cried.

"I know, and I want that too. But we can't right now. Not until they know."

"Why is this happening? Where is my baby boy?"

"Claire," he said through her tears. "Claire, listen to me!" he said more firmly. "Listen!" She quietened and he continued. "Honey, I have to go back on shift. Just stay strong, alright? For me, for Lena. I'll call you again in a few hours. You give her a big hug from daddy, alright?"

Claire's crying calmed, but she continued to sniff.

"Promise me!" Leo said.

"I will," she whispered.

"Good . . . I love you, honey. I love you and Lena so much."

"I know," she said. "We love you too. Please come back to us."

"I will," he said, clenching his jaw, fighting the emotion that suddenly surged up into his throat. "I promise."

He hung up the phone then and looked around his empty house. He stood there not knowing what to do. The truth was he still had a few minutes before he had to check in with Earl.

His eyes were drawn to the darkened hallway, and his body moved down toward Mickey's room. He stood in the doorway for a moment, eyeing his son's empty cot.

He moved into the room and stood beside it, looking down into it. He rested his hands on top of the white wooden frame, studying the blankets within. His legs suddenly felt weak and he lowered himself into a crouch, sliding his hands down over the wooden slats along the sides, curling his grasp around them. As he stared through those slats, those bars, into his son's cot, he was sure he could smell Mickey's scent. That beautiful, soft, baby smell.

Leo tightened his grip on the slats, rested his forehead against the cot and couldn't fight the tears any more as he mourned his missing son.

Stanley Barrick rested his head in his hand, but had so far kept his voice measured and calm. It wasn't every day he had a direct line with the President.

"So that's your recommended course of action?" President Turner's voice sounded down the phone.

"Yes, Mr. President," Stanley said. "There's nothing we can do right now but keep the town under quarantine and the zone barrier in place."

"There's been no indication that the ship will return?"

"No. However, our scientists are studying the environmental impact of its first visit. We're hoping we can build some kind of warning system from the data when it's complete. If the environment, the weather, etc, displays similar conditions to the first visit, it will raise an alarm. So we'll know about it."

"How much warning will we have?"

Stanley paused a moment. "Our estimates are, at best, maybe an hour or two, but it could be as little as twenty minutes, maybe less."

The President was silent a moment. "That's a damn shame, Stanley."

"It is, Mr. President. These things took the healthy, sir, and they categorized those left behind. We don't know why, but we do think it would be foolish to think they won't be back. Whether they will bring the healthy back, or whether they will come back for the others, or maybe a different town, we don't know. But that's why we need to keep the town quarantined. Just in case. If they come back for those left behind . . . I don't think there's anything we can do about it, sir."

"And what if they come back and choose another town next time? And then another. And another."

Stanley took a moment to steady his voice. "Then I would say we're in a whole lot of trouble, sir. Our weapons were ineffective. There will be nothing we can do, but sit back and watch."

"That's what I was afraid you'd say."

"I'm sorry, sir. We'll keep working on things. We've stood the CDC down for now, but we're keeping them on standby. According to the press, however, they're still working on the problem."

"Alright. I agree with your planned course of action. Keep the town quarantined. It's important that the rest of the world thinks it's just Victoryville, that this was a one-off attack and these things won't be back. We are walking a fine line and if we're not careful, this could cause a massive international collapse. Nerves are on the brink as it is, but if we can assure people that this tragedy will be confined to just one town . . . It's a tragedy what has happened, and we will do what we can to help the people of Victoryville, but if we have to sacrifice a small town for the sake of world stability, then that's what we need to do."

"Agreed, sir."

"Keep up the good work, Stanley. Keep me informed."

"Yes, Mr. President."

Day Four

Abbie made her way to the Chalmer house. There had been an announcement that a press conference would be happening this morning and a nervous excitement seemed to swell in the air as to the possibilities of what might be revealed.

As she crossed the street, she noticed Josh and Peter were standing on their porch studying something in the distance. She turned her eyes to where they were looking. About 500 meters away, where the town center's barricade gateway stood, a small crowd had gathered.

"What's going on?" she asked.

"Supplies are coming through from the Clean Zone," Josh answered.

"People are worried about getting their share," Peter told her.

"Looks like Roy Kenny's down there." Josh squinted, trying to pick people out of the crowd.

Peter shook his head and sighed. "Trust him to be in the thick of things."

"Roy Kenny?" Abbie asked. "He owns the hardware store right?"

"Yeah," Josh said, leaning against the porch post. "When I'm not at the VAC, I've been working there part-time. He's . . . an interesting character."

"And that's why I go to the hardware store across town instead," Peter said. "If you go into Roy's store, he'll bail you up with his conspiracy theories."

"Conspiracy theories?" Abbie asked.

"Roy Kenny is a paranoid delusionist," Peter told her. "I went to school with him. I should know."

Abbie studied the group in the distance. "Is he the skinny one in the black muscle-shirt?"

"Yeah," Josh said, "next to the guy in the wheelchair."

She eyed Roy Kenny in the distance. He stood, arms folded, talking to the man in the wheelchair. The wheelchair had what looked like an oxygen tank on the back, and something bright red in color attached to the side.

"The one in the wheelchair, is that the union guy?" she asked, noticing that the small crowd gathered seemed to be paying him attention.

"Magnus Bracks," Peter told her. "I hear he's a minor celebrity in these parts. The small town guy who's made waves in the statehouse."

"Roy Kenny is one of his biggest supporters," Josh said. "He's got posters up at the hardware store."

"Yeah," Abbie nodded, "I've seen him on the news."

Just then they saw the barricade gateway slide across and a jeep emerge. Armed bio-guards stood up in the vehicle and waved at the small crowd to disperse. The group eventually did so, but even from where Abbie stood, she could tell from their reluctant body language that they weren't happy.

"What are Magnus and Roy up to?" Karen's voice sounded behind them.

"Karen!" Peter hissed and pushed her back inside the door. "If they see you . . ."

"No one will report me, Peter," Karen said softly. "There are others doing exactly what we are. I saw Shonda-May, Abbie's neighbor. Her little boy Cassius is still with her. He's a Clean Skin. She must've hidden him when the military came around."

"When did you see her?" Peter asked.

A guilty look flashed across Karen's face. "Last night," she said. "I couldn't sleep. I came and stood by the window and looked out. I saw them scurrying around the back of their house."

"Did you see you?" Josh straightened.

Karen paused, then nodded.

"Karen!" Peter gasped.

"She won't tell," Karen told him. "She's hiding her boy too. She won't tell."

"You stay away from the windows from now on," Peter demanded. "You hear me?"

"I can't stay locked inside forever, Peter."

"It's not forever, it's just until they sort this mess out."

"And what if they don't sort it out?"

"They will. They've announced this press conference. They must have something to tell us."

"And if they don't, Peter?" Karen asked softly. "What do we do then?"

Peter's blue eyes looked away from hers. "Let's just wait and hear what they have to say."

Dr. Lysart Pellan sat on the couch in his apartment, not far from the Bateson Dermacell facility in the Clean Zone, sipping his third glass of shiraz. The gift from Harvey to celebrate the grand opening, was good. Very good. He felt guilty, though, now that his work was done, to be sitting in this apartment drinking this fine red, while so many others had been displaced. Poor Cheung had taken to sleeping at the facility, as his lodgings were now in the Striped Zone. Lysart had offered him a room, but Cheung had refused, perhaps too proud to accept charity.

Lysart took another sip of the wine. He'd meant to save the bottle for a special occasion, but he had needed some kind of consolation now, something to try and make him feel better. He took another sip from his glass and rolled it around in his mouth. Full-bodied, with a hint of spice, it did make him feel better, if only temporarily. Within moments of swallowing each mouthful, the guilt and unease would settle once more.

His mind mulled over the press conference that had just taken place. Part of him had wanted to turn it off, but part of him wanted to see just how far they would go. He clenched his hands as he thought about it, then lifted his glass to sip his drink. The White House press secretary, John Kramer, had made his way across the podium in front of the news crews, as if this was all in a day's work. The cameras began flashing like an electrical storm, a nervous frenzied pack awaiting answers. Kramer was clad in a sharp suit, perfectly poised, and his expression was confident: the perfect press secretary.

He'd tapped the microphone, cleared his throat, then begun. Lysart sat and watched as he addressed the media, offering a watered-down version of what Lysart knew to be the truth. Kramer had thanked everyone for their patience. He related how the various agencies had joined forces and had been working around the clock to try and understand and resolve the situation. He stated that the CDC were making progress in their search to provide answers, but they could not yet advise on the origin of the welts, nor could they speculate as to whether any allergen, bacteria, or virus was responsible.

He did add that, so far, nothing on record could be attributed to the welts, but they would continue to examine and investigate.

Lysart had ground his teeth at Kramer's words. There was nothing wrong with the Striped Ones! They didn't have any foreign bodies in their blood, nor in those stripes, and they didn't match anything on file because they weren't contagious. He couldn't help thinking of his daughters, and wondering whether he would ever get to see them again. He wanted desperately to reunite with them, to fix this problem, but right now his hands were tied.

After presenting his statement, Kramer had then thrown to the floor for questions and at this point the press conference went crazy. The cameras were flashing psychotically, voices calling desperately and hands waving to a chorus of "Mr. Kramer! Mr. Kramer!"

The press secretary pointed to a lady in the crowd. "Ms. Bennett."

"Thanks, John. You say that you've been unable to identify the reason behind these welts. Does this just mean the alien ship has infected the Striped Ones with some kind of alien bacteria? Something new to our planet that we can't yet identify?"

Again the press conference went crazy. John Kramer held his hands up and asked for calm.

"We are still investigating the cause of the welts. Right now there is no cause for alarm. The welts have not changed in the three days since this event occurred, nor have there been any other symptoms. We are confident that we will get to the bottom of this in due course. I am merely providing you with an update on where we are at the present moment." He turned and pointed to another reporter. "Ms. Fendel."

"Mr. Kramer, when will the *Striped Ones* be allowed to

speak in person with their *Clean Skin* loved ones?"

"Ms. Fendel, our primary focus has been on quarantining the town and getting to the bottom of what's happened. But I can tell you that within the next couple of days, we will be rolling out a series of video link calls so that communication can take place between any currently separated parties who have no other means of communication. Further information about this will be released in due course via the various media outlets." He pointed to another reporter. "James Ford."

"John, will there be compensation for the victims of the violent scenes during the segregation process?"

"I don't have an answer for you at this time." He pointed to another reporter. "Mr. Hames?"

"Mr. Kramer, what is the plan now? How long will the exclusion zones be in place?"

"As I said, we are still investigating. The exclusion zones will stay in place until we have further information."

"Mr. Kramer! Mr. Kramer!" Voices erupted and John Kramer asked for calm again with raised hands in a hushing motion.

"Why is that, Mr. Kramer?" one voice asked, and all eyes snapped to a reporter joining the press conference by video feed. "Richard Keene, CNN," he said, "and temporary resident of Victoryville." Silence fell upon the room.

"Mr. Keene." Kramer gave a nod.

Lysart thought the man looked familiar, and suddenly realized this was the reporter who had been at the Bateson Dermacell opening, the day of the Occurrence. He had been scheduled to have an interview with him that afternoon, but, alas, it had not gone ahead. The reporter had no marks. He was a Clean Skin, like Lysart.

"As you said yourself, Mr. Kramer," Keene continued, "there

have been no changes, nor any spreading of the welts since this happened. Doesn't that mean they're not infected with a contagion?"

The room remained quiet and eyes were darting between Kramer and the reporter on the screen.

"The zones in Victoryville must stay as they are until we've exhausted every avenue of investigation. This is for everyone's safety. As you know, we are also examining the Clean Skins, so this works both ways here."

"We're now at day four," Keene pursued, "and everyone remains unchanged."

"Mr. Keene," John Kramer smiled, "isn't your specialty environmental issues?"

Richard nodded. "Yes. And an extra-terrestrial spacecraft hovered over the town I was in and froze us for twenty-four hours. I'd say it made a significant environmental impact, wouldn't you?"

"Well, thank you, Mr. Keene, but I assure you the experts are investigating every possibility and they will make recommendations based on the facts as they know them to be. The *facts*, Mr. Keene. Speculating doesn't help; facts and hard evidence do. And as soon as we have hard evidence of what caused this and what these stripes mean, we will share it with the people and take the recommended course of action."

The room burst into questions again, and John Kramer held his hand up for quiet. "We are just commencing our fourth day since the phenomenon and these things take time. As I said, we are working hard at providing an answer, and as soon as we have one we will let you all know. Now, I thank you for your time. Good morning." John Kramer turned and swiftly left the podium to a chorus of "Mr. Kramer! Mr. Kramer!"

Lysart sat on his couch and contemplated Keene's question. He swirled the wine around in his glass, and downed the last mouthful.

These things categorized us and took our healthy, he thought. *And whatever did this, did it for a reason.*

What that reason was, Lysart had no idea. And that scared him. But what scared him more was that whatever did this, might come back. And if they did, the government knew it was powerless to do anything to stop them.

Who knew who would be left alive in Victoryville if they did come back.

Who knew how much time any of them had left.

Abbie jumped at the knock on the Chalmer front door. They were sitting and dissecting the press conference they'd just watched together, avoiding the latest news reports of traffic jams on the main highways leading out of the area. If the exodus continued, those left in Victoryville would soon be the only people for miles and miles around. Besides the military guarding the perimeter, that is.

Peter moved toward the door as both Abbie and Josh ushered Karen to the basement and then stood atop the rug.

Peter checked that everyone was in position, then opened the front door just enough to peer through.

"Roy." Peter spoke to the man standing outside, not relenting on opening the door any wider. "What is it?"

"There's a meeting," Roy answered quietly. "Out the back of Johnny Regalo's Pizzeria in thirty minutes. You should come."

"What kind of meeting?"

"The kind of meeting where we discuss what's happening to us, and what we can do about it."

"Roy—"

"Pete!" Roy cut him off. "Don't kid yourself! Something is going down here and we need to be ready to protect ourselves."

"We need to remain calm until they sort this out."

"They? You mean the folks sitting safe on the outside? The ones that did jack shit when those aliens came and did this to us? Or do you mean the Clean Skins hiding behind that wall?"

"Roy—"

"They're saying we're infected! They're scared! God knows what they're going to do to us. Don't be ignorant, Pete. Don't be stupid."

"*Stupid* is doing something rash, Roy!"

There was silence for a moment, before Roy spoke again. "You didn't change a bit while you were gone, Pete. You're still a gullible, stupid fool."

Josh's father didn't appear offended by the comment. "At least I'm not paranoid, Roy."

"Paranoia will keep my ass safe, Pete. Ignorance will get you killed!"

"*Ignorance* is acting without all the facts!"

"Ah, forget it!" Roy slashed the air with his arm. "Stay here and be fodder for the Clean Skin's experiments. They're just puppets on the military's strings. They've fenced us in for a reason, Pete. You mark my words. They've fenced us in and they ain't ever gonna let us out again! *If* they let us live at all."

"*If* they let us live?" Peter's face crinkled in confusion and anger.

"They think we're infected. They won't hesitate to wipe us out if they think it will save everyone else."

"You don't know that."

"Like hell I don't! Now, you want to hole up in your house and be a coward, then you go right ahead. *I* am going to stand up for me and mine. I'm going to stand my goddamn ground!"

Abbie heard Roy's feet stomp off the wooden porch and disappear. Peter stared after him, then scanned the streets before swiftly closing the door.

"Why don't we go?" Josh asked his father, as he shifted the rug and tapped on the hatch. "To Johnny Regalo's. I think we should go to the meeting."

"No," Peter shook his head.

"They might have information."

"No, Josh," he said firmly. "It'll be nothing but trouble. We stay here."

"Well, if they're going to cause trouble, shouldn't we know about it? Know what we need to stay away from?"

Peter shook his head as Karen emerged from the basement.

"The only information we're getting is from the news, Dad!" Josh raised his voice. "There was nothing in that press conference that we didn't already know."

Peter sighed. "Roy's always had something against the government and the military because they refused him entry years ago. They said it was for medical reasons, but Roy was convinced otherwise. He's been full of conspiracy theories ever since. He's been waiting for something like this to happen. He wants to prove that he's right, and they're wrong; that they're the bad guys."

"What if he's right?"

"No!" Peter said firmly.

Josh clenched his jaw. "If you don't want to go, that's fine, but I do! I want to know what's going on. I want to hear what they have to say."

"I said *no*, Josh!"

"You can't stop me!" Josh went to move past his father, but Peter grabbed his arm. There was a brief scuffle before Josh tore his arm from this father's grip. "I'm twenty-one years old, Dad! I'm not a kid!"

"You are while you're living under my roof!"

"Stop it," Karen pleaded. "Both of you!"

Peter glanced at his wife, then at Abbie, who stood uncomfortably on the outskirts of their argument. He looked back at his son. "Alright, I'll go. But *you* stay here. You hear me?" he pointed at Josh. "I want you to stay out of it."

Josh and his father stared at each other for a moment, their bodies tense.

"I'll go," Peter reassured him, "but you have to stay here with your mother."

Josh flicked his eyes to Karen, then looked back at his father, finally relenting with a nod.

Richard sighed heavily on hearing of more people packing up and leaving the towns surrounding Victoryville, and of reports of more looting and violence in some places. How long before the chaos broke out here in Victoryville too? The lack of answers, the military perimeter, the barricade between the Clean Skins and Striped Ones, the separation of people from their loved ones and thoughts of that spacecraft returning were creating a tension that was simmering away underneath. It made him nervous.

He ran his hand across the stubble on his jaw as he watched footage of dead bodies being removed from a road rage incident outside of Plympton, some eighty-five miles from Victoryville. One car had accidentally rammed into the rear of another, an argument had broken out, then gunfire had ensued. Next thing, he was looking at footage of protestors waving banners in some of the major US cities. Some seemed to be arguing for the civil rights of those in Victoryville, while others demanded the town be wiped from existence before the stripes spread. And in some places the two differing sides had come in contact, which resulted in violent clashes.

And this was what was happening on the outside. Victoryville itself, the eye of the storm, was strangely calm and that bothered Richard. He knew things wouldn't stay calm if the contagion theory wasn't resolved soon. The people needed answers so they could deal with what had happened, so they knew *how* to deal with what had happened to them.

How could the experts not have come up with an answer yet? If they'd found something that wasn't verifiable, if it was a new mutation, say, then why hadn't they just named it already and started working on a cure or vaccination? Why was John Kramer so eager to wind up the press conference after Richard's questions? Why was the government so scared of announcing what the people already knew in their heart of hearts? That they had no idea what the aliens had done to this small section of the population, or what they wanted from humanity generally.

Richard admitted to himself that it was hard not to think about what they'd done during that twenty-four hour blackout. Even though he awoke a Clean Skin, somehow he knew that he hadn't been untouched. He studied his features endlessly, searching for a sign that they had done something to him. He felt he was waiting for something to magically appear on his skin or burst through his chest. The thought was terrifying, like living with a ticking time bomb inside you.

What the hell had these beings done to the people of Victoryville? Where had they taken the missing? What did those stripes mean? The same questions circled endlessly in his mind.

More than anything right now, he wanted to know just how long he was going to be a prisoner in this town.

Abbie, despite some discomfort, had stayed at the Chalmer house, because she wanted to hear what Peter had to say about Roy's meeting. He didn't return until almost 2.00 p.m., and when he did he looked wearier than ever, the lines on his face like brackets accentuating his troubled blue eyes.

"What is it?" Karen asked, her features also weighted with stress. "What's going on?"

Peter closed his eyes and shook his head.

"What?" Karen grabbed his shirt in her fist.

"Roy Kenny's talking about putting together an outfit. He's calling it a resistance unit."

"What are they gonna do?" Josh asked, stepping forward.

Peter sighed. "Nothing, yet. But if the government or the military try and move in and do something to us, then Roy's little army is going to be ready to fight back and defend themselves."

"With what?" Karen asked.

"They've started stockpiling weapons."

"Roy sells guns at the hardware store," Josh added. "He's got stock, alright."

Peter nodded. "Some of the others have their own personal cache as well. And there was talk of stealing more from the military if needed."

"How are they going to do that?" Abbie asked.

Peter shook his head. "It doesn't matter. We stay out of it."

"If they attack the military, the military will attack back!" Karen said.

"I tried to talk some sense into them, but . . ." He shook his head again. "I'm a new face in this town to many. I'm a stranger. Roy is all fired up, and he's got Magnus Bracks by his side.

People know them and they're listening to them."

"Magnus?" Karen asked, unable to hide her concern.

Peter nodded. "Apparently, Magnus has been trying to reach the mayor, who is over in the Clean Zone, but Russo is refusing to take his calls. They have a history between them, and not a great one. Magnus isn't happy the town has been carved in half, nor with the way the Striped Ones are being treated. They're pissed the government fed the supplies through the Clean Zone first and that we got what was left over." Peter rubbed his forehead. "There were a lot of young men there. Men Josh's age, some even younger. They're worried about what's going to happen to them and their families, they don't like this segregation. Some have no family left at all, they're on their own here. This is a dream come true for someone angry and delusional like Roy and he's got Magnus Bracks on his side, who hates the mayor and is someone people in this town look up to. People are scared and those two will tap into that fear and exploit it, given half the chance."

"Isn't Magnus at death's door?" Karen asked. Abbie nodded in agreement. She recalled seeing him on the news before. Her father had expressed surprise that Magnus managed to be so influential in the life of the union considering his health problems. He was heavily overweight, had myriad illnesses, yet he refused to step down as union leader. He was a thorn in side of big business and a hero to many. Despite his physical weakness, people were afraid of Magnus and what he stood for.

"His pacemaker's working fine," Peter sighed.

"Why is there bad blood between Magnus and the mayor?" Abbie asked.

Peter sat down on the couch and looked at her. "Mayor Russo runs a building company, one that Magnus worked for. One day there was an accident on site. It's what put Magnus in

154

that wheelchair. He did his back and legs in pretty good. Anyway, Magnus applied for compensation claiming unsafe practices by the company, but it was rejected on a technicality. Magnus fought for years to have the decision overturned, but it never happened. Ever since, he's been heavily involved with the unions, and has done his best to be a pain in Russo's ass. He's a like a dog with a bone. Any chance he has to help defend the little guy, Magnus has been there. That's how he rose to the top and became the local union leader."

Karen shook her head softly. "Magnus is stirring the hornets' nest while Mayor Russo is over on the other side of the fence."

Peter nodded. "Him and Roy Kenny together could be dangerous."

"So what do we do?" Josh asked.

"We stay inside," his father told him. "We keep your mother hidden, and we stay the hell out of it."

Mayor Russo stared at the two men standing on the other side of his desk: Chief Blackstone, and Dr. Emile Preslen.

"The girl is a Clean Skin?" Russo asked.

"Yes," Dr. Preslen answered, "she wouldn't be here in the Clean Zone otherwise."

"But she gave birth to a Striped One?" Russo clarified.

"Yes."

"Have there been any other cases?" Russo asked.

"No. She's the first, but there are a couple of others due soon," Dr. Preslen answered.

"Do you think she may have infected anyone?"

"I don't think so, but I can't be one hundred percent certain given we don't know what the hell we're dealing with. We've been treating all our Clean Skin patients in full protective gear—masks, gloves, glasses—as a precaution," Preslen said. "I don't believe any risks were taken by my staff."

"So what do we do with her?" Russo asked.

"We need to put her in isolation," Preslen said. "We can't house her at the hospital given the risk of infection and certainly not with the traffic we're getting. We have two doctors and limited facilities. Every Clean Skin is coming in for the slightest head cold, panicking about having caught something. We're stretched as it is. Dr. Chee has set up a medical center in her clinic over in the Striped Zone. I think it's best if she goes there."

"If she's got the room for them," Blackstone spoke up. "No doubt her clinic is getting as much traffic as yours. Probably more given it's in the Striped Zone."

Russo studied the doctor. "Does she need to go to a clinic? Where is her home? Could we send her back there?"

Blackstone scratched his jaw. "We could, but it's in the Clean Zone. I'm not sure the neighbors will take that so well. A striped baby in their Clean Skin complex?"

Dr. Preslen agreed. "Look, we've tried to keep this quiet, but word has already spread around and it's left a lot of people uneasy."

"So what do you suggest?" Russo asked.

"She has to go into the Striped Zone," Preslen said. "We don't have the facilities to house them in isolation and there could be a potential risk of infection if we leave her here in the Clean Zone." Preslen shrugged. "To be honest, I'm exhausted and stretched, and I don't really care. But she can't stay here."

Russo stared at Preslen, then at Chief Blackstone. He tapped his pen on the table as his mind ticked over, then sighed heavily and gave a nod.

"Send her into the Striped Zone," he told Blackstone. "It's our only option. We can't risk an outbreak."

"It's weird, though, don't you think?" Blackstone asked. "That's she's a Clean Skin and the child is striped. I would've thought if it was infectious, she'd definitely have it."

"I'm inclined to agree," Dr. Preslen said, "but if there's one thing I know, it's that prevention is better than cure. These stripes are like nothing we've ever seen before. Until we know more, that striped baby, and any risk of infection that comes with it, needs to be removed. We simply can't risk the rest of the Clean Skin population for the sake of one child. She's gotta go."

"Agreed," Mayor Russo nodded, then looked at Blackstone. "See it done, chief."

Abbie walked toward the main street of Victoryville with Josh by her side. They were headed to the grocery store to stock up on supplies, given the delivery of fresh produce that morning. They were worried that looting might soon occur, considering what was happening in other towns, not to mention the group Roy and Magnus were putting together and what they might do.

Josh had insisted on accompanying her to the store, although she wasn't sure if he wanted to protect her as much as he wanted some space from his father. Although the altercation between father and son over Roy's meeting had been brief, she sensed friction remained. She understood the constrictions Josh felt living with parents at his age, and she knew the tension created by hiding Karen wasn't helping things either, not to mention the tension caused by the family's move here to Victoryville in the first place. It was clear that Josh hadn't quite forgiven his father for his indiscretion as yet—or being forced to move here.

As they approached the main street she saw a huddle of people gathered. In the center was Magnus Bracks, with Roy Kenny by his side. Abbie eyed the wheelchair in which Magnus sat, laden with its oxygen tank on the back. The chair was an electric, high-tech looking one and must've cost a pretty penny. She saw a bright red object latched to the side of the chair and realized that it was a megaphone.

Roy eyed Josh keenly and gave him a nod. Josh reciprocated cautiously, then looked at two young guys standing near his part-time boss.

"Langdon," he said to the taller blond one with two stripes. "Trent," he said to the shorter, stocky one with dark hair and one stripe. The two young guys gave Josh a nod back. They were the ones she'd seen Austin talking with the other day when she'd checked out the barricade for the first time. They worked at Roy's Hardware and hung out down at the gym.

"You heard the news?" Roy asked Josh, the side of his face giving way to a twitch every now and then, making two of his four stripes move with it.

"What news?" Josh asked.

"Apparently a Clean Skin girl gave birth to a Striped One." Roy's eyes narrowed, gauging the response. Abbie wasn't sure if Roy had even noticed her standing there yet.

"Where'd you hear that?" Josh asked.

"Wendy overheard the soldiers talking," Trent answered for Roy, motioning to a brooding teenage girl standing with them, with dark hair and three stripes. She nodded in agreement, fastening her heavily made-up eyes on Abbie.

Roy turned his attention to Abbie, giving her the once-over. His face twitched, then he looked back at Josh. "The soldiers said they were going to kick her out of the Clean Zone, given her kid's marked and all."

"Can they do that?" Abbie asked concerned.

Roy shrugged again and motioned to the barrier. "Can they do any of this shit?"

"If I know Mayor Russo, he won't let the kid stay in there, that's for sure," Magnus said, his voice wet with phlegm, as he reached for his oxygen mask and took a breath in. His eyes, their cloudiness no doubt caused by his many illnesses, stared at Abbie as she counted seven stripes over his obese chin and jaw, fighting with the eczema for space on his skin. "They think we're infected," he said. "They think we're below them. They'll throw it out like trash, mark my words."

"They better not kick that Clean Skin out here as well," Roy said tetchily. "We don't want her neither!"

"Just wait and see." Magnus eyed the barricade, smiling lightly to himself as though this were a game, and he was waiting for the next play.

Abbie looked around at the barricade, at the makeshift gate, and suddenly realized that was why Magnus and Roy were waiting there. She eyed the group, mostly men, aside from Wendy and an older woman, their faces pasted with unhappy scowls. And their stripes, of course. They looked like they were spoiling for a fight, ready to intercept any intruders into the Striped Zone. Josh seemed to notice it too.

"C'mon," he suggested, motioning her onward with a flick of his head. She followed, but not before glancing with concern at Magnus and Roy. And as she walked away, she felt their eyes burning into her back.

Kaitlyn Manner's whole body shook like she was a bag of rattling bones. She stared down at the child lying on the bed in front of her, feeling a little numb. The newborn was crying, its face almost as red as the welt that marked its chin. It made her cry too. The sound of this child she'd been waiting months to see. And now it was here, she didn't want it to be. At least, not like this.

How could she have given birth to a Striped One? She was a Clean Skin. This didn't make sense. Whatever this was, she must've been infected before conception. Or *through* conception. She screwed her hand into a fist and scrunched the bedsheets. *Damn that Blake Rogers!* Why did she listen to him? *"It's alright, you won't get pregnant,"* he'd said. Her mama had warned her to stay away from boys and liquor and now here she was stuck in this mess. Blake was long gone. He was the lucky one, finishing high school. And here she was, a dropout with a damn Striped One for a kid.

She felt her shoulders shake as she began to cry again, the hopelessness hard to shift. She'd lost count how many times she'd burst into tears now, and it had barely been a few hours since the birth. It was bad enough that this phenomenon had taken place, but for her mama to be out of town when it did, to be separated from her? Then to go through hours of giving birth, to finally meet this child that she'd decided to give up her whole life for, and then to see that damn welt down his face . . .

She looked at her baby again. His little face was screwed up, like he was in pain. Her chest seemed to crush in on itself. The sound of his cries were like claws deep in the muscle of her heart. She reached over to him and ran her finger along his cheek. It was so soft, so baby soft, just like she knew it would be. She'd been to the antenatal classes where they'd brought in real babies for them to see, to deal with, to change, to help feed with bottles. And watching him now, she knew that her little boy was hungry and scared and alone. He needed his mama. Just like she needed hers.

She ran her hand down to his chin, to the welt that marked it. It was so smooth too, like it wasn't even a welt, just a pink tattoo beneath the skin. She opened the swaddling around him and followed the mark down to the middle of his chest.

Why? Why him? Why my baby? What was wrong with him? Was he doing to die?

She began to cry again, as the sound of his own cries became unbearable, like a drilling in her ears. She relented and lifted him up, cradling him to her chest and began to rock him, anything to stop the noise. *Anything.* In a way, she kind of rocked herself too; she needed someone to hold her, but she knew that he needed someone to hold him too. And that's all they had for now. Each other.

She looked around at the small room in which they were keeping her. The doctor and nurses had left some time ago to "discuss" his condition with the authorities and, despite having just given birth to her first child on her own, somehow this seemed even more frightening. She didn't know what was going to happen to them. All she knew was that she wanted her mama.

And so Kaitlyn Manner sat there and rocked and rocked, trying to give her son what she herself desperately wanted, but couldn't have.

Stanley Barrick looked at the young scientist, one of many who had been working with Dr. Wattowski on analyzing the data from the Occurrence.

"We think we might have found a link," the woman said, tucking a pen behind her mousy brown hair, "as to why the ship chose that town."

"And what link is that?" Stanley asked.

"The readings we managed to get during the visit, the air samples from the weather station, showed a high percentage of mercury in the atmosphere."

"Yes?"

"Certain levels of mercury are normally found in Victoryville airspace due to the close proximity of the coal plant."

"The Clivecorp plant," Wattowski added. "Funnily enough, it's one of the backers of the Bateson Dermacell research facility, who have been helping with our initial study of the welts."

"Go on," Stanley said.

"The percentage of mercury present in the air increased during the visit," the scientist continued. "Now, we know this didn't come from the coal plant because everything shut down when the ship appeared, including the plant. Which means the increase of mercury in the atmosphere occurred as a direct result of the ship."

"And that means?" Stanley asked.

"It means," Wattowski said, "that we think the higher levels of mercury are a result of pollutants from the ship, which means we may have traced how the ship runs, or what may have partially burned off in the atmosphere on its approach."

"So?"

"So," Wattowski said, "it's a stretch, but it could indicate why this ship may have chosen Victoryville."

"Depending on their point of entry into the Earth's atmosphere, that is," the young scientist was quick to add. "There are many other plants similar to Clivecorp's around the world, many that produce higher levels of mercury pollution here in the US, but the Victoryville plant may have been the closest source to where the ship came down."

Stanley stared at her. "Closest source of mercury?"

"Yes," Wattowski said. "We think they were attracted to a strong source of a resource they recognized."

"Apparently that was why Bateson Dermacell located itself in Victoryville," the young scientist added. "Their key focus was research into the effects of pollution on the human population. That Clivecorp plant is the state's biggest polluter."

Stanley tossed this information around in his mind. "So how does this relate to the welts?"

Wattowski shrugged. "That, I can't answer. All we know is that these levels of mercury could provide us with a link as to why the ship chose *that* particular town, as well as perhaps telling us something about their home world and what they may have there."

Stanley exhaled loudly and rubbed the back of his neck. "Alright. Keep working on it. I need more than mercury."

Deputy Leo Cann surveyed the crowd gathered at the Victoryville interzone gate. He was a little nervous about the numbers, given he was "it" for law enforcement on this side of the wall. He thought briefly about asking for reinforcements, but decided the soldiers at the gate would be enough. He spoke into his comms set.

"I'd say there's near on fifty people now, chief, and more are coming down this way," he said.

"Alright," Chief Blackstone's deep voice said, "I'll give the soldiers at the gate a heads-up, tell 'em to be alert. Do your best to get those people to clear the area without making too much of a fuss. We just want to clear a path to release the girl."

"Will do," Leo replied, clicking off his comms and surveying the crowd again. He sighed, then leaned in to turn on his vehicle's warning lights. The red and blue began to flash, drawing the crowd's attention as he made his way toward them.

Abbie and Josh came back from the store to find the numbers had swelled in the crowd gathered around Magnus and Roy. There were maybe fifty or sixty now, and an excitable murmur swam through them like an electric current zapping from one conduit to the next. She saw a lone police car down the road, lights flashing. It took her a while to spot the owner. Deputy Cann stood talking with Magnus and Roy. Over their heads she saw the barricade's makeshift gate opening up and everyone seemed to pause at the sight.

Josh halted beside her too, then quickened his step to join the throng. Abbie followed, and they made their way around the side of the crowd to the front, to get a better view of what was going on. She saw the bio-guards spilling through the gates with their weapons raised, telling the Striped Ones gathered to move back. Deputy Cann was saying the same, waving his arms, but something caught the cop's attention. He suddenly called out to someone at the back of the crowd and started making his way toward them.

Abbie glanced to where the deputy was heading and saw Austin standing with another young guy atop the rickety roof of the old bank, opposite the gate. Austin was holding a small camera and filming the scene. The deputy made it to the building and started waving them down, but they were ignoring him. She turned back around and noticed Roy watching Austin too, a smug look spreading across his face as he returned his attention to the gate.

"Move back!" one of the bio-guards barked, using his weapon to motion the way.

The crowd moved as told, but only slightly, the ones at the front fighting to move against the ones at the back seeking a better view. Instead of backward, they seemed to fan around, forming a rough semicircle in front of the gate. Four soldiers were on the Striped Ones side of the barrier now, aiming their weapons as they pressed forward, and Abbie finally realized what was going on.

She heard the girl's sobs before she saw her. It was a sound that made her feel instantly uneasy, registering somewhere deep within her chest. Her eyes searched the gateway for the source, and then finally saw it in the form of a skinny young girl, fifteen at most, but maybe younger, being led through the gates from the Clean Zone by one of the bio-suited soldiers. Abbie recognized her as the girl she'd seen on one of the balconies of the apartment block the other day.

The girl wore a baggy shirt and shorts and carried something in her arms that she was holding close to her for dear life. It looked like maybe a sack of clothes, but Abbie knew that it wasn't. The girl's legs skittered along the pavement as though she was trying to fight the momentum of the soldier escorting her. Abbie's uneasiness grew and sympathy swamped her. It was clear the girl didn't want to leave the Clean Zone, but was being forced to do so.

The murmur of those gathered began to turn into shouts and accusations.

"What do you think you're doing?" Wendy, the teen with dark hair and heavy eye makeup, shouted at them.

"What's going on?" another yelled.

"Who's she?"

"She's a Clean Skin! You can't send her out here!"

"We don't want her!"

"Take her back!"

Once through the gates, the escorting soldier released her and turned back to the gateway.

"No, please!" the girl cried, reaching after him. "Don't leave me, please!"

165

The other soldiers began to fall back as well, and the girl tried to follow them. She managed to grab one of their arms, but they turned her around and pointed firmly into the Striped Zone, shouting, "Go over there, Miss!"

The girl was crying hysterically and Abbie suddenly realized her fears were true as the cries and screams seemed to be happening in stereo. It wasn't a sack in the girl's arms, but a baby. A tiny, newborn baby.

"It's the girl Roy told us about!" Josh's voice said beside her, aghast.

"Hey, you can't leave her here!" The yells from the crowd continued, attracting more passersby to the din.

She saw Trent call out, "Don't dump your trash out here!"

"This is our zone!" Langdon echoed. "You don't want it, remember?"

Just as the soldiers went to close the door a rock smacked into the gate, narrowly missing one of their heads. The soldier in question spun around and gave a fierce stare into the crowd of Striped Ones, trying to see who threw it. His comrades also turned around as another rock hit its target, smacking into the soldier's mask, cracking the left eyepiece. They all swiftly raised their weapons and aimed them at the crowd, while the young sobbing girl stood in their line of fire begging to be taken with them.

Abbie felt her chest drop to see the girl standing with her crying baby and four guns sweeping across her to the crowd behind. Abbie looked desperately for Deputy Cann, but he was still trying to coax Austin and the other boy down from the roof of the bank, although darting occasional nervous glances to the growing mayhem behind him. Abbie took an anxious step forward as more insults were shouted at both the soldiers and the girl.

"Enough!" they heard an amplified voice sound loudly over

the crowd.

The crowd of Striped Ones turned and parted to show Roy Kenny hand the red megaphone to Magnus Bracks. Magnus took it and raised it to his mouth as his eyes scanned the soldiers, the girl, and the crowd around him.

"What's the meaning of this, soldiers?" his deep voice wheezed into the megaphone.

The bio-guards glanced at each other, then back at him.

"Who is the girl and what are you doing with her?" Bracks asked.

"She's infected," they heard a deep voice boom, without megaphone, from back behind the barricade. Abbie saw the Victoryville chief step up to the interzone border, surgical mask across his face. "She can't stay in the Clean Zone," he said.

"So?" Magnus shrugged. "Who said you can dump her out here?"

"Her child," the chief pointed, "is a Striped One. They can't stay in here, Magnus."

"*She's* not a Striped One!" Roy shouted.

"We don't want her and we don't want the kid!" Langdon called out.

Magnus raised his hand to call for silence, then spoke into the megaphone again. "I asked a question, chief. Who said you can dump her out here?"

"An authority higher than you, Mr. Bracks," the chief told him.

"What authority?" Magnus asked. "Do you mean that Clean Skin coward, Mayor Russo? If he's the authority of this town, then why haven't we seen his face? He seems to have found the time to show it to the people on *that* side of the wall."

The chief ignored his question, motioning for the soldiers to close the gate, and then began to walk away.

167

The lead soldier motioned for his men to continue and they too turned to leave. The young girl reached for him again, but he turned and took her by the tops of her arms. "You have to stay here, Miss."

Another rock soared through the air and clipped the side of his mask and Abbie gasped at how close it had come to the girl's face.

"I'm warning you!" the soldier yelled at the crowd.

"Back off!" another soldier yelled holding his weapon's sight to his eye.

"Screw you!" someone in the crowd yelled.

More rocks soared through the air toward the soldiers and the still sobbing girl. One caught the girl in the back and she collapsed to her knees. Abbie instantly dropped her shopping and rushed forward, propelled by some kind of gut instinct. She skidded on the knees of her jeans and came to a stop behind the girl, holding her arms out in an arc to surround her protectively as the stones and bottles continued to fly. The girl looked at her with distraught crying eyes that reminded her of some kind of wounded, terrified animal. A rock hit Abbie in the shoulder and she groaned, but it was cut off by ear-piercing gunfire cutting through the air.

She threw her arms around the girl and curled over her and suddenly felt another body come to wrap around her own. She saw Josh, doing to her what she was trying to do for the girl. The sounds of the terrified, shouting, screaming crowd filled the air and as she looked up she saw the bios retreat back inside the Clean Zone and close the gate. Abbie raised her head and looked behind her to see the scattering crowd.

"Oh my God, he's been shot! He's been shot!" Wendy screamed. As Josh moved away, Abbie turned to see Austin on the roof, pale-faced, trying to lift the limp body of the boy he'd been standing with. A panicky Deputy Cann was holding his arms up to the building's roof and, within moments, a group of men ran over to stand beside him. Austin dragged the boy to the edge and lowered him down to the men. Abbie watched in horror as the boy's lifeless and bloodied body was quickly taken away in the arms of Deputy Cann and three other men.

"Screw you!" Trent yelled, picking up another rock and hurling it at the closed barricade.

Abbie curled around the girl once more.

"Enough!" Magnus bellowed into the megaphone.

The gathered folks looked at him, as he set his chair in motion toward Abbie. She stiffened in fright as he approached, alarmed at what might transpire.

"Get away from her," Magnus ordered.

"What are you going to do?" Abbie asked, her voice noticeably shaking.

"Move!" Roy stepped forward, reaching for her, but she wrapped herself tighter around the girl. Roy tugged at her, but Abbie smacked his arm away.

"Wait!" Josh yelled, arms out, pleading for calm before Roy retaliated.

"Get away from that stinking Clean Skin!" Roy yelled.

"She just a kid!" Abbie shouted back, refusing to move from the crying girl who still sat on the ground on her knees, rocking herself and her child.

"Move away!" Magnus ordered again. "Show me the child."

A scuffle broke out as Langdon and another guy pushed Josh back, then Trent grabbed Abbie and dragged her off the girl. Roy stepped in and tore the child from the hysterical girl's arms and brought it over to Magnus.

Abbie elbowed Trent away from her and moved back to the girl to wrap her arms around her, trying to calm her.

Magnus and Roy examined the child.

"One stripe," Magnus said, then he turned his attention to the girl as a murmur swelled through the crowd.

"Send them back!" Wendy spat.

"How do you propose we do that?" Magnus asked her. "Toss them over the barricade? They'll just toss her back."

"They shot Chris!" Langdon called back. "This happened because of her!"

"It was a stray bullet!" Josh spoke up. "They were aiming over our heads. I saw them."

Austin pushed through the crowd then, panting, and held his camera out to Roy and Magnus. "I got it on tape!"

Roy slapped him on the shoulder in a congratulatory manner and exchanged a glance with Magnus.

"Take your child," Magnus told the girl.

The girl, shivering in Abbie's arms, looked at Magnus, but was too frightened to move. Abbie stood, took the child and returned him to the girl.

"What are you going to do with her?" Roy asked Magnus.

"What can we do?" he shrugged. "She's garbage like the rest of us. She can stay . . . for now."

Everyone watched as Magnus eyed the barrier with menace, then turned his chair and headed back toward the row of stores to inspect the scene of the shooting. Roy and the guys who'd both grabbed and held Abbie and Josh followed. As the rest of the crowd dispersed a young teen boy with a scowl pasted across his face spat on the ground near the Clean Skin girl in passing.

Abbie looked at the girl sitting with shoulders curled, eyes closed, unable to do anything other than cry in distress.

Josh watched the others move away before asking Abbie, "What do we do with her?"

"I don't know." Abbie shook her head, concerned by the

stream of high-pitched screaming coming from the baby.

Josh looked around the streets, as though searching for an answer.

Abbie looked at him. "We can't just leave them here," she said, then lowered her voice. "Maybe your mom can help with the baby?"

Josh hesitated, but then gave a resigned sigh and nodded.

Abbie stood and reached her hand down to the girl, but she flinched away. The girl darted a glance at Abbie, her eyes falling to the welt on Abbie's chin.

The Clean Skin girl was scared and, of course, didn't know her from any of the other Striped Ones here, Abbie realized.

She knelt down. "I'm Abbie," she told her. "This is Josh. It's not safe for you to stay out here. You should come with us."

The girl glanced at her, then broke out crying again. "I want to go back in there." She looked back at the closed gate.

"You can't," Abbie told her gently. "They won't let you. Your baby is . . . come with us. You'll be safe."

She saw the girl looking timidly around the surrounding streets. Abbie did too. There were still a few Striped Ones standing in the distance watching them. She spotted Austin, standing with Langdon and Trent outside the hardware store. Austin's camera was pointed directly at her and the Clean Skin girl, filming them. It made Abbie feel uncomfortable to be the target of their attention.

"We have to move off the street," Abbie said firmly to the girl. "You can't stay here on your own."

The girl glanced around again, at the Striped Ones watching her, at the gate, then down at her child.

"Come on," Abbie said softly, and helped the girl to stand. Then she wrapped her arm around the teenager's shaking shoulders and walked her in the direction of Josh's house.

Richard Keene's eyes were absolutely glued to the screen. The shakiness of the person holding the camera only seemed to add to the intensity of the vision. He couldn't believe what he was seeing. The footage had been taken in the Striped Zone, where a Clean Skin girl had been banished after giving birth to a Striped One.

He wondered why they hadn't just put her in isolation rather than kick her out. The scene of the distraught girl being evicted from the Clean Zone was distressing enough, but what moved him more was seeing the Striped Ones who rushed to help her against the angry mob. He then watched the situation erupt into chaos with the accidental shooting of the boy on the rooftop . . .

The Victoryville shooting was the lead story dominating every newscast, with secondary discussion threads on whether or not the Clean Zone had been infected by the child and what this now meant for the Victoryville Clean Zone.

Some were outraged that the girl had been kicked out of the Victoryville CZ, some were outraged by the behavior of the mob of Striped Ones, and others were outraged by the actions of the soldiers.

So much outrage everywhere.

He noticed the focus across all stations was on the horrific elements of the incident: the throwing of rocks by the Striped Ones, the shooting of the boy by the soldiers, the eviction of the young girl and child, the threat of disease in the Clean Zone. Not one of them focused on what he saw was the *real* story here: that young woman rushing out despite the flying rocks and stones to help the girl. The Striped One trying to protect the Clean Skin.

It wasn't long before it was confirmed that the boy who'd been shot had died from his wound, a single bullet to the chest.

Discussion boards on the internet and social media feeds exploded with anger and hate and persecution. Richard had a bad feeling; he'd seen this happen before. He'd seen how one single tragic accident or one wrong court decision could ignite a fury that grew so large the effects were wide ranging and devastating. These incidents showed the dark side of the human condition: how humans were so wildly driven by their emotions, no matter how valid; how the flame of injustice could turn emotions so volcanic that all sense and reason were vaporized.

He didn't want this to happen here. People couldn't lose sight of the bigger picture, of what had happened to the people of Victoryville, of the phenomenon that had triggered everything since. Now was not a time to fracture, it was a time to unite; to be strong for each other. He wanted people to regain focus, to regain calm, before things blew out of control.

He wanted to tell the story of the striped woman who put her life on the line to help the Clean Skin.

Dr. Lysart Pellan paced his apartment torn as to what to do. The day's events had left him with a bitter taste in his mouth and a nauseous sensation in his stomach. First, the footage of that poor girl's eviction from the Clean Zone in Victoryville had rocked him. She'd been thrown out like some trash because she'd given birth to a Striped One. And it killed him because he knew that the child wasn't contagious, that it was an empty gesture. That welt simply meant the child had inherited a condition from his mother or father. That's all. They'd been thrown out for no reason, violence had broken out, and a young man had been accidentally killed in the process. A casualty of a very unnecessary conflict.

As soon as he'd seen the news he'd immediately called

Harvey.

"Have you seen the footage?" he blurted once Meeks had answered. "Of the Victoryville shooting?"

"Yes," Meeks said quietly, "I have."

"We could've stopped that."

"No, we couldn't have."

"It never should've happened!"

"Lysart—"

"The child wasn't contagious!" Lysart insisted. "We knew that. *They* knew that! She never should've have been kicked out and put in that terrible situation."

"It's out of our hands, Lysart."

"Is it? Maybe you're content with washing your hands of this, Harvey, but I'm not. That boy was inadvertently killed because we are keeping quiet about our findings!"

"It's the government's call, Dr. Pellan," Harvey said firmly, as though pulling rank. "Until they know more, until they are certain these things won't come back, they cannot divulge these findings. They must discover what those aliens are and why they categorized you first."

"What caused this is a separate issue, Harvey! These people are not contagious. It's not right to segregate them, to herd them away from everyone, to let people think that there is something wrong with them."

"There *is* something wrong with them, Lysart, they are all sick. That is why they have those welts."

"And we Clean Skins have defective DNA, Harvey! How does that make us any better than them?"

"I saw the footage, Lysart. That mob were savages. That had nothing to do with us. That's on them!"

"They think the child is contagious, Harvey. We are

responsible for that!"

"Homeland Security have the final word, Dr. Pellan. May I remind you that you signed the agreement. This is out of our hands. This is above us. *You signed that contract.* Don't do anything to jeopardize our lab!"

"Is that all you're worried about, Harvey? Your lab? Your funding? What about that dead boy? What about that girl tossed into the Striped Zone with a bunch of people who don't want her there? What about the life of that child? The life of that non-contagious child!"

"Dr. Pellan—"

"Professor Meeks," Lysart said heatedly, "perhaps this is an easier decision for you, given you are sitting back there in Washington, but it's not so easy for me. I'm the one trapped here in this town. I can see, can *feel*, what these people are going through."

"Dr. Pellan—"

"We are not just samples in a petri dish, Harvey! We are not here to raise the profile of Bateson Dermacell or be peace offerings to the aliens so they stay away from the rest of you! We are people. We are living and breathing human beings."

Meeks exhaled loudly. "Look, things will calm down in Victoryville and the government will sort this out in a few days. Until then, just sit tight and keep your mouth shut, Lysart. There is nothing we can do, so just drop it. For both our sakes!"

With that, Meeks had hung up. Lysart collapsed on the couch, trying to erase the images of the distraught young girl clinging to her baby, and of the boy's limp and bloodied body being passed down off the roof. He looked around his apartment, helpless. He had never felt so alone.

His mind wandered to his daughters over in Paris, no doubt watching this latest tragedy unfold on the news; wondering where their father was in Victoryville, perhaps relieved at not seeing him in the crowd at the gate, thinking him not involved.

But he was involved.

And he was ashamed.

All the work he'd done, all his life, was for the aid of others. He studied and resolved medical conditions, ultimately to help people.

Yet here he was, sitting idle and letting people die.

Abbie studied the young girl, cradling her child as she sat on the couch. The girl's eyes were red and puffy, her face pale and exhausted, her hair limp and dirty, and she was still so frightened. Abbie had had no choice other than to bring the girl home, because Josh's father had turned them away.

"What are you doing?" he'd asked, stepping onto the front porch as dusk fell around them.

"She needs our help," Josh told him.

Peter's eyes went wide. "She's a Clean Skin!"

"But her baby isn't," Josh told him. "They've got nowhere to go." He motioned to the end of the street: "We couldn't leave them there."

"She can't stay here, Josh," Peter shook his head.

"Why not?"

"Because, your—" Peter stopped himself, darting his eyes to the girl. "We don't want to draw attention to our house, Josh," he said, looking his son firmly in the eyes. "We have to stay out of it."

Josh went to speak, but stopped. Abbie heard the creak of the floorboards inside and knew it was Karen. Clean Skin Karen. Josh must've realized why his father didn't want to help, because he dropped his eyes guiltily to the floor and went quiet.

"It's okay," Abbie spoke up, touching Josh on the shoulder. "The baby seems to be settling now. They can stay at my place. I could use the company anyway."

"But," Josh's eyes darted down the street and back, "what about them?"

"We'll be okay. Magnus said she could stay and people seem to listen to him."

Josh looked a little edgy, but he didn't argue. How could he argue with the safety of his own mother? Especially after today's violence.

Abbie had taken the girl and her child and crossed the street to her house. As she did, she saw something move out of the corner of her eye. She looked over to her neighbor Shonda-May's house, and saw the curtains moving as though falling back into place. Had Shonda-May been watching them?

Approaching her door, Abbie suddenly remembered the shopping that she'd left at the barricade.

"Shit!" she whispered. She turned to Josh and asked if he'd go back and get her things. He'd nodded and jogged away.

As Abbie entered her house she felt a sense of sadness, the memories of her missing family rushing up to crash into her. Here she was, bringing a complete stranger and her newborn child to stay at her parent's house without their invitation. She thought about what they would've said, and saw their approving smiles; her parents were kind, always offering to help people and give back to their community. Even though tears threatened her eyes, Abbie felt a sense of pride. She was doing the right thing, just like her parents had raised her to do. They would be proud of her. It was all she could do to keep their memory alive right now.

Abbie ushered the girl to the couch and they sat there in silence for a little while, not sure what to say or do.

"I never got your name?" Abbie finally broke the silence.

The girl darted her eyes to Abbie, still shaking a little. "It's Kaitlyn," she said quietly. "W—what's your name again?"

"Abbie."

The girl nodded and her gaze fixed on Abbie's welt, her eyes tracking it from her chin to her chest. It was strange, Abbie thought . . . for a brief while there she'd almost forgotten she even had it, but now Kaitlyn's Clean Skin stares ensured it sat heavily upon her skin once more.

Kaitlyn looked down at her child. "Does it hurt?" she asked.

"What? The stripe?"

Kaitlyn nodded shyly, darting her eyes back to Abbie's chin.

"No," Abbie told her, "it doesn't hurt."

"And you don't feel sick or nothing?"

Abbie shook her head. Kaitlyn glanced at her and Abbie saw a faint relief wash over the girl as she tucked her thin, reddish-brown hair behind her ear.

"Is it a boy or a girl?" Abbie motioned to the child.

Kaitlyn sniffed and looked down at her child. "Boy."

"What's his name?"

"I don't know." Her young face flushed very pale. "I haven't even thought about that yet. I haven't had time with all . . ." Her voice trailed off as her mouth contorted, wanting to let out another cry.

"Well, you can name him now?" Abbie said gently.

Kaitlyn stroked the single stripe trailing down her son's chin. Abbie saw the exhaustion pouring from her. Her shoulders were stooped and eyes drooping.

"When did you have him?"

"This morning," she said softly, the tiredness seeping

through her voice.

"God, you must be exhausted." Abbie moved over to her. "Is everything alright? Do you feel okay?"

The girl looked up at her through glistening eyes. "I just want my mama."

Abbie felt her own shoulders slump at the girl's words. She nodded softly. "So do I," she whispered.

Kaitlyn stared at her, as tears slid down her cheek. "Did your mama go missing?"

Abbie nodded, fighting the lump that suddenly threatened to close her throat. "I lost my whole family."

Kaitlyn stared at Abbie for a moment longer, before her face curled into sobs. Abbie wrapped her arm around Kaitlyn's shoulders, pulling her into a hug, trying to comfort her. Although she soon realized that she was comforting herself as well. She suddenly appreciated just how much she needed someone to hold her and tell her things would be okay.

When Josh finally returned, he told her the shopping bags were gone. Someone had taken them. Abbie couldn't believe that someone could steal from another in these circumstances, but at the same time she wasn't surprised. Nothing seemed to make sense any more.

"I'm sorry," Kaitlyn said as Josh left again, and Abbie closed the door. "You lost them because of me."

Abbie gave her a smile. "It's not your fault."

Kaitlyn looked down at her son mournfully, exhausted.

Abbie moved over to the girl again. "I think you should rest now. Come on, you can take my sister's room."

Abbie led her upstairs and held the nameless boy, while the shattered young Kaitlyn lay down on the bed and swiftly fell asleep.

Day Five

Dr. Lysart Pellan sat back in his chair, running his fingers over his mouth. His coffee sat beside him, now barely warm. It had been ignored while he'd absorbed himself in the news report. There was something about it that had caught his interest. He'd replayed it over and over again. This reporter, Richard Keene, had taken a different angle on the Victoryville shooting. This man seemed to see what others could not. He wasn't going for the blood and gore that people fed on. He'd pulled the one solitary good thread out of that mayhem and he'd turned a spotlight on it. The one good deed, amidst the chaos and horror.

More than that, he'd noticed something else that others had been too blind to see over and above the violence and the shooting itself. Where some believed a striped child from a Clean Skin meant contagion, Keene had asked a question that gave Lysart a spark of hope that the truth might come to light. Keene had asked: if the baby was striped and contagious, then why hadn't the mother become a Striped One too?

Not only did the reporter ask this question, but he strongly implored the authorities to provide an answer.

Abbie stared at the TV, stunned. It was surreal to see her name and photograph up on the screen, as that strange mechanical noise buzzed on and off through the speakers. The reporter, Richard Keene, had done a story on the Victoryville shooting and had made her into some kind of hero.

"Oh my God, that's you!" she heard Kaitlyn say.

She glanced at the girl holding her son at the bottom of the stairs, then turned back to the screen and listened to the reporter's closing statement.

"The alien visitation, the riots, the looting, the protests, this boy's shooting in Victoryville, are tragedies. But despite this, glimpses of hope remain. The hope within humanity that, despite what has happened, despite the blockade around Victoryville, despite the barricade splitting this town in two, a Striped One could put aside resentment and assist a Clean Skin against the angry mob. This is the humanity I want to hold to. This symbol personifies the hope . . ." A still image appeared on the screen of Abbie on her knees, her arms wrapped around Kaitlyn and her son, ". . . that Striped Ones and Clean Skins will unite. I hope there are more people like Abbie Randell out there in this chaos, because what happens if the Striped Ones are not contagious? What if this young Clean Skin mother is proof that they aren't? What if we find out that the young Kaitlyn Manner was ejected from the Clean Zone for no justifiable reason? What if we let these barricades create a division between us that can't be undone? Just like the death of this boy in Victoryville cannot be undone. I think that is the real enemy we need to be wary of. I think people like Abbie Randell should be the ones we hold up as an example of how we should behave in these frightening and uncertain times. This is Richard Keene for CNN."

A knock at the front door startled Abbie. She opened it and

Josh stood there with a strange look upon his face. Concern. Fear. She saw him glance at the TV, then back to her.

"She's a hero," Kaitlyn said quietly, giving an unsure smile as she rocked her son.

"Er," Josh looked back at Abbie, "have you been outside today?"

"No."

"You should probably take a look," he said stepping back from the doorway.

Abbie stepped out onto her porch and the acrid smell of paint hit her immediately. The front of her parent's house had been graffitied. She moved back to take in the words painted in large black letters across the white walls of the house and gasped.

Go home Clean Skin bitch!

"What is it?" Kaitlyn asked, moving to step outside. Abbie rushed forward and threw her hands across the screen door, stopping her.

"It's nothing."

Kaitlyn looked at her with innocent eyes, the freckles sprinkled across her nose making her look that much younger.

"Then why can't I look?" she asked.

Abbie struggled to find the words and exchanged an awkward glance with Josh.

"You don't need to see it," he told her.

Kaitlyn unconsciously took a step back. "Is it bad?" Her voice trembled as she pulled her son closer to her.

"Just go sit on the couch. I'll be with you in a minute," Abbie told her firmly.

Kaitlyn's face paled, and she turned and ghosted away from the door.

"I'll see if I can find something to wash it off," Josh murmured. He went to leave, but suddenly paused. "Hey!" he shouted, waving someone off.

Abbie turned to see a few people standing around, gawking at the house. A couple of them were filming and taking photos.

"Get out! Go away!" Josh yelled, still waving as he made his way toward them. They quickly dispersed, but concerned, Abbie continued to look around to see if anyone else was checking out her house. The only thing her gaze caught was the outline of Peter Chalmer standing just inside the screen door of his house across the road. She held his stare for a brief moment before he stepped back and closed the main door, disappearing from view.

Abbie moved back inside, closing her door as well. Not sure how to feel, she put on a brave face and moved to where Kaitlyn sat on the couch still holding her son.

"Is everything okay?" Kaitlyn sniffed, her eyes wet and questioning.

Abbie nodded and sat down on the couch beside her.

"Are we in danger?" Kaitlyn asked.

"No," Abbie said, although she wasn't sure if it were true. "it's just kids."

Kaitlyn looked down at her son.

"How's he doing?" Abbie asked, trying to change the subject.

"Okay, I think . . . I'm sorry about his screaming last night." She looked at Abbie bashfully. "I don't really know what I'm doing. My mama was supposed to help me through this."

"I'm sorry I'm not much help." Abbie gave her a sad smile.

"No, you are. Thank you," she smiled awkwardly, "for letting me stay."

Abbie gave her a brighter smile. "It's no problem. I'm just glad you're both okay."

"I really wish I had his things. We'd bought lots of stuff, ready for his arrival, but it's back at our apartment."

"You and his father?"

"No," Kaitlyn shook her head, averting her eyes. "His father is long gone. Well, he's at college. That was the deal. His parents had money. They bought me and mama the nice apartment, so long as we never named my baby daddy or asked for anything ever again." She stared down at her son. "Their boy had potential, they said. Didn't want him to ruin his future." She gave a sad laugh. "They didn't care much for mine, though." She caressed the baby's cheek. "Or his."

The silence sat around them for a moment, as the boy gurgled and yawned and stretched.

"I think he's feeding well," Kaitlyn said, looking at her hopefully. "At least that's something."

Abbie nodded, studying the boy and the red mark down his chin. It looked somehow darker today. "You know, you should probably give him a name now."

"Well, I thought before I had him, that I liked the name Jackson. But now I see him I don't think he's a Jackson. Do you?"

Abbie shrugged. "I don't know. You're his mom. What do you think?"

Kaitlyn studied the sleeping boy for a little while, then seemed to nod to herself. "I think he's more of a Charlie, don't you?" She looked at Abbie for approval.

Abbie smiled, and gave Kaitlyn a nod. "Charlie it is."

Mayor Russo switched the TV off and looked at his acting

deputy, Graeme Shother, standing beside Chief Blackstone.

"It's a PR nightmare," Graeme said, shaking his head.

"That," Russo pointed at the screen, "was Magnus Bracks' doing!"

"Magnus didn't kick a teen mom out of the Clean Zone, Mike. We did," Graeme told him.

"It was too risky to keep her here," Russo said. "They're overloaded. Dr. Preslen agreed it was best to send her there."

"That doesn't matter," Graeme said. "What the people saw were soldiers forcing a scared young teenager into the Striped Zone against her will. *We* look like the bad guys here. It's the leading headline around the world. The aliens are second now. We look like assholes, Mike." Graeme exhaled heavily. "I really wish you had checked with the rest of the council before doing this."

"What?" Russo said, fighting to control his anger. "You're telling me you would've gone against medical advice and risked the entire Clean Zone?"

"I'm not saying that," Graeme snapped. "I'm saying that this is not a dictatorship, Mike."

Russo cast him a look that told him the comment was unfair.

Graeme held his hand up in apology.

"Look," Russo said, pushing his anger down, "we'll issue a statement clarifying the details from our end, and focus the blame on Bracks making trouble."

The chief sighed loudly and Russo threw him a glance.

"On that," Graeme said, "what do you want to do about Mr. Bracks? You think he's going to be a problem for us moving forward?"

"Bracks is always a problem," Russo said, unable to hide the venom in his voice. "In that respect he's a very reliable man." He turned to Blackstone. "Tell your deputy to keep an eye on him. He's in charge of the Striped Zone now, so it's *his* job to keep Bracks in line!"

"Is Deputy Cann going to be enough against Bracks and his supporters?" Graeme asked, raising his eyebrows and folding his arms. "He did jack when this particular episode went down."

"He was trying to get the two on the roof to come down," Blackstone countered. "It's an old building and it was dangerous. If they'd have listened to him, that boy would be alive right now."

"But they didn't listen to him, chief," Graeme said. "*That's* my point."

Russo shrugged. "Deputy Cann will have to be enough. He's a police officer and it's his job to keep the peace. That boy getting shot was the fault of Magnus Bracks, not me. He was in the middle of it with his goddamn red megaphone stirring up the people like he does. If Bracks makes any more trouble in the Striped Zone, then that's on the head of your deputy, Earl. He has the power to make arrests, so maybe he should use it once in a while. You make sure and tell him that!"

Blackstone didn't respond verbally, just stared stonily at Russo, then turned for the door. Graeme followed him. "I'll draft the statement, see if we can dig ourselves out of this mess."

Russo watched them leave, then exhaled loudly and slammed his laptop closed.

Deputy Leo Cann sat on one of the beds in an empty cell of the Victoryville police station. Leaning forward, elbows resting on his knees, his head was in his hands. He listened to the quiet of the police station, the emptiness. He felt awful. Guilty. A teenage boy was dead. Shot right in front of him, while Leo stood there, helpless. He could only watch as the boy's chest sprayed blood and his legs fell out from under him.

Leo rubbed his hands together as though trying to wipe the memory of the boy's blood covering them. He'd helped carry the boy to the medical center, but it was too late. Dr. Chee tried to revive him, but he was DOA. This was Leo's fault; he was supposed to be policing the Striped Zone. This shouldn't have happened.

He exhaled loudly in anger and frustration. He was outnumbered, he was running each day on only a few hours' sleep, and coping with his own loss. He couldn't do this alone. There were soldiers on the wall, but they never left their post. Even in their bio-suits they didn't travel further than they needed to. Besides, they answered to outside agencies, not the Victoryville PD.

What the hell was he supposed to do against an angry mob when it was sixty to one?

He hadn't said these things to Earl when they'd talked after the incident, but he hadn't needed to. The chief understood. Leo hadn't said a word when he answered the phone call, because Earl, in that deep voice of his, was quick to say, *"It wasn't your fault, Leo. Alright? There was nothing you could've done about it. It's a tragedy, mark my words, but there's absolutely nothing you could've done about it."* They'd talked briefly. The chief reassured him, told him to keep his mind fixed on the job until this situation was over, and if Leo needed it, there would be counselling for him to access. *"I know it's hard, but you need to accept it. The boy's death was a tragic, horrible accident. Just keep your head clear, and stay focused. There's going to be fallout from this, whether we like it or not. That's what you need to focus on. Keep your eyes and your mind sharp, Leo. Do your best to keep the people calm, and move them on if they start to gather again. And watch your back, alright?*

That's a priority. You're no good to the people over there if you're out of action." Leo had agreed. *"Good,"* Earl had said, *"let's keep the communications open. I want to hear from you every four hours. Got it?"*

Leo knew everything Earl had said was right, but it was still hard to shift the guilt. Still hard to erase the image of the boy's body collapsing. That poor kid had survived the phenomenon, only to die at the hands of a stray bullet fired by a fellow human being. A stray, unnecessary, bullet.

He sighed, thinking of Claire and Lena over in the Clean Zone, wanting desperately to be with them. At least they were safe, he thought. He just had to be strong and make sure that he made it back to them.

When this was all over, that is.

If it could ever be over.

He looked around the cell and his eyes fixed on the bars running along the face of the room. The bars, in long lines, that reminded him horribly of the stripes afflicting the people of this zone. Afflicting him. It made him think of the wooden slats down the side of Mickey's cot again . . . straight lines digging into horrible memories everywhere he looked.

He suddenly felt claustrophobic, and hastened to exit the cell, wrapping his hand around one of the bars and rolling the door shut behind him. The loud clang echoed around the empty station, reminding him again of his solitary state.

He took one last look at the row of bars before getting as far away from them as he could.

Abbie answered the phone with a thumping heart. It hadn't rung once since . . . since her family had disappeared.

"Hello?" she said tentatively.

"Is this Abbie Randell?" a male voice asked.

She paused wondering whether she should confirm it. "Who is this?"

"Abbie, my name is Richard Keene. I'm a reporter. Sorry for calling so late . . . I, er, I did a story on you helping that girl—"

"I saw it," she told him cautiously. "What do you want?"

"I was watching the news, and . . . I saw what they did to your house. I'm sorry if my story caused that to happen. Is everyone okay?"

"What do you care? You got your story."

"I didn't mean to put you in any kind of dangerous position," he said. "I thought what you did was very brave. I wanted people to see what you did, to celebrate your actions."

His voice was warm, it sounded kind. The silence sat for a moment.

"So, what do you want now?" she asked.

The reporter was silent again for a brief moment. "I just wanted to make sure you're alright. That Kaitlyn and the child are alright?"

"We're fine."

"There's been no other trouble except the graffiti?"

"No."

He exhaled heavily. "I'm glad to hear that. There're some weird things going on and people can start acting a little crazy in times like these. I didn't want my story to cause any more trouble for you. I want to make sure that people like you stay safe, Abbie."

"We are," she told him, adding, "so far."

"What's it like in the Striped Zone?"

Abbie pondered his question for a moment. "Are you looking for another story, Mr. Keene?"

There was another pause before he answered. "I'm looking for the truth, Abbie."

"Well, we're just the same as the Clean Zone . . . except marked."

"Tell me something Abbie, if you don't mind me asking, how is Kaitlyn really? Is she feeling alright, is she displaying any symptoms? Anything at all from being over there in the Striped Zone?"

Abbie looked to where Kaitlyn was asleep on the couch, Charlie swaddled beside her.

"She's just given birth. She's tired. She's adjusting."

"But she's not sick with anything? She's still a Clean Skin?"

"Why do you ask?"

"I'm just curious. How does a Clean Skin give birth to a Striped One? If it's contagious, shouldn't she have caught it?" He paused for a moment. "Like everyone else here in this town, I want to get to the bottom of this. The sooner we can drop those barricades, the better . . . if you Striped Ones aren't contagious, then we can do that, Abbie."

Abbie thought of Karen and the fact that she wasn't displaying any symptoms either. Nor Cassius, Shonda-May's little boy, as far as she knew.

"Abbie?" the reporter asked. His voice seemed so kind and gentle, but she didn't know if that was just his way of getting her to talk. The truth was, he was a stranger, and a reporter at that. She wasn't sure whether she could trust him.

"I'm just trying to find the truth, Abbie," he said. "Will you help me? Will you help free your town and get your life back?"

"My life back?" she asked, swallowing hard. "You can return my missing family?"

Silence poured down the line.

"Your whole family is missing?" he asked.

"Yes," she said, swallowing again.

"I'm so sorry, Abbie. I can't imagine—"

"I'm having trouble imagining it myself," she cut him off, "but it's true. The empty house around me is evidence of that."

Again silence filled the line. She felt bad for snapping at him. This phenomenon wasn't his fault. He was just as much a victim in this as she.

"Kaitlyn is fine. The boy is fine," she said. "Read into that, what you will, Mr. Keene. Goodbye."

Abbie hung up the phone, mulling over his words, then turned to stare at the sleeping Clean Skin.

Stanley Barrick glared at Colonel Levin.

"This could cause us a lot of problems."

"I agree," Levin answered, "but we always knew there was only so long that we could keep the truth hidden. If the welts don't change, if they don't experience any symptoms, they'll soon figure out that they're not contagious. They're not stupid."

"And now we have a Clean Skin girl living in the Striped Zone, which will only speed things up," Stanley added, as they sat in his makeshift office.

"I'd say you have a couple of days before they start thinking the government is lying and trouble breaks out," Levin said.

"Trouble has already broken out," Stanley said. "We've got a dead body to prove it."

"My soldiers fired overhead into the air. That kid shouldn't have been on the roof of that building. It was accidental."

"Tell that to public opinion," Stanley said bluntly.

Levin sighed heavily. "We could bring the zone barrier down, let them mingle, but still keep the town quarantined from everyone else."

Stanley considered the idea briefly. "We still don't know why they categorized the people. *That* is the problem here. They did it for a reason. So why the hell *would* they categorize the people, mark some of those people, if they had no intention of coming back?"

Levin shrugged again. "Well I, for one, have always thought there was no question that they were coming back."

Stanley stared at him.

"Why wouldn't they?" Levin asked them. "They got past our defenses with ease, they rendered us powerless to do anything against them. I have absolutely no doubt that they're coming back. For me, the question is when."

"I'm inclined to agree," Stanley said, "but we can't go out to the public and say that. The world will goddamn explode if we do. We suspended trading on the stock market to avoid a crash, we've got people leaving towns up and down the Eastern Seaboard, turning the whole area into one big ghost town, and we've had pockets of riots and looting and protests around the world. And that's just because this ship hovered over one town. *One* town. If we tell the people of the world that those things will be back and any one of us could be next, God knows what would happen! If those things are coming back we need to focus every ounce of our attention and resources on *them*. We can't be having to deal with mass unrest across the country or the globe, as well."

"I agree," Levin said. "We have to contain it and maintain world stability."

"So, how do we do that?" Stanley said.

"Aside from erasing the town from existence and convincing people the problem's been taken care of?" Levin said bluntly. "I'm all ears."

Stanley shot Levin a stony look. "We go with the long incubation story," he said, then shrugged. "Who knows, it could still be true. In truth, we know very little about any of it."

"That will buy you *some* time," Levin said, "but not much."

"We keep the barrier between zones in place. I want your soldiers on alert."

Levin gave a nod. "As always."

"We'll prepare another statement. Meanwhile I'll get our people to have a friendly chat with the media outlets about not inciting violence."

Josh Chalmer's heart kicked up a notch. Standing in the warehouse out back of the hardware store, Austin, Langdon and Trent were staring at him, having just loaded ammunition into the weapons they had been allocated.

"Are you in or not?" Austin asked, brow furrowed in annoyance.

Josh, nervous as to what would happen after the death of Chris, the boy on the roof, had come to the hardware store to try and find out. Now he wasn't sure coming here had been such a good idea. But still, he couldn't walk away. He wanted to know what Magnus and Roy's mob were going to do.

He nodded, "Y—yeah. Sure."

"Good," Austin said, walking up to him and thrusting a gun into his chest. "You know how to fire one of these?"

Josh took it in his hands and studied it. It was heavier than it looked. "Er, no."

Austin exhaled impatiently. "You should've been here when Roy showed us. You gotta catch up." He looked at Trent. "Teach him how to use this thing."

Trent stepped toward him as Austin and Langdon moved back into the front of the store.

Josh listened as Trent quickly showed him how to load the gun and use it. He only took half of it in, though. His mind was racing, thinking about what they were planning, how far they intended to take things.

"You think they'll actually use these on anyone?" Josh asked, holding the gun carefully in his palm as though it were a grenade with a loose pin.

"If they have to," Trent said. "They're not for show, you know. These are real guns with real bullets."

"Yeah, but the military are out there on the barrier. They've got some firepower behind them too."

"So have we," Trent said, looking down his nose at him, despite the fact that Josh was taller. Regardless of the height difference, Trent was broader than Josh and had clearly spent a lot more time down at the gym. He was strong and, from what Josh had heard, had been taking boxing lessons from Austin for a while now. Getting into a fight with Trent or any of these guys was not on Josh's list of things to do; they were on his list of things to avoid. At all costs.

"We're leaving soon," Trent said to him. "Be ready."

Josh nodded and watched him walk away, then looked back at the gun in his hands, wondering what the hell he'd just gotten himself into.

Abbie knocked softly on the door of Josh's house. It was late, but she didn't know what else to do. Peter answered.

"Mr. Chalmer—" she began before Peter cut her off.

"Is Josh with you?"

"No. Is he not here?"

Peter seemed to hiss angrily.

"We think he went to Magnus' meeting," she heard Karen's disappointed voice say from inside.

"There was another meeting?" Abbie asked.

"What do you want, Abbie?" Peter asked softly.

"I need to speak with Karen. Charlie, the baby, he's screaming a lot tonight and we don't know what to do. Can she come and take a look?"

"No," Peter said adamantly, "of course not."

"We don't know what to do," Abbie pleaded.

"Peter," Karen said softly.

"If they see you!" he hissed over his shoulder, then turned back to Abbie. "Look what they did to your house, Abbie. Tensions are high, and you go and take in that Clean Skin girl."

"What else could I do?" Abbie said. "Let them stone her and the baby?"

"It's too risky. Look how they've reacted to *your* Clean Skin. What will they do if they discover Karen? If you draw unwanted attention and she gets caught—"

"I wouldn't do that!"

"You're doing it *right now*, Abbie!"

Abbie didn't know what to say. "Can I bring the child here, at least?"

"Absolutely not! Take it to the medical center."

"But—"

"As far as people know, Karen is interstate. No one can know she is here. Do you understand?"

"Mr. Chalmer, I would never—"

"We helped you when you needed it Abbie, but you're doing fine back in your own house, so please don't come here again."

195

With that Peter closed the door. Abbie stood there for a moment, shocked.

She turned and slowly made her way off the porch and across the road, reading the ugly words smeared across her house. Words that Josh hadn't been able to properly erase, so they were now smudged thickly across the wall.

As she stepped on to her front lawn, she saw movement in the corner of her eye and looked over at her neighbor's house. There, in the darkened window, sat Shonda-May, watching Abbie, her brown eyes and skin silhouetting her further against the white underside of the curtain. As soon as they made eye contact, Shonda-May stepped away and closed the curtain. Abbie paused, staring at the window, and considered briefly whether Shonda-May could help with the child. But she felt a sorrow slowly build within her. A realization. She knew the reaction would be the same as Peter's.

Everyone was scared. No one was willing to help.

Josh Chalmer was crouched behind a parked car, staring, frozen, at the dead soldier laying in the distance beneath the streetlight. His whole body rattled in terror.

"Come on!" Langdon hissed, as he ran past toward their car.

Josh turned and stumbled, then righted himself and followed. As soon as he jumped into the car, it took off, tyres screeching. Those in the car burst into a cacophony of "Holy shit!" and "That was insane!" and someone gave a relieved laugh and punched the roof of the car.

Josh felt a hand slap around his neck and squeeze tight, and he bunched his shoulders in response.

"Did you even fire?" Langdon laughed. "Or did you just hide behind the car and piss yourself?"

A chorus of laughter broke out.

Josh didn't answer. He couldn't actually get his mouth to move. He looked down at the gun in his hands. The safety was still on. He'd never bothered to take it off.

"You better man up, Joshy," Trent sneered at him, "or you might as well bend over and let those Clean Skins fuck you!"

They broke out in laughter. All except Austin, whose hard eyes studied him from the front passenger seat.

"That's okay," Roy said from the driver's seat. "Josh will step up next time, won't you?" It sounded more like an order than a question.

Josh nodded, and managed a "Yeah."

They dumped the car and set it alight, then ran to the hardware store, where Magnus Bracks and others waited for them. On hearing the news of the soldier's death, the group were given slaps on the back and firm nods of approval for being brave and "doing what had to be done". Phrases like "Justice for Chris" and "An eye for an eye" were murmured, and someone else said something about "survival of the fittest".

Josh's hands, still shaking, were sweaty and he wiped them on his jeans. Wendy came up to him and threw her arms around his neck, pulling him into a tight hug.

"You did good, Josh," she said. "Those weapons will help us. We need to be able to protect ourselves if they come for us."

He heard snickering laughter and saw Langdon and Trent watching them. He pulled back from her, but she kept her hands on his shoulders a moment longer, smiling at him. She turned and walked away, and Austin moved to stand next to him.

"Looks like you're in with Wendy," he said.

Josh glanced at him and shook his head. "No, she's just being friendly."

Austin laughed under his breath. "Yeah, she's been *friendly* with a few of the guys here."

Josh glanced at him, then forced a smile as though he shared Austin's sentiments. Anything to hide the terror he felt within.

"Hey, look," Austin said, nudging him with his elbow, "if you froze up this time, don't worry about it." Then he turned and his taller, broader frame leaned in closer. "Just make sure it doesn't happen again."

Josh stared at him.

"You've seen what people are saying on Facebook and Twitter about us," Austin said. "Some of those outsiders want to wipe us out. If they try to, or if those damn aliens come back, we have to be ready to defend ourselves. 'Cause no one else will give a shit about us, I promise you that. We defend ourselves or we die." He poked his finger, which felt as hard as a marble, into Josh's chest. "You piss yourself again, I'll do more to you than the Clean Skins or those aliens will." Austin stared at him briefly, his dark-brown eyes fierce, then he relented and gave Josh a friendly slap on the shoulder. "Come on. Let's go celebrate our haul."

Josh watched Austin walk away. Petrified, and not knowing what else to do, he followed.

Lysart paced his apartment, two news reports circling in his mind with overwhelming ferocity. The first was another story by that reporter, Keene. He'd written a follow-up on the girl, Abbie Randell, who had saved the Clean Skin mother, Kaitlyn Manner, and her child. Her house had been defaced with cruel words, her kindness treated as though it was a crime. But what got to Lysart the most was that Keene had spoken with Abbie about the health of her house guests and had confirmed that Kaitlyn was not displaying any symptoms. Keene then posed theories and questions to his viewers: If this could occur, if a Clean Skin could live in the house of a Striped One, then didn't it mean that whatever this was, it wasn't an airborne contagion; and if Kaitlyn could give birth to a Striped One, and have that exchange of bodily fluids and still not be affected, then didn't that mean this contagion wasn't transferred through bodily fluids either? And if this contagion wasn't transferred by air or fluids, then how could it be transferred? Was it transferred at all? Did this mean there wasn't a contagion? Most Clean Skins and Striped Ones had interacted for over twelve hours before the segregation took place. If the Striped Ones were contagious, then why had no Clean Skin suffered any symptoms? Keene then posited that if he had come to this conclusion through observation and no medical testing, then why had the CDC and government not come to this same conclusion? And if they hadn't come to this same conclusion, then what had they discovered? What were they hiding?

The second report, however, worked to crush Keene's speculations: the government released a statement saying that their testing, although currently inconclusive, had not yet ruled out an alien virus with a long incubation period, and therefore, the segregation between the Clean and Striped Zones would remain in place until they could rule out or confirm the presence of an alien virus.

Lysart was astounded that they could release such a lie to the people. His initial testing had been clear. There was no contagion.

He was a scientist and he believed that everything had an explanation, but why the population of Victoryville had been categorized by these things, he didn't know. What he did know, however, was why the government was keeping segregation in place, why they were keeping the town in quarantine: in case the aliens came back. And if they did, the government knew it was helpless to do anything. So they were going to keep the town fenced off and wait and see if the aliens came back to finish whatever it was they had started. At least, the government was hoping that was all the aliens would do when they returned.

Regardless, it was clear the people of Victoryville had already been tainted, so if they were the cost of saving everyone else, then it would be a small price to pay.

And that price included Lysart's life. He thought of his daughters in France with their mother, constantly wondering if he'd ever get to see them again. Then he thought of that young mother thrust into the Striped Zone with her baby. The girl's own mother, according to news reports, was trapped outside the town somewhere.

This couldn't go on. If the lives of the people of Victoryville were still in danger, if they were going to be left here like bait for the alien's return, then they had the right to the truth, they had the right to know.

And they had the right to be reunited with their loved ones before it was too late.

Abbie awoke to the sounds of distant yelling. Arguing. She got out of bed and moved to the window. She saw Josh exiting his house, slamming the door behind him and striding angrily across his front lawn to the pavement. Glancing up, he saw her at the bedroom window. He seemed to pause for a moment, then changed direction and headed for her front door.

She pulled on a robe and walked downstairs to open it, turning on a couple of lights as she did. Josh marched straight in and began pacing her living room.

"What's wrong? What's going on?" she asked.

Josh continued to pace. "My damn father! He forbids me to go to any more of Magnus' meetings. He doesn't understand. I'm doing it to protect mom! I'm keeping an eye on them, trying to figure out what they're up to. Trying to figure out if they know about her or any of the Clean Skins who are hiding, and what they'll do about it, if they do. He doesn't get it!"

The energy flowing through him scared her a little. He was on edge. She didn't really know him that well, but she could tell that this was more than just an argument with his father about Magnus' meeting.

"What's wrong? What's happened?" she asked.

"I didn't have anything to do with that soldier's death!" he said vehemently.

Abbie paused a moment. "What soldier's death?"

Josh continued to pace, shaking his head. "It's all over the news . . . things got out of hand. It was Roy. It was all Roy. I had nothing to do with it."

"Nothing to do with what?"

Josh kept pacing and ran his hand over his face as though trying to wipe the images away. Abbie moved to the TV and turned it on. A weather report was on, but she read the news scrolling underneath:

More violence in Victoryville tonight. One soldier dead, one injured, as tensions rise.

Abbie turned back to Josh. "So what the hell happened?"

Josh slumped on the couch, leaning forward to put his head in his hands. Abbie wasn't sure what to do, but moved to sit beside him and tentatively put her arm around his shoulders.

"Josh, *what* happened?"

He looked at her briefly and she saw tears threatening his

eyes. He clenched his jaw, and lowered his head into his hands again.

"Josh . . ." she said gently.

"They've started looting and stockpiling," he eventually blurted out. "Magnus and Roy are convinced the government are lying to us. They think something bad is coming. They think the Clean Skins and those outside are going to do something bad to us . . . Magnus keeps giving warlike speeches, saying that we have to prepare to defend ourselves, that we won't let them do anything to us, that we won't go down without a fight. They've gathered everyone's personal cache of weapons, but Magnus says it's not enough. Roy's started taking groups out to rob what they can and tonight they decided to hit some soldiers."

Abbie felt a weightlessness fill her stomach.

It was fear.

"No one was supposed to get hurt . . . but one of the soldiers went for his weapon and Roy shot him. Just shot him." Josh shook his head as if trying to get rid of the memory.

"You were there?" Abbie asked, trying to contain any judgment.

Josh sniffed back his tears. He glanced at her, then nodded. "Roy and Austin asked me to go. Langdon and Trent were there too. I think they were testing me, testing my loyalty, so I went. I was curious about what they were doing, how far they were taking things."

"Oh God, Josh . . ." Abbie whispered.

"I didn't fire a single shot! As soon as Roy fired, the other soldier fired back, and then the guys joined in and they were shooting at each other. The soldiers were outnumbered. I just ducked for cover and watched it go down. Roy had a choice. He could've just wounded that soldier but I saw what he did. He wounded the soldier and when the guy tried to get up, Roy shot him clean in the neck. He didn't have to shoot him again, but he did. He killed him!"

Abbie squeezed Josh into a hug, resting his head on her shoulder. The fear within her zoomed up to terror level.

"They all got in on it," Josh continued. "Even Austin. Afterward, they celebrated. They were high-fiving, saying what a good haul they got from the soldiers . . . like that soldier wasn't killed. Like the other wasn't hurt."

"Austin, too?"

Josh nodded. "He said it was payback for Chris' death. He said that with the aliens out there and us locked up in the town, the rules no longer apply. It's just life and death now. Survival . . . I—I couldn't move, couldn't say anything. I just didn't know what to do."

"What did Magnus say about it? He didn't approve, surely?"

"He didn't say anything. Roy told him what happened and Magnus just gave him a nod, as if to say 'it had to be done'."

Josh stood, shrugging her off and started pacing again. "What am I going to do?"

Abbie looked at him, not sure what to say. She watched him as he paced, tortured by what he'd witnessed, scared by the decisions in front of him.

"I don't know what to do." Josh shook his head in disbelief.

"Did you tell your father?" she asked.

"God no! He saw the news and asked, but I told him I wasn't there. I said I didn't know what they were planning."

"Just stay away from them, Josh. Don't go back there, just stay away."

"I can't," he argued. "They're dangerous. If you're not with them, then you're against them. Roy made comments to me about my old man, saying he needs to harden up, saying he needs to reassess where his loyalties lie. They're threats, I know it! If they find out that we're hiding mom . . ."

"Go to the police, then."

"Are you crazy? I have to keep them on side. I have let them think that we're okay, that they don't have to worry about us."

"The police can help."

"No, they can't! Deputy Cann is on his own over here. You think he can do anything? He's out of his depth."

"Josh, I really think you should stay away from them."

"*God*, you sound like my father! You have no idea. It's not that simple, Abbie!"

"Is everything okay?" they heard Kaitlyn's small voice asking from the top of the stairs.

Abbie and Josh looked up at the sound.

"It's fine," Abbie called back quickly, not wanting to alarm the teenager.

Josh turned suddenly and headed for the door.

"Josh!" she called, but he ignored her, vanishing through her front door.

Day Six

Richard Keene woke to his phone ringing. He picked it off the sleeping bag he lay on and answered.

"Harry?"

"Richard, where are you?"

"I'm still at the Civic Hall. Why?"

"We, er, may have a little problem."

"Yeah, what's that?" Richard asked as he stood up, grabbing his pack and making his way to the balcony where it was quieter.

"I had a visit from Homeland Security."

"You did?" Richard stepped out into the early morning air.

"As a matter of national security, we've been asked to report responsibly and avoid speculation."

"What?"

"They said people are on edge and the slightest thing could trigger unwanted outcomes. There're claims of inciting violence and the like. We've got the eye of Big Brother firmly upon us."

"Us?"

"You better watch yourself, kid. The questions you've been asking must be ruffling some feathers. Your name came up a few times."

"Is this just us or is this industry-wide?"

"Industry-wide, apparently. I put in a few calls. It looks like everyone has politely been asked to watch what they say. If anyone is found to be inciting violence, then measures may be taken."

"Well now, isn't that interesting." Richard felt the hairs on the back of his neck prickle.

"It is, kid, but this is serious. They're watching you."

"Must've hit a nerve, huh. So much for free speech."

"Oh, they were sure to word things carefully. It was a simple request all in the name of keeping the peace and not fueling mob violence."

"I'm not fueling violence, I'm been imploring people for kindness and calm. What they don't like is the questions I'm raising to *them*."

"Look, just be careful, alright? I gotta go."

"Thanks, Harry."

Richard ended the call. He leaned against the brick pillar beside him, which formed part of the Victoryville clock tower. Resting his hands on the railing, he stared at the distant barricade and its guards, then looked beyond into the Striped Zone.

His curiosity was absolutely burning now. Just what was it about the Striped Ones that scared the government so?

Mayor Russo gave Chief Blackstone a hard look. "What the hell is going on over there, chief? Is your deputy *actually* doing his job?"

"Deputy Cann is covering the Victoryville Striped Zone on his own. He has to sleep sometime."

"A soldier was shot and killed on Victoryville soil. I've had the state governor on the phone chewing my ass! They're sending in more soldiers because they think we can't police our own people. After the press we got sending that girl out of the Clean Zone, this is a goddamn nightmare!"

"Yes, it is," Chief Blackstone nodded calmly.

"What are you doing about it?"

"What *can* we do about it? One soldier is dead and the other is recovering from surgery. I'm waiting to speak with him to see if he can ID the shooters, but until he comes to, there's not much I can do. There appears to be no other witnesses. At least, from what I can gather, given I'm over here in the Clean Zone." Blackstone said the last part with a hint of condescension. "Of course, with your permission, I could grab one of those bio-suits and head over there—"

"No!" Russo cut him off. "Your job is here in the Clean Zone."

"Then what would you have me do, mayor?"

"You can start by talking to Bracks," Russo fumed. "I'll bet you any money, he knows who's behind it."

Blackstone regarded him for a moment, lips pursed, then conceded a nod. "I'll have Leo pay him a visit."

"Don't just get him to pay a visit, Earl, get him to lay down the law," Russo warned. "This happened because he stirred up the crowd the other day. If we have any more trouble . . .!"

"We'll do our best within the constraints of the law, mayor. We can't go accusing anyone without evidence."

"Then find a way! Have him tailed or something."

"I'll have Deputy Cann do what he can, *within* the law.

Bracks, of all people, is the last person you want to accuse you of unlawful activity, don't you think?"

Russo clenched his jaw, fuming at the calmness with which Blackstone spoke. He couldn't recall ever seeing the chief upset or on edge. *How the hell could be so relaxed about things?*

Regardless, he knew the chief was right. If he gave Bracks an inch, the man would take a mile. Magnus was just waiting for him to put a foot out of line. Russo had to watch his step and play things by the book. He couldn't let that man win.

"Just..." Russo paused, trying to push down his anger. "Just do what you can, chief. But do it fast, and thorough."

Blackstone tipped his hat and left.

Richard stared at his ringing phone. He didn't recognize the number.

"Richard Keene," he answered curiously, walking along the corridor of the Civic Hall, having just washed one of his shirts in the bathroom basin.

"Mr. Keene," the male voice responded, but silence soon filled the line.

"Yes." Richard prompted the caller. "Who is this?"

He heard the man sigh. He sounded nervous, unsure.

"Have you heard the latest reports of what happened in Victoryville?" the man asked.

Richard stopped walking. He glanced around the corridor, then slipped into the nearby accessible bathroom, locking the door behind him.

"Who is this?" he asked again, dumping his pack on the ground.

"Have you heard the latest reports of what happened in Victoryville?" the man repeated.

"Yes, I have. A soldier was killed at the barrier. Why do you ask?"

Silence, for a moment, before the man spoke again.

"Things are getting out of hand . . . but you're doing well, Mr. Keene. Don't stop digging."

Richard paused as he tossed the words around in his mind, letting them sink in.

"Do you know something?" Richard asked, staring blankly at the wall in front of him. "Can you help me?"

"Just keep asking the same questions you have been," the man said. "If you smell a rat, then chase it. Don't give up."

And with that the man hung up.

Richard immediately called the number back, but the man did not answer. Dropping the phone to his side, he gazed at the wall a moment before turning around. He caught his reflection in the bathroom mirror and stared back into his own eyes. He tapped the phone against his thigh as his mind ticked over, then he grabbed his backpack and set off to work.

Abbie heard a distant rumbling that made her pause. She placed her knife on the table and moved to the living room window, peering out through the sheer curtain. A flutter of panic raced around her chest when she saw a tank rolling down her street, followed by two military vehicles containing heavily-armed soldiers.

"What's going on?" Kaitlyn asked from behind her.

Abbie didn't dare speak as the tank approached her house.

"What are they doing?" Kaitlyn asked, coming to stand beside her.

The tank rolled by, along with the vehicles, and Abbie paid close attention to the weaponry the soldiers were equipped with.

"It's a show of force," she told Kaitlyn. "It's a warning."

"Because of what happened last night?"

Abbie nodded. "A soldier was killed, one was wounded. That won't go unpunished." She squeezed her eyes shut for a moment before opening them again. "I don't know what they were thinking to attack the military like that."

"You think Josh is in trouble?"

Abbie stepped away from the window and turned to Kaitlyn. "I don't know, but you must never speak of what you heard last night to anyone."

Kaitlyn stared back at her.

"Do you hear?" Abbie said firmly. "Don't speak of it again, Kaitlyn. For all our sakes."

Kaitlyn nodded and Abbie moved off to the kitchen, her stomach clenching tightly as she did.

Deputy Leo Cann entered Roy's Hardware, located in the row of stores along the main street, just down from the interzone gate. He'd been told that he'd find Magnus Bracks here. The store looked empty. He figured not too many people were up for DIY under the circumstances. He looked over to the two cash registers and saw Langdon Swan manning one. Austin Saller stood beside him. He knew Austin a little from seeing him at the gym and, of course, had heard the recent rumors that he'd been pushing steroids there.

Leo approached and gave them a nod, eyeing the cabinet beside them that displayed an array of guns. He noted there were several gaps, however, and suddenly wondered what type of gun had been used by the people firing on the soldiers last night.

"Deputy," Austin said, bringing his attention back to them.

"I was told I could find Magnus Bracks here," he said glancing around the store. "You seen him?"

He heard the motor of Bracks' electric wheelchair before he saw him.

"Deputy Cann," Bracks greeted him, emerging from an aisle, "to what do I owe this pleasure?"

"Mr. Bracks," Leo greeted him. "I wondered if I could have a word with you?"

"Yes?" Bracks wheezed a little, then inhaled from his oxygen mask.

"Is there somewhere we can talk in private?" he asked, noticing that Austin and Langdon, now joined by gym buddy Trent Ford, were watching them.

"I'm in a store." Magnus waved his hand about. "Where do you suggest we go?"

Leo surveyed the surrounds again, letting his eyes linger on Austin, Langdon and Trent, until they got the hint to at least pretend they were busy.

"Have you heard anything about that shooting last night?" he asked Bracks, placing his hands on his hips.

Bracks shook his head as Leo studied the seven stripes running down his large chin and jaw. "Only what I've seen on the news."

"You've heard no talk on the street as to who might've been involved?"

"No." His cloudy eyes stared lifelessly at Leo. "Should I have?"

Leo shrugged. "Well, you seem to be a man of the people, Mr. Bracks. You certainly had a few gathered around listening to what you had to say the other day. The day that kid was killed." He made sure to look Bracks firmly in the eye as he said

211

that last part. "I just thought maybe one of them might have let something slip about this shooting."

Bracks stared back for a moment, then shook his head. "I'm afraid not, deputy, but I'll certainly keep an ear to the ground. It's a terrible thing, what's been happening here of late. It must've been hard for you having to carry that dead boy's body all that way to the doctor."

Leo stared into Bracks' cold eyes, trying to remove the image of the boy's bloodied, limp body from his mind. He couldn't help but swallow his feeling of guilt. The truth was, that boy's face had haunted him ever since. If only they'd gotten down off that roof when he'd asked . . .

"You're right, Mr. Bracks, things have been getting out of control of late," he said, matching Bracks stare for stare. He remembered Earl's words, that this wasn't his fault. And Earl was right. It wasn't. But it *was* his job to try and make sure it didn't happen again. "I would really appreciate it, if you could use your connection with these people to help keep them calm. We don't need any more trouble than we've already had. Between these welts and the . . ." Leo couldn't bring himself to say the word aliens, ". . . whatever did this . . . there are bigger things we need to be dealing with here."

"I agree, deputy," Bracks said, a cold glint to his eyes now, as though he knew a secret. "I'll keep my ears open for you. And I'll do what I can to help protect the people of this zone."

Leo regarded him, not exactly comfortable with Bracks' words or the look in those lifeless, cloudy old eyes of his. He glanced over at Austin, Langdon and Trent, who gave him sullen, resentful looks in return.

"Well, thank you, Mr. Bracks. I'll be sure to let the chief and mayor know of your compliance, helping to keep our town safe," Leo said coolly.

Bracks gave a smile, but it didn't reach his eyes.

Leo turned to the cash register. "I see some gaps in the cabinet," he said to Langdon, motioning to the display of guns. "Know who bought them?"

Langdon pouted his lips and shrugged his shoulder. "Don't know. They were sold when I wasn't here."

"People are arming themselves against the aliens," Austin added.

Magnus nodded. "You can't blame people for protecting themselves."

"I guess not. But defense and attack are two very different things according to the law." Leo said, before turning and walking away.

He left the store feeling anger swelling within, an aggressiveness that was alien to him. This wasn't him, this wasn't his style. He didn't like it. He wished to God he could tear that barrier down and get things back to normal. But he knew that wasn't going to happen anytime soon. He was trapped in the SZ, just like everyone else.

He got in his car and slammed the door, leaning his elbow up on the window frame and catching sight of his reflection in the side mirror. He stared at the single red welt running down his chin, then raised his fingers to rub it, as though hoping it would come off. It felt like nothing was there, as though it had been drawn on with one of his daughter's crayons. He huffed loudly, looked over at the gray barrier fence separating him from normality, then put the car in gear, and headed off to do another patrol.

Mayor Russo hung up the phone and rubbed his forehead. He'd been on calls all morning, trying to keep the military at bay. Given their soldiers were attacked, they were insisting on stepping in and taking over in Victoryville. Russo had to utilize his smoothest persona with the state governor, among others, to allay everyone's fears and keep martial law at bay. If he let the military in, Victoryville would no longer be his. And what the hell would that look like to his constituents? To the world? A mayor, and a chief, who can't run their own town? In the end, he'd compromised by allowing the military to run some patrols, announcing to residents that a 9.00 p.m. to 6.00 a.m. curfew would be imposed. He figured it wouldn't hurt to give whoever did this a little scare anyway. But at the end of the day, Victoryville was his. And he would make sure everyone knew that.

Even Bracks.

He thought briefly of Nicola, craving one of the neck massages she would give him when he was stressed, but quickly pushed her from his mind. He had to focus. He had to remain in control. He needed to see Victoryville through this testing time. This was a massive challenge, but also a massive opportunity. If he kept this town together, it was a sure bet he would be a candidate for the next state election; maybe even oust the governor from his job. Hell, maybe he could even try for a federal position one day . . . but first, he had to make it through this.

Chief Blackstone had confirmed that the wounded soldier was awake after his surgery, but couldn't identify his attackers. There were approximately five offenders, but their faces had been covered with bandanas and the like. Blackstone also confirmed that Deputy Cann had paid that visit to Magnus Bracks, who, according to the deputy, came across as nothing but helpful and obliging.

Of course he did, Russo seethed.

So Victoryville had been splashed all over the news again, for the wrong reasons. He'd been on calls with councillors and they were expressing doubt about his leadership, Patty Duke making no secret of the fact that she blamed him for the Clean Skin girl expulsion fiasco. If Russo wasn't careful he would face a drubbing in the next election. Or the others might even plan a coup to remove him from office. His gut instinct, his gut reaction, was to go into a PR drive as though he were in election mode. He was making plans to pull out all the stops and make as many appearances as he could. Anything to show the people of Victoryville that he cared and that he would do what he could to stop the violence.

There was one small problem, though. That barricade. How could he keep all his constituents happy when he could only visit half of them? He could wear a biohazard suit, he supposed, but he felt as though that didn't exactly give the right impression. *I want to speak to you, constituents, but I don't want to get too close and catch what you have!*

He sighed and mentally shrugged. *You'll just have to work on one side at a time,* he told himself. *Half is better than none.*

Besides, he thought, perhaps a little crudely, *who knew whether the Striped Ones would still be here come the next election?*

Abbie, by midmorning, and after several more drive-bys by the military to make their increased presence obvious, had grown concerned for Josh. She'd left Kaitlyn at home, and after receiving no response when she knocked on the Chalmer front door, walked down toward the town center looking for him. She kept seeing the expression on Josh's face when he left her house the previous night. After what he'd seen, he was understandably upset. Should she have gone after him?

She instantly regretted having left her house when she saw the military presence at the interzone gate. The tank was parked there on full display. Several soldiers stood on lookout posts erected on the Clean Skin side of the barrier. She could see the barrier had been reinforced with covered scaffolding, to give it some height, a good twenty meters across either side of the gate. This gated section of the barrier along the main part of town was now a full-on wall, and several soldiers paced along the front, eyeing her carefully. Their weapons were angled toward the ground, but their hands were wrapped firmly around them, ready to raise them in an instant. One of their own had been killed, another injured. Revenge would be on their minds.

Unsurprisingly, there were no civilians standing around today. She moved her eyes away from the soldiers and turned around to view the roof where the boy, Chris, had been accidentally shot. Two deaths, now, in a matter of days.

She heard a car and turned around to see the deputy pulling up alongside her. He wound his window down.

"You alright, Abbie?" he asked.

"Yeah," she said, "I'm just looking for a friend."

The deputy nodded. "I saw you on the news." He studied her a moment, his tired eyes dropping to the stripe on her chin. "It was a brave thing you did." He glanced at the wall, then to her. "I wish there were more people like you around. Helping, instead of hindering."

She thought of Magnus and Roy and the guns. "Me too."

"So who are you looking for?" the deputy asked. "I'll keep my eye out for them."

Abbie suddenly wondered whether she should mention Josh, given what he'd become embroiled in. She glanced around the empty streets and at the gate, her mind roiling, then she looked back at Deputy Cann. She trusted him. He'd been trying to get those guys down from the roof. He cared. Maybe he could keep an eye on Josh too.

"Josh Chalmer," she said. "He's about five foot ten, shaggy

216

blond hair, twenty-one years old." She pointed down her street. "He lives opposite me. His family moved here a couple of weeks ago."

She saw a look of sympathy cross the deputy's face. "Bad timing."

"Yeah."

"When did you last see him?"

Abbie paused again, then said. "Last night. Late."

The deputy regarded her a moment, then gave another nod. "I'll keep an eye out for him."

"Thank you," she smiled.

"No problem." He gave a small smile back, then glanced around the streets. "Maybe you should go home and wait for him there."

"I will," she said. "I'm just going to take a look around the center of town, then I'll head back."

"Alright," the deputy said, "stay safe, Abbie."

"You too."

She watched the deputy drive away, then swallowed hard as she moved toward the strip of stores on the right-hand side that made up the Striped Zone half of the main street. Most of the stores seemed to be closed, but she found a couple open— one being Roy's Hardware. Given Josh worked there part-time, when he wasn't working at the VAC, it was the most likely place to look. She hesitated, considered turning back like the deputy had suggested, but thoughts of Josh and what trouble he might be in made her muster the courage to continue. She forced herself to enter the store. If Josh wasn't around, one of his co-workers might know where he'd gotten to.

Entering, she immediately saw Austin near one of the two counters talking with Langdon, Trent, and couple of younger guys. They stopped when they saw her. She glanced quickly down the aisles, saw no one else, so she decided to approach them.

"Hi," she said to Austin, "have you seen Josh?"

Austin pursed his lips and shook his head.

Abbie studied him, trying to read any regret on his face from the previous night's events. She merely saw a defiant shiftiness in his dark eyes. The other guys were the same.

"If you do, could you tell him I was looking for him, please."

Austin shrugged his muscled shoulders. "Sure."

The group stared at her silently. Their eyes were untrusting; the stripes running down their chins like exclamation marks of anger. She darted a glance to the gun cabinet beside them, saw it was near to empty. She felt uncomfortable, the way they looked at her, so she gave a quick nod, then swiftly departed.

Fearing Josh was in trouble, Abbie wanted to scour the streets to try and find him, but not knowing him that well, how could she gauge where he might hide at a time like this? Besides, the deputy was on it. He'd keep an eye out. She decided to return home, to Kaitlyn and Charlie, thinking it would be best that she remain where Josh could find her. *If* he wanted to find her, that is.

Sure enough, hours later, just as she was really starting to worry, Josh knocked on her door. He looked exhausted, like he hadn't slept.

"Deputy Cann said you were looking for me."

"Are you okay?" she asked ushering him inside.

"Did you say anything to him?" Josh asked, he looked anxious, but a little vague at the same time. Spaced out.

"No, of course not. Are you okay?"

He didn't answer, just slumped on her couch. Kaitlyn was sleeping upstairs with Charlie and the TV was off, so they sat in silence.

"Where have you been? Have you been home?" she eventually asked him.

Josh shook his head. "I don't know," he slurred with exhaustion.

Abbie looked at him as a strange feeling prickled inside. Something seemed off. "What do you mean, you don't know?"

Josh stood and began to pace slowly, like he didn't know what to do, or was maybe confused.

"Josh, what's wrong?" Abbie stared at him. "What aren't you telling me?"

He continued to walk around her living room; his eyes looked a little glazed, his face had fallen slack.

"Josh, are you okay?" She scrutinized him carefully, worried.

He kept pacing, shoulders slumped like he didn't hear her. He was acting weird, his feet shuffling along the floor.

"Josh, are you drunk?"

He stopped moving then and just stood staring into space.

"*Josh!*" Abbie stood from the couch and moved over to him. "Are you on drugs on something?" She took him by the shoulders and turned him to face her. "Did you take something?"

He stared at her with a glazed expression, then moved into her kitchen. She followed him in, and he looked around, then moved back into her living room. He sat down on the couch, almost falling into it. He sat for a moment, swaying a little, then looked as though he was lying down, stretching out.

Except that, as she watched, she noticed the stretch didn't retract. His body was stiff as a plank, and as she watched his face she saw his eyes roll back into his head.

"Josh?" She moved over to the couch.

It didn't take her long to realize he was having a seizure of some kind. His stiff body gave way to uncontrollable shaking that sent Abbie's eyes wide.

"Oh God," she whispered, taking hold of his shoulders. "Josh. Josh!"

She went into action, quickly recalling her first aid training, a requirement to be a swimming coach. She lifted his legs up on the couch and rolled him on his side.

"Kaitlyn!" she yelled out. "Kaitlyn, wake up!" She turned back to Josh. "It's okay," she told him. "It's okay. It's going to be okay . . . KAITLYN!"

She heard the rhythmic pattering of Kaitlyn running down the carpeted staircase and turned to face her.

"Go get Peter Chalmer. *Now!*"

Kaitlyn saw Josh's convulsing body and her eyes flew wide with shock.

"Now!" Abbie yelled again.

The Clean Skin girl moved toward the door, her eyes hesitantly scanning for threats before she exited.

Abbie tried to keep Josh on his side as much as she could, but his body was hard to control. She heard Kaitlyn yelling and thumping on the Chalmer door across the street. Moments later Peter burst through Abbie's door and moved toward his son. She stepped out of the way.

"Should I call an ambulance?" she asked.

"Just give us a moment," Peter told her, watching Josh carefully, hand gently resting on his shoulder. "Go get his medication off Karen."

Abbie raced past Kaitlyn, across the street and entered the house. She explained what was going on and Karen quickly handed her the medication Peter was talking about. Abbie raced back across the street and gave it to Peter.

"What's wrong with him?" she asked.

"He has epilepsy," he told her, studying the medication carefully, then sighed heavily. "He just started this pack two days ago. I think he's missed a dose!"

Abbie and Kaitlyn stood back and watched as Peter took care of his son, waiting for the seizure to end and coaxing him back to consciousness. Josh eventually slurred some words to indicate the seizure was over. Peter straightened his body to make him more comfortable, and requested a blanket which Abbie swiftly fetched.

"Is he going to be okay?" she asked, handing the blanket to Peter.

"Yes. He'll sleep for a while now, and he'll be tired for a few days, but as long as he takes his medication he should be fine."

Peter sat down on the couch beside his sleeping son, and looked at Abbie, then over at Kaitlyn. Charlie began to cry, so Kaitlyn jogged upstairs to her son.

"Does it happen often?" Abbie asked, taking Peter's focus off the young Clean Skin girl.

Peter shook his head. "Not so much any more. We've managed to get a good handle on things." He exhaled wearily. "I guess these past few days have taken their toll, though. Stress can bring it on. Lack of sleep. And he must've forgotten to take his meds."

"So we just let him sleep now?" she asked.

Peter nodded. "We need to keep an eye on him, but yes, we just let him sleep it off now. I'll make him check in with his doctor once he's back on his feet."

"How long will he sleep for?"

Peter shrugged. "It depends on the seizure. Sometimes it's just an hour or so, sometimes it's several hours."

"Should we move him to a bed or something?"

"No." Peter's eyes darted to Kaitlyn who was walking down the stairs with Charlie in her arms. He turned back to Abbie. "Just let him be for now. When he wakes up I'll take him home." Peter shot an accusing glance at Kaitlyn. Abbie could sense that Peter did not want to be here with the Clean Skin girl, did not want to be associated with her in any way that could possibly get Karen caught.

"I'll keep watch over him," Abbie reassured Peter. "You should go back and tell Karen he's okay."

He nodded, studying his son, then stood from the couch. "You call me no matter what happens," he admonished her with a pointed finger.

"I will."

Peter readjusted the blanket and ran his hand quickly over his son's hair. He threw Abbie one last glance, then ignored Kaitlyn as he left.

Once Peter was gone, Kaitlyn moved to stand beside her. "Is he going to be okay?"

Abbie nodded, letting out a long breath, relieved that it was over. Although, as she exhaled, she noticed how tight her chest felt.

"Shit," she muttered, moving for the stairs.

"What?" Kaitlyn looked after her.

Abbie went to her room, found her bag and Ventolin spray and inhaled long and deep. She only needed one this time. She'd gotten the spray into her lungs before the spots had appeared in her vision.

"You've got asthma?" Kaitlyn asked.

Abbie nodded. "Yeah. But it's okay. I'm fine."

Dr. Lysart Pellan sat back in his chair. He'd just sent a response to Mary Rodriguez's email thanking him for calling in on her children, who were now in the care of Mary's neighbor. He was pleased that Mary was doing okay, but felt for her being confined to a local school gym with other Striped Ones from their area whose houses were located in the Clean Zone. John Seevers, too, had responded to his email, confirming that he was doing well and thanked him for passing on his medication to the soldiers. John was one of the lucky ones. His house was located in the Striped Zone, so he'd been allowed to return to it.

Lysart reached forward and picked up the framed photo of his ex-wife and daughters from its place on his desk. He stared sadly at it, wondering if the madness would ever be over, or whether, perhaps, the government would confine everyone to this town indefinitely; wondering whether Victoryville would become a living museum for the outside world to gawk at.

He removed his glasses, lowered his face into his hand, smoothing his forehead and rubbing his tired eyes.

The phone suddenly rang, startling him, especially as it wasn't his cell phone, but the home phone. He placed his glasses back on and reached for the handset, hoping it was his daughter, Marissa.

"Hello?" he said, putting it to his ear.

"Dr. Pellan," a man's voice answered. He recognized it from his brief conversation earlier that day. It was the reporter Richard Keene. Lysart hadn't answered any of the calls to his cell phone, but the reporter had found his home number.

"Yes?" He played dumb.

"Do you know who this is?"

Lysart didn't answer.

"I'm going to suggest you do," Keene offered, acknowledging the silence. "Otherwise you would've made that call from a public phone box."

Still Lysart didn't answer.

"I'm a reporter, Dr. Pellan. You knew I'd investigate the cell number and find out the details of my mystery caller. And given your profession, I think it's safe to assume that you are a smart man who wouldn't risk being found out if you didn't want to be."

Lysart remained silent while he thought things over. "And where are you making your call from?" he eventually asked.

"A public phone box."

Lysart nodded to himself. "What do you want?"

"The same thing you do. I want the truth."

"What makes you think I can give you the truth?"

"You called me, Dr. Pellan. You wanted me to find you. You started this."

"But who says I have the power to finish it?"

"Well, perhaps if we talk . . . maybe I could help you?"

Lysart's mind ticked over again, suddenly wondering if he'd made a horrible mistake. His eyes fell onto the photograph: his daughters, his ex-wife. Then he skimmed over the emails, left open on his laptop, from his colleagues.

"Dr. Pellan, if there is something the people should know, then they should know it. You want them to know it, that's why you called me. Let me help you."

Again Lysart was silent.

Keene seemed to sigh, quietly, patiently. Lysart figured he must be used to sources clamming up. "Listen, you think about it," the reporter said. "I'm going to go grab a coffee at Leinsel's Cafe in an hour."

Keene hung up and Lysart placed the phone back in its cradle. He tapped the fingers of one hand on his desk, moving them as though playing a rhythmic pattern on the piano. It's what he did when he was lost in thought. Playing the piano was something he'd done as a child, something he still did to relax. However, he had not yet shipped his piano to Victoryville, so it remained at his ex-wife's house in Washington. God, how he missed it.

He pursed his lips and moved his fingers to his laptop and looked up Leinsel's Cafe. The reporter had provided him an option to meet in person. The cafe was in the Clean Zone, not far from the Civic Hall. Pellan checked his watch: two hours until curfew.

He tapped his fingers on the desk again, picturing Harvey Meeks in his mind, and wondered what he should do.

Abbie placed a cup of hot chocolate on the coffee table in front of Josh.

"Hey," she smiled gently.

He looked a little groggy as he sat up. He rubbed his face and squinted as though the lights were too bright or his head hurt or something.

"How are you feeling?" she asked.

"How long have I been asleep?"

"A few hours."

He glanced out the window at the darkness, then looked around the room, his face falling a little. He looked down at the floor. "You saw it?" he asked quietly.

Abbie nodded. "You had me worried for a moment there. We got your dad. He came over and made sure you were alright."

"We? Oh, Kaitlyn. Where is she?"

"Taking a shower."

Josh nodded glumly. "So I had a whole audience. Great."

"It's nothing to be ashamed of Josh. You have a condition, that's all. And it's controllable."

He nodded, refusing to make eye contact with her.

"Hey, you wanna know how many times I've had an asthma attack in front of people?" Abbie tried to make him feel better. "Hell, I had one when the military first came, remember? I had a whole audience then, you were there, your dad. Shit happens, right?" she shrugged. "We have medical disorders and sometimes they get the better of us, but we deal with it and we move on."

"Getting short of breath doesn't quite compare to having a seizure and rolling around like some kind of freak show, Abbie," he said bitterly.

"You think turning blue and collapsing to the floor is any better? Gasping for breath and wheezing like you're drowning or choking?"

Josh glanced at her, then turned away, rubbing the back of his hand across his chin. She studied the three stripes that marked him.

"Why didn't you tell me?" she asked gently.

He didn't answer her.

"You thought I wouldn't understand? You should've told me, Josh. What if something happened and I couldn't help you."

"It turned out fine. I just forgot to take my meds."

Abbie stared at him, and he looked at her, confused.

"What?" he asked.

"How long have you had it?"

He reached forward and took the hot chocolate and sipped it. "My whole damn life."

"And you're still ashamed of it?"

Josh looked back at her, a slight furrow in his brow.

"I thought you'd be used to it by now?" she shrugged.

"I don't tell people because they tend to go all weird on me, and judge me. Like you are, right now."

"I'm not judging you for having the condition, Josh. I'm just curious why you hide it."

"It's no one's business. Besides, people freak out when I tell them. They don't know how to handle it, so I just don't tell them."

She gave a sympathetic smile. "People sometimes avoid what they don't understand."

He shook his head. "You have no idea what it's like. Asthma is a lot more common and understood."

"Maybe."

"No maybes. Being out of breath is kinda normal. Their brains can process that. But you have an *episode* in front of someone, you flip around on the floor in front of someone, then you see it in their eyes every time they look at you again. They don't understand it and it makes them uncomfortable. It's lost me more things than I can count."

"Like what?" she asked gently.

"Girls don't tend to like it. One dumped me after I had a seizure in front of her. She didn't dump me exactly, but was suddenly too busy to see me. I read between the lines, took it as over. She didn't know how to handle it. It scared her."

Abbie felt a sadness wash over her. "She was a fool, then. She wasn't worth it."

"I lost my spot on my high school football team." His face filled with sadness, and she thought she saw his eyes glint with tears. "The coach loved my tryout, was very enthusiastic, then found out I had epilepsy, and that ended things. He said I couldn't be on the team as the risk was too great. If I got a head injury . . . I was a *good* player. The coach had hinted I might

227

make quarterback, but . . ."

Abbie moved to sit beside him and placed her arm around his shoulders.

"Forget it all, it's not worth it," she told him. "Our lives are a little tougher than other people's, but that doesn't mean we have to suffer, Josh. That's exactly why I took up swimming, you know. Best thing for asthma sufferers. I could've been scared, but I faced it head on. My parents were good like that," she smiled sadly. "They always encouraged me to not be a victim. They raised me to treat my asthma as an annoying condition I had, not a life-threatening thing that should rule my life. They encouraged me to carry on as normal. To take it on the chin and be a fighter."

Josh laughed sadly. "I wish my parents were like that."

Abbie studied him seriously. "Your father seemed pretty calm, like it was nothing. He seemed to prescribe to that way of thinking."

"Yeah, we always treated it like it was nothing. Nothing to be spoken about, unless necessary . . . but I was always the fragile one. My younger brother was the normal one. That's why my mother cries every night because he's gone. She lost the normal one."

"Josh!" Abbie scolded him. "That's not fair. She cries because she's lost a child. Just like I cry because I lost my family. You can't hate her for that."

He clenched his jaw, a troubled, guilty look crossing his face.

"You need to stop feeling sorry for yourself. When Kaitlyn went over to your folks house, your father came running straightaway. I saw him. I saw the way he burst into this house. I saw the way he looked at you. He would do anything for you. He loves you."

"Why didn't he think of that before he screwed everything

up? We wouldn't even be in this shitty town if it wasn't for him!"

Abbie sighed. "This town's not so bad . . . at least, that's what I always thought. I've lived here my whole life."

"You'd change your mind if you saw what else was out there."

Abbie looked at him, a little offended by the condescending tone in his voice. She brushed it off. She knew he was hurting, angry at his father and embarrassed by what had happened.

"People screw up, Josh. Unfortunately, that's what we humans do . . . but we can also forgive."

Josh placed his elbows on his knees and rested his head in his hands. "Everything is just so messed up," he said quietly.

Abbie squeezed him closer, running her hand up and down his arm in consolation.

"We just need to stay strong. Things will work out. They have to. We just need to keep our heads and not do anything stupid."

She heard him sniff and felt a lump gather in her own throat at the thought of his sadness; of the people who had died; of her missing family; of the aliens; of her own loneliness.

Josh took a moment, then seemed to push his sorrow aside and raised his head. "Have there been any updates?"

Abbie shook her head. "No, but Victoryville is still all over the news. More people in surrounding towns are leaving. If it keeps up we'll be the only ones left on the Eastern Seaboard. No one wants to be anywhere near us."

Josh's jaw clenched momentarily, then gathered himself to say, "Thank you for . . . for taking care of me."

Abbie smiled softly. "What will we have left, if we don't take care of each other?"

A moment of silence passed as Josh met her eyes. Sitting side by side, their faces were close, and she thought he might kiss her.

But a knock at the door interrupted their bubble of intimacy.

Abbie quickly stood and answered it. It was Austin.

"Yo, Josh," he said, spying him inside, entering the house uninvited. "There's another meeting. You gotta come."

"What? Now?" Abbie asked.

"Yeah." Austin glanced over his shoulder at her.

"He needs to rest," Abbie told him.

"No, I'm fine," Josh said quickly standing and slipping his meds into his pocket.

"Josh—" she began in protest.

"I'm fine," he said adamantly, his eyes showing he was still determined to hide his condition.

"What are you, his mother?" Austin said, his face screwed up.

Josh gulped down the hot chocolate, then looked at Austin. "Just give me a second," he said, and disappeared upstairs to the bathroom. Abbie hoped he was taking his meds.

"What's going on?" she demanded of Austin.

His dark eyes regarded her. He looked a little on edge, a slight sheen of sweat glistened on his forehead. "It's a private meeting."

"Why? What are you guys up to?"

Austin stared at her as he moved out onto the porch, but he didn't answer.

"Don't cause any more trouble for this town," Abbie said.

Austin's brow furrowed. "The only people causing trouble for this town are the goddamn outsiders and those Clean Skins.

Who do they think they are, herding us like this? Not telling us anything? They're the ones up to something!"

"Is that you talking, or Roy Kenny?'

Austin gave her an angry look. "No one speaks for me."

"Just don't do anything stupid!" she pleaded.

His frowned more intensely. "It's not us you should worry about. It's them," he said, pointing down the road in the direction of the interzone gate. "We're just trying to protect ourselves." He took a step closer to her, his larger, athletic frame intimidating her. "You should be careful about what you say, you know. You better decide which side you're on, because if the shit hits the fan, it'll be us against them, and we won't be protecting no traitor."

"Traitor?" Abbie said, appalled.

"Yeah," he said, then glanced inside, motioning to the staircase. "Where you hiding that Clean Skin?"

Abbie went stone-faced, recognizing the veiled threat. Austin's dark eyes rested on hers, then he motioned to the graffiti still visible on her house. "You should watch yourself. You're marked in more ways than one." He dropped his eyes to the stripe running down her chin, then looked at the graffiti again.

Before Abbie could respond, Josh came back down the stairs and exited the house.

"Josh?" Abbie called nervously, trying to halt him.

He glanced over his shoulder, his face hard to read, as he moved off down the street with Austin.

Richard finished his second cup of coffee and looked at his watch. Ten minutes until the cafe closed and thirty minutes until the curfew came into play. He sighed, scrunching a napkin in his hand and tossing it into the empty cup. He really hoped that Dr. Pellan would show, and the fact that he hadn't meant the man was afraid. Which, in turn, must mean that he had something pretty important to say.

Richard checked his watch again, then glanced around. He suddenly noticed a man of Anglo-Indian descent staring at him through the front window of the cafe. It was Dr. Pellan. Richard recognized him from the Bateson Dermacell opening and the photos he'd seen while researching his mysterious caller.

Dr. Pellan abruptly turned and began to walk away from the cafe.

Had he changed his mind?

Richard stood, threw some money on the table and made his way out onto the street. He saw Dr. Pellan, tall and trim, wearing a hat and scarf, walking up ahead. The man glanced over his shoulder as though to check Richard was following him. The reporter did so, keeping his distance, wondering where Pellan was leading him. *Somewhere quiet without witnesses?*

He followed the scientist to a car that was parked in a darkened corner of a deserted, fenced lot. For a moment Richard wondered if Pellan could be trusted, whether he should blindly follow this man. But it wasn't the first time he'd taken a risk for a story. He glanced around him, scanning his surroundings to be sure that they were alone. Harry had warned him to be careful and now here he was in a dark, deserted lot with a stranger.

Richard patted his jeans pocket, wanting to feel the pocketknife he always carried with him on the job. He was grateful all over again for having grabbed his backpack the morning he'd left his hotel. It was all he'd had on him since he'd been hauled onto that bus and taken to the Civic Hall. His tools of the trade.

He saw Pellan disappear into the driver's seat of the car parked in the corner against the tall wooden fence. That corner of the lot was so dark he could no longer see Pellan at all. Richard walked slowly around to the passenger side of the vehicle, glancing around quickly, then opened the door and got inside.

Pellan sat staring out the windscreen until Richard was settled, then the doctor turned his face to him. Richard studied the hat and scarf he wore, and thought that by trying to disguise himself like that in this weather, Pellan was actually only drawing more attention.

"Richard Keene," Richard said, extending his hand, a peace offering.

Pellan looked at it, then extended his own. "Lysart Pellan."

Richard nodded as they shook. "We were supposed to do an interview the afternoon of the Occurrence."

"Yes," Pellan said. "And now here we are."

"So, Dr. Pellan, why did you call me?"

Pellan exhaled slowly, and the seconds seemed to pass by. "I don't really know."

"Yes, you do," Richard told him.

"Okay, I know why. But I'm still not sure that I should have."

"You work for Bateson Dermacell. Your background is in genetics, but your specialty is dermatology. I assume you're the one who was assisting the CDC with the initial investigation. You know what's behind these welts, don't you?"

Pellan considered the question, the streetlights in the distance shining off his round, thoughtful eyes. "No," he said. "I don't know what caused these welts."

"But you know something?"

Pellan exhaled loudly, then reached out and took hold of the steering wheel, tapping his fingers against its surface.

"What I know . . . I've been forced to sign a confidentiality agreement . . . by Homeland Security."

"Homeland Security?" Richard felt the hairs on his arms constrict.

Pellan looked over at him, "If I tell you . . . ?"

Richard nodded, comprehending Pellan's hesitation. "Okay. Jesus." He was suddenly incredibly curious and rather terrified of what it could be. When Pellan had called, Richard thought it might be to do with a hunch the doctor had. He didn't realize that Pellan knew something concrete that had been classified from the top.

"Is it bad?" Richard asked. "I mean it has to be, right?"

Pellan looked out the windscreen again. "*It* is not bad. But what caused it . . . I don't know."

Richard frowned, but before he could speak he saw movement. He turned to look out the windscreen and saw three people enter the parking lot. For a moment he froze, wondering what was going on, whether Pellan had somehow set him up, but when he peeked at Pellan's face, he knew the doctor was just as surprised as he.

They both sat still and watched as one man led the other two people into the parking lot then stopped. He turned to the others, one hand in his pocket, no doubt on a weapon, and the other he held out for something. The other two figures, a man and a woman, gave a nod, as the man pulled an envelope out of his coat and handed it to the first man. The first man opened the envelope, pulled out what looked like a wad of notes and fanned them. He gave a nod to the couple, then walked further into the lot and along the fence to a point in the corner, barely fifteen meters from where Richard and Pellan sat.

The man bent down, then lifted and dragged a sewer grate back. They couldn't hear what was said, but from the man's hand movements, it looked like he was giving them directions of some kind. Richard's eyes moved back to the parking lot entrance, and through the opening, in the distance, he could see the barricade and he understood immediately that this man was helping the couple escape into the Striped Zone. The couple gave a nod, then slowly they disappeared into the hole. The first man pulled the grate back into place. He glanced around, thankfully not seeing Richard and Pellan sitting in the car in the darkened corner. Then he left.

Richard and Pellan sat quietly for a moment, trying to digest what they had just witnessed.

"If I tell you," Pellan said breaking the silence, staring at that grate, "and you report this story . . . we will both be forced into hiding. Do you want that?"

"Forced into hiding? Where can we hide in this town?"

Pellan shrugged. "You see my point."

Richard turned to stare out the windscreen again, registering the streetlights in the distance. They were like beacons, just like the story . . . the truth right there in front of him, but just out of reach. Harry's words seemed to cycle through his mind again. *Be careful, kid.*

"Is it something the people should know?" Richard asked him.

Pellan glanced at him and nodded. "Yes, I think it is. You are already very close to the truth. You just need to take that last step."

"Why is the government keeping it quiet?"

"They are trying to keep control. Maintain order . . . but they are also protecting themselves. Right now they want to keep Victoryville quarantined—away from the rest of the population."

"Because of a contagion or in case those things come back?"

Pellan stared at him, but did not reply.

"Could the repercussions be bad if people are told the truth?" Richard asked.

Pellan shrugged. "Who knows how people will take any news given to them."

Richard sighed, nervous at the choice in front of him. "But the people should know?"

"Yes. I believe they should."

Richard nodded, his mind ticking over.

"Why do you want this story? Really?" Pellan asked him.

"The same reason everyone else does. Answers. I want to know where my missing crew are. I want to know why I can't go home to my apartment in New York. I want to know if this thing, this virus, if it is a virus, will kill me eventually. I want to know if this is the beginning of the end. I want to know if this Occurrence, this phenomenon, will be the end of us all, the end of mankind."

Pellan looked at him with sympathy. "I wish to know many of those things too, Mr. Keene. But I can't answer all of them myself. I know only a little."

Richard's breath hissed in frustration and he combed his fingers through his hair. "We're going around in circles here, doctor. You need to tell me what you know, so I can decide from there whether this is a story that needs to be told."

"You're prepared for the repercussions? You're prepared to go into hiding?"

Richard stared at Pellan. He thought of Harry, but realized that right now he didn't have much left to lose. What could be worse than his current situation?

"Yes. If the story needs to be told to the people, then I will tell it. You obviously think it needs to be told or you wouldn't have contacted me." Richard narrowed his eyes. "Why *did* you contact me? Why me, of all the reporters out there? Because I'm on the inside? Because I'm here in Victoryville?"

Pellan's eyes took him in for a moment. "Because of your humanity, Mr. Keene."

Richard stared back waiting for him to elaborate. Pellan turned to stare out the windscreen again.

"Like you, I have done my research. I've seen the stories you've done in the past. You care about this planet, Mr. Keene, and you care about its people." Pellan watched him. "Since this phenomenon occurred, the other news reports have focused on the blood and the gore; the rioting and the deaths. They fed on the consequences, the terror, the disintegration, the sensationalism. But you . . . you focused on humanity, on hope. You showed people the light in the dark, the good in all this bad. You showed people what they must hold to, and what they must not give in to." Pellan looked away briefly. "The story you did, when the boy got shot . . . everyone else saw the violence and the anger and the carnage, but *you* saw the striped woman risking her life to protect the Clean Skin."

Richard nodded to himself. "Abbie Randell."

Pellan gave another sad smile. "And you were the only one who bothered to learn her name, and to learn the young mother's name. You were the only one who bothered to check on them and do a follow-up story. That is what I'm trying to do here, Mr. Keene. I want to help the Abbie Randells of this world. To free them. The Abbie Randells deserve the truth. No more lies."

Richard nodded gently. "What is it, Dr. Pellan?" he finally asked. "What truth do you know that will change my life and send me into hiding?"

Pellan stared at him with tired, resigned eyes.

"Tell me." Richard said firmly. "I want to know."

Stanley Barrick stared at the readings on the screen that the technician, Gavin—wearing yet another Metallica shirt—and Dr. Wattowski were displaying for him.

"You can see here minor spikes of the concentration of mercury in the atmosphere," Wattowski said.

"So, what does this mean?" Barrick asked.

"It means several stations across North America have detected slight spikes in mercury, similar to what we detected around Victoryville during the Occurrence. Some of these locations have nearby coal plants, some don't."

"These have been detected since the ship disappeared?"

"Yes. Since the ship disappeared. These are lower levels than Victoryville though."

"So what are you saying? They're still here? Or have we got more than one ship?"

"It looks like there's only the one ship," Gavin answered, "because all the readings have been recorded at different times."

"We think the ship is moving around," Wattowski added. "It's hovering."

"Hovering? You think it's choosing another town?" Stanley asked.

"We don't know. These spikes, although similar, are very clearly not at the same levels of the Victoryville Occurrence. Perhaps it's because the ship is at a higher altitude. We don't know, of course, but we're thinking that when the readings match the Victoryville levels, that's when we'll know it's descended and could show itself again."

"So, at worst, we could have, what, a few minutes to register it?" Barrick asked.

Wattowski nodded. "Yes."

"A few minutes?" he repeated.

"Yes. A ship of that caliber, I suspect, could cover ground relatively quickly."

"So these other towns are at risk?" Stanley asked.

"Sir," Gavin interrupted. "I don't think it's going to hit another town."

"Why?"

"Because," he pulled up a map showing where the readings were picked up, "the areas where the mercury spikes have been detected in the atmosphere are all within the vicinity of Victoryville. They've been up and down the east coast, yes, and as far inland as Texas, but they're still relatively close to Victoryville. If these readings are caused by the ship, then it's sticking around its original target."

Stanley straightened as he stared at his colleagues. "So you believe the ship is still here, and you think, if it's going to hit again, that it will target Victoryville?"

"We don't know that for sure," Wattowski said cautiously.

"Give me a percentage of probability?"

Wattowski and Gavin exchanged a look.

"I'd say . . ." Wattowski mused, "about seventy percent."

Stanley nodded, looking at the map and focusing on the location of Victoryville and the nearby readings.

"Get me the president's office on the line," he said Colin, who stood beside him.

"Yes, sir." His aide hurried away.

Stanley pulled out his phone and dialed Rita Hogarth, CDC.

"Mr. Barrick?" she answered.

"Dr. Hogarth," he said stepping into a quiet room. "We think the ship is still here, and we think it's going to target Victoryville again."

"You do?"

"Yes, Dr. Pellan was right," he said, staring blankly out the window. "The aliens categorized the population for a reason. And they're not done with them yet. So be ready. We might need to bring the CDC back on board."

Mayor Michael Russo sat alone at a corner table in Segal's. The lights were dim, his third glass of red was almost gone, and the remnants of his pasta primavera lay scattered across his plate. This was the table he and Nicola would always take. They would sit here because there was a large indoor plant positioned just so, to offer a little privacy from the other diners. Although there were no other diners tonight. But that's why he still wanted this table over any other. Owner Rory Segal had set it up especially for the two of them. In a town like Victoryville, the mayor was as close to celebrity as they came.

Not that Nicola or Rory were here any more. They were part of the missing.

He'd had to get out of his apartment that night, needed a change of scenery. He'd just received word of more looting taking place in the town. A liquor store, some of the homes of the missing. He knew who was behind it. He had no doubt that somehow, in some way, it would lead back to Magnus Bracks.

Russo sighed and ran his hand over his face. He felt as though he was standing on the edge, all his hopes and dreams on the verge of collapse if he couldn't keep control of the town. He pictured Nicola sitting opposite him, wondered what she'd say about the situation. He knew she wouldn't have said much. Outside of jewelry, shopping and beachside holidays, she didn't really have an opinion about anything. He could just picture his father, though. That bastard would've said something alright.

When he'd inherited his father's business, he knew that

running a construction company was not what he wanted to do with the rest of his life. But, at the time, he needed it and he acknowledged it was a moderately successful business, one he could raise up and sell off. His father had left the company to him, hoping that he would then pass it onto the son he would surely have, and keep it in the family. But that was never going to happen. No, Russo had set his sights on achieving more than his old man did. After a few years of running the company and winning key contracts with both local and state government, he had turned his attention to politics. His aim had been to start out in local government, and he'd been a councillor for twelve months before running for mayor. And as soon as he had won that sweet spot, he'd handed the day-to-day running of the company to another, while he focused on other things. The timing couldn't have been better. He'd finally won the last of the litigation with Bracks and could put it behind him, had eventually sold his father's business to another.

The previous six months of his life had been soaring at a wonderful pace.

Then this phenomenon happened. Nicola was gone, and Victoryville had taken a turn for the worse. While he was mayor.

This was the greatest challenge of his professional life. If he couldn't lead Victoryville through a time like this, then he could kiss any aspirations of a transition into state and federal politics goodbye. He could not let Bracks destroy everything he'd worked for. Michael Russo was worth more than that. He *deserved* more than that. He would not let Bracks take what was rightfully his.

Abbie lay in bed, desperately wanting sleep. She'd been awake for hours, unable to switch her mind off the endless thoughts crowding it. Austin's veiled threat had been at the forefront, of course, closely followed by the look Josh had given her as they'd left. She couldn't read it at the time, but the more she concentrated on that image, the more she was convinced the look was part scared, part wary, part lost, part hopeless. Part desperate. He'd been sucked into something he wasn't quite sure how to get out of. He'd started down that path to protect his mother, but was he now in too deep?

And then there was that moment between them on the couch . . . had he been about to kiss her? She wasn't sure of her feelings. If it had been the Josh in Mona's Cafe a week ago, then maybe. However, she wasn't sure about the Josh of the last couple of days. He seemed to be a different person. Or maybe just a different version; one that was adapting to its surroundings. One that thought he was adapting to survive.

She kept picturing Peter's silhouette, too, at the front door of his home, watching her as they'd discovered the graffiti on her house. That image seemed to float there, haunting her. She pictured Karen hiding down in their basement, waiting to come out. She thought of Kaitlyn sitting on the couch that first day, with her then-unnamed son in her arms, terrified. She pictured the image of Shonda-May, her neighbor, pulling away from the curtains. She recalled her conversation with that reporter Richard Keene over the phone. She kept hearing his calming voice saying, "I'm looking for the truth, Abbie."

She thought of her parents, then, and her sister, and had to wonder again where they were. Wonder whether they were alright. Wonder if they were dead. Six days had passed. The house was so lonely without them. Ghostly. Every creak in the wood sounded amplified, every silence felt like a sentence, a curse.

She looked at the items on the bedside table. She'd brought pieces of her family into the room with her, to stay by her side at night. Her father's baseball cap, her sister's perfume, her mother's cell phone that she kept charged.

What would she do if they really were dead? If they weren't coming back? What would she do if her entire family had been wiped out? How could she face tomorrow knowing that for sure? That any hope of them returning alive was gone. How would *she* adapt to survive without them? This town and her family had been all she'd known. Was that enough to enable her to survive any turn of events? Maybe Josh was right. Maybe she was naive. Maybe it was time she grew up and faced the real world.

But how could she face this life alone?

Marked.

Segregated.

Would she even get a chance at life? Or would these aliens return and take it from her. Was she just waiting things out, not knowing her true fate? She'd heard the rumors and the debates, seen the protestors, seen the strange people holding signs and welcoming the aliens back. She'd seen what people were saying about Victoryville on social media. These strangers, speaking with such authority about the town and its people, what we should and shouldn't have done.

So what would happen if the aliens did come back? What would they do to those left behind in Victoryville? Take more? Or kill more?

She felt tears begin to run down her cheeks, but didn't wipe them away. There was something soothing about them, consoling. Something she could use to exhaust her, to tire her out enough to push her over the precipice into sleep. She clung to her tears in the hope she would fall asleep and then waken to find it had just been a bad dream. But she knew that wouldn't happen.

Six days . . .

It had been too long to be a lie.

And among everything else that troubled her mind were thoughts of what Josh was getting caught up in with Magnus and Roy, right now, and what news would be awaiting her in the morning.

Dr. Lysart Pellan awoke in the darkness to the sound of his phone ringing. He picked up the handset beside his bed.

"Hello?"

"Dr. Pellan, it's Richard. I've made my decision."

Lysart sat up a little, resting on an elbow, and rubbed his eyes. He looked at the clock and saw it was 2.59 a.m. When he'd parted with Keene earlier that evening, no decision had been made as to whether to run with the story or not. Lysart had simply told the reporter what he knew and Keene had agreed to take some time to think the matter over before making the critical decision. But now, it would seem it had been made.

"I'm going to run the story," Richard told him.

Lysart nodded to himself in the darkness. "I see."

"I'm writing it now. It should be finished in a few hours. I'll then record my post and send it to my editor with instructions not to go live with it until later this afternoon. That will give us time to hide in case they send the military for us."

"Yes."

"I'm sorry for the late call. Or early, as the case may be," he laughed quietly, tiredly. "I just wanted to let you know, so you had as much time as possible to put plans into motion."

"Thank you."

"No. Thank you, Dr. Pellan. You're right. The people need to know this. They need to be with their loved ones. They shouldn't be separated. Whatever caused this..." Keene sighed sadly. "Whatever caused this, if they come back... God knows who will be left. If time is short, then people need to make the most of it and be with their loved ones."

"Agreed."

"Do you have family in Victoryville?"

Lysart pictured his daughters in his mind. "No."

"Then where will you go? Do you have a place to go?"

"Yes," Lysart assured him, "I'll find somewhere."

"Yeah. It's probably best you don't tell me."

"Do you have a safe place, Mr. Keene?"

"I'll find somewhere . . ."

"Very well," Lysart told him. "Stay safe, Mr. Keene."

"You too, Dr. Pellan. Again, thank you."

"Write well, Mr. Keene. Write carefully. Speak truthfully."

"I will."

With that they ended the call and Lysart placed the phone down on his bedside table. He threw his sheets back and dropped his legs to the floor, letting out a small huff of resignation for what he knew in his heart had to be done.

Day Seven

Richard stood in the empty bathroom and squeezed his tired eyes shut. "Yes, I know what I'm doing."

"Kid, this is serious shit you got here," Harry hissed quietly into the phone, as though trying to hide his voice from others. "Are you sure this is true? If we run with this and it's not—"

"It is."

"There could be all kinds of repercussions from this, you understand? And I'm not just talking about the government here. Who knows how the people will react when they find out they've been lied to."

"Hopefully they'll react with relief that they're not contagious and reunite with their loved ones."

"Yeah, most will. But some will be damned angry with the government for withholding the truth and keeping them apart!"

"Only for a moment. Only until their brains wrap around the real reason as to why they did this, why they tried to keep this secret."

"To tell you the truth, that's what I have the biggest issue with here," Harry told him. "That they think these goddamn fucking aliens will come back. That's why they're keeping the town quarantined?"

"The authorities can't find a reason for the categorization, Harry. They're scared."

"But does this necessarily mean the aliens'll come back?"

"No one knows, Harry. But they went to the trouble of categorizing people. And if they do come back, the government knows that they'll be powerless to do anything about it, so they're just going to leave Victoryville chained up to the post like some sacrificial goat, and hope that keeps these aliens away from everyone else."

"Goddamn aliens. Never thought I would see the day that shit came true."

Richard felt his shoulders soften with inevitability. "Don't use the word 'aliens'. Try 'extraterrestrials'. It sounds better. Friendlier. I hope."

"Does it? Still sounds rather fucked up to me."

Richard sighed heavily. He slumped down on the closed lid of the toilet. "Oh, it's fucked up, alright."

"I'm sorry, kid. Listen to me going on, when I'm here miles away and you're the one stuck there."

"It's okay, Harry. You got a right to worry too."

There was a pause on Harry's end, then a ruffling muffled sound as though he were running his free hand over his face.

"You're sure about this?" Harry asked again. "You're one hundred percent sure you want to go with this and put a big freaking target on your back?"

Richard stared at the bathroom floor. He pictured Lisa and Benny's faces. Pictured the faces on the walls showing images of the missing. He recalled the couple he'd witnessed waving to each other over the barricade. Then he remembered that footage of Abbie Randell running out to shelter Kaitlyn Manner and her newborn baby. The Clean Skin teenage girl who had just given birth to her first child, separated from her mother and removed from her home thanks to the Victoryville quarantine.

"Yes," Richard said firmly. "If these things are coming back and there's a chance that I could die, then I want to do what I can before that happens. I want my death to count. I want the truth to be told. The Striped Ones aren't contagious." He stood up and stared at his reflection in the mirror. "I'm prepared to face the consequences. Are you?"

Richard heard a tapping noise as Harry thought things over one last time.

"The scoop of the century?" Harry asked. "Sure. I'll run with it. My days are numbered anyway."

Richard smiled regretfully.

"You better get to hiding, kid," Harry said.

"I'm just about to leave. Make sure you don't run it until 5.00 p.m. to give me a few hours' head start to disappear as best I can in this town."

"Will do."

"You, ah, better watch your back, too, Harry."

"I'm the captain, kid. It's my job to go down with the ship. Get out of here," he said, then swiftly hung up.

Richard stared at himself in the mirror one last time. He took a deep breath, quickly pocketed his phone, and headed for the nearest exit.

Stanley Barrick watched the TV in disbelief. He closed his eyes and lowered his head into this hands. *"Jesus Christ..."*

"Mr. Barrick?" Colin called from the doorway. "The president's office is on the phone."

Stanley exhaled heavily. "I bet it is."

Abbie's mouth fell open and her whole body went numb. She collapsed to the carpeted floor on her knees, as she stared, glued to the TV. There was silence around her. It was as if the whole world had paused. Nothing moved, no one spoke. It seemed as though every living thing in existence held its breath and hung on every single word of the news report airing. And this was the second time it was being shown. It was as if the news station knew that people would not understand the first time, that they would need to hear it again. And again.

The reporter, Richard Keene, spoke into the camera. He sat before a plain background, framed from the chest up. He spoke slowly, carefully, in that calming voice she recalled from their phone conversation. His green eyes held a sadness to them, his unshaven face and unkempt curly hair seeming to confirm the state of his address. He was telling the world bad news, trying to break it as calmly as he could. And what he had to say was, to put it mildly, earth-shattering.

Richard spoke to camera as though he sat in a confessional box: a home video, a final broadcast from a man who would never be seen again. Abbie's eyes glazed over as the information pounded through her head and her heart, while the rest of her body sat numb. The welts weren't due to any virus or bacteria. They weren't due to any radiation or the like. There was no contagion. They had no answer for it. All they knew was that the people of Victoryville had been categorized by the visitors, as though part of some kind of experiment.

"It's really true?" Kaitlyn's voice was light and shaky with shock, as she reached for the remote. "Do you have instant replay?" Kaitlyn fumbled with the remote and replayed the report again, clearly needing to hear it one more time.

Abbie stared at the TV and saw her face reflected in Richard Keene's. She raised her hand to her face, to her welt, trying to view it in the reflection. It wasn't clear though, and she needed to see it now more than anything. She quickly stood and ran upstairs to the bathroom. Pushing the door open, she moved straight up to the mirror over the basin, and her eyes fixed on the stripe running down her chin and neck. Again she raised her hand to her face and ran her fingertips along the welt, right down to where it ended over her heart.

So it was true. There was a reason why only some of them had been left marked.

The aliens had categorized the Striped Ones as defective.

The thought scared her immensely. That those things, whatever they were, had done this to her on purpose. That this was not just some random side effect of their visit. Not an alien contagion accidentally transferred, nor a kind of radiation that only some people had been susceptible to. These aliens had weeded her out from the others—the Clean Skins—and branded her as inferior. According to what Keene had said, all those marked with the welts were ill in some way. The Clean Skins were carriers of defective genes, and all those missing had been healthy. Her family, mother, father, sister, had been healthy. And for this they'd paid the price. They had been taken.

She stared at the stripe, noting that it seemed so much darker now, as though the truth behind it had branded her further. This one stripe, marking her as damaged goods. Her asthma, something she'd never been ashamed of before, was now to be forcibly worn like a badge of indignity for all to see.

She felt herself shaking at the enormity of it. This phenomenon that had changed Victoryville in the blink of the eye, had also categorized the town in the blink of an eye. She suddenly thought of the three stripes branding Josh: his epilepsy, his seafood allergy, his nut allergy. She wondered what Peter's stripes were for? Or Charlie's? She wondered what defective gene Kaitlyn carried. Is that why Charlie was striped? Did she pass something onto her son? Or did he receive it from his absent father?

"Tell me what's going on?" Kaitlyn tearily demanded from the doorway, cradling Charlie. "What does this mean? What's going to happen to us?"

Abbie turned to face her and saw the fear in the girl's eyes: a teenage first-time mom with her few days' old son. It was such a strange picture. This girl, so young, so naive, yet she had this baby to take care of. A child with a child.

Kaitlyn pointed to Abbie's welt. "Is that because of your asthma?"

Abbie nodded.

"Well, what's wrong with Charlie? They said he was fine in the hospital?"

"Kaitlyn—"

"What's wrong with me?" She was crying now. "I gave him something, didn't I? I'm a Clean Skin. That means I made Charlie sick, didn't I?"

"Kaitlyn," Abbie said, taking hold of her shoulders, "don't panic! It might not be anything to worry about."

"But he's striped! That means he's sick!"

"That doesn't mean it's bad!" Abbie said firmly. "Look at me, I've had asthma my whole life, but I'm fine. Whatever it is, it doesn't have to be a bad thing!"

"But what about what did this? They said they might come back?" she sobbed, bordering on hysterical. "Are they going to hurt you and Charlie? Why did they mark you?"

Abbie stared at her, gripping the girl's shoulders firmly, but had no answer. The truth was, she wondered the same thing.

What the hell *did* this mean? Why had the aliens marked them? And what the hell *would* they do when they came back?

Dr. Lysart Pellan felt his shoulders slump as he watched the news in the cheap out-of-the-way motel he'd found in the Striped Zone. It hadn't been easy, but he'd traveled here through the early hours, scarf wrapped tightly around his neck and chin, hat worn low over his eyes, trying to stay hidden. He'd surreptitiously made his way back to that parking lot he'd been in with Richard, found the sewer gate, and made his way through the dark, murky tunnel until he'd made it to the other side.

Knowing that Harvey, the CDC, and the government, would soon work out that he was the one who had fed Richard the information, staying in the Clean Zone was no longer an option. He found a motel, took a room, and had been waiting nervously for the news to break.

Second thoughts were flooding through him now as he watched the TV and saw the chaos breaking out, not just in Victoryville, but across the world. The people of Victoryville were angry at the lies they'd been told, scared at the probable reason the government was keeping them prisoner in the town. Residents began to gather along the Victoryville barricade between the zones, tensions rapidly rising. Some Victoryville residents were barricading themselves in their homes. Others stood peacefully not far from the growing mobs, holding signs and imploring whatever did this to return to Earth. More people from surrounding towns were fleeing, crashing through roadblocks and creating even worse traffic jams than when the phenomenon had first occurred.

They were no longer scared of a contagion. They were scared that the aliens would return for those they'd categorized.

And it was Lysart's fault.

To make matters worse, a new story was breaking, reporting that an arrest had been made at Bateson Dermacell. And there, Lysart saw, was Cheung being taken away by soldiers for questioning. *Cheung!* He had forgotten about poor, innocent, Cheung.

This isn't what he had wanted. He didn't want the violence, the death. He'd intended that the truth would set them free, that families would be reunited. He wanted to be allowed to see his own family. He wanted to be with them while he could, in case whatever did this, returned. He wanted Victoryville and the world to unite, not segregate further.

He stood shakily and turned the TV off, unable to watch the footage any longer, unable to listen to that strange mechanical grinding noise any longer. He moved over to the minibar in his room, grabbing the first bottle his hands took hold of and tearing the cap off, guzzling the fiery liquid within, desperate to calm himself. Desperate to try and wash away the horrendous mistake he'd made.

Abbie stared at Josh as he paced her living room. As soon as he'd heard the news he'd knocked on her door. When she answered it, the two of them couldn't help staring at the other's stripes.

"I can't believe they lied to us," he paced. "I can't believe Magnus and Roy were right!"

Abbie stood silent, not sure what to say.

"They knew," Josh said. "They knew the government was up to something. They were right."

"Josh," Abbie said weakly.

"The government thinks those aliens are coming back," Josh said, "and they are just going to sit back and let them have us!"

"What happened last night? At the meeting?" she asked, petrified of what their little group might do now.

"He said they were holding something back. I should've known! Mom never got sick staying with us. Why did we fall for it? *Goddamn it!*"

"Josh," she tried to focus his attention, "what happened at the meeting last night?"

He stopped pacing and turned to her. "Magnus told us that Deputy Cann had been by to see him."

"He doesn't support what Magnus is doing?"

Josh shook his head. "No. He asked about that soldier who was shot."

"And?"

"Magnus played the concerned citizen, but laughed as he told us. The deputy has no proof, so he can't do anything. He knows it, Magnus knows it. Besides, he's outnumbered over here."

"But surely he could get reinforcements? The bios could assist."

Josh shrugged. "They can't do anything without proof."

"So, what? The deputy and the military are just going to stand by while Magnus and Roy stockpile weapons and create a private army?"

"Without proof, they can't do anything. Magnus says the deputy's not a threat anyway. If he keeps asking questions, then Magnus will talk him around. Cann works for the same authority that separated him from his family for being a Striped One. He was tossed aside like the rest of us. Why fight something he can't win? It's not worth his life."

"But the authorities didn't know at first. They didn't know it wasn't contagious."

"No, but once they learned the truth they never lifted those barricades either, did they? Those Clean Skins did this! They drove us out. They wanted us kept away from them."

"That would've been a government decision, Josh. The local authorities here wouldn't have known. You think the government would keep the chief and the rest of the Clean Skins in the loop and not us?"

"I guess we'll never know. Besides, it doesn't matter. Not to Magnus."

"I can't believe this," Abbie shook her head. "What about those Striped Ones with family on the other side? What do they think they're going to do?"

"There're only a few in Magnus' group that have family on the other side," Josh said. "Most lost their families during the Occurrence or they're here in the Striped Zone. Some are orphans, some lost their kids. They're all angry and hurting, and they're scared of those aliens. They want to punish someone and the Clean Skins are in their sights."

"But the Clean Skins are victims just as much as us. They're trapped in this town too."

"To Magnus' group, the Clean Skins are everyone who are not us, Abbie. The Clean Skins, whether they're on the other side of that barricade, or outside the town, are all the same. He says the Clean Skins will sacrifice us in a heartbeat if it means saving themselves."

"Josh, you don't know this—"

"Do you know what they're calling us, Abbie? They're calling us zebras, making all these jokes. To them we're just injured meat left out in the sun, waiting for some animal to come along and end us!"

"Who said that? Magnus?"

He ignored her. "I should go find them. I need to see what's going on now this news is out. I need to know if mom's in danger."

Abbie stared at the three red stripes down his chin. His looked darker, too, somehow, but it wasn't the truth that had made them that way . . . it was the shadow of uneasiness in his eyes. The eyes of an angry person on the brink. She wanted desperately to pull him back from that place, but didn't know how.

He noticed her perplexed stares, and seemed uncomfortable. "I'm going down to the gate."

"I'm coming," she blurted, wanting to make sure he didn't do something stupid.

He looked at her as he moved to the door. "No. Stay here—"

"I said, I'm coming! I want to know what's going on, too." Her voice was firm, as Kaitlyn appeared at the top of the stairs. Abbie threw her a glance. "Lock the door behind me, Kaitlyn. Stay here!"

Kaitlyn nodded, cradling Charlie, and Abbie followed Josh out the door.

✕

Chief Earl Blackstone answered his deputy's call.

"Leo, what's going on?"

"Chief, they're gathering at the gate again. There're at least as many folks as last time, maybe more."

Blackstone sighed. "You've heard why?"

"Yeah," his deputy answered after a pause, "I saw the news."

"So you know this gathering ain't going to be good,"

Blackstone warned.

"Yeah, I know. Magnus and Roy are there, in the middle of things again."

"Jesus . . ." Blackstone sighed and closed his eyes briefly. "Go speak to them, try and defuse whatever it is they're planning on doing. I'll come down and meet you at the gate."

"I think that's a good idea, Earl."

Abbie and Josh made their way toward the gate and saw Magnus, Roy and their crew gathered around. Magnus was speaking vehemently into his megaphone, the union man, well rehearsed in giving speeches, in full swing. The crowd gathered around were animated, waving arms and calling things out in reply to the big man in his wheelchair. As they got closer, Abbie saw that some of them were openly carrying their guns. Her eyes darted to the soldiers on the gate, who were on alert, holding their weapons firmly, ready for any trouble.

"The undeniable truth is," Magnus' wheezy voice called, "that they *lied* to us! This whole time they kept us locked up here in the SZ like we were lepers! They discriminated against us because of our welts! Our lives could still be in danger, because they failed to allow full disclosure. They took from us the ability to decide our own fate."

The crowd roared loudly, as Abbie and Josh joined the throng. She saw Deputy Cann trying to fight through the crowd to reach Magnus.

"Well, I say *no more!*" Magnus roared, and the crowd roared back.

Abbie looked around nervously. The crowd looked twice the size of the one that had gathered the other day. Most were young males, some older men, and there was the odd female present. She spotted Wendy, then her eyes locked with

Austin's. His gaze seemed to challenge her, as if to say that he was right, she was wrong, and she must choose a side. He looked edgy, like he was spoiling for a fight. She saw him flex his hand and crack his knuckles. Abbie looked away and found Roy's eyes on her. She didn't like his look either, but he gave her a nod, acknowledging her presence. She wanted to tell him that she wasn't there in support of them, but to see for her own eyes what was going on.

Deputy Cann reached Magnus then and tried to speak with him, but Austin quickly shouldered him out of the way.

"No more will we put our lives in *their* hands!" Magnus continued. "We don't need them! We will protect *ourselves* from whatever did this. The government and those Clean Skins gave us the SZ, now we're going to keep it! The SZ is *ours*! And we will defend it and our people with *everything* we've got!"

The crowd erupted in applause, but it was caught short by another booming voice. They turned to see one of the soldiers with a megaphone of his own.

"Everyone remain calm and clear the area!" he told them. "Please return to your homes. I repeat, everyone please calmly clear the area and return to your homes. Further information will be provided to you in due course."

"Fuck you, man!" someone yelled, and the crowd vocally volleyed the words onward.

"Please disperse immediately!" the soldier called back.

"This is our territory now, asshole!" Trent called.

"You're goddamn liars!" Wendy yelled. "We're not listening to you any more!"

"If you don't return to your homes, we will clear the area forcibly," the soldier continued.

"Just try and move us!" Langdon said, holding his arms out wide.

"You step a foot over that line and we'll shoot you!" Roy yelled.

Deputy Cann was still trying to talk to Magnus, but Austin kept blocking him. Abbie saw the deputy scan the crowd around him, hand firmly on the weapon at his side, as though sizing up his options.

"Clear the area!" the soldier called. "I won't warn you again!"

Someone threw something at the soldier then, and he had to duck. It missed him, but hit the megaphone he held and cracked it, and the crowd cheered. The other soldiers aimed their weapons, as more bottles and cans sped their way. Abbie automatically stepped back, sensing the flame of heated emotion flaring through the crowd. She knew this wasn't going to end well. She exchanged a worried look with Josh.

A strange sound like a whistling noise came from the soldiers at the gate.

"Teargas!" someone yelled.

Suddenly the crowd began to disperse, running in all directions, as a thick cloud of smoke and chemicals began to fill the air. A guy standing in front of Abbie spun around and bolted, knocking her to the ground as he did. Josh reached for her, but had to retract his arm and fight to keep his balance as bodies rushed past and over them. Abbie glanced around through the spreading smoke and saw Austin struggling with Deputy Cann. He landed a crunching punch to the deputy's face, which sent him crashing to the ground. Langdon stepped in to land a swift kick to the cop's stomach. Panicked, Abbie managed to scramble to her feet and turned back toward Josh. Austin was now crouched beside him, slipping a gun into his hand. She looked for the deputy again, but the ground was now empty where he'd been laying. Her eyes began to sting and she had to squeeze them shut to ease the pain. When she opened them, she saw Austin running to join Roy, who had begun firing at the soldiers. The gunfire noise was so loud both Abbie and Josh flinched and covered their heads.

"Jesus," Abbie yelled, eyes burning. "Josh!"

"Go!" He waved her away. "Get out of here!"

"Come with me!" she yelled back.

"Just go!" he shouted, then ran off, disappearing into the clouds of smoke.

Abbie coughed, stumbling around in the smoke, her eyes burning, her nose running, her throat dry. She didn't know where she was going, she just ran desperately in the direction she thought was home.

Mayor Russo paced his office, while Chief Blackstone watched. Today had offered nothing but bad news. First, the revelation that the Striped Ones weren't contagious, meaning that their removal of that Clean Skin girl made them look like even bigger assholes. Then came the news of the riot at the interzone gate. Tensions had boiled over. Dozens were injured, shots were fired, mass panic and violence ensued. And there at the center of it all, stirring things up, was Bracks.

Magnus goddamn Bracks.

"At least they're not contagious," Blackstone said, but it wasn't in his usual laid-back style. The chief's face was tense. "That's a good thing. That barricade can come down. The sooner it does, the sooner things can return to normal."

Russo stopped and turned to stare at him. "Normal?"

Blackstone looked back at him. "Normal in that our town doesn't need to be divided any more. I sure as shit didn't mean ... goddamn *aliens* categorizing us ... that shit ain't normal."

"You saw what happened out there today," Russo pointed

in the general direction of the barricade. "Magnus Bracks created a riot! You and Cann need to sort that out before any barricade comes down. We need to protect the Clean Skins."

"I think it may take a little more than me and the deputy to settle things over there."

"Obviously!" Russo's voice went up a few octaves. "Because Deputy Cann did *shit* out there again today!"

"He was one man against an angry mob that formed and reacted very quickly. What did you expect him to do?" Blackstone said, raising his voice.

"His *job!*"

"He has been doing his job! On his own. And might I add, mayor, he's been doing so while dealing with the loss of his son, being separated from his wife and daughter, and dealing with whatever the hell that stripe on him means!"

"He should've arrested Bracks when I *first* asked for it!"

The chief paused a moment, biting his tongue. "Look, I'll get some back-up from the military. We'll take that barricade down, and go sort things out."

"No. You sort things out first, *then* the barricade comes down."

"Mayor, they think we Clean Skins have been working with the outside on this. They think we've been lying to them. If we keep that barricade in place, that will only confirm their theory."

"I don't care what they think," Russo said, picturing Bracks' face as he did. "I'm not risking the lives of the people on this side of the fence to appease the *feelings* of the Striped Ones. We lower that barrier, they'll be looting and causing havoc over here. I won't have that!"

The chief put his hands on his hips as he stared back. "You don't think we should take this to the council for a vote? I think

261

Graeme would prefer that. And Jeff, Patty and Darryl."

Russo looked coldly at the chief. "I said no. The barricade stays in place until I'm sure the Striped Ones pose no threat to the Clean Skins of Victoryville. I've made my decision." There was no way he was going to risk his life or the safety of things on this side of the wall while violence played out on the streets of the SZ. As far as he was concerned, political correctness could be damned.

Blackstone stared at him, eyes still red from the teargas down at the gate. The chief had arrived there too late, the riot already in full swing, and he could only stand there and watch helplessly as the bios fired warning shots, sending the people vanishing into the smoky cloud of chaos.

"Don't look at me like that, chief."

"Like what?"

"Like I'm white privilege personified."

"Well," he shrugged, "I'm sorry, but right now you're acting like it. You're sitting there while just outside your door all hell is breaking loose and you don't seem to care because you're safe in here."

"I do care," he said through gritted teeth. "I've told you to sort it out. *Then*, the barrier can come down. So go out there and calm your people down."

"*My* people?" he said, eyebrows jumping to the top of his forehead. "What's that supposed to mean?"

"Look—"

"No, I get it." Blackstone held his hand up. "You think I'm stupid. I know why I was hired for this job. You white folk in power thought a black Chief of Police would be good to help keep the minorities in check. But guess what, mayor? Over that fence, a bunch of white boys are leading that fiasco. If they'd been black, you would've shut them down days ago."

262

Before Russo could respond Eva burst through the door, startling them both. "Mayor!" she panted, "turn the TV on. It's Bracks!"

Richard, alarmed, watched the live feed on his new prepaid cell phone. There was a report about Homeland Security paying a visit to CNN. He'd tried to call Harry from a pay phone, but there had been no answer, and now Richard worried about what was happening to him. Switching to another station, he watched, horrified, as the latest events from around the world showed a mix of reactions, some violent, to his exclusive story. But of all the concerning events, the one that struck him the most was the one here in Victoryville. A riot had broken out, teargas had been used on the crowd, and soldiers and civilians had been wounded in an exchange of gunfire. What shocked him most of all as he watched the shaky amateur footage, was that he'd recognized Abbie Randell there. She'd been knocked to the ground, trampled, and was stumbling her way up through the choking smoke, trying to get out of there. She looked terrified. *What the hell was she doing there?*

The news then cut to what they were claiming was an exclusive video released just moments ago from a man at the center of the Victoryville riots. A man claiming to be the leader of the Striped Zone: Magnus Bracks. Richard paused when he saw him. He rolled on-screen in a wheelchair, an oxygen bottle attached, possibly some other medical paraphernalia, and the red megaphone he'd used to stir the riots. The man looked to be in his fifties or sixties, but it was hard to tell. He was Caucasian, overweight and his receding gray-brown hair had been pulled into a little ponytail at the back. As the camera zoomed in, Richard saw that he had dry, pale skin, blotched with sunspots and broken capillaries. His amber eyes were cloudy and flecked, and the man's double chin was large and flat like a dinner plate. But what caught Richard's attention most was that this man had not one, but *seven* welts running down his chin. Given that number of welts, this man had to be his own deadly, walking time bomb.

"I am Magnus Bracks," his rough voice said to the camera, "and, as of this moment, I am in charge of the Victoryville SZ." It had been recorded on a simple system, the microphone picking up the ambient room sounds and the bystanders somewhere out of frame.

"We," Magnus continued, "were herded like branded cattle into this area, segregated from the rest of you to await our fate. I concede the government may not have known at first whether we were contagious, but once they did, they decided to leave us here. Some of us had been removed from our homes, because they were deemed to be in the Clean Zone. Some of us have had family members removed by soldiers. Homes have been robbed. Those Clean Skins in the government, and in the military, left our town quarantined because they think those aliens are coming back. And if the aliens do return ... they're going to stand by and let them have us. Those Clean Skins left us here in the SZ because they were afraid.

"We know that *something,* not of the Earth, did this to us. They categorized us for a reason. They took our healthy from us." Magnus' eyes lowered for a moment, before he looked back into the camera. "My thoughts and prayers go out to the families of the missing ... I hope they didn't suffer. Whatever did this, took them from us because they were healthy. And we were left behind: the Clean Skins, carriers of faulty genes, and us Striped Ones who are the ill. That is why I'm sending this video to you all; to tell you that we don't need you. We don't need the Clean Skins and we don't need those of you on the outside. We will fortify our boundary and keep ourselves safe. Because if whatever did this comes back ... they'll come for the

Clean Skins next, or the rest of you. We, the Striped Ones, will be safe. We are ill, they don't want us, that is why they marked us. And here's the funny thing: the government and the Clean Skins kept us at bay to protect themselves, but what they ultimately did was protect *us*." Magnus' eyes hardened. "So we are going to keep that boundary in place. Here, in the SZ, Clean Skins are not welcome. You will not put our lives at risk any further. South of Ventnor Avenue, in Victoryville, is striped territory. Any Clean Skins found to be trespassing will pay a heavy price. You will not taint us with *your* curse, Clean Skins. You will not draw the aliens back here to us," he said as a slight smile curled the corner of his mouth. "We, the Striped Ones, the sick and diseased ones, will be safe. It's not survival of the fittest, it's survival of the sickest. This is the time of the stripes," he said. "The weak have become the strong. We will be the survivors of this apocalypse."

The video ended and Richard sat there, everything numb, except his heart, which thumped against his ribcage like a racing thoroughbred. He couldn't believe this man had been so bold as to openly declare war on the Clean Skins. Bracks was clearly convinced that the Clean Skins were working with the government, that they were responsible for the treatment of the Striped Ones. And there was every chance that the aliens could return. Bracks was right, the Clean Skins, aside from a dodgy gene or two, were healthy. If those things came back, they presumably wouldn't want the ill and the diseased. Magnus himself was a poster boy for that; a man skating on the edge of death. If those things came back, they would target the Clean Skins or the outsiders. And Richard knew the outsiders would be hoping that the Clean Skins would be first.

He began to pace the alleyway in which he stood. He suddenly wondered whether escaping into the Striped Zone had been such a good idea now, given he was a Clean Skin. But he couldn't go back either. Where the hell would he go now that

Magnus had declared hostility toward Clean Skins caught in the Striped Zone? He would need to hide his chin and neck. His mind rolled ideas around, trying to consider his options. He kept seeing the footage of the riot in Victoryville: the teargas, the gunfire, Abbie Randell stumbling terrified through the chaos.

He stopped pacing, then, and thought of the young Clean Skin mother, Kaitlyn, who Abbie had taken in. His heart began to race even faster and his palms began to sweat wondering just what danger he had put them both in now. The people of Victoryville knew the Clean Skin girl was at Abbie's. That's why her house had been vandalized. So what the hell would Magnus Bracks do about it, if Clean Skins were no longer welcome in the SZ?

Whatever it was, he had to stop it. He couldn't fix the damage he'd caused throughout the town, throughout the world, but he could try and help Abbie and Kaitlyn.

He had to do what he could to fix the terror he had just brought upon them.

Deputy Leo Cann slowly awoke to a cracking headache. He opened his eyes and it took him a moment to realize he was lying on a concrete floor of some kind. He lifted his head and surveyed the room he was in. Some kind of storeroom. He saw mops, buckets. Where the hell was he? And how the hell did he get here? He tried to remember what happened last. He remembered the riot and the smoke. Then he remembered Austin trying to force him away from Magnus Bracks . . .

He'd been trying to stay calm, and in turn was trying to keep the young, strong Austin calm. Leo had been so relieved to hear that he wasn't contagious, all he wanted to do was go to Claire and Lena, but then this mess had broken out. So he'd been trying to play it as calm as he could, knowing how important it was to make it out whole. But it hadn't worked. Austin had been edgy, and somehow Leo knew it wasn't just an adrenaline rush boosted by the crowd around him. No, Austin looked like he was being boosted by something else, something chemical, something synthetic. Earl had told him about the reports of steroid use, but Leo was starting to think that maybe it was something else Austin had been dealing. *Methamphetamine?* Austin had been too worked up and he'd been spoiling for a fight. And all Austin's boxing down at the gym had worked, because his punch had been hard and fast and had dropped Leo quickly, leaving him seeing stars. He didn't have time to react before he received a boot in his gut, and then . . . well, he didn't remember much after that and figured that was why his head was throbbing like it was.

He moved to push himself up off the floor. It was hard work given the state of his head, but he did. He swayed and felt the back of his skull. His fingers came away with congealing blood. He went to rest his hand on his gun, needing some reassurance, but his holster was empty. His eyes quickly confirmed that it was gone, as was his comms gear.

"Shit," he whispered.

He moved over to the door of the storeroom and pressed his ear against it. He heard voices outside, but couldn't make out what they were saying. He placed his hand on the doorknob and tried to gently and quietly twist it, but it was locked. He rested his forehead against the door for a moment, trying to catch his breath, let his aching mind think. He looked around, thinking the mop and bottles of cleaning fluids could make for weapons, but if he was where he thought he was— somewhere Austin had put him—then he knew they wouldn't do much good. He'd seen Bracks' supporters down at the gate. Many of them had been armed, and now one of them was roaming around with his own gun. Depending on how many were on the other side of that door, a mop and bottles of cleaning fluid would only do so much.

He exhaled heavily and moved to sit back against the shelves opposite the door. He realized there was nothing he could do but wait. Wait until someone came in who he could try and talk some sense into, or wait until Earl realized he was missing, and he or the military came in after him.

Either way, until then, he was in a real goddamn mess.

Mayor Russo slumped into his chair and lowered his head into his hands.

"He's out of his goddamn mind." Chief Blackstone shook his head, still staring at the TV in shock.

Russo finally looked up. "You think?" he said sarcastically. "He just declared war on Clean Skins!"

"I heard what he said!" Blackstone bit back.

"Mayor," Eva put her head around the door, "word is that the site it was uploaded to has crashed from all the hits, but it's already gone viral on hundreds of other sites." She disappeared at the sound of the phone ringing.

Russo looked at Blackstone. "What the hell are we going to do about this? The Victoryville SZ just declared war on Clean Skins and anyone else who tries to cross that wall. This is a goddamn nightmare!"

"I'd better put in a call to Leo, make sure he's okay." Blackstone straightened and headed for the door, just as Eva came back, a nervous look on her face.

"Mayor," she said nervously, "I have a Colonel Levin on the line."

"Jesus Christ," Russo whispered, closing his eyes.

Dr. Lysart Pellan knocked carefully on the door. He wasn't sure what he was doing here, but he had nowhere else to go. After receiving the call from Harvey Meeks, which he hadn't answered, he'd been terrified that the government might use the phone to track his location. He immediately destroyed it and left the motel as soon as he could.

It cut him a little inside to know that his daughters would not be able to contact him, but he told himself that he would call them as soon as he had a safe moment to do so. Then he'd been struck by the harsh reality that their phones, too, would probably be hacked and his calls traced. His head and shoulders drooped. He'd done this to be able to reunite with his family, but the truth was he'd now pushed them further away. How long did he have, hiding from the security forces in this small town?

The door finally opened and Dr. John Seevers stood there.

"Dr. Pellan?" he asked, confused.

"John," he smiled sadly.

"What are you doing here?" he asked, darting his eyes cautiously to the street behind him.

"I, er . . . I had nowhere else to go."

John stared at him, studying his face, as understanding slowly dawned across his own. "You?" he asked. "You were the one who spoke to that reporter. You made the discovery?"

Lysart stared back, but didn't answer the question. Instead he motioned indoors. "May I come in?"

John glanced behind him into the house, pausing for a few seconds, then closed the door over a little more. "I'm sorry, Dr. Pellan, I can't . . ."

Lysart's face fell a little.

John's face looked both nervous and ashamed. Lysart eyed

the red stripe running down his chin. "It's not safe around here. Things have gone crazy."

"I know," Lysart said gently, "that's why I'm here. I need somewhere to stay, John."

His colleague averted his eyes, shook his head. "I'm sorry, Dr. Pellan. You're a Clean Skin."

The words hit Lysart like a slap in the face.

"I can't have a Clean Skin here," John told him. "It's too risky. They'll find out. I'm sorry." John went to close the door, but Lysart stopped it.

"I'll stay hidden," he said, his voice weak, his eyes pleading. "Please. I won't cause you any trouble."

"I'm sorry. I can't. You have to go. Please don't come back here." With that, John closed the door in Lysart's face. He stood there in the dark, staring at the wall of wood in front of his face that was John Seevers' front door, an utter feeling of hopelessness swallowing him.

He turned around and faced the deserted street. It seemed to echo how he felt inside. He was alone, cut off from his family, and hunted by those in authority who would make him pay for sharing the truth.

He was a Clean Skin stuck in the Striped Zone with a target on his back in more ways than one.

Abbie and Kaitlyn panicked when they heard a knock at her back door, which led off the kitchen. They both looked at each other and Kaitlyn's eyes went wide with fear. *Why would someone knock on the back door?* For a moment Abbie worried that it was soldiers, come to arrest her for being at the gate during the fracas. But she hadn't done anything. And she certainly didn't condone what went down. Her mind raced as she blinked her still stinging eyes.

"Maybe it's Josh," she said standing from the couch. "Maybe he's hiding from someone."

"Be careful!" Kaitlyn whispered.

Abbie wiped her swollen red eyes, then headed into the kitchen to snatch up a knife as she made her way to the back door. She placed her hand on the doorknob.

"Who is it?" she said firmly, trying to sound brave.

"It's Richard Keene," a man's voice answered quietly, "the reporter. We spoke on the phone."

Abbie paused in shock. He was the last person she expected at her back door. She pulled the curtain back and peered out the window. The man was looking over his shoulder, but turned back to face her at the movement and flash of light. She recognized him from his news stories.

"What do you want?" she asked.

"Can I come in?"

"Why?"

"To talk. Please." There was a desperation in his eyes, a pleading, a sorrow. She studied his Clean Skin stubbled chin, then looked up as a loud bang and yelling sounded in the distance. Richard flinched, looking toward the sound, then back at her, worriedly. Then they heard what sounded like gunfire.

She dropped the curtain and took hold of the doorknob again.

"Are you sure?" Kaitlyn whispered loudly behind her, standing by the door to the living room, clutching a small statue she'd grabbed from the TV cabinet.

Abbie shrugged nervously. "I can't leave him out there. He's a Clean Skin."

She unlocked the door and Richard Keene quickly slipped

inside.

"Thank you," he breathed, panting a little with nerves, and darting his eyes to Kaitlyn.

Abbie locked the door again, straightening the curtain. Richard was taller and trimmer than he looked on TV, wearing black jeans, an olive green T-shirt, and a dark-brown jacket with a red backpack slung over his shoulder. He held his hands up in surrender, looking at the large knife in her hands, that she now realized she'd been holding up defensively at him.

"I'm not here to cause any trouble," he said in that calming voice of his, sea-green eyes imploring hers. "I promise."

She studied the reporter a moment, and believed his words.

"What do you want?" she asked.

He lowered his arms a little, although he still held them in a placating manner. "You've seen my report? You know the truth about the stripes?"

Abbie nodded.

"I'm on the run. The government . . . there will be questions they'll want answered about the revelation." He swallowed nervously. "I saw the news, the riot. I saw you there among the crowd, and I saw the video Magnus Bracks released afterward. I was worried that you might be in a whole lot of trouble." He looked over at Kaitlyn. "Both of you." He turned back to Abbie. "You heard what he said about the Clean Skins?"

Abbie nodded, lowering the knife. "I didn't know what that meant," she said. "They know she's here. They've always known she's here. He let her stay because Charlie was a Striped One like the rest of us."

She saw Richard's eyes fall to her chin and neck, eyeing her welt, fascinated.

"Charlie?" he asked.

"Kaitlyn's son."

"Oh," Richard glanced at Kaitlyn again.

"I don't know why things would change now," Abbie added.

"I don't know either," Richard told her. "But I wanted to make sure you're alright. I wanted to make sure no harm came to either of you," and he looked at Kaitlyn again. "It's the least I could do."

"That's why you came here?" Abbie asked. "To the Striped Zone? You must've known it was dangerous."

Richard sighed. He pulled the curtain back and glanced out the back door window, then finally dropped his hands, resting against the wall behind him. "I crossed over before Magnus made his announcement."

"And you're still here?"

He gave a sad smile, eyes dropping to her welt again. "I wanted to make sure you were alright first. I saw you in the riots, saw Bracks' video, knew Kaitlyn was here."

She studied him again, brow furrowed a little, her fear softened by his kindness. It looked like he hadn't slept, and the clothes he wore, she was certain, had been the same in his last few reports. She eyed him sympathetically. She had been marked, but at least she hadn't been displaced from her home.

"It just kinda blew up," he continued. "I wanted people to know the truth but I never thought it would turn out like this. I thought this would unite people again, knowing the Striped Ones weren't contagious. I never meant to put anyone in harm's way."

Abbie looked at Kaitlyn, still hiding back by the doorway to the living room, statue in hand.

"Well, we're fine," she said, trying to ease his mind. He looked like he had enough to worry about. Then she added, "Thank you, but we're okay."

He smiled, motioning to the knife in her hands. "I can see that now. You're taking care of yourself just fine."

She gave him a brief, awkward smile in return, then finally put the knife down on the kitchen bench near her. "What will you do now?"

Richard shook his head. "I don't really know."

"Do you have somewhere to go?"

His face fell a little. "No, but I'll figure something out."

"It's dangerous out there. It's not safe for someone like you. A Clean Skin."

Her words seemed to hang in the air, and the silence sat for a moment, she eyeing his clean chin, and he her marked one.

"I know," he eventually said, "but I'll be okay. I made my bed. Now I guess I have to lay down in it."

They heard what sounded like more gunfire in the distance. They both looked over at the closed door, and Richard peered behind the curtain again.

Abbie stared at him, feeling uneasy about sending him away. Out there into the night, out into the chaos.

"You can stay here tonight," she said, then quickly added, "in the basement."

Richard looked at her a little surprised. "I don't want to burden you."

"You wanna go back out there?" she asked bluntly.

He didn't answer.

Abbie shrugged. "I'm already harboring one Clean Skin. What's two?"

Richard stared at her, his eyes thoughtful as he mulled things over.

"No one saw you come here, did they?"

"No," Richard shook his head, "I don't think so."

Abbie shrugged again. "Well, if you stay hidden until this blows over, we'll be fine."

His mind seemed to visibly turn over, until a resignation washed over him. His eyes and shoulders softened. "You're a good person, Abbie. That's why I wanted to make sure you were okay."

She gave him a sad smile, then held her hand out and gestured him toward the kitchen table. "Have you eaten? You look like you could do with a meal."

Richard moved over to a chair and sat down, running his hands through his curly brown hair. He sighed heavily, gratefully.

"Thank you," he said quietly. "I really mean it. Thank you."

Mayor Russo was walking a very fine line. He had managed to stall the military and state governor with talk of local police intervention first, to ensure things didn't escalate unnecessarily. The riot had been broken up by the soldiers and things seemed to have calmed for now, but everyone's patience was wearing thin. Very thin. Homeland Security had given him a window of forty-eight hours to resolve the situation and deliver Bracks to them, before the military would move in and do it themselves. Thankfully, because of their efforts at keeping the peace in certain pockets around the country, and around the world, for that matter, their attention and resources were stretched. And that bought Russo time.

Chief Blackstone knocked and entered his office. Russo eyed him expectantly.

"Leo isn't answering my calls," the chief told him with a serious look.

"What does that mean?"

"I don't know," Blackstone's eyes narrowed. "He may have his hands full after that riot, in which case taking my call isn't high on his list of priorities, but . . ."

"But?"

"I got a bad feeling."

"So what do we do?"

"For now the crowd has dispersed, thanks to that teargas from the soldiers at the gate. I'll give him a couple of hours in case he's attending to arrests. If I can't get a hold of him by then, I'm going in."

Russo held up his hand. "We don't want to do anything rash, chief."

"Rash?" Blackstone said irritably. "And there I was thinking you wanted me to clean this up?"

"I do, but we need to be smart about it and not just go in guns-a-blazing."

"If my deputy is in trouble, I'm going in there after him," Blackstone said firmly.

"And if something happens to you, who will enforce things this side of the wall? We need to think of the Clean Skins too, chief."

Blackstone stared at him and Russo didn't like the accusation in his eyes. "We need to think of everyone equally."

"Give your deputy a couple of hours and if you don't hear from him, then we try to resolve things another way."

"What way?"

Russo sighed heavily, giving him a deadly serious look. "We negotiate."

"Negotiate?"

"With Bracks. We dangle a carrot in front of him. *Me*. It's what he ultimately wants: my attention. If your deputy doesn't respond, I'll talk directly to Bracks and get him to retract his statements."

"You think that'll work?" Blackstone said, unable to hide his skepticism.

"It's me he wants, chief. I'm the one he's been after all this time. I've been ignoring his cries for attention, so maybe it's time I give him what he wants. It'll work. It has to. If it doesn't, the military will go marching in there and . . . God knows what will happen then." Russo gave him a worried look. "Victoryville has been in the press enough. I don't want to give them another bloodbath to feed on. We have to contain this ourselves, and fast. Quickly and quietly. We've got forty-eight hours."

Day Eight

Richard awoke to the sound of a faraway baby's cry. He blinked his eyes open and it took him a moment to register where he was: on a foldaway mattress on the floor of Abbie Randell's basement. He looked up at the small window high on the wall, and saw daylight streaming in around the edges of the curtain. He looked at his watch and saw that it was early morning. He yawned and stretched, then lay there some more, thinking about the past twenty-four hours.

And the mess he was in.

And the mess he had caused.

It had been late when he'd arrived at Abbie's the night before, and after a brief chat at the table about all that had happened since the phenomenon, the two women had announced that they were going to bed. Abbie looked tired, and not just because of her red swollen eyes from the teargas. Richard himself was exhausted, having worked through the previous night on the story. He was actually relieved at the thought of turning in for the night.

Abbie had helped Richard with his makeshift bed, while Kaitlyn watched from the top of the basement stairs as if to make sure Abbie was okay. Richard smiled to himself, pleased the two women were taking care of each other. When Abbie left him for the night, he heard her lock the door to the basement. It unnerved him a little to be caged in, but he guessed he couldn't blame them. He was a stranger, and given the circumstances of the phenomenon and Magnus' declaration, they didn't really have the need to trust anyone right now.

He heard the creaking of floorboards overhead, the sound of movement, of someone walking around. The child's cries slowly ceased. Someone came down the stairs to the ground floor and light suddenly poured in around the door to the basement, as if the living room curtains had been drawn. He focused on the gap beneath the door and saw a shadow halt in front of it. A few seconds passed, then he heard the door being unlocked. The shadow moved away.

He took that as a signal that it was time to get up now. He yawned again, scratched his fingers through his hair, then rubbed his eyes and stubbled jaw. He threw the sheets back and made his way to the small bathroom in the corner of the room.

He soon made his way cautiously up the stairs and opened the door. He made his movements slow and obvious, not wanting to frighten anyone. As he closed the door behind him, he looked up at the stairs and saw no one, then he walked across the empty living room. He moved over to peer out through the sheer curtain covering the large window. The street outside was empty.

"Careful." Abbie's voice gave him a fright. She was standing in the doorway to the kitchen that fed off the living room. "Don't let anyone see you."

"I know, I'm sorry," he apologized, stepping away from the window.

"Would you like some breakfast?"

Richard nodded and said, "Thank you," and watched as she

279

disappeared into the kitchen. He followed her and saw her standing at the bench, her back to him. "Can I help?" he asked.

She turned around with a plate of toast. "It's only toast, I'm afraid." She placed it on the table. "My groceries are a little thin on the ground. There was supposed to be another delivery of supplies yesterday afternoon, but the riot . . . well, if it's safe, I'll head out and see if I can get some more today. Hopefully they'll try and redeliver the supplies, but after what's happened, I don't know."

Richard nodded. "They may try and starve the SZ in order to gain compliance."

She motioned for him to sit, and he did so. "Coffee? Tea?" she asked.

"Coffee, please."

She poured a cup and handed it to him. He smiled a thank you and took a sip, the warm full-bodied flavor comforting to him. He watched Abbie as she prepared some toast and coffee for herself. Based on his research, she was twenty-three years old, soon to be twenty-four. She looked a little different in the flesh, her long dark-brown hair framing a soft, attractive face, which he noted held an expression that was equal parts sad, tired, worried, even lonely. He remembered her saying that her whole family was missing when they'd spoken on the phone, and the thought evoked his sympathy.

She moved over to the table and sat across from him. He eyed the welt that traced down her chin and neck again. Her blue-green eyes, still a little pink from the teargas, looked at his.

"Did you sleep well?" she asked, as though trying to shift his focus.

He nodded. "Yes, I did. Thank you again for giving me somewhere to stay. I needed the rest."

"No problem."

"Did Charlie keep you awake?" Kaitlyn asked, walking into the room with the child in her arms. "He had a bad night."

Richard shook his head. "No, I was exhausted. Didn't hear a thing down there." He eyed the child in her arms. "So your mother's out of town?"

Kaitlyn nodded. "She's in Wyoming. She went for my aunt's fiftieth birthday. It was just supposed to be for a few days. It was too risky for me to go, flying when I was nearly due."

A silence befell the room, all of them thinking about that simple decision her mother had made to go to her sister's and the consequences for Kaitlyn, who had stayed behind.

"We've been talking on the phone. I miss her," Kaitlyn said, "but in a way, I'm kinda glad she's not here. She might've been taken if she'd stayed. At least I know she's safe. For now."

They exchanged a concerned look before a knock at the door stole their attention.

Abbie stiffened, her eyes darting to the doorway then back to Richard.

"Shall I go to the basement?" he asked.

"Just stay here," Abbie said, getting up and closing the kitchen door behind her.

Richard sat in the closed room with Kaitlyn, and heard muffled voices. Whoever had been at the door was now inside the living room. The voice was male.

Charlie began to cry and Kaitlyn looked at Richard worriedly.

"Josh!" he heard Abbie call.

Suddenly the kitchen door opened and a guy around Abbie's age stalked in. He stopped abruptly when he saw Richard and quickly whipped out a handgun, aiming it at him. Richard threw his hands up in surrender.

"Whoa! Easy!" he said.

"Who the fuck are you?" the guy asked.

"Josh, no!" Abbie pushed the arm holding the gun down, so that it pointed to the floor. "What's wrong with you?" she hissed.

Josh narrowed his eyes at Richard, darting them to his Clean Skin chin. "You're that reporter. The one who did the story."

Richard nodded.

Josh turned to Abbie, looking at her like she was crazy. "What's he doing here?"

Abbie tried to answer, but her response was hesitant and she faltered.

Josh cut her off. "Are you out of your mind? He's a Clean Skin! Is he doing another story?" Josh turned to Richard, an accusing look upon his face. "Are you doing another story?"

"No," Richard said, hands still steady and held up.

"He had nowhere else to go," Abbie answered for him.

Josh looked at her like she was crazy. "Are you nuts? Magnus has just declared war on the Clean Skins and you take *another* one in?"

"That's *exactly* why I took him in!" Abbie argued back.

Josh looked at Richard and raised his weapon again. "What do you want? Are you running another story? Are you trying to get us killed?"

"No, Josh. Not at all," Richard said in an even tone.

"You saw the graffiti on her house, right? They don't think she's the hero you made her out to be."

"Well, they're wrong. She is a hero," Richard said, maintaining his calm. He saw Abbie glance at him. "I was trying to focus on the good people, and not the destruction, Josh. Not the people like Magnus Bracks. People like him deserve nothing."

"So, what are you doing here then?"

Richard shrugged. "I wanted to see that Abbie and Kaitlyn were alright. I wanted to make sure I hadn't caused them any harm."

"Well, you have!" Josh spat. "Everyone knows about her now. Everyone knows that she took in a Clean Skin. Magnus has declared the SZ as an exclusion zone for your kind. What do you think that does to her now? You being here."

"My *kind*?" Richard asked. "There's only one kind here, Josh. Human beings. Marked or not, we're all humans."

"You know nothing about what it is to be marked. Don't you put yourself with us!"

"Josh," Abbie said, "put the gun down. What the hell do you even have that for? Get it out of my house!"

He looked at her. "Everything's going to shit out there, Abbie," he told her. "Trust me, we need protection."

"What happened to you last night?" she asked. "You took off in the riot. I saw Austin give you that gun. Where did you go?"

"Not in front of him," he said, motioning to Richard, then lowered his gun and stepped closer to her. "Don't tell him anything, Abbie. If they find out you're snitching . . ."

"Who?" Richard asked, brow furrowing. "If who finds out?"

Josh gave him a hard look, then turned back to Abbie. "Get him out of your house! It's too goddamn risky."

"I'm not buying into this, Josh," Abbie told him. "This is *my* house! I will not be threatened or coerced by Magnus or Roy. *Or* Austin!"

Josh's eyes flew wide for a moment at the mention of their names, then paused and asked. "Austin?"

"Yeah," Abbie nodded. "The other night when you took off with him, while you were upstairs, he warned me to choose which side I was on. It was a threat, Josh. A veiled one, but a threat nonetheless."

Josh shook his head. "It's not safe to have them here, Abbie."

"He'll stay in the basement."

"Abbie—"

"It's not just the fanatical Striped Ones, Josh. It's the government and the military. He's not safe out there."

"The government?" He glanced at Richard.

"Homeland Security are not happy I unveiled the truth to the people," he told Josh.

The young man stared at him for a moment, then looked back at Abbie. "All the more reason you need to get him out of your house Abbie. *Think* about it!"

"This is my house, Josh! Well, it was my parent's house, but seeing how they've disappeared, it's now mine. I know they would support me in this. Magnus Bracks won't tell me what I can and can't do in my house, *nor* who I have stay here! You need to stop listening to what they tell you. They're warping your mind. They're using this phenomenon to manipulate people."

Josh stormed out of the kitchen, saying, "Come and watch this!"

Abbie followed him out, as did Kaitlyn, albeit meekly. Richard stood from his seat at the table and followed too, moving cautiously. They stood around the TV and watched the news.

"They've been showing it all morning," Josh told her.

Richard saw amateur footage of the streets of Victoryville, of the houses and letterboxes which had now been painted with thick red stripes.

"People are marking their houses," Josh explained, "letting

everyone know that they're Striped Ones. The unmarked houses belonging to Clean Skins are being ransacked."

Richard sunk down to the couch in shock.

"Magnus is getting people to pledge their allegiance," Josh said.

Richard shook his head hopelessly. "What does he think, he's leading some kind of revolution here?"

Josh shrugged. "He says they're not going down without a fight. That they won't stand being treated like dogs. He's fighting the oppression."

"Oppression of who?" Richard asked angrily. "The Clean Skins are people just like you. The Clean Skins are caught up in this as well."

"No, they're not," Josh told him. "We're ill, diseased. At the first sign of trouble, the Clean Skins threw us in here, forced us away, like we were trash—"

"They thought it was contagious," Richard interrupted him. "You had the welts, what did you expect them to do?"

"Yeah, and when they learned it wasn't contagious, they kept us here." Josh stared at him. "You obviously thought it was wrong of them to do that, that's why you did your story."

Richard closed his eyes and lowered his head into his hands, the regret rushing through him like an avalanche.

"Something out there did this to us," Josh told him. "Whatever it is, it's coming back. And I think Magnus is right. If they do come back, they're coming back for you Clean Skins!" he pointed at Richard. "*Not us.* So the tables have turned now, reporter. Now, it is *us* keeping *you* out!"

Richard looked up and saw the threat in the younger man's eyes.

"Josh," Abbie said softly, shaking her head, "listen to what you're saying."

"No, Abbie! Be smart! These Clean Skins are dangerous. They're targets for Magnus and Roy, for the government, and for the goddamn aliens! Get them out of your house."

"And will you do the same?" she challenged, folding her arms across her chest, obviously referring to something of which Richard wasn't aware.

Josh seemed to suck in the air around him as though she'd just slapped him. He lurched closer to her and pointed his finger in her face, making Richard tense. "If you draw any unwanted attention, Abbie," he warned, then stepped back and headed for the front door. It slammed closed behind him, and the three of them sat in silence for a moment, soaking in what had just happened.

"Friend of yours?" Richard asked, breaking it.

Abbie looked at him, her eyes sad and afraid. "I thought so," she said quietly.

Richard sighed. "He's right, though. I should leave."

"No," Kaitlyn blurted, cradling Charlie close to her chest. "If you go, then I have to go," she said, frightened. "I don't want to go. I can't go out there."

Abbie turned to her. "It's alright, Kaitlyn, you don't have to." She took the young girl's shoulders and pulled her into a hug, comforting her. As she did, she looked over Kaitlyn's shoulder at Richard. "Nor you."

Richard watched her carefully. "Are you sure, Abbie?"

She nodded, her eyes shining with tears. "If we all stick together, we'll be okay," she said. "Besides, if you leave . . . I'll have no one."

A heavy sensation filled Richard's chest as he thought of his missing crew, of being stuck here in Victoryville on his own.

He watched the two women hugging: the Striped One and the Clean Skin. And somewhere in the darkness of the misery and chaos that surrounded them, that little light of hope shone through again. The hope that shone from within Abbie. The hope that had drawn Richard here like a moth to the flame.

Deep down, despite how dangerous it was, he was glad that she was letting him stay. He wasn't sure he could face the brutality of the streets right now. Besides, the image before him was something he felt compelled to protect. He didn't want to leave until he could ensure it would remain safe.

Stanley Barrick reviewed the press release that they were about to issue. With input from several experts, it very carefully laid blame on the irresponsible behavior of reporter Richard Keene and attempted to quell fears. They couldn't debunk Dr. Pellan's theory, so the focus was not on the CDC and the government withholding information, but rather protecting people from the chaos that had ensued thanks to Mr. Keene's sensationalist story and reckless disregard for the safety of the people.

He slid the paper across his desk to Colin, who quickly hurried out of the room to have it issued through the proper channels.

"My soldiers have confirmed that Pellan's apartment was empty," Levin said. "His cell phone and his belongings were there. He'd be a fool to enter the SZ with what's going down, but you never know. He'd be a fool to stay in the Clean Zone too. Anything from his family?"

"No. His ex-wife is in Paris with their daughters. They're being watched," Stanley said. "Is there an update on this Magnus Bracks?"

"No. We've increased the military presence around the town, along the wall and at the gates, but we're on standby. I'm not sure why you gave the local authorities forty-eight hours to handle things themselves."

"They wanted to handle things discreetly. That's our preferred method too."

"They haven't been handling things very well so far."

"No one knew how far this Bracks guy would take things."

"Well, we're watching the clock and waiting, but if things begin to turn away from discreet, we'll go in regardless."

"Any more violence?" Stanley asked.

"Things have been quiet since the riot, but overnight the Striped Ones have marked out their houses, and empty homes belonging to Clean Skins are being ransacked. They've also been daubing Bracks' slogans around the place: *The Time of The Stripes*, *The Weak Become The Strong*, and the like. Most residents are staying in their homes, but some have tried to flee over the wall and out of town through the blockades. We're sending them back until we're given the order to remove the barricades and blockades. The press are all over it, of course. They're hungry for another video upload from Bracks."

Stanley nodded. "Well, we've put our own plans in motion. A media package is being put together on Bracks and his history with the unions. It will be ready to air straight after the press release goes out. It won't paint him in a particularly nice light, which may help persuade his followers to think twice about what they're doing."

"Good. What's the latest from the CDC?"

"Well, they're pissed at Pellan for granting the interview and making them look bad. They want this cleaned up as much as we do. There may be no contagion, but they still want to further study the residents. While there's chaos in Victoryville, there's no chance they can get the opportunity."

"You know, we could forget the media package and just take Bracks out before he has the chance to take this further?"

Levin said, eyes firmly on his colleague's.

Stanley shook his head. "If we put a bullet through his head now, we risk making a martyr of him to his followers in the SZ. We can't do that. Can you imagine the outcry if some sniper takes him out? How will that look? The cowardly government hiding in the shadows and shooting a sick man in a wheelchair, who's on the verge of death? No, that will only fan the flames. We've got enough to deal with."

"Well, as soon as that forty-eight hours is up, we're going in and we will remove him one way or the other," Levin said bluntly.

Stanley nodded. "Agreed. Just keep a close eye on it for now and report back to me."

Deputy Leo Cann finally heard the door to the storeroom unlocking. He tensed, holding onto the snapped mop handle he had decided to brandish. The door opened and Roy Kenny stood there, face twitching. He kept back a little, staying out of reach should Leo come out swinging.

"I wouldn't advise that, deputy," Roy said, motioning to the handle in his hands, as an armed Langdon Swan and Trent Ford flanked him.

"What the hell are you doing, Roy?" Leo shook his still aching head.

"I should ask *you* that," Roy said.

Leo looked at him. "I'm trying to do my job. Trying to keep the peace and stop people from getting hurt."

"Yeah, you did a real good job of that," Trent smiled snidely.

"*What are you doing*?" Leo asked again, accentuating the words, eyeing each one of them as he did. "Why did you lock me up in here?"

Roy shrugged. "We're trying to stop *you* from getting hurt, deputy. This ain't a fight you can win. So you best just stay out of it."

"What?"

"Magnus has declared the SZ out of bounds for the Clean Skins. When those aliens come back, they're going for them, not us. We'll be safe over here, and we don't want any of them near us. If they try and come for us, we'll kill 'em."

Leo spoke through clenched teeth. "This will end badly, guys. I'm telling you. You will go to jail."

"Says who?" Roy asked, tilting his head back to eye him down his nose, face twitching nervously. "A new world is upon us, deputy. It's only a matter of time before those aliens come back and the rest of the world ends up like us. The way I see it, the old law don't apply no more. There'll just be us, the Clean Skins, and the aliens. Your badge means shit around here now."

"How long do you think it will be before people know I'm missing? They probably already do. The chief would've tried to call me after the riot."

Roy shrugged. "You can walk out of here any time you like, deputy, so long as you keep on walking and stay the hell out of things."

Leo stared at him. "You know I can't do that, Roy. I'm in charge of policing the SZ."

"No, you ain't in charge of nothing no more! And the quicker you understand that, the better. I don't got much patience for slow learners."

Slow learners? Leo thought, feeling like he was staring at one. His eyes moved to scan the background behind Roy, and the faces walking past. They all seemed to have weapons.

"Hey!" Roy yelled at him. "Eyes front!"

"Alright, fine," Leo said, realizing there wasn't any point in

290

trying to talk them down. He wasn't equipped to talk down a whole warehouse full of armed hostile people. "How about you just give me back my gun and let me walk out of here."

The three men laughed.

"What you're doing right now, holding me here against my will, that's jail time right there," he told them firmly. "Not to mention the assault of a police officer, and theft of my weapon."

Roy stopped laughing and his face fell flat.

"Don't be stupid, Roy," Leo said firmly. "Let me go."

"See, I don't think you understood my request, deputy. I'm not getting a strong feeling here that you're going to walk away from this."

"I'm not going to try and stop you, Roy. I know I'm outnumbered. I just want to leave. With my gun."

"You're going to run to the chief, though. I can see that in your eyes."

"I see it too," Langdon said, nodding, sniffing. "He's going to squeal like the little pig he is."

"Get the chair," Roy ordered Trent, who nodded and disappeared.

Leo's hand tightened around the mop handle. "Roy, don't be stupid," he pleaded.

Trent came back with the chair. "How we doing this?"

Leo tensed up again. "Roy?"

"We gave you a choice, deputy. Can't say we didn't give you that." Roy raised his gun and aimed it at Leo's face. "Hands up."

"Roy?" Leo felt his body flush with sweat, and his heart beat double-time.

"Get 'em up!" Langdon yelled, also aiming his gun.

Trent started making his way into the room with the chair. Leo's eyes darted between the three, trying to think of a way out, but quickly realized there wasn't one. The two weapons aimed at his head made any move with a broken mop null and void.

So did thoughts of Claire and Lena, and not seeing them again.

"Don't be stupid," Roy threw Leo's own words back at him.

He exhaled and dropped the mop handle he'd been holding. Langdon rushed in, threw his arm around Leo's throat and yanked him into the chair that Trent had placed down. They grabbed his arms and twisted them behind his back, and he felt his handcuffs being ripped off his belt and snapped around his wrists. Langdon grabbed a fistful of Leo's hair and pulled his head back, as Roy peered into his face.

"We were hoping, as a Striped One, you'd be more supportive of our cause, deputy," Roy said, face twitching. "Maybe you just need a little longer to think about where your loyalties are."

"My loyalties? My wife and child are Clean Skins, Roy," he told him through gritted teeth. "What do you expect me to do?"

Roy gave a nod to Langdon who let his hair go. "Or maybe," Roy said, ignoring his words and stepping back, "you might just need a little persuasion to walk away and forget about all of us?"

Leo felt a crack across his right cheekbone as Trent's fist flew past his face. It was followed by a blow from the left as Langdon caught his jaw. Leo hunched over as he spat blood out onto the floor.

"More?" Langdon asked Roy eagerly.

"Nah," the hardware store owner said. "Let him think on that a while. We can give him some more encouragement later."

Leo stared at the blood splattered floor, his head throbbing double-time, as the three of them left, locking the door behind them.

Abbie watched Richard, concerned. He sat on the couch, his elbows on his knees, his head sunk in his hands. They'd just seen the latest update on the news. The government had issued a statement in reply to Richard's story on what they were calling Pellan's Theory. Both Richard and Dr. Pellan were made out to be villains, troublemakers wanting to cause a sensation, with little regard for the human consequences. Both were now wanted by federal agents to answer for their actions. Richard was wanted for questioning, but a warrant was out for Dr. Pellan's arrest. Photos of both men were displayed on the screen with the word "Wanted" underneath. Victoryville residents were encouraged to call a number on the screen should they have any information on their whereabouts.

"Jesus Christ," Richard whispered, shaking his head. He looked up at Abbie. "Do you think your friend will call me in?"

Abbie thought for a moment, then shook her head. "No." She couldn't explain to Richard about Josh's mother, that he wouldn't want to draw attention to the street.

"Are you sure?" he asked.

She nodded. Then added, "For now."

Richard breathed out and combed his hands through his hair. "I can't believe they plastered Dr. Pellan's face up there like that, like he's some criminal. I mean, we knew it was a risk, but ... I guess we hoped things would turn out differently. God, I hope he's alright."

Abbie moved to sit on the couch beside him. "Do you have any family out there, Mr. Keene?"

Richard looked at her. "Rick. Call me Rick."

"Rick." She gave him a nod.

"I have a sister. Adopted. Tom and Margaret, my parents, adopted us both when we were young, from different families," he said sitting back in the couch. "They're all fine. They're in Iowa." His eyes seemed to stare off into nothing.

"Your real parents?" she asked.

"They died. Car accident. Them and my brother. Sally, my adoptive sister, her mother was a single parent. She died of cancer when Sally was just three."

Abbie nodded in sympathy. "At least they're safe," she said. "I'd love to know where my family are."

"Yeah." Richard thought of the framed photographs he'd seen around the house the evening before, of Abbie's family; noticed items throughout the house, left untouched, as though their owners had only been there yesterday, as though Abbie was expecting, or hoping, that they would soon be back. "I can't imagine what it must be like to have your family disappear like that," he said, "but at the same time, I know what it's like to be left alone like that. So suddenly."

She gave him a sad smile, a slight shine to her eyes.

"I wish I knew where the missing were," he said. "I lost two colleagues, two friends . . . but I'm rapidly losing hope that I'll ever see them again."

"Me too," she whispered, listening to the empty quiet of the house around them. Even Charlie was quiet. Kaitlyn was upstairs feeding him.

Richard looked at the TV screen. "I just thought the people deserved the truth," he said quietly. "I never thought things would end up like this, that people like Magnus Bracks would—"

"You couldn't have known," Abbie tried to reassure him.

"Something out there did this to us, Abbie," Richard turned his face to her, his eyes imploring. "Something our experts can't explain did this to *all* of us. We need to unite, not fracture like this. That's what I wanted. It's what Dr. Pellan wanted: people to reunite with their families. Who knows how much time we have left? These things could come back and take more of us. I don't want to spend what little time we may have left fighting each other, do you?"

Abbie shook her head, her face softening with sympathy. "I'm not fighting anyone. That's why you and Kaitlyn are here." She smiled gently. "I'm glad you told us the truth."

They stared at each other in silence for a moment, then turned to watch footage rolling on TV of the newly-marked houses in Victoryville, and the red spray-painted slogans scrawled over stores and parts of the barricade fence. Ugly words that spoke of hate and war.

This is the Time of the Stripes!

The Weak Become the Strong!

Mayor Russo waited calmly. He was sitting alone in his office, the door closed, silence around him. He always closed his door for important phone calls, the kind where he needed to concentrate and ensure every word he spoke was careful, calculated, and clean. A politician was nothing if he couldn't wield words. And the truth was, this was probably going to be one of the most important phone calls of his career.

Magnus Bracks was cunning and Russo had to be prepared for that. So far in their dealings, Russo had managed to stay a step ahead of him. But he was smart enough not to take that for granted. Things could change at any time. They almost had. It was the most important lesson he'd ever learned from his shrewd father: never turn your back, never assume you can trust anyone, don't take anything for granted.

But maybe he had. Taken things for granted. Maybe that's

why Bracks seemed to have gotten the upper hand. Maybe Russo had become too complacent in his Clean Skin. And maybe that's why the chief's accusation of his privilege had stung.

He thought of the footage he'd seen that morning of houses in the Striped Zone defaced with the sickening thick red stripes and graffiti. The welts, once considered a mark of something heinous, were now being celebrated and embraced with pride. They believed the aliens had marked them because they didn't want them. The Striped Ones now believed they were safe. They believed that Clean Skins, like Russo, were next on the alien's hit list and that the outsiders would just stand back and let it happen. Somehow, the tables had turned and if he wasn't careful, the Clean Skins would become the greater victims in this.

Russo closed his eyes briefly, slipping his fingers beneath his glasses to rub his tired eyes. *You are not a victim. That's not how this is going to go. Just sort out Bracks and you'll get Victoryville back. You can still turn this around. Save the town, save your career. Don't let Bracks win. Don't let that asshole—*

"Well, if it isn't Mayor Russo," Bracks' wheezy, rough voice said through the phone. "To what do I owe this pleasure?"

"This isn't a pleasure, Mr. Bracks," Russo said, straightening his glasses. "I think you know why I'm calling."

"Do I? Well, I'm not so sure," he wheezed. "You see, I tried to contact you a number of times recently, but you wouldn't take my calls. So forgive my confusion, mayor, about your sudden interest. Did you finally find time in your diary to squeeze me in?"

"As you're well aware, things have been more than a little crazy since this phenomenon occurred. My attention and focus has been tied up with many other things—"

"Like taking care of your Clean Skins on the other side of

that wall?"

Russo paused, exhaling measuredly. "What is it you want, Mr. Bracks?"

There was silence for a moment. "I think I made that clear in my video. I take it you saw it?" Magnus wheezed and coughed up a chuckle. "Oh, you must have. That must be the reason for this call."

"You've incited riots and you've made open threats against Clean Skins, Mr. Bracks. You realize charges can be laid against you."

"So lay them. You won't be around much longer to see them enforced."

"Mr. Bracks, I'm calling you to appeal to your better judgment. Now it's confirmed that the Striped Ones are not contagious, we would like to take down the barrier—"

"No one is taking down that barrier."

"It's not *your* barrier. It's the town's."

"Don't hide behind the town, Russo. That was *your* barrier to keep us out. Now *we've* decided we want to keep it. So now it's ours. *Ours.* And we're keeping *you* out."

"There are Striped Ones who wish to be reunited with their Clean Skin family members, Mr. Bracks. And vice versa. The barrier will come down, we will end this peacefully, and you will hand in your arms."

"Says who?"

"Says the law. This is not a fight you can win. Have you seen the military presence along the wall? The other units at the camp on the outskirts of town? The only reason they're still there and not here is because I'm holding them off. If you don't end this peacefully, they will go into the Striped Zone and take it from you."

"They can try."

"They can and *will* take it from you, Mr. Bracks. They are the military. You and your band of merry men are no match for them. Don't let it come to that. If they do go in and you somehow manage to make it out alive, they will haul your ass into court, and then into prison. Is that what you want?"

"To see you in court again?" Magnus' voice dripped with menace.

Russo was silent for a moment. "Mr. Bracks, I really hope you're not doing all of this just to get at me."

"Well, now, that depends. Is it working?"

"No, it's not. It is only putting innocent lives at risk. But then again, that's your specialty, isn't it, Magnus? Putting people's lives at risk."

"What's that supposed to mean?"

"This phenomenon has *nothing* to do with what happened to you those many years ago on my construction site. That was a different time, a different world. We spent years in and out of court arguing who was at fault, and the courts ruled in my favor. *You* didn't take the necessary precautions that day, Magnus. *You're* the reason you are in that wheelchair, not me and not my company. Do not turn the events of this phenomenon into a tool for your revenge against me. If you do, you will ruin countless people's lives, including your own. Learn from the past, Magnus. Don't let your actions create mistakes that you will then have to live with for the rest of your life."

"You know nothing of my life!" Magnus hissed. "You know nothing of the pain I went through, of the torment of this chair, the sting of those medical bills. All you know is how to stand there on your two perfect legs, smile for the crowd in your expensive suit, and look at your pretty Clean Skin in the mirror. *You* put me in this chair, Russo, and for that I hate you. But you really are an arrogant son of a bitch if you think this is only about you. You're just the face of everything I have fought against my whole life. You aren't worth spit to me. You step a foot over here into the SZ and we will kill you. That's how little you mean to me. So you stay the hell over there in the Clean Zone and leave us be. We don't want you. We don't need you. And the sooner those aliens come back and take you, the better."

"Mr. Bracks—"

"You are a waste of space and you will *not* control our lives any longer! Whatever power you think you had, you just lost it, Russo. I own this shit now. And however this turns out, I promise you, if I go down, I'm taking you with me. All. The. Way."

Bracks hung up, and Russo sat there, listening to the sound of the dial tone.

Richard, using his laptop, spent the morning drafting and redrafting a statement to refute the government's lies. He must be up to his seventh or eighth draft by now. Often he found it rewarding, writing when he was fired up and passionate about something, but this was so different. As much as global warming, pollution, palm oil, and all of those things angered him, he could always write with a clear mind in the pursuit of informing and educating others. But this time, he was actually frightened of his own words. What reaction would they ignite? Could more people be hurt or killed as an indirect result of his reports? Was he better off staying silent? Or was it important that the people have another voice to equalize the playing field? Was it important that Dr. Pellan not be victimized for ultimately doing a good deed?

"Coffee?" Abbie asked as she walked down a few steps into the basement.

He looked up at her and gave a defeated smile. "I think that might be a good idea. I need all the help I can get."

She smiled back and motioned for him to come out of the basement.

"Kaitlyn sleeping?" he asked Abbie as he entered the kitchen.

"Yeah, she's been trying to sleep when Charlie does," Abbie told him, then glanced over her shoulder. "Those kids are 'round-the-clock work, huh?"

Richard chuckled. "Definitely not for the faint of heart."

"She's handling it well, though, given her mother's not with her. She's frightened, but she's stronger than she looks."

"Yeah," Richard nodded, "I can't imagine how tough this must be on her. Being a teen mom is one thing, but to do it under these circumstances is another."

They exchanged a look of agreement as Abbie sat down at the kitchen table opposite him.

"How's the new report going?" she asked.

"Not so great," he confessed, taking a sip of his coffee, contemplating things. "Which is strange, you know? Writing narrations for my reports has always been my thing, and taking up causes is what I do. But this? This has shaken me a little. I guess I've learned a valuable lesson on the real power of words."

"You told the truth," Abbie said, studying him. "There's no shame in that. You haven't learned the power of words, you've learned the power of the truth. Sometimes it hurts."

Richard gazed back at her. She was a virtual stranger, yet somehow he felt like he had known her for a long time. It was odd, he thought, to feel so comfortable in her company after so little time.

"You seem older than your age," he mused.

Abbie smiled and shrugged. "I'm a swim coach. I teach kids. Let's just say I quickly learned that I had to be the adult."

Richard broke into a soft laugh. She grinned and laughed in return.

"God," he shook his head, "I can't remember the last time I laughed."

"Me either," she said with a warm smile.

"So you're studying?" he asked.

"You've done your research."

"Actually, no. I saw some textbooks in the living room before."

She took a sip of her coffee. "I was studying literature, but I've changed things around so that I can become an English teacher."

"Yeah?"

She nodded. "For a while there, I didn't really know what I wanted to do with my life. But teaching the swim classes made me realize that I like being around kids. I like seeing them learn and evolve." She shrugged. "My dad taught Little League. We used to go and watch the games on the weekend. And my mother always had her nose in a book. I guess I inherited my path in life from them." A melancholy briefly touched her features. "Life has a funny way of taking you places."

"That it does. So you're studying by correspondence?"

"I was supposed to move to the city, but my father got laid off from his job. He sold farm equipment, but the drought slowed things down. Some blamed the Clivecorp plant for affecting things," she shrugged. "Anyway, it was cheaper to stay here, work and study part-time." She paused, her mind ticking over for a moment. "And I guess a part of me didn't want to leave. This town is all I've known."

He nodded. "It's a big world out there. It can look a little scary when you're watching it from the outside, but once you're in it, you just become part of it. Symbiotic."

"And you?" she asked. "Did you always know that you wanted to be a journalist?"

Richard nodded. "I did. Well, at least from high school. When I was a kid I wanted to be a marine biologist. But yeah, I developed a love of travel and a fascination for people and animals. Mother nature just amazed me," he said. "It's such a wondrous thing, but I also realized that it could be a horrible thing. Mother nature has the power to be devastating. And then I learned that man often made things worse. As I got older, I saw that bad things were happening to people and animals around the globe, and I wanted to do something about it. I thought, hey, mother nature can be cruel and there's not much we can do about that, but why do we need to mess it up and make things worse? I guess it just evolved from there."

"And the environmentalist was born," she nodded, her eyes thoughtful. "So what's been your biggest story?"

"Besides this?" he smiled.

"Well, yeah," she smiled back, maybe blushing a little.

He turned his chair around slightly and rested his head back against the wall and trawled through his memory. "The biggest one, that I was at ground zero for, was probably the oil spill in the Gulf of Mexico."

"The Deepwater Horizon tragedy?" Abbie said.

"Yeah. The deaths of those workers was terrible enough," he continued, "but seeing the damage done to the ecosystem there afterward was horrifying. It was a fucking disaster," he shook his head. "In between reports I volunteered to help clean things up. I mean, seeing animals covered in this thick, brown crap, the dead ones washing up on the shore . . . it was just awful. I felt so ashamed to be a human, seeing what we'd done to them. Then there's the health effects on the humans themselves, living in the area, that they're still discovering today." He shook his head again. "Did you know there're over 27,000 abandoned oil wells in the Gulf of Mexico? Some dating back to the 1940s? And tens of thousands have been reported as badly sealed." He shook his head again, sighing sadly. "Man is sometimes a monster . . . but that said, I do remember the number of people who turned up to help. People from across the world, donating their time to try and help sort out the mess."

Abbie nodded, looking down into her cup. He watched her a moment.

"Sometimes humans disappoint me," he said, "but sometimes they surprise me too. Sometimes they give me hope . . . Like you did."

She looked up at him again.

"You rushing out to help Kaitlyn against the mob was like all those people coming down to the beach to help the animals."

She stared at him. "And like you for exposing the truth the government was trying to hide. For trying to reunite people before it was too late."

He smiled a little sadly. "I'm not sure my actions can be held in the same regard, Abbie. So far I've caused more damage than good."

She opened her mouth to respond, but her words were interrupted by a knock at the door. She instantly tensed and they locked eyes.

"Go to the basement," she said, standing up.

She headed for the front door, but Richard couldn't bring himself to hide. Instead, he moved up behind her, but stood out of sight of the open doorway.

"Hello?" Abbie said, then seemed to pause as though she

recognized the person.

"Ms. Randell?" a familiar voice said. "You don't know me but I—"

Richard pulled back the door, startling Abbie. "Dr. Pellan?"

Lysart was both shocked and relieved to see Richard inside Abbie Randell's house.

"Mr. Keene?"

Richard grabbed Lysart's shirt and pulled him forward. "Get inside, quick!"

Abbie closed the door and stared wide-eyed at the two of them.

"What are you doing here?" Richard asked.

"I could ask you the same question?"

"I came to see that Abbie and Kaitlyn were alright," Richard told him.

Lysart nodded. "And I thought you might. Or rather, *hoped*. I came to see if Abbie had heard from you."

"Are you alright? Have you seen the news?" Richard asked.

Lysart nodded. "It would seem I am a wanted man."

"I'm sorry, Dr. Pellan. I had no idea things would turn out like this."

"Don't be, Mr. Keene. I saw your report. It was done well. I would have said nothing differently. You had no idea the reaction would be this, nor did I. But it is what it is, and we must face the consequences."

"What are you going to do?" Richard asked him.

"I don't know. That is why I was looking for you."

Richard nodded, then glanced at Abbie. "I'm sorry, Abbie, but would you mind if Dr. Pellan stays for a few moments to discuss things?"

Abbie nodded. "We can't leave him out on the street now, can we?"

"No one recognized you on the way here?" Richard asked to check.

"No, I don't think so," he said taking off his hat and unwrapping the scarf from around his neck and chin. He watched as Richard moved to the window and peered out.

"There're a lot of unfriendlies around here," Richard told him.

"Yes. So it would seem."

Richard ushered him through to the kitchen and Abbie poured him a coffee.

Lysart sipped the drink, relieved at the warmth rolling into his empty belly, closing his eyes briefly to try and hold onto the feeling.

"So what do we do?" Richard asked.

"I have no idea. You, it would seem, have choices. They only want to question you. You could hand yourself in and they may not charge you with anything too serious. I, on the other hand ... If I turn myself in I will go to prison. Or, who knows? Perhaps I might even disappear altogether."

"Surely not?" Richard asked.

"I am a wanted man, Mr. Keene. You are merely guilty by association." Lysart pulled out a folded newspaper from the inside pocket of his bulky coat and laid it on the table. The tabloid headline glared out at them:

Pellan's Theory Erupts into Chaos!

"The phenomenon has a name," Lysart told them. "Pellan's Theory is everywhere. Some are starting to call the visitation the Pellan Phenomenon. This event which has taken place, this event that has stolen our loved ones, that has marked us, this *evil,* is now known by the name of Pellan."

Richard sighed heavily and sat back in his chair. Lysart glanced at Abbie's troubled face as she stood leaning against the counter watching them.

"What do you know of this Magnus Bracks?" Lysart asked, turning back to Richard. "What is behind this madman's thinking?"

Richard shrugged. "I don't know much, but Abbie might know something."

The woman tensed as they both looked at her.

"I know very little," she said, shaking her head. "Josh is the one who has been going to their meetings."

Lysart turned to Richard. "We expected a reaction. We expected people to be angry. But we expected that anger to die down when they realized the importance of reuniting with their loved ones. This Magnus Bracks is trying to keep that anger burning. He is fanning the flames of ignorance."

"I know," Richard nodded, "but how do we stop him?"

"We can't," Lysart shrugged. "We are Clean Skins. We are the enemy now. And if we go out there and someone recognizes us, who knows what they'll do. Whether they deal with us themselves, or whether they hand us over to the government, either way, we're in deep trouble, Mr. Keene."

The three let silence sit between them.

"I'll call Josh," Abbie suggested. "We'll find out what he knows, see if he can help in some way."

"You think he'll actually help us?" Richard asked skeptically.

Lysart saw a hopeless look cross Abbie's face.

"I don't know."

"Another one?" The young Clean Skin girl that Lysart had seen on the news stood in the kitchen doorway. She seemed to pause as she studied Lysart's face. "Pellan's Theory," she murmured. "You're Dr. Pellan?"

Lysart's shoulders sank as he turned to lock eyes with Richard.

"It's okay, Kaitlyn." Abbie moved toward her and ushered her out of the room. "I'll explain everything."

The two women left and Lysart heard their footsteps padding up the staircase he'd seen when he'd first entered the house. He raised his eyebrows at Richard.

"What are we doing here?" he asked the reporter. "It is dangerous for them."

The reporter seemed to sigh and nod, and his eyes fell guiltily onto the table in front of him. "I know, but like you said, we caused this. We need to face the consequences." He looked determined. "If we're going to stay anywhere, it might as well be here in the eye of the storm."

"I think the eye has passed now," Lysart said quietly. "The storm has begun to ravage us."

Mayor Russo eyed the chief carefully.

"Are you sure about this?"

Blackstone looked resolute. "Deputy Cann is AWOL. I need to find out what happened to him. The Striped Ones aren't contagious, so I'll be safe. And careful. I'm not stupid."

Russo couldn't help the nervous look he knew was pasted across his face.

"We give this a try," Blackstone told him. "Me, *alone*, trying to talk some sense into him. As far as I'm aware, Magnus has no beef with me."

"And if he decides he does? Guilty by association and all that?"

The chief shrugged. "Then we deal with that then. But if you want to keep this quiet and out of the press, then we need to keep the military out of it. This is our last chance to do that. If it doesn't work, then we have no option but to send the military in. We need to end this, mayor. This *cannot* go on any longer."

"Alright," Russo said, resigned. "Give it a try. But the second you sense trouble, get the hell out of there and back into the Clean Zone."

"Will do." With that, Blackstone tipped his hat and left.

Abbie paced the living room waiting for Josh to come. Richard and Dr. Pellan waited in the basement. Given Josh's reaction to the reporter, Abbie could just imagine the reaction if he saw Dr. Pellan there too. She'd sent Kaitlyn upstairs and told her not to leave her room. This conversation had to be between her and Josh alone. One Striped One to another.

"Hey," he appeared at her screen door, giving her a little fright.

She spun around and quickly walked over to let him in.

"What's going on? I got your message?" he asked, stepping inside.

She noted the dark circles under his eyes, the three welts running down his chin, his dirty hair.

"Have you been taking your meds?"

Josh stared at her with a look that said it was none of her business.

In the background she saw a car drive down her street. Langdon and Trent were within, along with a couple of other younger guys. They were armed, and proudly displaying the fact.

Josh glanced around to see what she was looking at. He turned back to her. "What did you want?"

"I just wanted to know the latest. What's going on with Magnus and Roy?" She fidgeted nervously.

Josh's narrowed eyes were wary. He dropped his eyes to her hands, then he glanced around the house, through to the kitchen, then up the staircase. "Where's the reporter?"

"In the basement," she figured the truth was the best bet. "He promised to stay hidden and he has been."

"Abbie," Josh stepped closer, lowering his voice, "you need to get him out of here, seriously. Magnus has been on a call with the mayor and he's riled up."

"The mayor?" she asked. "What did he say?"

"He asked Magnus to stand down."

"I take it he didn't agree?"

Josh looked at her strangely. "Of course not! This is Magnus we're talking about. He thinks it's great. He had the mayor make a personal call to *beg* him to behave. Magnus is ruffling feathers and he is loving it! People are listening to him, the *mayor* is listening to him. He's got the Clean Skins scared and he's got reporters from around the world calling him. Magnus has become the figurehead of the Striped Ones!"

"Are you kidding? He's not the figurehead of me. Do people think what he's doing is right?" Abbie couldn't believe it, her face contorting in disbelief.

Josh nodded, a little disbelief showing on his face too. "With those seven stripes, Magnus is the most Striped. If the aliens come back, then he is probably the safest person in the whole town. He's wearing his stripes with pride. He's the sickest *and* he's the safest. He says that's why he's destined to lead the Striped Ones, because he knows what it's like to suffer, and he'll be the one left standing in the end."

"Jesus Christ," Abbie muttered, lowering her head into her hands.

"They heard people were trying to flee, so he's got guys out there, armed, securing the Clean Skin border, making sure no one else tries to cross over. That's what that patrol was about just then. Someone ratted out a Clean Skin hiding in this house and they dragged him out, beat the crap out of him and dumped him at the wall." Josh started pacing the carpet.

"Oh my God, Josh!" Abbie stared at him wide-eyed. "Please tell me you weren't part of it?"

Josh looked at her, but darted his eyes away. "Of course I wasn't . . . I mean, I was there, but I didn't do anything."

"Josh!"

"What could I do, Abbie?" he shouted, holding his hands out questioningly. "Magnus ordered me to go along. There was a group of them, I couldn't stop it happening! There was only one of me."

"Enough, Josh!" Abbie raised her voice too. "This has to stop! You're getting in too deep!"

"You're right! I *am* in too deep. I can't get out now. They're . . ." He paced agitatedly. "Austin and the guys, they're all jacked up on stuff that's keeping them awake and alert."

"What kind of stuff?"

"I don't know. Austin knew this drug dealer, a striped guy, so he got stuff to keep everyone awake and wired."

"On edge you mean," she said, studying him. "Have you been taking it too?"

Josh averted his eyes.

"Josh?"

"I had to. They were all standing around, watching me. I had to!"

"Goddamn it, Josh!"

"I told you, I'm keeping an eye on them!" he pleaded with her. "I have to know what they're up to. If they find out about mom, I can warn her, get to her before they do."

"Josh—"

"No, Abbie!" he said harshly. "There are whispers about how a small section to the south-west isn't protected by the military. Some people headed out that way and they haven't been seen again. That means the military didn't send them back, and that must be because they weren't caught. Do you understand? People can still escape Victoryville and head out into the countryside. Magnus' focus is on the Clean Skin border right now, he wants to see what the mayor will do after their little conversation. Once the border is under control, they're going to start running patrols to see if they can find the gap. They're talking about building a wall out there and fortifying the whole area. So I have a small window to get mom out if needed. I just need to stick close to them for now to see if this will blow over, or whether I need to get her the hell out of the SZ!"

"Are you kidding me? Build a wall? They're going to cage us in? They're going to do *exactly* what they're hating the Clean Skins for doing to us?"

Josh shrugged. "They're marking their turf while they can, while there is confusion and chaos around the globe over whether the aliens will be back."

"Do they really think they're going to get away with it? Forget the mayor or the state governor. Do they really think that the President of the United States and the military will just sit back and let them declare their own territory?"

"Come on, Abbie, they're leaving us for the aliens! The president doesn't give a shit what happens here in Victoryville!"

"Try to carve out your own independent little corner of the

country, and I bet he would!"

"Abbie, everything's changed. The same rules don't apply. This phenomenon has changed *everything*. We're not living in a normal world any more. These aliens are going to come back and fucking destroy us. Life as we know it is gone, Abbie!"

"No, Josh. It's only gone if we let it go."

"Abbie, you haven't been out there. I mean *really* out there. You have *no* idea!"

"Then take me to the next meeting!" she blurted.

Josh paused, staring at her, aghast. "No way, Abbie. It's not safe."

"Screw you, Josh! I'm sick of you insinuating that I'm naive, that I know nothing about life because I've never left this town. You tell me I don't know what's going on out there, then show me! Let me see for myself."

"Abbie, it's too dangerous for you."

"Why? Because I'm a woman?"

"No, because you're harboring Clean Skins!"

Abbie's face tightened. "Magnus doesn't know about Richard and he said Kaitlyn could stay."

"For now!" Josh told her firmly. "He said she could stay '*for now*'. They want the Clean Skins out of the SZ, Abbie. If you try and stand in their way . . . striped kid or not . . ."

Abbie felt a cold sensation wash over her. "Have they said anything? About me? About Kaitlyn?"

Josh averted his eyes.

"Josh, you would warn me, wouldn't you?"

He spun his face back to hers. "Of course!"

"So what did they say?"

"Look, it's just not safe for Clean Skins here. You should tell Kaitlyn to get out. *And* that damn reporter! Tell them to jump that wall or sneak out into the countryside. They'll be fine."

"But is it safe for them to leave? You said they're guarding the wall. What if they get spotted?"

"Well, that reporter got in somehow. He can get them out the way he came."

"I crossed over before Magnus declared his little war," Richard said, emerging from the basement.

Abbie glanced at him nervously. Josh did too, but with harder eyes.

"Things were still relatively calm when I snuck across," Richard continued, moving calmly, cautiously toward them. "I think there's little chance of me going anywhere now. Not after that story and my 'Wanted' face splashed across the news."

Abbie looked at Josh and saw him harden his jaw. He pointed accusingly at Richard. "You're putting everyone at risk by being here."

Richard shook his head, using that even-toned voice of his. "But no one knows I'm here, Josh. Except you. If no one knows, then there is no way I can cause trouble for Abbie."

"They know Kaitlyn is here!" Josh hissed at Abbie. "If they come for her, they'll find him, and what do you think they'll do then?"

"They would harm the man who sought to free them with the truth?" Dr. Pellan stepped out now too. Both Abbie and Richard looked hesitantly at him.

"Jesus, Abbie!" Josh cried. "You got him here too?" He spun back to face her. "What the hell are you doing?"

"He's the one who uncovered the truth, Josh!" she said. "And Rick is the one who brought the story to the people! We would still be in the dark if it wasn't for them. We owe them something."

"Rick?" Josh queried.

Abbie frowned, confused that out of everything she just said, her use of "Rick" was what Josh chose to focus on.

Richard stepped closer. "Do you have any idea what the mayor or the military are going to do now?"

"You were eavesdropping?" Josh accused.

"Sorry," Richard shrugged, "I'm a reporter. Old habits die hard. You mentioned Magnus pissing off the mayor?"

"So?"

"So, if the mayor can't control this, you don't think they'll send the military in?"

"The military have been through here and they left."

"That was before," Richard told him.

"If this isn't contained, they will send in the big guns," Dr. Pellan said gently to Josh. "And the military don't tend to ask nicely twice. I'm surprised they've waited this long."

Josh's face flashed concern as his eyes darted across the three of them.

"Mr. Keene and I were talking," Dr. Pellan said. "We think it might be a good idea if we post a video of our own, asking for restraint from both sides. We don't want people thinking we agree with what is happening. We must stand against it. We must voice our opinions, a sense of reason."

"But won't they be able to trace you somehow?" Abbie asked worriedly.

"I have ways," Richard told her. "Dummy accounts and the like. It's a necessary tool of the trade sometimes when chasing stories of this caliber."

"Haven't you caused enough trouble?" Josh asked him. "You wanna go stir up some more?"

"Like what Magnus is doing?"

"Our intention is not to make trouble, Josh," Dr. Pellan

explained. "Just insert a voice of reason. This whole situation has blown out of control."

Josh shook his head and began pacing again.

"When is the next meeting with Magnus?" Abbie asked him.

"Soon," Josh answered, checking his watch. "Just under an hour."

"Take me with you. Rick and Dr. Pellan will stay here and upload their video."

Josh stopped pacing and stared at her.

"Let us help you, Josh," she pleaded softly. "You don't have to handle this on your own."

Richard hit upload and sighed loudly. He cast his eyes to Dr. Pellan, who stared back in contemplation.

"Let's hope this one goes better than the last," Dr. Pellan said, sitting in a chair, resting elbows on his knees, hands clasped.

Richard nodded, leaning against the wall as he sat on the floor of the basement, legs straight out and crossed at the ankles.

"They definitely won't trace us? Identify the location of the upload?" Pellan asked.

"No," Richard shook his head. "They give us dummy accounts that are linked to random servers in different countries for our safety when we're undercover or in war zones."

"War zones?" Pellan questioned.

Richard looked back at him. "Well, right now it feels we're riding pretty close to that here."

Dr. Pellan nodded. "So your server will protect us from the government. But are we safe from the people of Victoryville?"

"That, I don't know."

"The young man was tense," Dr. Pellan noted. "He is on edge."

"It sounds like he's in a little too deep with these guys."

"Victoryville is not safe for anyone, I think. Striped or otherwise."

"No. What do you make of his talk about escaping into the country?"

Dr. Pellan shrugged. "It could be a possibility. But it would be a risk. If we were captured? Military or otherwise . . ."

"Do your family know where you are?" Richard asked, bringing his feet up and resting his arms on his knees.

"No," Pellan looked down. "They know I'm in Victoryville, but they do not know that I've left my apartment."

"When did you last speak to them?"

"I spoke to one of my daughters after it first happened. They were fine. On holiday in Paris with my ex-wife."

Richard nodded to himself. "Have you been separated from your wife long?"

"A while . . . we don't speak much. I've been somewhat estranged from them all. It is something that I have been trying to remedy these past years."

Richard gave the doctor a sympathetic smile.

"And you?" Dr. Pellan asked.

Richard explained about Tom and Margaret and his sister, Sally, back in Iowa, that he had been an orphan.

"How did it happen?" Pellan asked. "Your parents?"

"Their car collided head on with an overtired truck driver. My mother died on impact and my father and older brother died later in hospital."

"You weren't in the car?"

"I was five when it happened. My grandmother was taking care of me while my parents watched my brother in his school play. They never made it home."

"I'm sorry to hear that, Mr. Keene. That must've have been hard on you."

"It was," he agreed, staring off into the distance. "I just remember my grandmother hugging me, saying how grateful she was that my mother didn't take me with them that night. She raised me for about five years, then she passed. That's when Tom and Margaret adopted me." His mind drifted off as he thought of his parents and Sally, wondering if he would ever see them again. "They've been good to me. Raised me like their own."

Dr. Pellan glanced at the floor, then looked back up at Richard. "No girlfriend? Wife?"

Richard shook his head. "Broke up with the last one about six months ago," he said. "She found someone who would be around for her more often. Apparently, I was so busy trying to save the world that I forgot about her."

Dr. Pellan gave a sympathetic smile. "Ah, passion for one's work. A blessed curse I know too well." Richard looked at him enquiringly and Dr. Pellan elaborated. "I have been married to my work for some time. Why do you think my wife divorced me?"

Richard looked at Pellan with a rueful smile. "Just as well, I guess. Otherwise you might not have been able to work so hard to discover what you did. And then where would we be?"

"Probably still in the Clean Zone and not hunted by all and sundry."

A chuckle escaped Richard's lips. "This is true."

Dr. Pellan sighed, his face falling serious. "I am not so sure about escaping into the country. We could try going through the sewer system again, but we would need to traverse some ground to reach that crossing point."

"The sewer system? That's how you came across?"

"Yes. You didn't?"

"No. I just walked until I found an unguarded section of the barrier, and climbed over."

Pellan stared at him, a smile creeping across his lips, which eventually gave way to laughter. "That would've been a lot cleaner and easier, I think."

Richard laughed back. "Yes, I think so."

Their laughter slowly fell away. "Either way we are not ordinary Clean Skins, Mr. Keene. We are wanted men, wanted Clean Skins. Hiding here in Abbie's basement is the safest option for now. Hopefully the military will step in, order will be restored, and then we can leave."

Richard nodded, his mind wandering to Magnus' meeting. "I wish I could've gone to that meeting with Abbie."

Dr. Pellan's eyes scrutinized him gently. "You feel responsible for her, don't you?"

Richard pondered this. "I wouldn't say responsible for. She's been taking care of herself. But . . . I don't know. I shone a spotlight on her, brought her to everyone's attention. She's a good person. She deserves to be safe. I'd like to see that happen. Maybe the break-up with my ex taught me something after all. Something about not just looking at the bigger picture, but paying attention to the detail as well, to the people around me." His mind tossed around this thought for a moment. "There's nothing I can do about this phenomenon. I can't save Victoryville from this . . . but maybe I can try to protect those who matter most. Abbie, Kaitlyn, Charlie, you."

Dr. Pellan gave small smile and a nod. "Abbie *is* a good person. And brave. Who else would take in the three most well-known Clean Skins in Victoryville?"

Richard stared back at him. "Exactly."

"All we can do is wait and hope, Mr. Keene."

Richard nodded, contemplating Pellan's words, as his mind wandered again to Abbie, and Magnus' meeting.

Abbie tried hard to control the nerves shaking her body. She couldn't stop fidgeting and shoved her hands into the pockets of her jeans to steady them. She had to look cool and calm, like she wanted to be here. It felt somewhat reassuring to have Josh by her side, but at the same time, she was worried. The gun he carried made her nervous. The fact that he'd been keeping himself awake on drugs made her even more nervous. If anything went wrong, what would he do? Would he side with Roy and Austin for self-preservation? If it meant protecting his mother, would he sacrifice her?

Magnus, it would seem, was holed up out the back of the hardware store, in the small warehouse. He'd taken up residency in the office tucked away in the corner. It must've been where he'd recorded the video message. There were about fifty or so people milling about, most with weapons: handguns tucked into jeans, rifles slung over shoulders, hunting knives strapped to thighs. She could understand this response if it were the aliens they were planning to fight, but it wasn't. They were preparing to fight their own kind.

They all seemed to stare at her: some curiously, some suspiciously, some threateningly. She was a new face to many and she certainly didn't look hungry for a fight like the rest of them. She tried to keep her expression even, showing no emotion or judgment. She recognized some of the faces, people she'd seen around town, but as she looked at them now they seemed like total strangers.

"What's she doing here?" Austin asked, giving her the once-over.

"She wants to be part of this," Josh answered.

"Yeah?" Austin asked, his voice dripping with skepticism. "She still got that Clean Skin at her house?"

Josh glanced at Abbie, unsure what to say.

"You mean the mother of that striped kid?" Abbie responded. "Yeah, she's still there. Along with her striped son."

Austin grunted, then motioned for Josh to follow him, and the two disappeared out to the front of the hardware store.

Abbie stood there on her own and surveyed the scene. She could see Magnus in the office to her right; the blinds were up, affording her a view through its window. He was deep in discussion with Roy Kenny, who looked armed to the teeth. Abbie recalled Josh's story of Roy shooting that soldier, and tried hard to wipe the disgust from her face.

She glanced around at the others, saw a mixture of ages. The youngest looked about fourteen, the oldest in his seventies. There was only a scattering of women. She saw maybe four or five with weapons, although there were a few more posted at a temporary cooking station, serving up meals like it was some kind of honorable war effort they were engaged in.

She saw Langdon emerge from the doorway of a small room to the left. As the door swung open and closed, she could've sworn she saw Deputy Cann inside. It was only brief, a flash, but she thought she saw him sitting on a chair in there. *What was Deputy Cann doing here?* Something about it seemed odd. The way he sat, his head hunched over. *Was he here voluntarily? Or was he here against his will?*

"You're new?" she heard a woman's voice say behind her. Abbie turned to see Wendy standing there, her dark hair pulled back in a long plait, the dark eye makeup taking the smoky look to the extreme.

"Yeah," Abbie said, then held out her hand. "Abbie Randell."

"I know who you are," Wendy nodded. "You're the one that took in that Clean Skin."

Abbie dropped her hand. "Yeah, I did."

"So what are you doing here, then, if you're a sympathizer?"

"Excuse me?"

The girl just stared back at her.

"I'm here because I care about what happens to Victoryville," Abbie told her, then glanced around the room again. "It's my home."

"Your home is striped territory now."

"Yeah. And in case you haven't noticed, I'm a Striped One too."

"I see that," Wendy motioned to Abbie's stripe. "Only one though."

Abbie stared at the three welts rolling down the girl's chin and neck. "So?"

"So, out of all of us, you should be the most careful. If those aliens come back and take the Clean Skins, and they decide they want more, who do you think they'll come back for next?"

Abbie stared at her, confused.

"You single stripes will be at the top of their list," Wendy told her. "And being a single stripe, you're at the bottom of ours."

"And . . ." Abbie said firmly, wanting her to get to the point.

The girl shrugged. "You should be real careful about who

you side with. Side with the Clean Skins now and when they're gone, who's going to have your back? No one. Side with us, then we'll do what we can to protect you."

"Yeah? And what's that?" Abbie turned to face her. "Whatever did this marked us and stole our healthy while the might of our military sat helpless. What is it, exactly, that you think you can do to protect me?"

"Who said I'm talking about when the aliens come back?" Wendy's dark eyes were hard. "We might have a long wait before they show up again. I'm talking about watching your back now. Not too many people 'round here are happy that you're harboring that Clean Skin, you know." The girl waved her arm around the room. "You'd be wise to show our group a little more respect."

"Is that a threat?" Abbie glared at her.

Wendy stepped closer, putting her face up in Abbie's. She was slightly taller and somewhat imposing with the rifle over her shoulder. "No, that's just a piece of advice." The girl stared at her to make a point. Then she gave Abbie a smirk, turning to head over to where Josh and Austin now stood huddled and talking by the food table. Abbie watched as the girl threw her arm around Josh's neck, glancing over her shoulder at Abbie once more.

Abbie shook her head, blowing out a short sharp laugh. *So that was what* that *was about.* The girl had her eye on Josh and wanted Abbie to stay away.

"Don't mind Wendy," Roy Kenny said beside her. Abbie spun to face him. "She's a passionate girl, that one." He smiled, showing his yellowed, crooked teeth. "But her heart's in the right place. She's got her loyalties in line."

"Let me guess, and I don't?" Abbie's frustration was starting to boil over.

"I don't know, do you?" Roy stared at her, the left side of his face giving a twitch every now and then. She wondered if it was related to one of the four stripes marking him.

"Look, I'm here because I care about my community. Why is everyone second-guessing my intentions?"

"This has been going on for over a week now. What took you so long to show up?"

Abbie stared at him, searching for an answer. "Josh was coming. He was relaying the information. He told me to stay at home."

"How's that Clean Skin of yours?"

Abbie didn't answer him.

"She still there?" Roy asked, staring at her, twitching.

Again she didn't answer him.

"You realize Magnus has declared the SZ a Clean Skin free zone?"

"Yeah, I saw the video."

"And she's still there with you?"

"She's fourteen years old, Roy. What would you have me do with her and her newborn son? Her *striped*, newborn son. Kick them out on the streets?"

Roy shrugged, pouting his lips. "Not my problem. And she shouldn't be your problem neither."

Abbie fought hard to bite her tongue from saying something she shouldn't. She saw Langdon disappear into the room off to the left. She watched carefully and caught another glimpse of Deputy Cann. She saw him, saw his face this time. His *bloodied* face.

And the deputy saw her.

"What are you doing with the deputy?" she asked.

Roy moved to block her vision of the room. "Ain't no deputy here."

"I just saw him—"

"No, you really didn't," Roy said firmly, his face in hers, his eyes threatening. He pulled back and sniffed, looking around the warehouse. "Ain't nobody seen the deputy for a while now." His eyes came back to hers and a shiver went through her bones. "It's good that you're here, Abbie. *Finally*," he told her, leaning in again as if telling her a secret. "But as long as that Clean Skin is in your house, your loyalties are divided. As long as that Clean Skin is in your house, no one here will trust you. You understand?"

He didn't wait for a response. Before the words had even settled into her brain, he was already walking away.

She glanced at the closed door of the room they were keeping Deputy Cann in, then her eyes slowly, worriedly, scanned the warehouse again, her body beginning to shake with shock. Her eyes fell on a young boy walking past the open roller door leading to the back parking lot. She froze and her mouth fell agape. It was Justin from her swimming class. A twelve-year-old boy walking around with a shotgun slung over his shoulder. She went to go after him, but Josh caught her arm.

"What'd Roy want?" he demanded.

She looked around, then back to the roller door, but Justin had gone. She turned back to Josh. "They have Deputy Cann here."

Josh stared, but didn't answer.

"I saw his face, they beat him," she said.

Again Josh stared, guilt sliding over his face, but he said nothing.

"You knew? Jesus, Josh!"

"Cool it," he said quietly, "don't create a scene."

"You have the deputy hostage!" she hissed quietly.

"No," he said, then hesitated. "There's nothing he can do.

He's outnumbered. They're just keeping him out of the way so he doesn't cause trouble."

"So, he's a hostage then?"

Josh and Abbie turned at the sound of laughter to see Wendy and Austin huddled and talking, their eyes fixed on her.

"Why do I feel like the enemy here?" she muttered.

"This is why I tried to tell you to stay away. They don't like that Kaitlyn is in your house, Abbie. I gotta listen to their comments all the time. I'm guilty for hanging out with you. It puts *me* at risk. If they think I side with you, then they don't trust me. I'm walking a fine line here."

"You realize they've enlisted twelve-year-old boys, don't you? I just saw a kid from my swimming class with a rifle over his shoulder."

"It's out of my hands, Abbie!" he hissed. "I'm keeping an eye on things, but right now there's nothing I can do to help anyone."

Just then a young guy, who'd been manning the front of the store when Abbie arrived, ran into the warehouse and up to Roy Kenny. He whispered something in Roy's ear, then Roy swiftly turned and ran into Magnus' office. Abbie and Josh watched them exchange words, then Magnus motioned to the blinds. Roy moved over and pulled them down, then the door to the office closed. Abbie looked at Josh. His eyes were warily fixed on the closed office door.

"What's going on?" Abbie asked.

"Don't know," he said. "Maybe you should go."

Abbie glanced around the room again and was inclined to agree. They didn't want her there. And the truth was, Josh was right. If they didn't trust her, then it would affect his place with them, and it wasn't right to put Josh's life at risk—or his mother's—just to satisfy her own curiosities.

She nodded, "Alright, I'll go."

"You want me to walk you?"

"No, I'll be fine. Stay and find out what's going on." She went to leave, but then stopped. "Don't let them hurt the deputy. And look out for that young kid, Justin. Alright?"

Josh nodded, then motioned for her to leave as he moved over to another group of armed men. As Abbie turned to go, she caught eyes with Wendy. The girl raised her index finger to her mouth. At first Abbie thought Wendy was telling her to be quiet, but then Wendy traced her finger down over her chin and neck, reminding Abbie that she was a single stripe.

Abbie stared at Wendy's three stripes, and thought of Josh's three stripes, then she turned and left. As she did, she gave the door to the room the deputy was being held in one last glance, hoping he would be alright.

Only a couple of guys milled about on the street outside, keeping watch. Otherwise the streets were empty. She shoved her hands in her jeans pockets again, as they still rattled with nerves. *What the hell were they going to do to the deputy?* And what the hell was *she* going to do about it? She felt wracked with guilt for walking away, but what could she do against all those armed people. She started to understand how Josh must've felt when they'd shot that soldier or beat that Clean Skin. Helpless. Outnumbered. Concerned with self-preservation. Survival.

But she could call the chief. She could tell him what she knew.

As she passed by the gate between the zones, she eyed the soldiers atop the barricade, as they watched her in turn. They looked a little edgy. It was then that she made out Chief Blackstone standing with them, and she wondered why. She paused a moment, staring at him. Did she run and tell him? She looked back to the hardware store and saw the guys on guard keeping a watch on her.

Maybe the chief already knew Magnus was holding the deputy? Maybe that's why that young guy ran in and told Roy. The glimpse she'd had of Deputy Cann's bloodied face flashed in her mind, but she let it go. He was still alive, and it looked like the chief was getting ready to go in. *Let him handle it*, she thought.

She turned her eyes away from the chief and the soldiers at the gate. She thought it strange that the soldiers remained in their bio-suits. It was as though they wanted to keep their faces hidden. She found it a little unnerving, and somewhat ironic that the streetlights reflected off their face masks to give them an alien appearance. It only made her think of Wendy's words, about how the single stripes could be next on the list of potential vanishings after the Clean Skins.

"Hey, Abbie." The voice made her jump. She turned to see Austin jogging out from the shadows of the parking lot behind the warehouse.

She stared at him. "What do you want?"

"It's not safe to walk by yourself."

She eyed his tall, gym-toned frame. "I'm fine," she said, and began walking toward her home.

"No," he said, moving in step with her. "I'll walk you."

She glanced sideways at him, but kept walking.

"If you're here to make threats, don't bother. Wendy and Roy have done that already."

Austin gave a little chuckle. "Yeah, Wendy's got a thing for Josh. What's going on with you two, anyway?"

She looked at him. "Me and Josh?"

Austin nodded.

"Nothing. We're just neighbors," Abbie said. It was the truth, but she also thought it best to ensure a little distance was kept between her and Josh, especially in front of Austin.

Austin nodded in contemplation. "I think he likes you."

Abbie didn't respond.

"I mean," Austin shrugged, "Wendy's all over him and he hasn't given in yet. The other guys think he's crazy for not tapping that. With all the shit that's been going down, who'd turn down a lay, right?"

"Josh can do what he likes."

"Yeah, but he won't," he said. "He's protective of you."

Abbie glanced at Austin. "He's just looking out for a fellow Striped One."

"He's gotta be careful, though, you know. That boner he's got for you could land him in trouble."

Abbie stopped and stared at Austin. "Why? Because I have a Clean Skin in my house and he shouldn't be consorting with my kind? I thought you weren't here to make threats?"

"I'm not," Austin stopped as well, turning to face her. "I don't make threats, Abbie. I make promises."

"So then what are you promising?" Abbie demanded, folding her arms.

"Shit is getting real around here," Austin told her, his two angry red stripes standing out on his olive skin despite the lack of light. "This Striped Zone has finally got some leadership and the Clean Zone is worried. If shit is going to go down between the two, then we need Josh. We need his loyalty. You can't get in the way of that."

"I'm not getting in the way of that."

"Yes, you are. You're protecting that Clean Skin, and Josh is protecting you. That can't work. He can't fight the Clean Skins and protect you at the same time. He has to choose. And the only way he can choose you is if you dump that Clean Skin bitch and her kid. He can't have it both ways. So you're either with him or against him."

"You can't tell me what to do, Austin. You can't tell anyone what to do. This is Victoryville, USA. We have free speech, we have rights."

"Not any more. The aliens took that away when they stole our healthy. What we have now is two sides fighting for survival."

"No, we have three sides," Abbie told him. "The Striped Ones, the Clean Skins, and those of us who want to live in peace!" She turned to stalk off, but Austin grabbed her arm and yanked her back so violently she almost lost her feet.

"I haven't finished!"

"What's wrong with you?" she said, trying to pull her arm from his grip, but he didn't relent. "How can you do this?"

"This is *my* town!" he spat.

"Yeah? Well, it's my town too!"

"Those Clean Skins tried to hand us over to the aliens. Well, fuck them!"

"Not all Clean Skins!"

"This is your last warning!" he hissed, squeezing her arm so tightly it made her gasp. "Get rid of her or we will take *both* of you out!" He pushed and released her arm at the same time, and she fell to the ground. He stepped toward her and spat at her viciously. It landed on her cheek and she turned her face in disgust. She held her body still, her heaving chest the only movement, and watched from the corner of her eye as Austin glared, then turned and walked away.

Richard and Dr. Pellan turned to the basement stairs on hearing the front door of the house closing. They glanced at each other then slowly, carefully, ascended to find out who it was. Richard pressed his ear to the door and listened. He couldn't hear any voices, so he figured it must be Abbie returning from the meeting. He slowly twisted the handle and opened the door a crack. He heard movement coming from the kitchen. The front door was closed, so he decided to take the risk.

He opened the door wide enough to slip out through the crack, then quietly made his way to the kitchen. He peered in and saw Abbie standing at the counter with her back to the door. She was wiping her face with paper towel.

"Abbie?" he said quietly.

She jumped in fright and turned around to him. Her eyes shone wet with tears.

His body instantly tensed. "What's wrong? What happened?"

She turned away, holding the back of her hand up to her nose. He heard her sniffing.

"Abbie?" he said softly, moving to place his hand on her shoulder and turn her around. "What's wrong?"

She looked at him as tears spilled down her cheeks.

"Hey..." he said gently. He took hold of both her shoulders, trying to peer into her face which she had lowered to the floor. "Abbie, tell me what's wrong."

She let out an audible sob and he felt her shoulders shake.

He pulled her into a hug. "It's alright. It's okay," he tried to soothe her, as she cried into his T-shirt.

"Is she alright?" Pellan's concerned voice came from the doorway.

Abbie pulled away from Richard, her face wet and flushed pink with emotion.

"What happened, Abbie?" Richard asked, one hand still resting on her shoulder.

"They threatened me."

"Who?" Richard asked.

"All of them," she said, wiping her face. "They want Kaitlyn out. Austin said that if I didn't get rid of her, they'd take us both out."

"Was it just talk, or did he mean it?" Richard asked.

"He meant it," Abbie said, rubbing her arm, which was red and beginning to bruise.

"He did that to you?" Richard asked, eyeing her arm. "Austin?"

She nodded, wiping her cheek with the paper towel again. "He spat in my face after pushing me to the ground."

Dr. Pellan sighed loudly and shook his head.

Abbie gave a cough, wheezing a little, then fished through her bag for something. She brought out a Ventolin spray and inhaled.

"Are you okay?" Richard asked, realizing that must be the reason for her welt.

She nodded, inhaling another spray.

"What about the group? Did you learn anything from them?" Richard asked, feeling concern brewing within.

"They have boys as young as twelve down there with rifles slung over their shoulders. And they've got the deputy."

"The deputy is helping them?" Pellan asked, astounded.

Abbie shook her head, wiping her face again. "No. They're keeping him locked up in a storeroom."

"Hostage then," Pellan said.

Abbie nodded. "His face was bleeding bad. They'd beaten him."

"Jesus," Richard exhaled.

"Something happened just as I left," Abbie told them. "Roy

ran into the office with Magnus and they closed the blinds and door. Josh and I thought it was a good idea that I leave. I saw the chief at the barrier gate. It looked like he was going in."

"Things are getting serious, now." Pellan shook his head in disbelief.

Richard nodded in agreement, then looked back at Abbie. She returned his glance, as more tears brimmed in her eyes.

"I'm really worried for Kaitlyn," she said. "She's only fourteen, for God's sake. She can't defend herself."

"Why?" Kaitlyn's voice sounded from behind Dr. Pellan.

They all turned.

"Why are you worried?" she asked, staring at them. "Why do I need to defend myself?" Her face paled. "Are they coming for me?"

"Kaitlyn . . ." Abbie stepped forward, but Dr. Pellan cut her off, turning to the girl and wrapping his arm around her.

"It is alright, Kaitlyn. We won't let anything happen to you. As long as you stay here with us, you will be fine."

Kaitlyn looked at Abbie, questioning, pleading.

"We won't let them take you, I promise." Abbie said, determined to keep Kaitlyn and her baby safe.

Charlie's cries rang out from upstairs then, a timely interruption.

"Come," Dr. Pellan gave a warm smile and ushered Kaitlyn toward the stairs. "Introduce to me to your son."

Richard and Abbie watched them disappear, then turned to face each other again.

"Don't go to any more of those meetings," he told her gently.

She shook her head, "I won't." The emotion seemed to twitch at her mouth, and she moved past him into the living room to slump on the couch. He followed, sitting down beside her.

Richard watched as Abbie closed her eyes. "How did this all happen? How did everything turn so bad so quickly?"

He sighed. "Fear . . . fear of whatever did this. Fear of what will happen next. Desperation. It makes people do stupid things."

"They're saying the aliens will come for the Clean Skins next," she told him sadly, dejectedly.

"I know," he nodded, absentmindedly massaging his stubbled chin and jaw.

"Then they say the aliens will come for me, because I'm a single stripe."

He stared at her, at the red welt running down her soft, smooth skin.

She gave a short, sharp laugh. "I'm the lowest of the low. Single stripes aren't worth much in the SZ apparently."

"They're worth more than a Clean Skin," he told her.

She looked at him and smiled, but her face quickly scrunched up with emotion. "What's happening to us?" she gasped, as tears rolled down her cheeks. "Why would the aliens do this? If they wanted to kill us, then why didn't they just do it when they were here the first time?"

Richard moved closer and wrapped his arm around her shoulders, pulling her gently to rest against him.

"I wish I knew, Abbie," he whispered. "I really wish I knew."

Chief Blackstone walked slowly, carefully, toward Roy's Hardware. The soldiers at the gate had reported seeing people coming and going from there. As Blackstone approached, he saw a couple of striped teens standing guard by the door.

Armed.

It didn't surprise him that Roy's Hardware was their hub of operations. If it could be called that: *hub of operations.* Indeed, he doubted a bunch of angry, armed civilians would have much organization about them. But that's also what made them dangerous. Their foolishness. Add to that Roy's paranoia and conspiracy theorising, and on top of that put Magnus' hate for the mayor and what he represented . . . it added up to a whole load of trouble.

He breathed out measuredly and sharpened his focus.

As soon as he'd appeared at the gate, one of the guard teenagers had run inside. Magnus knew he was coming. As he neared the door, he held his arms up in the air peacefully. The two young guys on the door, one white, one black, were ready and suspicious. They raised their guns in Blackstone's direction.

"Trent, Lewis," Blackstone said calmly, recognizing them. "How y'all doing?" If there was a time for Blackstone to lean on his laid-back southern style, now was it.

Trent and Lewis glanced at each other, then returned their eyes to Blackstone.

"What do you want?" Trent barked defensively.

"Wondered if Magnus was around. I wouldn't mind the opportunity to speak with him. You think that's possible?"

Again, they glanced at each other.

"I'm alone, boys," Blackstone told them. "I just want to talk."

"Why you armed then?" Trent questioned.

Blackstone looked down at the SIG Sauer sitting in his holster, then looked back to Trent. "I'm a police officer," he said mildly. "It kinda comes with the job."

Trent eyed him with a scowl, then motioned for Lewis to

go pass the word. All the while Trent aimed his shotgun at Blackstone.

"That yours?" he asked Trent, motioning to the gun he held.

Trent didn't answer, scowl still in place.

"You know how to fire that thing?" Blackstone continued.

Again Trent didn't answer, but the furrow in his brow grew.

"They're pretty dangerous things in the wrong hands, you know," Blackstone said conversationally. "You fire one of those things and kill a man, that ain't ever going to leave you. It's bit like gunpowder residue. It sticks where you least expect it." Blackstone pointed to his own temple. "Right up here."

Trent sniffed and glanced around the streets angrily. His square jaw clenched, his stocky body tensed.

"Still," Blackstone continued, "there're worse things. Like prison. Now there's a nightmare you can't erase."

"SHUT UP, CLEAN SKIN!" Trent shouted and aimed his weapon more firmly in Blackstone's direction.

"Whoa, now!" the chief said, raising his hands higher. "Just making conversation, Trent. I used to play baseball with your old man, you know. I'm sorry he's gone now."

"I said SHUT UP!"

"What's going on here?" Roy Kenny appeared at the door with Lewis by his side.

"Roy," Blackstone gave a nod. "I was just wondering if I can have a word with Magnus."

"Why's that?" Roy asked chin out defiantly, face twitching like it did.

"Well, now, I think you know why. But either way, I think it's best discussed in private." Blackstone motioned to Trent and Lewis.

"Anything you wanna say to Magnus, can be said to me," Roy told him.

"Okay, that's fine," Blackstone nodded. "Can I lower my hands and step inside?"

Roy examined him for a bit, then said, "Let him through."

Trent threw Roy a questioning look, but lowered his gun. Blackstone lowered his hands and went to step forward, but Roy raised his weapon.

"Uh-uh," he said. "You keep your hands high, chief. You can step inside, but you keep your goddamn hands high."

Blackstone paused, but raised his hands again to step inside the hardware store. He found it dimly lit; only one of the store lights was on, the one shining over the cabinet where the guns were usually kept. It looked empty, however, which made Blackstone nervous. He briefly wondered how many guns it had held and how many guns were now out there in people's hands.

No one else seemed to be about. Down at the far end, though, he saw light shining beneath the doors leading to the warehouse out back.

"What you wanna say?" Roy demanded.

Blackstone turned to him, saw the weapon pointed at his gut. "I want this madness to end, Roy. People are getting hurt, people are dying. This ain't going to end well for anyone."

"No, it ain't," Roy agreed. "Those goddamn aliens will make sure of that."

"This is my point. We don't know what the hell we're dealing with here. We've got enough going on, we don't need to turn on each other."

"You Clean Skins already did that when you kicked us out!"

"We're dealing with an alien life-form here, Roy. They didn't know if you were contagious—"

"Not at first, but when they found out, you left that goddamn wall in place to keep us penned up!"

"No, Roy, *I* didn't," Blackstone stared at him. "We found out the same time you did when we saw that reporter's story on the TV. This was way out of our control. This was in the hands of the government and the military. Now, me and the mayor want to bring the wall down and reunite Victoryville. But we can't do that with y'all threatening violence against the Clean Skins and the outsiders."

"Fuck the Clean Skins, chief! Fuck the outsiders! And fuck you!"

"Roy," Blackstone said, retaining his calm, but noticing a pleading tone sliding into his voice. "I've known you a long time. Magnus, too. This is *madness*—"

"Of course it's madness, Earl!" Roy used his first name. "Aliens have come and they have taken our healthy. They have come and raped the Earth, and they will come again. For *you*!" he pointed. "It doesn't matter how far we go back. It's about survival now. You Clean Skins have a death warrant on your heads. And just like when this first happened and you Clean Skins didn't want anything to do with us, well, now we don't want anything to do with you! So stay the hell away!"

"*Goddamn it,* Roy!" Blackstone hissed. "If you don't let us drop that wall, if you don't end this madness, they will send the military in and you will lose. Trust me, no matter what you think you got going on over here with this little group of yours, you *will* lose."

"Is that a threat? You threatening me on striped soil, chief?"

"No, Roy, it's not a threat. I am trying to talk some common sense here. You want to survive, then this is how you do it. Drop your weapons and stand down before you get everyone in here killed."

"I am not handing the SZ over to Russo." Magnus' wet voice wheezed from a darkened aisle. Blackstone turned to see Magnus roll out in his electric wheelchair. He'd been sitting there listening the whole time. Magnus sucked in a breath from his oxygen mask, staring at him, while Langdon Swan moved up behind him, rifle in hand. "So you make sure and tell the mayor that."

"Magnus," Blackstone shook his head helplessly, "what do you think you're going to achieve?"

"Sovereignty of the Victoryville SZ in the wake of this new apocalyptic age. Security. Making sure we're nowhere near you when those aliens come back."

"Do you think that will really matter? What they did, we had no control over, Magnus. Our weapons were useless. Our radars didn't pick them up! If they come back here, there ain't nothing anyone can do."

"It does matter," Magnus wheezed. "If we don't have much time left, then we're going to live it the way we want to. Away from you Clean Skins."

Blackstone sighed, scratching his face as he looked at the ground.

"You can't declare the Victoryville SZ as yours, Magnus. No one in the history of the United States has been able to do that, so what makes you think, with the military lined up outside your door, that you can be the first?"

"When the aliens come back, there won't be any military left," Magnus said plainly. "They're a healthy bunch who passed their physicals. So we just need to hold it until then."

Blackstone gazed at the man before him, sick in more ways than one . . . or, rather, seven.

"Is that all, chief?" Magnus asked. "Is there anything else Russo wanted you to ask because he was too chickenshit to leave the Clean Zone himself?"

"He didn't ask me. I volunteered."

"And why's that?"

"I want to know where my deputy is." Blackstone stared hard, locking eyes with the man, despite the dim lighting.

"Deputy Cann?" Magnus asked, tilting his head to the side as though in contemplation.

"You know of any other deputy I have left?" Blackstone couldn't help the condescension in his voice.

"I can't say I've seen the deputy for some time." Magnus sucked in another breath of oxygen.

"Yeah," Roy agreed quickly. "Some seem to think he hightailed it out of here a couple days back."

"And made it past the military blockade around the town?" The condescension remained in Blackstone's voice.

"Maybe he got lucky, found a gap," Roy shrugged.

"He hasn't been returning my calls."

Roy stared back. "Guess he don't want to be found then."

"If he'd left his post, I don't imagine he would answer, chief," Magnus told him.

"I know my deputy, Magnus. He's a good man. He wouldn't abandon his post."

"So?"

"So that means y'all have killed him, or y'all are holding him somewhere, keeping him out of the way."

"That's quite an accusation, chief," Magnus said.

"It is, but I've been working this job long enough to know when I'm right and when I'm wrong. And this feels right."

"Feelings won't stand up in court now, will they?" Magnus said, a slight smile on his face. "You make sure and tell Russo that, you hear?"

Blackstone continued to stare at Bracks for a moment. "I

want my deputy back. You need to give him back, or they will storm this place."

"Wouldn't that be dangerous for your deputy, though?" Roy asked lightly. "I mean, if you *feel* that he is here somewhere. I mean, he could get hurt. Shot or something. Caught in the crossfire."

Blackstone stared narrowly at Roy Kenny, his eyes filling with hate. "If he was here, that is." The chief's voice dripped with contempt and a seriousness that seemed to increase the intensity in the room.

"I guess that leaves you in a quandary, doesn't it, chief," Magnus said. "You got a choice to make. Send in the big guns and risk your deputy's life. Or stay the hell away and see if he lives."

"This won't be my decision to make," Blackstone told him. "Time is running out before the military will step in and take over Victoryville. You can't control this, Magnus."

"I'm doing alright so far."

"*Goddamn it*, be smart!" Blackstone yelled in frustration. "They will crush you, Magnus! This is the United States military we're talking about. They will *annihilate* you!"

Magnus wheeled his chair as close to the chief as he could, and stared up. "I told Russo that if I go down, I'm taking him with me. He will be known as the mayor who stood by and watched Victoryville destroyed. Now, you can send those forces in and it'll be just like you say. Everyone will get killed. But know this, chief: I will start with your deputy and any other hostages I may or may not have. You want to protect the innocent? Then stay the hell away and I'll let them live. Clean Skin or not."

"Magnus—"

"I'm done, chief," Magnus said. He waved his pudgy arm in the air, turning his chair around and rolling away.

"Magnus!" Blackstone barked after him. Langdon and Roy quickly stepped forward and grabbed Blackstone by the arms and dragged him toward the front door. They pushed him through, and he stumbled forward a few steps before steadying himself. He turned to face them.

"You got thirty seconds, chief," Roy said, "to get out of the SZ before I start shooting."

Blackstone stared at Roy and the three young men who lined up, weapons raised: Trent, Lewis, Langdon. A row of ignorance, the stripes running down their chins like smears of angry blood beside the weapons held up to their eyes. Their hatred was pointed at him, but it was ultimately flowing in an aimless direction. Regardless, he knew they were done talking.

Blackstone began to step backward, aiming for the interzone gate, refusing to turn his back on them immediately.

"Twenty seconds!" Roy called, and Blackstone picked up his pace.

"Open the gates!" he called over his shoulder to the soldiers manning it. "Open the gates!"

"Ten seconds!"

Blackstone looked over his shoulder to see the gates beginning to open.

"Five seconds!"

He spun around and raced for the gates, sliding through just in time to hear shots being fired, and laughter ringing out.

In safety, behind the wall, he bent over panting, catching his breath. He glanced up to see one of the soldiers looking down at him.

"They just fired in the air," the soldier told him. "The assholes were just playing with you."

"No," Blackstone shook his head and stood upright, "they ain't playing."

He pulled out his phone and dialed Mayor Russo.

Richard roused from sleep and opened his eyes. He flinched in fright at the sight of someone standing over him. As his eyes grew accustomed to the dim light, he made out the shape of a rifle over someone's shoulder and peered at the face to see it was Josh.

Abbie stirred at Richard's flinching, but didn't awake. Her head lay on Richard's chest, her arm across his waist, her warm body against his. His own arm was draped around her shoulders, holding her to him. It's how they'd fallen asleep after talking, after he'd comforted her. Leaning back against him, she'd fallen asleep, and Richard, tired also, had slowly brought his legs up onto the couch and gently brought her down to lie alongside him.

Josh's eyes appraised them both, lying together on the couch like that. Richard studied him, trying to read his face, trying to gauge what was going on in his mind; wondering if Josh and Abbie were together or whether this guy just wished they were.

Josh's face was hard, his eyes even harder.

"She was scared," Richard whispered quietly, not wanting to wake Abbie. "Your friends threatened her," he said accusingly, unable to stop his own face from hardening.

Josh didn't respond, he just eyed the two of them lying together. His face was angry, his eyes hurt. He gave Richard a cold look, then turned to leave.

"Josh!" Richard whispered after him.

The young man swiftly swung back and pointed the rifle in Richard's face, the barrel a fraction of an inch away.

"*Don't* talk to me," he hissed quietly, then pressed the

barrel hard into Richard's cheek. "You stay away from me, Clean Skin."

Richard's heart pounded in his chest as he watched Josh walk out the door, slamming it shut behind him. Abbie jolted awake, her hand grabbing onto Richard's side, making his body flinch.

"What? What is it?" Abbie asked groggily.

"It's okay," Richard told her, sliding his hand onto her forearm. "It must be the wind or something."

Abbie took in the sight of them lying together, then looked into Richard's face. She awkwardly pushed herself up and away from him.

"I'm sorry," she mumbled, rubbing her eyes.

"Don't be," he said, dropping his legs to the ground and sitting up. "I needed the company too," he smiled. Where she sat, the streetlights shining in around the curtains illuminated her face in a soft glow. The half-light shadows hid her welt and he could tell what she would look like without it.

Beautiful. Just as she was with the welt.

She stared back at him for a moment, then said, "Thank you. For being there, for listening."

"You can only bottle it up for so long, Abbie," he told her. "You've been so brave for everyone else's sake, soldiering on, it's time someone was there for you."

She looked down at her lap briefly. "You're going to make me cry again."

"Sorry," he said softly.

Her face broke into a beautiful, rather sad, smile. Then she reached out from the shadows and slid her hand onto his. "Thank you," she whispered.

He curled his fingers around hers, gripping them reassuringly. "Any time."

She gave his hand a squeeze, offered one last smile, then rose and disappeared upstairs to her bedroom. Richard watched her go, exhaling and running his hand through his hair. He felt strange inside. Torn. Developing feelings for Abbie wasn't something he'd planned on. But the truth was, he could've lain there with her all night. Something just felt so comfortable, so right about it. And as much as she'd needed someone, the truth was, he'd needed someone too.

Was he falling for his muse because of this phenomenon? Was he just falling for the person who embodied the hope he held for the future? Or was he falling for *her*. He pictured Josh standing over them with his rifle, and his face hardened a little at the thought of what he and his friends might do.

He heard the stairs creak and looked up to see Dr. Pellan descend. Richard looked at him questioningly.

"Kaitlyn was scared. She couldn't sleep," he explained. "I stayed in her room until she did. I guess I fell asleep as well."

"Same here," Richard said, eyeing the empty couch. He stood and moved over to the basement door. "After you," he gestured to Dr. Pellan. The doctor smiled and disappeared through the door. Richard took one last look around the house, moved over to lock the front door, then followed Pellan down into the basement.

Deputy Leo Cann spat more blood on the ground. Austin had a mean right hook.

"C'mon, Leo," Roy said, standing behind Austin. "I know you know more than you're letting on."

Leo looked up at him, face bleeding, cheeks swollen, jaw hurting.

"What plans does the chief have?" Roy asked. "He must've discussed possible tactics with you if things turned to shit.

How many military they got on standby?"

Leo spat again. "You starting to realize you're out of your depth, Roy?"

Austin looked at Roy, who gave a nod of approval. Austin swung another crunching punch at Leo's face. The pain radiated out over the whole side of his face, sending blood splattering across the floor. Leo groaned, squeezing his eyes shut. He wasn't sure how much more of this he could take.

But he'd try, praying that Earl would get him out of there soon.

Abbie sat up in bed at the sound of a loud banging on her front door. She looked out the window and saw Austin standing there. Langdon and Trent were further back on the lawn, scanning the street. He banged again then stood back and spotted her at the window.

"Let me in!" he shouted a whisper. "It's Josh!"

Abbie's breath caught. She threw back the sheets, pulled on a jacket and exited her room.

"Who is it?" Kaitlyn asked.

"Go back in your room. Stay there!" she said, pushing Kaitlyn back and closing the door. She ran down the stairs as Austin banged again. "I'm coming!" she called out, reaching the bottom of the stairs.

"Abbie!" Richard whispered, peering out through a crack in basement door.

She quickly moved over and pushed him back too. "Get inside! It's Austin! Be quiet!"

"Abbie!" he tried to argue, but she closed the door on him and locked it.

She moved over to the front door and opened it. Austin

barged in, splatters of blood on his pale-blue T-shirt.

"Where's Josh?" she blurted, eyeing the mess on Austin. "What happened to him?"

Langdon and Trent followed Austin in, eyes darting around, casing the place out.

"Where is she?" Austin demanded.

Abbie froze.

"Upstairs," he ordered the other two. "Go!"

"No!" Abbie stepped forward to stop them, but Austin grabbed her and held her back. She watched in horror as an armed Langdon and Trent ran up the stairs.

"Austin, no!" she begged, trying to pull away from him. "Don't do this!"

Josh burst through the door then, puffing and sweating like he'd been running to catch up. "Austin! What are you doing?"

"We need more leverage!" Austin spat back at him, as Kaitlyn's screams rang out from the second floor.

"If you hurt her, they'll kill us!" Josh argued urgently.

"They won't touch us if we have hostages!" Austin said.

"We've already got Deputy Cann, we don't need another!"

Austin stepped his larger form up to Josh. "Do you have a problem?"

"No, I just—"

"They're Magnus' orders!" Austin stabbed his finger into Josh's chest.

Abbie watched in horror as the two men dragged a crying Kaitlyn downstairs, while she held a screaming Charlie in her arms. Abbie tried to move toward them, but Austin caught her by the hair and pulled her back.

"Stop it! Leave her alone!" she yelled, struggling to free

herself, but was cut short as a crack of pain spread across her cheek and suddenly found herself on the floor.

"Hey!" Josh shouted, moving toward them.

"Whose side are you on?" Austin yelled, throwing Josh back against the wall. "We need this Clean Skin for leverage! Cann is striped, he ain't worth shit, but she is! They won't risk her!"

Abbie, still on the floor, cheek throbbing, watched Kaitlyn struggling with the two men as she begged them to let her go. "Please! Don't hurt me! Don't hurt me! Please!"

"Shut her up!" Austin yelled, and Langdon punched her hard in the face. Kaitlyn fell limp, smacking her head on the banister on her way down to the floor. Abbie held her breath and watched in horror as Charlie fell from her arms. Thankfully, Trent scooped him up before he hit the ground. Then she watched as Langdon grabbed Kaitlyn and threw her over his shoulder.

"Let's leave the kid here!" Trent said, putting Charlie on the ground.

"No!" Austin said. "He may be striped, but he's still a kid, and the military don't like shooting kids!"

Trent gave a nod and picked Charlie up again.

"Get out of here!" Austin ordered and his two accomplices made their way out the front door. Austin then grabbed Josh's shirt in his fist. "Are you with us or against us?"

"I'm with you," he said, although Abbie could hear the terror in his voice, and saw his chest rising and falling rapidly.

"Good!" Austin exited the house and Josh looked at Abbie. She pulled herself up off the floor, as they heard her neighbor's voice berating the intruders.

"Stop! What are you doing? Put her down!"

Josh and Abbie raced through the front door to see

Shonda-May standing on her front lawn, phone in one hand and baseball bat in the other, as some of their other neighbors' lights flickered on at the sounds breaking the night.

"Put her down or I'll call the cops!" Shonda-May said again. Abbie's heart lifted.

Austin raised his gun, but Abbie ran out with her hands in the air. "No! No! No!"

"Mommy?" Shonda-May's little boy came running out of the house. Shonda-May's dark face turned pale. "Cassius, no! Back inside!"

"He's a Clean Skin!" Trent said, pointing.

"Well, well," Austin grinned. "Look at that, more leverage."

"Cassius, inside. *Now*!" Shonda-May scolded.

"Don't move!" Austin held his gun on her, reaching out and grabbing Charlie from Trent with the other. "Get him!" He motioned for Trent to move, and he did so, marching over to grab the little boy.

"Oh, no!" Shonda-May's eyes flew wide. She swung the bat at Trent and they began to scuffle. Abbie tried to rush to her aid, but Josh held her back.

"No!" she struggled against him. "Austin, don't do this! They're innocent! They never hurt anyone!"

Trent managed to disarm Shonda-May, but she continued to fight, clawing at him and smacking him with the phone, but he swiftly cracked her over the head with his gun and Shonda-May fell to the ground in a heap, unconscious.

"Let's go! Quick!" Austin whispered, running off into the darkness with a shrieking Charlie. His two accomplices followed, Langdon carrying an unconscious Kaitlyn and Trent carrying a screaming Cassius, who was calling for his mother.

"NO!" Abbie screamed, trying to free herself of Josh's hold. He stood behind her, arms tightly wrapped around her, but he didn't let her go. More lights flicked on in the street.

"Abbie, stop it!" Josh begged, cheek pressed against hers, mouth to her ear. "They'll kill you!"

Abbie landed an elbow into Josh's ribs. He groaned and let her go and she scrambled to her feet. "We have to stop them!"

"What are you going to do?" he yelled at her. "They're heavily armed, Abbie! *What* are you going to do?"

They both stopped as they saw the porch of Josh's home light up. They looked across the street and saw Peter's shadow through the screen door.

Josh raised his hands to his head, pulling at his hair. His eyes were panicked. "I have to get my mother out of here," he whispered.

The sound of banging from inside her house caught their attention then. Someone was trying desperately to break through the basement door.

Richard rammed the door with his shoulder, groaning at the pain it sent through his arm.

"Abbie!" he called desperately. He no longer heard the voices of Austin and his friends, or the screaming of children, and Kaitlyn's screaming had stopped earlier. Richard's heart pounded like nothing he'd felt before, trapped in the basement, unable to do anything to help.

"I'm sorry," Dr. Pellan said, stepping back from him. "There was nothing we could have done. They would have killed us." Dr. Pellan had stopped Richard from trying to break out of the basement. The doctor, stronger than he looked, had thrown his hand over Richard's mouth and pulled him back from the door. Richard fought at first, but Pellan's whispers had somehow broken through to his common sense.

"It's no good," he'd begged. "They will kill us. We can't help them like this. As soon as we walk out that door they will shoot us like dogs!"

They heard the basement door unlock. It opened and Abbie stood there, distraught, her cheek swollen and pink.

"They took Kaitlyn and Charlie," she said, shivering with shock. "They took the neighbor's little boy too. He was a Clean Skin as well."

Richard latched onto her arms, moving them out into the living room. "Where did they take them?"

"The hardware store, I think."

Dr. Pellan emerged behind them, his hand held out placatingly. "They were going to use them as leverage. We heard. It's okay, that means they will be safe for the moment. They need them alive."

Richard held his hand up to Abbie's swollen cheek. "Are you okay?"

"Shonda-May!" she suddenly said, turning for the door. "She's unconscious."

They turned to see Josh carrying the woman inside. He placed her on the couch, then threw Richard a savage look as Abbie moved to her neighbor's aid.

"Did you know they were coming here?" Richard asked Josh accusingly.

"If I did, I would've told them about you," Josh said through his tight jaw.

"Josh!" Abbie looked at him shocked.

He threw her a dark look, then moved for the door. Abbie went after him.

"What are you going to do? You're not going back there?"

"No," he shook his head hopelessly. "The chief came to speak with Magnus and Roy. He knows they have Deputy Cann.

It was their last chance. They're gonna send in the military now. Magnus sent Austin to get Kaitlyn to hold them back. They have the deputy, but the more hostages they have the better."

He turned to leave again, but she stopped him. "So what *are* you going to do?"

Richard saw the serious, tense look Josh gave her. "I'm getting my mother the hell out of here before they come back."

"Josh, it's too dangerous!" Abbie latched onto his arm.

"She can't stay!" he argued, pulling his arm away. "How long do you think it will be before Kaitlyn gives up those two?" He pointed to Richard and Dr. Pellan.

"She would never—" Abbie countered.

"Magnus and Roy will get it out of her! They gave the deputy a beating, trying to get information out of him. Did you see Austin's shirt? That was the *deputy's* blood!" he said. Suddenly a thought seemed to dawn on him. Josh angrily pushed her back against the opened door, his arm scrunching her shirt in his fist. "She knows about my mother, doesn't she!"

Richard quickly stepped forward and threw his arms between the two, pushing Josh away from Abbie. Josh threw a punch at him, but he moved so it caught his shoulder.

"Stop it!" Abbie begged, as Richard raised his fists up in defense. He was by no means a fighter, but he'd do it if he had to.

Josh swiftly pulled his gun and aimed it at Richard, but Abbie knocked it away.

"*What are you doing?*" She pleaded for him to come to his senses.

"I'm telling you, when they find out, they will come back for those two!" Josh said. "If they realize you've been hiding them as well, they will punish you, Abbie! And if they realize they can't trust you, they won't trust me. I have to get mom out

351

of here before they find her too!"

"How Josh? Between the military and Magnus' men, how?"

"We'll go south-west while they're busy with their hostages. I'll make sure they get through! Dad's striped, so he can walk around freely."

"Don't do this!"

"Come with me!"

"What?" A furrow crossed Abbie's brow.

"Ditch them and come with me!" Josh said, leaning closer to her.

Abbie stood, speechless.

Richard exchanged an uneasy look with Dr. Pellan, who stepped forward. "If the military come in, they will end things, Josh," he said quietly. "We just need to be patient."

"Not now Magnus has leverage," Josh said, shaking his head. "This could go on for days." He looked back at Abbie. "Come with me."

Abbie glanced at Richard, then at Dr. Pellan, then back at Josh.

"We have to hurry, Abbie!" Josh insisted. "We have to go now!"

She shook her head. "I can't leave, Josh. What about Kaitlyn, Charlie," she glanced at Richard and Dr. Pellan, "them?"

"They're as good as dead, Abbie," he said desperately. "Come with me! We'll hide out west."

"Hide where? We can't hide from the aliens, Josh," she said softly. "There's no hiding from anything any more."

"We stand a better chance than we do here!"

Abbie shook her head and stepped back from his grasping arms. "I'm sorry, Josh. I can't just leave Kaitlyn and Charlie to a fate decided by Magnus Bracks. I won't leave them."

Richard, watching the two of them carefully, saw Abbie look over at him.

Josh flashed Richard a dark look, then snapped, "Fine! You want to side with them, you want to die with them? Fine. You're on your own!" He pointed angrily in her face, then left, slamming the screen door shut behind him.

Richard watched Abbie as she stared after him, then, lowering her eyes, she leaned back against the door, sliding down to the floor hopelessly. Richard moved to crouch in front of her and squeezed her shoulder. Abbie buried her face in her hands and sobbed. Richard breathed out heavily, looked over at the unconscious woman lying on the couch, then over his shoulder at Pellan.

"What the hell are we going to do now?" he asked him.

"I don't know," Pellan answered, rubbing the back of his neck. "I honestly don't know."

Deputy Cann, sitting hunched over in the chair, had dozed off. Whether from exhaustion, lack of food and water, or whether the beating he'd taken had left him with a concussion, he wasn't sure. But he awoke with a start at the sound of the door opening and people, more hostages, being forced into the small room.

He recognized Rachael Manner's daughter, the Clean Skin mother who had been evicted from the CZ with her striped child. She lay unconscious on the floor, her hands bound in front. Her screaming child was placed beside her, along with another young, distraught African-American boy.

"What the hell are you doing?" he asked Langdon and Trent.

"Leverage," Austin told him from the doorway. "To make sure your friends don't do anything stupid."

"Goddamn it, Austin!" Leo said. "You have me for leverage, let them go!"

"You ain't a Clean Skin, deputy. They're worth more."

"They're kids, for God's sake!"

Austin and his accomplices left the room, locking the door and leaving him alone with the unconscious girl and crying children. He eyed them all, panicking at the thought of what Magnus Bracks was planning. The young boy in particular was quite distressed.

"Hey," he said to the crying boy, trying to calm him. "Hey, it's okay."

The boy didn't look at him, he just banged on the door and cried for his mother.

"Hey," Leo tried again, "it's okay. Your mom will come get you soon, alright?"

The boy's scared dark eyes looked at him, but then he turned back to the door and started crying again. Leo didn't blame him. God knows what he looked like right now with his battered and bloodied face. The boy probably thought he looked like Frankenstein's monster or something. He sure felt like it the way his face felt tight and puffy and was throbbing and thumping.

"What's your name?" he asked the boy, trying to ignore the pain in his head. "Mine's Leo. Can you tell me your name?"

The boy didn't answer, just kept his back turned and kept on crying, calling for his mother. Leo looked over to the screaming, fidgeting baby lying next to the unconscious girl. He closed his eyes a moment and lowered his head again. He felt so helpless; beaten, handcuffed, weaponless, surrounded by screaming children. He had to do something, but couldn't think what. He tugged on his handcuffs in frustration.

Then he suddenly remembered that he still had a spare

key to the locked cuffs.

They'd been no good to him before, because he was handcuffed through the back of the chair. But now there was someone in the room who could get the key and unlock the cuffs for him, he may just stand a chance.

He looked at the unconscious girl again. He stuck out his foot and tried to shake her awake.

"Hey," he said, trawling his memory for her name. "Kaitlyn?" He shook her again but she didn't stir. He saw the young boy looking over his shoulder, watching him. Leo turned his attention back to him. "Hey," he said, "I know you want to see your mom. I can help you. My name is Leo and I'm a cop. Do you know what a cop is?"

The boy looked at him with his dark, wet, terrified face.

"I'm Leo," he said again, as softly as he could. "I'm a policeman. Did your mom ever tell you what a policeman is?"

The boy nodded hesitantly.

"I try to help people," Leo said gently, wondering whether the boy's mother had told him good things about the police, or bad. Would this kid trust him? "And I can help you get back to your mom, but I need you to do something for me."

The boy looked at him, eyeing his bloodied and battered face.

"What's your name?" Leo asked.

The boy didn't answer.

"My name is Leo. What's yours?"

"C—Cassius," his weak, quiet voice eventually said, as he huddled against the door, still terrified.

"Hi, Cassius," Leo smiled, feeling his cut lip and bruised cheeks sting and throb. "I'm going to help you get back to your mommy, Cassius, but I need you to help me with something. Can you do that?"

Cassius looked at him, wiping the back of his arm across his nose.

"Can you do that, Cassius?" Leo asked. "Can you help me? I have a key in my pocket and I need you to get it for me. Can you do that?"

The boy looked at the door and started crying again.

"I know you're scared, Cassius. I am too. But I can help you. I promise, I'll help you find your mommy. I just need to have my hands untied first. If you help me get the key, I can untie my hands, and then I can take you to your mommy."

The boy looked at him.

"Will you help?" Leo asked him, trying to smile again, trying to ignore the terrible ache in his head.

The boy just stared.

Leo motioned with his head, to his pocket. "My keys are just in there, in my pocket, but I can't reach them. I know you could reach them, Cassius."

The boy wiped his face again, seeming a little calmer now.

"What do you say?" Leo asked him. "You help me get my keys and I'll take you to your mommy."

The boy stared at him for another moment, then finally stood up.

"That's it." Leo smiled again and tried to angle his body to make his right pocket accessible. "They're just in this pocket here."

The boy moved over cautiously to stand in front of Leo.

Suddenly gunfire rang out, making both of them flinch. Leo eyed the doorway and listened. It sounded like it was coming from the street outside.

They heard it again.

"Cassius," Leo said urgently, "help me with my key!"

The boy started crying again. More gunfire sounded, closer this time.

"Cassius, come here!" Leo said. "Move away from the door. It's not safe!"

The boy glanced at him then back at the door. More gunfire rang out, and someone ran past the door shouting, "He's been shot! They got Lewis!"

"Jesus," Leo breathed. The chief or the military were making a move.

More gunfire sounded.

"Get behind me! Now!" Leo barked to Cassius. The boy looked at him, petrified. "Cassius, get behind me, behind my chair!" The terrified boy did so, bawling as he squeezed into the tight space behind Leo's chair. The girl on the ground began to stir. More gunfire and shouting ensued. Leo reached his leg out and tried to move the baby further into the corner, tried to shake the girl awake. She stirred again, but didn't open her eyes.

He turned his face to the door again, hoping to hell that whoever came in would make sure they looked before they fired.

The door suddenly burst open, giving him and Cassius a fright. Roy and Langdon charged in, grabbed Leo in a headlock, bent him forward and unlocked the cuffs, then dragged him roughly out the door.

Chief Blackstone watched as Roy dragged his deputy in sight of the doorway leading to the warehouse out back. Leo's face was bloodied and swollen, blood spatters covered his shirt and cuffs still dangled from one wrist. Roy pressed a pistol against his temple.

"There, chief, you got your evidence," Roy yelled. "Now pull back or I will blow your deputy's brains out!"

Blackstone locked eyes with Leo, giving him a look of solidarity. He wanted Leo to know that he was doing what he could to get him out of there. He'd started the assault along with a small military contingent, and had progressed into the store. One of the soldiers had killed the young man on the door, Lewis, in an exchange of gunfire. But Blackstone couldn't think about that boy right now. Right now, Roy was holding up their progress with talk of executing the hostages, starting with his deputy. Blackstone had insisted on proof that Leo was still alive.

"You alright, Leo?" Blackstone called.

His deputy managed a nod. "They got kids in here, Earl—" Leo's words were cut short by Roy cracking him across the head.

"Keep your mouth shut!" Roy yelled, then looked at Blackstone. "I'm warning you, chief. Pull back or I'll kill him. You know I will."

Blackstone evaluated the situation. He'd insisted on being given authority for the assault, since he knew those involved, and now the leader of the military unit was looking at him for his next move. Blackstone gave a reluctant nod, and motioned back to the street.

"Pull back," he told the soldier.

The soldier eyed him a moment in question.

Blackstone gave a sharp, definite nod.

"You don't give up gained ground," the soldier whispered.

Blackstone looked at him. "When they're threatening to execute children, you do," he said with finality, then motioned for them to pull back.

The lead soldier reluctantly obeyed, and the unit slid

carefully back to the doorway.

Blackstone looked at his deputy. "I'll get you out of here, Leo. Just hold tight."

Leo gave him a nod, before he was swiftly yanked back into the warehouse.

Mayor Michael Russo squeezed his eyes shut as the state governor yelled down the phone.

"I know it's your town, Russo, but it's in my state! What the hell is going on. Why are they pulling back?"

Russo exhaled. "They started the assault, but Bracks is threatening to execute Clean Skins if we don't back down. He has the young mother who was kicked out of the Clean Zone, her newborn baby, and another Clean Skin boy about four years old. Not to mention our deputy."

"So what are you doing about it? I've got the National Guard ready to go."

"Colonel Levin has stepped in. He's brought in their best negotiator to see if he can secure the hostages' release. We had no choice. They had a gun to the deputy's head."

"What's your chief of police doing?"

"He's down at the gate helping the negotiator."

"This is out of hand. You should've shut this down a long time ago. So shut it down *now*!"

"We're trying to, governor. We're trying."

Russo hung up the phone, only to have it ring immediately. He picked it up.

"Mayor," Eva said, "Deputy Mayor Shother is on the line. He's demanding to speak with you."

Russo sighed heavily. *Aren't they all*, he thought. He'd been fending off calls from the other members of council all day.

"Tell him I'm a little busy right now," he said.

"He said he won't take no for an answer."

"Well, he's just going to have to," Russo said and hung up again.

Dr. Lysart Pellan turned the TV on, wanting an update on what was happening with the siege. It wasn't too long after Austin had left that the sounds of gunfire had erupted.

Richard had encouraged Abbie to sit on the couch and had locked the front door. Shonda-May, the neighbor, was still out cold.

"We need to get her to a doctor," Abbie had said worriedly.

Lysart moved to the woman, cupping the back of her neck. He'd felt something wet and pulled his fingers away to see they were covered in blood.

"Do you have ice, Abbie?" he asked.

She nodded and made her way to the kitchen.

"Jesus!" Richard breathed, his mouth agape as he stared at the TV.

Lysart turned toward it, as Abbie came back with a bag of frozen corn in her hand. The three of them stared silently at the parade of images. Someone had recorded the siege from the apartment building overlooking the gateway. As the replay ended, they saw more recent amateur footage of Chief Blackstone discussing tactics with military personnel, behind the inter-zone gate on the Clean Skin side. The body of the young man shot in the siege, a Striped One, lay on the ground near the doors of the hardware store. Abbie wondered who it was, whether she'd seen him around at the VAC, but the way his body lay meant she couldn't see his face on the footage.

"Why aren't they moving in?" Abbie asked. "Why are they stopping?"

"Magnus probably announced his hostages," Richard responded.

A newsreader came back on screen and said they would try and speak live with the Clean Skin resident who had taken the footage in just a moment, then proceeded to replay the footage of the earlier assault, when the military stormed the front of the store. According to the newsreader, one Striped One was confirmed as dead, while it was believed other casualties remained inside the hardware store.

Abbie finally handed the bag of frozen corn to Lysart, and he held it to the back of Shonda-May's head. He watched as Abbie moved to the curtains and peered out. She closed them again and seemed to think for a moment, then looked at both Lysart and Richard.

"Maybe you two should go with Josh?" she said.

The two men stared at her.

"Josh's right. If they find out you're here . . ." she said softly, shaking her head. "They'll want as much leverage as they can get, now the military is trying to move in."

"I don't think Josh would welcome our company right now," Richard told her.

Abbie stared at him. "Magnus and Roy are serious, Rick. They could kill you."

"And if they found out we were here, they could kill *you*, Abbie. I'm not running away and leaving you to face that alone."

"But this could be your only chance."

"She's right," Lysart pondered. "We may not get another chance to escape. Magnus and Roy are busy right now, as is Austin. We could make our way back to where that sewer tunnel is."

Richard stared at him. "If you want to go, Dr. Pellan, don't let me hold you back. But I can't—"

"Rick—" Abbie protested.

"I'm not going to leave you here alone with those crazy assholes running around, Abbie!"

Lysart listened to them, the concern they had for one another. He studied them thoughtfully and saw something in their eyes. It made him recall when he was a younger man. He mused on lost chances, his age, of what he had to gain by running to the sewers, or to the country. He knew he had nothing out there now. He knew the government would eventually catch up with him. He knew there would be a price to pay, regardless.

He looked down at the unconscious woman who had tried to help them, whose son was now a captive of Magnus, then he looked back to Abbie and Richard. He thought of the young Kaitlyn and baby Charlie, and he knew then that his fate was sealed. He couldn't abandon these people. He had to do what he could, to help save those who stood a chance of having a life after this mess was over.

"We stay," he said softly.

Abbie and Richard looked at him.

"Richard's right. We can't run away. So we stay," he said firmly, focusing his attention on Abbie. "You helped us when we needed it, Abbie. So we don't abandon you or Kaitlyn now."

Deputy Leo Cann, cuffed once more, sat still while a groggy Kaitlyn Manner fished in his pocket for his spare key ring. Her hands were bound, so it was a little awkward, but she eventually managed to hook her fingers on the small loop of keys and drag them out.

When they'd brought him back to the storeroom after the standoff with the chief, Kaitlyn had come to. She'd done her best to soothe her screaming baby, although she couldn't hold him properly with her hands bound like they were. Leo had worked hard to calm all three of them, and once that was accomplished, he'd thought about what to do next.

He'd told her they had to play this very carefully. For now, there was no threat of being caught in the crossfire as the military had pulled back, which was something at least. But he wasn't sure how much time they had before the military pressed forward again. Or before their captors snapped and did something stupid in desperation. And he knew it would be stupid. Most of the young guys, from what he could tell, were on some kind of stimulant. They were overtired, they were on edge, and they weren't thinking straight. A very dangerous combination.

Kaitlyn, unsteady on her feet, with a black eye and bleeding head, was presently unlocking his cuffs. Now he had to pick his moment to make a move. But he had to be careful about it. He and Kaitlyn were outnumbered, and if he made a wrong move he would be killed. And not only that, his actions could get Kaitlyn and the two children killed. Whatever he did, he had to leave them out of it.

For now, he was just going to sit there and pretend he was still bound, until the right opportunity presented itself.

Mayor Russo sat at his desk, head resting in his hands. Chief Blackstone had been reporting on the events down at the gate, but he didn't need to. Russo had the TV on, watching the news reports, and his heart sank further with every minute that passed. Victoryville was a mess. An absolute disaster spread across every media agency and affiliate website that existed.

These events were drawing as much attention as the alien visitation had. He'd stopped checking the social media feeds a while back. Seeing the town being described as "Victimville" and "Savageville", along with images of the town graffitied with red stripes and blood splatters, was too much to bear.

Russo knew it would be hard to recover from this. Things had gone too far. He'd let them go too far. He should've let the military go in when they first wanted to, before there were hostages involved. He'd made decisions without consulting the council and they had backfired. Now he would need to face the consequences.

Had Magnus Bracks won?

Even if the military stormed the place and killed him, Bracks would still win. He'd held true to his promise that if he was going down, then he was taking Russo with him. And he was. Bracks had been taunting him and Russo had fallen for the bait. He had, in his arrogance, ignored the man until it was too late, until the hole was dug too deep. All Russo could pray for now was that the hostages make it out alive.

The door to his office was flung open and Graeme Shother and Patty Duke stormed in. Eva came with them, trying to halt their advance.

"I'm sorry, mayor," Eva said, looking harried. "They wouldn't wait for me to announce their arrival."

Russo motioned for Eva to leave the room as Graeme and Patty came to a stop on the other side of the desk.

"So you sent in the military without informing us," Graeme said. "Anything else you'd like to share with us while we're here?"

"I was going to call you," Russo said.

"Really! When?" Graeme threw back. "Perhaps if you'd answered one of my calls we could've discussed it!"

"I wasn't left with a choice. I had to make quick decisions regarding the safety of this town, so I did," Russo said. "I was going to brief you all—"

"Well, we're here now," Patty said, her striped face less than impressed as she placed her hands on her broad hips.

"How did you make it into the Clean Zone?"

"Graeme let me in," she told Russo, folding her arms and pinning him with a hard stare. "I'm not sure if you've heard, but we're not contagious, so that wall should be taken down."

"It stays as long as the Striped Ones threaten the Clean Skins."

"Enough with the delay tactics," Patty said. "Tell us what's going on."

"Not everyone is here," Russo said. "You'd like me to update only half the Council?"

"Well, it's better than none!" Graeme said.

"Bracks took the deputy hostage," Russo said, trying to contain his anger. "The chief went to speak with Bracks, but he was threatened and forced to leave. Left with no other choice, the military moved in. However, Bracks managed to secure more hostages in the meantime. As you can see things have moved fast. Had I stopped to put things to a vote, then God knows how many hostages the man would have now!"

"We look like fools, Mike," Graeme seethed. "Things never should've gotten this far!"

"It's unacceptable!" Patty nodded firmly.

"Look, I understand you're angry, but I had no other choice," Russo told them. "I had to act. The military will take the building soon and clear this up."

"At what cost? More lives?" Graeme said.

"It never should've been allowed to get this far," Patty agreed. "You let your relationship with Bracks get in the way of things. You brought this on the town, and you need to pay for what you've done!"

"Pay?" Russo frowned at her.

"I'm sorry, Mike," Graeme shook his head, "but you just lost your seat on the council. We've seen to that."

"Graeme." Russo stood from his chair, holding his hand out to placate the man. "Wait a minute, this was Bracks' doing."

"Enough!" Patty said. "The council has taken your lead and made a few decisions without your input. The first being to remove you from this office."

"Excuse me?"

"This town has been damaged enough, Mike," Graeme said. "We need to pull it together again before those things come back."

"You can't do this," Russo told them. "The constituents voted me in."

"You really want to go down that road?" Patty asked condescendingly. "You want us to put this to a vote after all that's happened? After people find out you let your petty dispute with Bracks lead to this?"

Russo wanted to wipe the look off her peroxide-haired, overly made-up face.

"Don't worry, Mike," Graeme said, "we can make it look like your choice. You can keep that seat until the military sorts this mess out. And when it does, that's when you resign from your position and take the stink away with you."

"And that's when Mayor Shother and myself, Deputy Mayor Duke, will take over the reins and give this town the leadership and support it deserves," Patty said.

"May I remind you, you're *acting* deputy mayor, Graeme. At my behest! You weren't voted in."

"Check your emails, Mike," Patty said. "I've outlined the

relevant clauses we will be using to remove you from your position if you do not go quietly."

"You can't do this," Russo said, although his voice wasn't quite as firm as he would've liked.

"Yes, we can, Mike," Graeme said, "and if you're smart, you'll do this the easy way. You can walk or we can push. It's up to you."

With that, Michael Russo watched as Graeme and Patty stormed out of his soon-to-be ex-office.

Day Nine

Abbie sat on the couch beside Richard. Upon waking, Shonda-May had been taken by volunteer ambulance personnel to Dr. Chee's clinic to have her head injury checked. Shonda-May had wanted to go after her son, but they had managed to convince her that it was too dangerous, that the chief and the military were working to get her boy back safely, that she would just get in the way. Abbie told her that Deputy Cann was also a hostage, and she was sure the deputy would look out for Cassius. The fact that Shonda-May had been so unsteady on her feet helped to convince her that she needed medical attention first.

It was all over the news now, that Clean Skin hostages were being held in the SZ. The military had pulled back to the interzone gate while negotiators worked to free them, but that could change at any moment. The dead body of the Striped One still lay outside the store in a pool of blood. Abbie wondered why the Striped Ones had just left him there like that. Was Magnus making some kind of statement by leaving the boy's body on display. Or were they concerned about being shot if they retrieved him.

Abbie felt helpless, but taking the same advice she'd given

Shonda-May, they had decided to stay at the house and let the chief and military try and retrieve the hostages.

She witnessed Josh sneaking out in the darkness with his parents in tow, placing something, perhaps a key, in a pot plant out front. It must've taken him some time to convince them to leave. She watched as their shadows bled into the night and couldn't help feeling a tightening in her gut. She hoped they would be safe. She hoped they would make it.

Dr. Pellan retreated to the basement. Abbie wasn't sure whether he wanted to be alone, or whether he was leaving her and Richard alone, but his mood was introspective. They'd watched the news coverage for a while, but then they turned it off, unable to stand waiting to see what was going to happen. They sat in the near darkness, listening to the quiet, wondering if Kaitlyn and Charlie were okay, whether the deputy and Cassius would be okay. Wondering whether someone would come for Abbie and the two Clean Skins she harbored.

But no one came.

Exhausted, she eventually lay down, her head resting beside where Richard sat. He told her to sleep, promising that he would stay awake. It took her a while to relax and let herself go, but fatigue eventually crept in, as Richard stroked her hair, soothing her. She kept replaying the scene of the young men taking Kaitlyn, Charlie and Cassius away, kept wondering what they were doing to them, kept wondering what would happen to baby Charlie if they did something to Kaitlyn that couldn't be undone.

She awoke suddenly at the sound of voices in the street. It was early morning, around dawn. She looked up and saw Richard pulling back from the window.

"What is it?" she asked.

He shook his head. "I don't know. Something's going on. People are headed toward the gate." He grabbed the remote and turned the TV on, but a commercial was playing.

Abbie regarded Richard and saw how tired he looked. "I'm sorry, I didn't mean to sleep so long."

He smiled, the dawn light casting his stubbled face in a peachy glow. "It's okay. You needed it."

The news came back on then and the reader announced a breaking story. Abbie and Richard sat to attention. According to the news anchor, apparently more hostages had been taken by the Victoryville SZ. The footage was shaky, but from what they could tell, there was a small mob dragging some people toward the parking lot at the back of the hardware store. It looked like it was again being recorded from the apartment block beside the interzone gate. Abbie squinted her eyes, scanning the crowd, desperate for a glimpse of Kaitlyn, wondering if they were moving her somewhere. Perhaps the chief had been successful in negotiating her release.

But then she saw someone else. Her jaw fell and her eyes flew wide open.

"Oh my God!" she breathed as her blood ran cold.

"What?" Richard asked.

Abbie stood, pointing at the screen. "That was Karen. That was Josh's mom!"

"What? You're sure?"

Abbie stood, shocked. She nodded, still pointing at the screen. "That was Karen. That was Karen. Go back and replay it!"

Richard fumbled with the remote as Dr. Pellan appeared at the doorway to the basement.

"What is it?" he asked.

Richard replayed the footage and the three of them stared at the screen. Abbie moved right up to it. As soon as she saw Karen again she blurted, "Pause it!"

Richard did.

"There!" Abbie pointed to Karen, then she suddenly gasped in horror. "Oh my God, they got Peter too! Where's Josh?"

Richard stood from the couch and Dr. Pellan moved closer. Richard let the footage roll.

"They got them," Abbie said breathlessly. "They didn't make it! They've got them! What are they going to do? We have to help them!"

"This is shocking news," the news anchor said, as the telecast jumped back to the studio. "Reports from the scene indicate that a crowd is gathering at the back of the hardware store. It is unknown what is about to take place, however we've been told the military on the gate are on alert..."

"Oh my God! We have to go! We have to do something!" Abbie was panicking.

Richard and Dr. Pellan looked at each other.

"We can't just sit here!" Abbie pleaded. "Josh and Peter are striped. Magnus doesn't need them. Who knows what he'll do!"

"Abbie," Richard said, "do you have some makeup we could use?"

She looked at him in confusion.

"If we give ourselves fake stripes, maybe we can move around unnoticed?"

Dr. Pellan's eyes lit up at the idea and he looked at her eagerly.

She hurried upstairs to her bathroom. She raced back with some lipstick and blush and they swiftly set about turning themselves into Striped Ones. She grabbed her father's Little League baseball cap and handed it to Richard to wear low over his face, while Dr. Pellan wrapped his neck in his scarf and donned his hat.

Within minutes they were ready and they began to jog down the street toward the warehouse. The closer they got the more people they saw. As the report had suggested, the small crowd was gathered around the back of the warehouse, in the small parking lot and loading bay. She looked for the source of the shaky camera footage on the news and saw someone standing on one of the balconies of the apartment block by the gate, but the camera couldn't capture what was going on behind the warehouse. She noticed that the number of soldiers at the gate had increased and they were on alert, dressed in full combat gear, but not yet making any attempt to enter the SZ. She saw the chief standing with another man who was talking on a phone.

She and her two companions walked to the back of the gathered crowd. Whatever was happening, it was happening right outside the back doors of the hardware store's warehouse. Abbie found a spot where she could see, and there, in the center of it all, were Peter, Karen and Josh on their knees. Josh's face was bruised and bloody. He'd been beaten, as had Peter. Karen was crying profusely, begging for their lives. Magnus sat in his chair to the side, eyeing the three captives contemptuously.

"Is the front of the warehouse secure?" Magnus asked.

"Sure is!" Roy said, pacing in front of the Chalmer family, eyeing them accusingly. He paused briefly to spit on the ground in front of Peter.

"Magnus." Justin, Abbie's swimming student, came jogging out holding up a phone. "They want to talk to you. They want to know what's going on."

"Tell them to hold," Magnus' phlegmy voice said, as he motioned for Justin to head back inside.

"What are we going to do with them?" Langdon asked, motioning to the Chalmer family.

Austin put his face right in Josh's and glared. "I say we teach them a lesson!"

Gavin Taylor, data technician for NASA, groaned as part of his sandwich fell onto his AC/DC shirt. Munching away, he reached for a napkin and tried to mop up the sauce that had smeared across the shirt.

The screen before him beeped and data flashed up on his screen. He looked at it, seeing fresh environmental readings of what they'd been tracking.

He tossed the napkin and what was left of his sandwich aside and moved closer to his screen to review what it was telling him. He studied the new readings carefully, swallowing his mouthful as a realization hit him. The mercury level was showing in a much higher concentration than the previous readings.

He quickly wiped his hands on his jeans and pulled up another screen to check the source of the readings. It was from a weather station located in Richmond.

"Shit," he whispered to himself. This was the first reading back in the state of Virginia since the initial Occurrence. He checked the mercury level again. Definitely higher than those previously recorded in the other states.

"Dr. Wattowski!" he called out. "You better come take a look at this!"

Richard saw Abbie begin to move forward through the crowd, but he caught her arm and pulled her back.

"Wait!" he whispered. "Let's find out what they're going to do first."

She stared back at him confused and frightened. He kept a firm hold of her, not wanting her to do anything stupid. *Surely Magnus wouldn't harm them*, he thought. *Not here in front of all these people. Josh and Peter were Striped Ones, for God's sake.*

"Just wait," he begged Abbie in a whisper. "They're probably just going to use them as more leverage to stop the military."

The tension of her arm pulling against his hand eased off and she stood still beside him. Richard exchanged an anxious look with Dr. Pellan who stood on the other side of her. Their chins had fake stripes running down them, but if anyone looked closely enough they would see they were a ruse. Neither man had shaved in days, so the stubble had made it difficult. Their hats were pulled low, and Dr. Pellan had his red scarf, but whether it was disguise enough for two of the most well-known Clean Skins, Richard wasn't sure. In fact he was downright worried about it—standing there, surrounded by aggressive Striped Ones.

"I knew you were up to something!" Austin spat at Josh. "You were supposed to follow us back to the warehouse last night and you didn't. So I checked up on you. Saw you sneaking out your Clean Skin mother!"

"One of our own!" Roy shook his head, leaning over Josh, then turned to face the crowd. "Running around behind our backs! Making out like he was with us, and the whole time he was harboring a Clean Skin!"

"*Fuck*, Roy," Josh pleaded with him, "she's my mother!"

Richard looked at Magnus and saw his mind ticking over as he contemplated Josh.

"Please!" Peter begged. "We didn't want the military to take her when they first came. That's all!"

"What if we were contagious?" Magnus questioned. "You would risk your wife?"

Peter looked at Magnus. "We didn't know. We just panicked. All this talk of aliens . . . we just wanted her to stay with us. I swear, that's all."

"That's why you've been hiding in that house!" Roy pointed accusingly. "That's why you never came out to support us."

"At least he was honest," Magnus said, eyeing Josh.

"Yeah," Trent stepped in front of Josh. "And while we were fighting the soldiers and Lewis was killed, you were sneaking away like a goddamn coward!"

Austin grabbed Josh by the hair, pulling his head back. "You been spying on us? Huh? Feeding *them* information?"

"He's smart," Magnus nodded, the seven stripes running over his fat chin stretching and contracting as he did. "He was keeping an eye on his enemy."

"Enemy?" Roy looked at Josh again. "Is that what you think we are?"

"You betrayed us, man!" Langdon spoke up. "You betrayed us and then you ran like a fucking coward!"

"Why, Josh?" Wendy moved beside Langdon. Her voice sounded teary, regretful. "How *could* you?"

"How could I what?" Josh yelled at her angrily. "Protect my family?"

"Josh!" Peter said, looking at his son, eyes pleading for steadiness. Peter turned back to Magnus. "Look, we don't mean any harm to anyone. Just let us go and we won't be any trouble, Magnus. I swear. Josh hasn't been reporting on you to anyone."

"The Victoryville SZ is mine," Magnus wheezed. "This here," he circled his pale pudgy arm about, "is mine. That Clean Skin," he pointed to Karen, "is trespassing."

"Jesus Christ, Magnus, she's my *wife*!" Peter's voice raised an octave. "She's not a trespasser! She lives here!"

"You hid her from us, and then you tried to run!" Roy

pointed at him. "That's deceitful, Peter. That's what that is!" He began to pace again.

"What about that Clean Skin girl?" Peter argued. "The one that had the striped kid!"

Josh looked at his father.

"We got that Clean Skin bitch inside," Austin said.

"So," Peter argued, "you never accused Randell for taking her in! So why us now?"

"Dad!" Josh warned, eyes wide.

"That was before we found out the Clean Skins lied to us," Magnus replied in his rough voice. "Back then, she was just trash who had a striped kid. Things are different now."

"So?" Peter asked.

"So, that Randell bitch will get hers!" Austin spat.

Richard tensed. He exchanged another look with Dr. Pellan, then took hold of Abbie's arm again. "I think we should go," he whispered. "Now."

Abbie looked at him, perplexed. "We can't leave them!"

"So what do we do?" Magnus called to the crowd, raising a heavy arm as far as he could. "What should we do with the Clean Skin and these traitors?"

The crowd started yelling all manner of things. Richard noted, however, that some people looked frightened about what was happening, their eyes darting around, as though they wanted to walk away, but were too scared. *They knew*, Richard thought. *They knew things had gone too far.*

Magnus held his hand up to his ear. "Do we set them free? Or do we punish them?"

Roy's pacing stepped up a notch and he ran his hand back and forth over his closely-shaved skull, his face twitching occasionally. Austin moved agitatedly, shaking his legs and flexing his hands, his glare still fixed on Josh.

"Goddamn it, Austin!" Josh pleaded. "Don't do this!"

"You're a fucking traitor!" Austin accused. "You lied to my face! You said you were with us!"

"She's my *mother*!"

"You fucking lied to us this *whole* time!" Austin shouted back.

Wendy wiped an angry tear from her cheek, smudging black mascara, then lunged forward and kicked Josh in the side, making him curl in pain. "You piece of shit!"

"We can use the Clean Skin as more leverage," Magnus thought aloud, studying Karen.

"Yeah! Leverage!" someone yelled.

"No, you should punish them!" Trent shouted.

Roy suddenly stopped and pulled out his pistol and held it to Karen's forehead.

"Roy, no!" Peter lurched toward him, arms raised in a peaceful gesture. "Please, Roy! You know me. We went to school together, for God's sake!"

Roy stared at Peter, mind ticking over. "Betrayal has a price, Pete."

"Don't, Roy!" Peter pleaded. "Please, I'm begging you."

"We have to do something," Abbie whispered to Richard.

Richard's hand pressed her arm. "If they're going to kill them, they'll kill you too!"

"What, Pete?" Roy asked. "What will you offer us in trade not to kill your wife?"

"I'll trade anything you want, Roy! Anything!"

"Anything?"

"Yes! Don't hurt them, please," Peter begged, turning to Karen and Josh. "They're my family, I love them."

"Yeah?" Roy asked. "How much do you love them?"

Austin barged forward, shouldering Roy out of the way. "Enough talk! No trade! Just do it!" he yelled, then held up his pistol and fired.

Peter Chalmer's head flew back, and his body followed.

"NO!" Josh screamed, jumping to his feet and tackling Austin to the ground.

"Austin!" Magnus barked, eyes wide with shock.

"Jesus!" Roy panicked, stepping back, eyeing Peter's dead body.

Karen threw herself on Peter, wailing in despair.

"Oh my God!" Abbie suddenly lurched through the crowd, tearing away from Richard's grip, but he went after her. He caught her and threw his arms around her to stop her. "Abbie, no!"

Some of those in the crowd turned around and looked at them, wondering what was going on. Richard held her tightly, dragging her back, "Abbie, please!"

Up ahead Roy was watching Josh and Austin scuffling on the ground, as was most of the crowd. Richard saw Roy look around at Magnus for his next move. They were panicky. They hadn't planned on that happening—Austin shooting Peter. Karen screamed and wailed, and turned her attention to Josh, moving toward him. but Roy quickly stopped her. Magnus motioned for Roy to take her inside with the other hostages. He tried to, but Karen fought, sinking her teeth into his hand. Roy cried out in pain, pushed her back, and she lunged at him, hands clasping around his throat, but he raised his gun and fired. Richard watched helplessly as Karen, shot through the chest, fell to the floor in a heap. They heard Josh screaming as Austin stood and started laying into him with kick after kick. Trent and Langdon began to join in. And that was the moment Richard knew all hope was lost.

"JOSH!" Abbie screamed.

Richard heaved and swung Abbie around and began to drag her away.

"Hey!" someone yelled, noticing him forcibly removing her. "What're you doing?"

Richard ignored the voice and kept moving, as Abbie cried and looked over her shoulder. "We can't leave him!"

Dr. Pellan quickly followed them.

"Hey!" someone else yelled and grasped Dr. Pellan's scarf. His neck yanked back with the movement and he spun around as it was pulled from his throat.

Richard yelled in pain when someone hit him hard in the back. He let Abbie go and turned around.

"Hey! Hey! It's Pellan's Theory!" a woman shouted, pointing at Dr. Pellan.

"Shit!" Richard muttered as a man walked up to Pellan, knocked off his hat and grabbed his face. In the scuffle with the scarf, the makeup stripe had smeared across his cheek.

Dr. Pellan pushed the man away and stepped back, but the man simply stepped forward.

"You're Pellan!" the man pointed. "You're the Clean Skin who was working for those lying assholes!"

"No, I brought you the truth!" Pellan said, stepping backward.

"Leave him alone!" Abbie threw herself in front of him, holding her hands out against his attacker.

"You're that Randell bitch!" The man pointed viciously as an angry crease furrowed his brow.

"And he's that reporter!" the woman accused, pointing to Richard.

"What are you doing here?" the angry man asked, then looked at Abbie. "You harboring them, too? You selling us out?"

379

Richard, Pellan and Abbie walked backward, keeping an eye on the four or five people moving toward them. Just then they heard another shot ring out. Everyone turned to see Austin standing, still holding his gun, and Josh, unmoving, on the ground.

Richard quickly grabbed Abbie's arm and caught Pellan's eye, and while the crowd was distracted, they ran for their lives.

Lysart looked over his shoulder as he ran away from the warehouse area with Richard and Abbie. The group harassing them hadn't noticed their departure yet, their attention fixed on Austin and the commotion caused by the gunshot. Lysart and his companions disappeared around the corner of the hardware store, out of view of the maddened crowd. All three ran toward the interzone gate.

"Please!" Lysart called out to the bio-guards manning it, wiping his chin. "Please, let us in! I'm a Clean Skin!"

The chief stepped forward, eyeing him cautiously. "What the hell's going on back there?" he asked. "We heard gunfire."

"Hey!" they heard a shout and turned to see a group spilling out from behind the warehouse.

Lysart eyed the mob reforming, then looked back at the soldiers. "Please! They just killed three people!"

"What?" the chief's face fell.

They heard more shouts and looked back to see the armed mob jogging toward them.

"Teargas!" the chief yelled to the soldiers, pulling on a mask. "We're going in!"

Lysart saw the gate open and a mass of armed soldiers head toward him, shooting teargas. He spun around to see the mob approaching from the other way.

"Dr. Pellan!" Abbie yelled, waving at Lysart to follow her and Richard as they turned and ran back toward her house. He followed them, wanting desperately to get out of the way of the two groups about to clash.

He ran as fast as he could, catching up to them. "If they come for us they'll go to your house, Abbie!"

"We'll go to Josh's!" Abbie panted, darting a glance at the clashing mob behind her.

As they neared the Chalmer house, she ran straight to the pot plant, retrieved the key she saw Josh hide the night before and unlocked the door. They rushed in, slammed the door shut and locked it again.

"Stay down!" Richard hissed, and the three of them dropped to the ground. They held still for a moment, panting, before Abbie peered out the window.

"They're coming!" she said, spinning around and moving to the middle of the kitchen. She threw aside the rug that lay on the floor. Lysart saw a hatch, which Abbie quickly lifted. "This is where they hid Karen!" she told them.

They heard a smash across the street, and Abbie moved back to the window. Lysart followed and saw some of the mob who had made it through the teargas and soldiers, smashing windows and kicking down her door. Abbie covered her mouth in terror.

Lysart eased her back from the windows.

"What are they doing?" she cried, tears rolling down her face. "They killed them! They killed the Chalmers, and now they're going to kill us!"

Lysart pulled her into a hug. He wanted to tell her it was going to be alright, but he honestly wasn't sure it would be. He released Abbie and moved to the window to peer out again. He spied Austin among the small mob at Abbie's house. He stood on the porch scanning the surroundings, then suddenly looked across the street at Josh's house. Lysart threw himself back from the window, shepherding Abbie and Richard behind him.

"What?" Richard asked. "What is it?"

"Austin," he whispered in dread, "I think he saw me."

Abbie, huddled on the floor with Richard and Dr. Pellan, held her breath. They heard someone rattle the knob on the front door, and her body tensed in fear at the sound. She looked at Richard and motioned to the opened hatch. She saw his green eyes study the opening, then look over at Dr. Pellan and motion for him to go first. Dr. Pellan shook his head.

"You two go," he whispered. "I'll cover it up."

Abbie and Richard shook their heads. The doorknob rattled again, more violently this time.

"Go!" Dr. Pellan hissed.

Richard motioned for Abbie to move, and just as she did, the front door burst open with a loud, frightening bang. Abbie's eyes widened in terror as Austin, Langdon and Trent tumbled through. She quickly scuttled to the opened hatch, but she knew it was too late. She heard thudding footsteps crossing the room, and as Richard and Dr. Pellan moved to counter the invaders, she heard the sickening sound of bodies connecting.

She spun around to see Dr. Pellan wrestling with Langdon, and Austin fighting with Richard. She didn't take either Pellan or Richard for a fighter, but didn't have time to worry about that. Trent was rushing at her. She ducked beneath his swooping arms, throwing the hatch shut, not wanting Richard or Pellan to fall down the gaping hole as they fought. She lunged for the kitchen counter, to a wooden block loaded with knives. She grabbed hold of the largest one, as Trent latched onto her hair and pulled her back. She yelled in pain and swiped the knife around at him, but Trent jumped back, avoiding it. She automatically ducked at hearing a gunshot, and the cupboard beside her head spat splinters of wood. She looked up to see Austin with his gun out, and Richard trying to wrestle it from his hands.

Trent lunged at her again, but she held the knife firm, viciously swinging it as he got close. She knew she was done for if he managed to disarm her. She had to hold onto the knife for dear life. Trent knew it too, and he began grabbing things off the counter—plates, cutlery, chopping boards—and throwing them at her and the knife. She cringed and cowered, as things hit her hard, darting her eyes to the others. Austin was throwing vicious punches at Richard's face, which were connecting with such ferocity that his blood splattered on the wall.

"No," she screamed, swiping the knife at Trent again, "leave us alone!"

She heard another gunshot, then heard Dr. Pellan moan. Langdon stood back from the doctor who cradled his stomach, blood pooling out and covering his hands.

"No!" she screamed again as Trent caught her off guard and hit her hard across the face. She smacked into the counter on the way down to the floor and the knife spilled from her hands.

"Bitch!" Trent spat, kicking her knife away.

Austin yelled out in pain then, and Abbie glanced over to see that Richard had plunged a pocketknife into Austin's shoulder and knocked the gun from his hand. But Trent rushed at Richard.

Abbie blinked to clear her vision, resting her eyes on the kitchen knife on the floor. She looked back to see Langdon punching a wounded, bleeding Pellan, then saw Austin and

Trent, who had now overpowered Richard, kicking him as he tried to crawl away.

Shaking with the horror of what had happened to the Chalmer family, and what was happening to the three of them now, Abbie somehow scrambled to her feet and grabbed the knife. She wasn't quite sure how she was moving; it didn't feel real, it felt like something deep inside had taken over and was moving for her. A sound came from her mouth. It was loud. A scream. A roar.

"Hey!" Austin yelled in panic, realizing she was off the floor. Trent, however, didn't have time. His back was to her as he kicked Richard, and it was that back that Abbie plunged the knife into, still screaming wildly as she did.

Austin charged her, but not before she managed to plunge that knife another two times. Trent collapsed into Langdon, clasping his back, as Austin grabbed her. She felt a pain at her wrist as he made her drop the knife, then she saw his angry dark eyes as he raised his fist and landed a crunching blow to her face.

She hit the floor again, saw feet at her face, but couldn't move. She blinked heavily, all sound seemed distorted. Her nose was probably broken and she tasted blood in her mouth. She looked up and saw Austin reaching for the kitchen knife. Black spots filled her vision and she wanted to cry for help, but couldn't seem to find the air to do it. She tried desperately to breathe in, then suddenly realized why she couldn't.

She was having an asthma attack.

And her Ventolin was back across the street in her house.

She gasped loudly, wheezing with all her might, trying to suck air into her closed-down lungs, as the black spots became more prevalent.

"He's dead!" She picked out Langdon's garbled voice as he knelt over Trent.

Austin turned back to her, a look of pure hate upon his face. He moved to her, holding up the bloodied kitchen knife.

Everything felt as if it were in slow motion then. Breathless, she looked over at Richard and tried to reach for him, but his back was turned to her. His body was limp, motionless. She didn't know if he was just unconscious or whether he was dead already. Caught in her airless vacuum, her eyes moved to Dr. Pellan, his entire stomach red with blood, but still he moved. He was reaching for something, grabbed it, then raised his arm. Austin's gun, which had spilled across the floor in the tussle with Richard, was in his hands.

She heard a loud noise. Through the black spots clouding her vision, she saw Austin's throat burst open. Shot from behind, his wide-eyed body collapsed and fell onto her with a thud. He was choking and gurgling, his weight adding to the pressure in her airless lungs. Another two shots fired. Abbie saw Pellan's body bounce and Langdon's head fling back. They'd fired at each other. Langdon's body fell onto the floor.

Abbie looked back at Austin lying across her. His eyes were open, but she saw no life within them any more; his blood poured over her. She didn't have the strength to move him. She couldn't even move herself. She saw Pellan's limp body slide down to the floor, lying in his own pool of blood on the other side of the kitchen, his eyes blinking heavily at hers. Then she eyed Richard lying there so still between them.

She didn't know how long she hadn't breathed for, but she knew her face was blue. After everything that had happened, after all the violence she'd seen, even though she lay here now covered in Austin's blood, this was how she was going to die. This asthma, which had always been a controlled threat, would now be the thing to kill her.

And Dr. Pellan's bloodied body, and Richard's battered body, would be the last things she would ever see.

Stanley Barrick burst into the operations room.

"Report!" he yelled.

"It's happening again!" Wattowski called. "I don't know how. As soon as the alarms went off it was there! It was that fast!"

"Get me vision," Stanley barked. "Get me status! What the hell is it doing!"

"On it, sir!" Gavin yelled.

"My units are on the move," Colonel Levin reported, listening to something through a comms channel in his ear. "They got no weapons, they got no juice! Systems are down! The ship's blocking us again."

"It's just hovering, like before," Wattowski called.

"Where?" Stanley barked.

"Victoryville."

Abbie opened her eyes slowly. It took her a moment to realize where she was. Still lying on the kitchen floor, Austin's body still weighing her down.

But something felt different.

She looked around at the carnage, the bodies strewn across the kitchen floor, could hear that familiar mechanical buzzing noise. *Had that been there before? During the attack?* It was loud. Louder than before. Where was it coming from? She could hear the sound of wind rushing wildly outside.

Suddenly Richard moved, groaned.

He's still alive!

Her eyes widened with hope as she stared at him. Richard rolled onto his back and raised a hand to his face, feeling along his bones and stared at the blood smeared across his fingers. Abbie's brow crinkled. From what she could see, his face looked uninjured, just bloodied. There was no swelling, no bruising. It was odd.

Then suddenly she gasped.

She realized she was breathing.

Normally.

Richard looked over at her. "Abbie?"

She stared wide-eyed at him. "I can breathe," she whispered.

Richard gave her a puzzled look, his mind ticking over, then he scanned down his body. He suddenly sat up, hands patting himself down. "I'm . . . not injured," he said, confused.

They heard Dr. Pellan groan, as he slowly pulled himself to sit up. He stared at the two of them for a moment, dazed, then frantically began to tear open his bloodied shirt and search his bare stomach wildly for signs of the bullets that had penetrated him moments earlier. He stared at Abbie and Richard, stunned.

"The bullets are gone," he whispered.

The three of them looked around at their assailants. They didn't move. Abbie rolled Austin's dead weight off her with a grunt and stumbled shakily to her feet.

"What happened?" she asked, looking down at her torso still drenched in Austin's blood. "What's happened?"

Richard, too, got to his feet, surveying the carnage again. The mechanical buzzing sounded louder. The windows rattled a little.

Abbie took deep breaths. She was breathing with such ease. Her lungs had never felt this light before, so free.

"My lungs," she said, as though thinking aloud. "I can breathe . . . they're so clear."

Richard helped Dr. Pellan to his feet.

"I was having an asthma attack," she continued. "I should be dead. How can I suddenly breathe?"

Richard moved to her and took her gently by the shoulders. "Abbie, it's alright," he said softly, pulling her into a hug.

"I should be dead," she said again into his shoulder, wrapping her arms around his back. "Am I dreaming?"

Richard shook his head, moving her back at arm's length. His green eyes gazed at her, just as concerned as hers were. "No. This isn't a dream, Abbie. You're alive. We're all alive."

"But they're not." She pointed to the three unmoving bodies. Richard released her and they just stared.

"They died before it happened . . ." Dr. Pellan said, astounded, looking at the bodies.

"Before what happened?" Abbie asked.

"It," Pellan said, still a little dazed, a little shaken. "*It* must've happened again."

Abbie and Richard stared at him.

"None of us could have survived this." He indicated the bloodied kitchen, opened his shirt and examined his bullet-free torso. "We were dying, we should *not* have survived this." He looked back to Richard and Abbie. "Something made us survive. Something took those bullets from me. Something healed us."

"But I'm still here," Abbie said. "They're Striped Ones." She pointed to Austin, Langdon and Trent. "They're dead, so shouldn't I be, too?"

Richard's attention suddenly turned to the window. It looked dark out, like the sun had disappeared behind a bank of clouds. He peered out. "The mob across the road, they're picking themselves off the grou—holy . . ." he said, eyes turning upward. "You need to take a look at this."

Abbie and Dr. Pellan moved to the window and saw what Richard was looking at: the massive black ship hovering above their town.

"Oh my God . . ." she whispered. "They came back."

Dr. Pellan nodded vaguely to himself, looking back at the bodies on the floor. "We killed them before it happened," he said quietly. "We killed them. They were dead. This phenomenon, the aliens, whoever they are . . . they can heal, but they cannot resurrect the dead."

Abbie, shaking, stared down at Trent and his bloodied back from her knife attack. "Josh?" she suddenly blurted. "Was he dead? Did he die?"

"I don't know," Dr. Pellan answered.

"What about Kaitlyn? Charlie?" she asked. "The soldiers were moving in!"

Richard looked back at her. "Let's go find out!"

Stanley moved to stand behind Gavin's chair. It had been a long twenty-four hours watching as the ship hovered over the town, powerless again to do anything.

But suddenly, the comms had come back online.

And the ship was still there . . .

"What is it?" he asked Gavin.

The technician motioned to a row of screens. "Data, sir," he said. "A whole lot of data."

"Like last time? What does that mean?"

"No, they uploaded a whole load of data to our systems. Like, huge! A massive amount of data."

"But that's what they did last time," Stanley said, eyes fixed on the screens and the scrolling information.

"No, sir," the technician said. "Last time they downloaded our information. They took from us. This time they're uploading it. They're giving to us."

"Giving us what?" Stanley asked. "Viruses? Are they trying to take our systems down?"

"No." The technician selected one of the packets of data and opened it. He read it for a moment. "Holy shit," he whispered.

"What?" Stanley said.

The technician looked at him. "It's in English." He looked back at the screen. "And Chinese. And Spanish. And . . ."

"What is?"

"I don't know. It looks like some kind of medical, scientific . . ."

"Beta cells . . ." Dr. Hogarth read aloud over their shoulder. At first sign of the ship reappearing twenty-four hours ago, Stanley had brought her back in. "Pancreas . . . insulin . . ." She glanced at them, then shouldered her way closer to the screen, scrolling down the data. The room sat silent while she scanned through it. Then she paused and stood back up. "This," she looked at them, "looks like a medical file for someone with diabetes."

The room stood silent as they stared at her.

"Diabetes?" Stanley screwed his face up.

"Open another data packet," Rita ordered the technician. He did so and she immediately scanned through the file while the room remained silent. She stood up, a shocked look on her face, pointing to the screen. "This mentions electrical activity in the brain . . . this could be epilepsy." She moved to the next file, then the next, then the next, before she stopped and turned around, wide-eyed, chest rising and falling with excitement.

"Chromosomes," she whispered to herself. "They've been studying us. I . . ." She looked at the screen, then back to them again. "I think these . . . I think these might be cures."

Deputy Leo Cann stood at the door to the storeroom, listening. He was shaking a little. He knew it had happened again. The Occurrence. He'd woken up on the floor. The first thing he did was check to see that Kaitlyn and the children, now hiding in the roof space, were okay. As soon as he'd heard the gunfire earlier, he'd gotten off the chair and made them all climb into the ceiling space. Now that he checked on them, they were still there.

That's what confused him.

Both he and the baby were Striped Ones. Kaitlyn and the boy were Clean Skins. And they were all still here. No one was missing.

And that's when he noticed his head felt okay, his face no longer swollen, his ribs no longer hurting.

He clasped hold of the door handle, praying that Claire and Lena were alright; that the ship hadn't taken them instead.

He heard voices and footsteps and looked up to the manhole in the roof. Kaitlyn peered down and he motioned for her to close the cover. She did, and he grasped hold of the old hammer he found tucked away at the back of a shelf. It would have to do.

Suddenly he felt the doorknob turning.

He stepped back and raised the hammer high, ready to hit Roy or whoever came through that door.

It burst open and there stood the chief, gun aiming in his direction.

"Earl?" he said, shocked.

"Leo!"

"What the hell is happening?"

"It happened again."

"I know. Where's Roy?" Leo panted.

"That's what I'm trying to find out. Where're the other hostages?"

"Kaitlyn!" Leo whispered loudly up to the roof. Earl's eyes followed his voice. "It's okay! You can come down now."

The hatch shifted and Kaitlyn peered down warily.

Earl glanced at Leo, then waved someone outside forward.

"Help them down," he ordered the two soldiers who had moved into the room. Then he pulled out a second pistol from his belt and handed it to Leo. "You alright? Your face, it's . . ."

"Healed," Leo said taking the gun and giving him a nod of thanks. "You ready?"

Earl gave him a firm nod. "Yeah, let's finish this."

Richard walked cautiously down the street with Abbie and Dr. Pellan, their eyes fixed on the black ship that covered the sky above them; the wind was whipping around strongly, blowing Abbie's long hair about her face. The mob across the road watched them, but didn't try to attack or follow. They were too scared, eyes fixed on the massive ship hovering above the town.

Abbie stuck close to Richard's side, her hand clinging onto his arm. He found it reassuring. The interzone gate was open and some of the soldiers stood in front of the hardware store, pacing around confused; some were still picking themselves up off the floor; some staring fixedly up into the sky. They, too, were scared. Confused. Stunned.

The mechanical noise coming from the ship suddenly

increased in volume and they covered their ears and looked away, as the ground seemed to vibrate beneath their feet. When Richard opened his eyes again, the sunlight was upon him. He looked up into the sky, and it was gone . . . the ship had disappeared.

Just like that.

The three of them stood in the middle of the road staring at each other, staring at the empty sky overhead, but they were strangely calm. They weren't afraid. The aliens hadn't stolen anyone this time. Hadn't killed anyone.

They had healed them.

They had saved their lives.

"Come on," Richard said.

They turned the corner and moved to the parking area where the mob had originally gathered. Some were still there, but no Striped Ones screamed at them, or came charging at them. Everyone was confused and frightened by what had happened. Richard noted that their stripes seemed faded now, nowhere near the deep red color they'd once been. Abbie's was lighter, too, he saw.

As they made their way carefully to where Josh, Peter and Karen's bodies had been, Richard saw they were still lying where they'd fallen. They had died before the second Occurrence. Abbie raised her free hand to cover her mouth as tears fell down her cheeks, the confronting truth of Josh's death hitting her. Richard pulled her into another hug, wanting to ease her pain.

He looked over Abbie's crying frame to where Magnus and Roy were. Magnus sat in his wheelchair, staring at his shaking hands. The blotchy eczema that had once clung to his face was gone; the seven stripes that had once stained him were faded. Richard's eyes grew hard, watching as Magnus slowly, shakily, stood from his wheelchair. Roy moved as if to catch him, but

Magnus waved him away and began to take steps.

"Goddamn it, they healed us!" Roy exclaimed, hand held to his cheek. "My face ain't twitching . . . my gut don't hurt!"

Magnus took a few more steps, nodding to himself as he stretched his back. A huge smile broke over his face. "Well, I'll be . . ."

Richard felt a an anger flame up in his belly and Abbie gave voice to his thoughts.

"How could you?" she yelled at Magnus, breaking free of Richard's arms. "You killed these people! You don't deserve to be healed!"

"Abbie!" Richard pulled her back to him.

"You're murderers!" she yelled.

Magnus' cold stony face turned to hers, as some of those still gathered began to drift away. Shocked and terrified, they were retreating to their homes.

"You said the aliens were going to come back," she shouted. "Well, guess what? They *did*! And everything you did was for nothing, because they healed us! They weren't trying to wipe us out, they were trying to heal us!"

"Screw you!" Roy said, stepping their way.

"No, screw you!" Dr. Pellan said, stepping forward. "No one's missing this time. They didn't attack us. They helped us!" He held his hands out, using them to accentuate his words and make them understand. "They were trying to help, that's all!"

"Get out of my territory, before I kill you, Clean Skin!" Magnus growled.

"There are no territories any more," Richard told him firmly. "We've all been healed. We're all the same now. Equal. I guarantee you, within hours, those barriers will be down, and you'll be thrown in jail for what you did. Both of you." He shot Roy a venomous look.

Roy raised his gun and Richard tensed. However, Roy stopped short as a voice sounded behind him.

"I wouldn't, Roy." A bloodied Deputy Cann emerged from the warehouse with a gun pointed firmly at the hardware store owner. "I *really* wouldn't!" Leo said, through clenched teeth.

Roy looked over his shoulder at the deputy, shocked to see him. "How'd you get out? Where'd you get that gun?"

The chief emerged behind the deputy, gun raised also. "I told you I wanted my deputy back, Roy."

"Abbie?" they heard the shaky voice of Kaitlyn calling. She emerged from behind Deputy Cann, holding Charlie to her chest, the hand of Cassius in the other.

"Kaitlyn?" Abbie ran over to her, and the girl fell into Abbie's arms, sobbing uncontrollably as she stared at the bodies of the Chalmer family on the ground.

Richard looked over at Magnus. "It's over."

"Get her!" Magnus barked at Roy, motioning to Kaitlyn. "We'll do a deal!"

Abbie looked up horrified as Roy lunged and Richard shouted, "No!"

But Deputy Cann fired, hitting Roy in the thigh and dropping him to the ground. "*Enough!*"

Magnus moved for his chair, but the chief turned his weapon on him.

"Don't move, Magnus," he said firmly, giving him a hard stare. "*Don't move!*"

Dr. Pellan quickly stepped forward and tore the gun from Roy's hand. He stood back, facing what was left of the crowd. No one tried to fight them. Instead, the final few now turned and ran away.

Magnus darted a steely, clear-eyed stare from the deputy to the chief and back.

"Do you know who you're messing with?" Magnus' voice sounded strange without his phlegmy wheeze.

"Yeah," the chief nodded, "a murderer who's going away from a long, long time."

"I didn't kill anyone." Magnus' eyes glinted with satisfaction.

"Yeah, you did," Richard said. "You may not have pulled the trigger yourself, but you killed with your words of hate, and I will do my damnedest to make sure the penalty is the same."

"As will I," Dr. Pellan nodded.

"You?" Magnus questioned doubtfully, then turned to the chief. "These two are wanted by Homeland Security. They're the ones you should be arresting."

The chief flicked his eyes to them, but kept his gun on Magnus. "No, I think I got the ones I want right here."

Richard gave Magnus a satisfied look.

The slight smile on Magnus' face faltered a little.

"Miss Randell?" the chief called.

"Yeah?" she looked over at him.

"Go tell the soldiers out front that I have Magnus Bracks and Roy Kenny, leaders of the Victoryville massacre."

Magnus snarled as Abbie moved away from Kaitlyn. She glanced down at Josh's lifeless, beaten body. He was face down. He'd been shot in the back of the head.

"With pleasure," she said, taking Cassius' hand and leading the hostages away.

Afterward

Stanley Barrick sat on his couch sipping a Scotch on the rocks. His feet were up on the coffee table, his tie loosened, his shirt untucked. He was in somewhat of a numb state, overtired from the craziest eleven days the world had ever seen—two days of blackout, and nine days of meltdown in between.

After the second blackout, the ship had disappeared again. Many believed that it had gone for good this time, that they had done what they had come to do. Others believed it was still out there somewhere, just waiting to descend once more. A whole realm of amateur astronomers were now searching the skies every day, waiting to catch another glimpse. The mechanical buzzing noise reported in the town seemed to have stopped, and the environmental readings seemed normal. However, NASA were continuing to scan the skies and measure the levels of mercury in the air. Watching. Waiting.

Quite honestly, although he'd been expecting it, he was still a little shocked by the second Occurrence and concerned for what this meant for their futures. They had mountains of data to review. It would take them months, maybe years, to go through it all, but early indications were that Rita Hogarth was right. The uploaded data pointed to potential cures for many of the illnesses that plagued mankind. Furthermore, it potentially explained the reason behind the disappearances of the healthy. It would seem that during the blackout of the first Occurrence, the visitors had downloaded our information and studied the healthy, the Striped Ones and the Clean Skins. Given what transpired during the second Occurrence, the theory that the healthy were used to fix those who remained seemed to make sense.

The healthy were, after all, still missing. The aliens had not returned them.

Stanley, like many in the world, wasn't sure how he felt about that. The fact that these aliens had used the people of Victoryville like this. Yes, they had potentially provided the human race with cures that would save thousands, maybe millions, of lives, but were we supposed to be happy about it? The cost of those cures had been some other thousands of lives.

And for what price? That's what Stanley worried about the most. Why would alien beings do the human race a favor? There had to be more to it. Wattowski's theory, that the ship had selected Victoryville because it had been attracted to the high output of mercury in the area, was of interest. Clivecorp had been fined in the past for its high readings of the toxic substance. Analysts were claiming this direct link—the pollutant produced by Clivecorp and the pollutant produced by the ship—could be the driver for their visit, suggesting the "visitors" could want our mercury, and the cures were perhaps some form of prepayment for that.

"Mercury," Stanley muttered, sipping his Scotch.

Of course, they wouldn't tell the public that just yet. Who knows how they might react to news of a potential third visit? Then again, after two, did it really matter any more? Whatever these things wanted, the human race was powerless to stop them from taking it.

He watched the replay of the president's address, a show of leadership to allay fears. Turner just told the people what they already knew: that the aliens had indeed returned and the strange phenomenon had occurred again. The people of Victoryville had blacked out, yet this time when they awoke, no one was missing. Everyone in Victoryville was accounted for, Clean Skins and Striped Ones. The president noted there was one major difference from the first time, however—it appeared the Striped Ones had been healed of their illnesses. But the president said nothing about the mercury link, or the data upload of the cures. They didn't want to get people's hopes up until the data was verified. Still, he gave enough of a positive spin to keep the people of the world pacified. For now.

Once order had been restored in Victoryville, several CDC units had been dispatched into the town. Testing was underway to confirm whether the genetic defects of the Clean Skins had also been rectified. The president asked for everyone to continue to remain calm while further investigations took place, but Stanley felt that such exhortations weren't really needed. There was something very different about things this time. People seemed less afraid. No one else had gone missing. The sick were now healed. This second visit hadn't cost the people of Earth anything.

Yet.

News coverage from around the world showed most people had retreated from the streets, incidences of looting almost ceased and angry mobs were dispersing. Something good had occurred, and they couldn't quite bring themselves to act badly in the face of that. Some were even calling it a miracle. Even Victoryville was peaceful, despite the atrocity that had taken place prior to the second Occurrence.

The reporter, Richard Keene, and scientist, Dr. Pellan, had

handed themselves over to the authorities, while they also, along with Deputy Cann, Chief Blackstone and town resident, Abbie Randell, had brought those responsible for the Victoryville killings to justice. The Magnus Bracks problem was under control.

Stanley sighed as he finished off his drink and considered having another, thoughts of his part in the town's combustion were haunting him. The truth was he wanted to drink the whole bottle, but he knew he would regret it in the morning. Tomorrow was another day, and there was a lot of cleaning up yet to be done. There were continuing investigations, there were barricades to be torn down, and who knew? There was always the chance that this mysterious phenomenon could occur yet again.

In fact, he was certain it would.

Richard sat in his apartment in New York and scrolled down the comments to his news story on the outcome of Dr. Pellan's case. He smiled, content. Although there were some who thought both he and Pellan had acted rashly, most supported what they had done in bringing the truth to light. Richard had gotten off more lightly than Dr. Pellan. He'd been slapped with a heavy fine and charged with several offences, but his lawyer quickly had them quashed. And Harry Dean made sure his legal costs were covered.

Dr. Pellan was up against heavier charges, namely, the ones brought against him by Homeland Security, but also that of the death of Austin Saller and Langdon Swan. A top criminal lawyer by the name of Thomas Calhooney came to his defense, free of charge. Calhooney was one of the best, and he never missed the opportunity for a little limelight. Dr. Pellan's case was the biggest the world had ever seen and Calhooney did his best to bring the house down. Public opinion was on Pellan's side, and in the end, he was cleared of the deaths of Austin and Langdon; they were ruled as self defence, and the charges brought against him by Homeland Security were rather uniquely pleaded out behind closed doors. Pellan's sentence was to serve some time in prison, then spend the rest of it confined and monitored in his home. His time spent in custody during the trial meant that once the verdict was handed down, his time behind bars had already been served. Calhooney, for good measure, saw the charges against Abbie for Trent Ford's death quickly dismissed also.

Richard had been there throughout Dr. Pellan's trial, covering it for CNN. It was the only story Richard had agreed to, having told Harry he needed some time off. Harry agreed, just telling him, "Whenever you want to hit the saddle again, kid, the door will be open for you."

Richard knew he couldn't focus on another story, because Victoryville was still very much inside his head. While people had moved onto Pellan's trial, word soon got out that there had been a massive data upload during the second Occurrence. The government advised it was analyzing the data from the alien upload and would report back when they knew more. Between the mysterious upload and talk of whether the phenomenon would occur yet again, the pressure on them was mounting. Still, Richard felt as though what happened in Victoryville had not really been dealt with properly. Rather, it had been quickly swept under the rug: a black spot, a very dark time in US history, as the world moved on to attend to more "pressing" matters.

Mayor Russo had stood down from his office, the stigma of the events something he, along with the rest of the council, were keen to distance themselves from. It soon came to light that the mayor's adversarial relationship with Magnus Bracks had served as a catalyst for the Victoryville siege. Russo was in full PR drive, though, working hard to rescue his career, offering to do his duty and testify against Magnus Bracks. He wanted to ensure the man was put away for life, and as Russo took the stand to do so, the smug look he gave Bracks screamed there was no love lost between the two.

The barrier between zones was quickly torn down, the military perimeter gradually dismantled, and movement in and out of the town eventually went back to normal as the CDC and various scientists began their testing on the survivors.

A massive effort was mounted to match orphans with families who wanted to adopt a survivor of the alien visitation, to repair damage to houses, and to thoroughly catalogue each survivor. The government had officially declared the people of Victoryville free of contagion. However, both the Striped Ones and the Clean Skins were now required, by law, to attend regular checkups every three months to ensure nothing about their health, or their DNA, changed over time. Richard, along with the other survivors of Victoryville, would be tracked by the government for the rest of his life. He felt a bit like an ex-prisoner in that regard, checking in regularly to his parole officer.

So, there was a massive effort to get the town back on its feet, and volunteers arrived to help boost the medical and police staff numbers, and do what needed to be done. As Richard had hoped, the people he remembered coming to the beach to help the animals injured in the Deepwater Horizon disaster, had come to help Victoryville.

As time passed, and the ship had not reappeared, the government realized that they could not keep the residents—now referred to by the press collectively as the Healed Ones—hostage any longer and they were finally allowed to leave. Not that many did, however. The aliens may have gone again, but fascination with the town remained.

Before long, the first tourists arrived in the town, eager to get a close-up look at some Striped Ones. For this very reason, few of those with stripes had wanted to leave the town. Forever marked, although the stripes were faded and faint, they would always be a freak show to outsiders. They would always be a memory of that ship, and of what happened in that town. And what could happen again.

Still, things almost seemed normal. Well, as normal as they could be with the mystery of the visitors still unresolved, with the faded stripes as a constant reminder, with the healthy still missing, and with the continuing government surveillance.

Although the Clean Skins had more anonymity—no one could identify them at a glance like the Striped Ones—Richard felt as though he may as well have been Striped. His face was too well known now and anonymity was something he would never experience again. Assimilating back into the general population was something he couldn't do. And not just because his face was well known. It was because he simply couldn't just sweep things away like that and return to normal. The people out there, outside of Victoryville, needed to know what really happened. And future generations, he thought, needed a reminder of what the human race could have become had it given in to fear and hate. What Victoryville had almost given itself up to.

He'd met with Dr. Pellan several times while covering his trial. The man had aged before his eyes. Shocked by all that had happened, he was surprised that he too had become a central figure in the story; that Pellan's Theory was now a part of world history.

"My hands are clean, Mr. Keene," he'd said during one visit, "and yet I feel they are stained with blood."

"If you hadn't shot Austin, he would've killed Abbie. You saved her. And Langdon was going to kill you. *Almost* did kill

403

you."

"Yes. But how many others did I hurt by unleashing this truth upon the population?"

"If people hurt others, they did that themselves, Dr. Pellan. All you did was help set the truth free."

Dr. Pellan had nodded sadly, events weighing upon him greatly. "Professor Meeks was always hounding me to step into the limelight. Now, here I am."

"Yes. Here we all are. But we can do some good with this attention, Dr. Pellan. Help me. Help me write a book on what happened. Let's tell people what really occurred. What it was like on the inside. Our stories, the stories of those in the town, they need to be told."

Pellan looked thoughtfully at Richard for a moment before nodding. "Alright, I will." Then he smiled, melancholy. "I don't think what I have to say will please Professor Meeks much though."

Richard nodded. "Well, as Abbie told me once, that's the power of the truth. It hurts."

So, the scientist had agreed to help with the book Richard was writing on the Victoryville phenomenon. Clearly, Dr. Pellan also wanted the events in the town to never be forgotten. He wanted to share what he saw.

And Richard knew that people would listen. For good or ill, Victoryville had become the town synonymous with alien contact. Forget Roswell, that was a joke. Richard, Dr. Pellan, Abbie, Kaitlyn, Josh, the Chalmers, and even Magnus and Roy: the world knew their names, and Richard didn't want them to ever forget. Both he and Abbie, along with Dr. Pellan, were making sure of that. This wasn't just about the big picture of the alien contact; this was about the detail of the individuals whose lives were turned upside down by their fellow man.

Whether they had wanted it or not, the three of them had

inadvertently become the spokespeople for the Striped Ones and the Clean Skins, and they had to use their new positions wisely. Richard, given his status as a reporter, had been called upon for endless interviews afterward, but Abbie and Dr. Pellan had also been dragged in, and to their credit they had accepted the responsibility.

Richard stared at the photo displayed at the top of the article he'd been reading. It was a shot of Pellan in the witness stand, which also captured his two daughters sitting in the row behind his lawyer. Richard smiled, pleased that Dr. Pellan had finally been reunited with them, although he regretted that they had to see their father like that, cuffed like a criminal, standing in orange coveralls.

Richard recalled sitting in the Victoryville police station in one of the little cells with Dr. Pellan as they awaited their fate after handing themselves in. Dr. Pellan had looked at him, studied the dried blood that covered their healed bodies.

"We are lucky men," Pellan had said.

"Yeah," Richard said, although his voice didn't portray a man who felt lucky after what he'd witnessed that day, nor looking at the cell in which he sat.

"We've been given a second chance," Pellan told him.

Richard nodded, looking down at the hands in his lap.

"We've been given a second chance," Pellan said again.

Richard looked up, and saw Pellan was looking past him. He turned to see what Pellan was staring at and saw the chief escorting Abbie into the cell next to theirs.

"We've been given a second chance," Pellan said yet again, carefully, accentuating each word.

Richard looked back at him.

"Don't waste it, Mr. Keene," Pellan had told him. "Life is too short."

He saw Pellan glance at Abbie again, and Richard turned to look at her too. She noticed his stare, and gave him a tentative smile. He returned it.

"Don't waste it," Pellan repeated, tilting his head back to rest on the wall behind him, and closing his eyes.

Sitting in his apartment's study, Richard came out of his reverie and sighed. He turned his eyes away from the article and picked up his dictaphone, deciding to play back one of the recordings he'd made of his musings.

"We believe that the aliens took our healthy and they used them to heal us. The government is still trying to decipher the full implications of the data upload they gave us, but whoever these aliens were, it seems they tried to save the human race. But what have they saved? Sometimes I think they have saved a lot of good: the Abbie Randells, Dr. Pellans, Deputy Canns, Chief Blackstones and Shonda-Mays of this world. But I also see the Magnus Bracks and the Roy Kennys and can't help wishing they'd been taken instead of the healthy.

"To save the human race from illness and disease the cost for the people of Victoryville was great. Many out there are still angry that these beings stepped in and made this decision for us. That they took us over, probed our bodies, our research, and played God. I'm sure most people of Victoryville would rather see their healthy returned than see their illnesses healed. Have the healthy gone for good? Or are they still alive somewhere? We may never know the answer. And we may never meet the aliens that did this and get the chance to ask why.

"Regardless, I don't think we can live in a world where we wait and wonder. I see this as a second chance, a new beginning. I see this as an awakening. The phenomenon created a brutal society where survival of the fittest, or should I say, survival of the "sickest", almost tore us apart. The aliens were trying to heal us, and we nearly destroyed ourselves in the process. That was our primal response. We gave in to fear and hate. Maybe that's what this was about? Maybe this was a test. To see how we would react. To see what this species, alien to *them*, would do. And if so, what did we show them? Were they impressed by our rate of destruction? Or were they disappointed at how quickly we crumbled?

"You know, I think that's why they showed themselves to the people of Victoryville when they came back the second time. They wanted us to see them. And they didn't remove the stripes when they came back. If they could heal us, then they could have removed those stripes, but they didn't. I think they left the stripes as a reminder. A reminder of what almost happened. A reminder of what not to become, of what not to do again. To remind us that we are not alone. That this is our second chance. Or maybe, our last chance. We were sick and dying before, the Striped Ones, the Clean Skins, but now we are collectively the Healed Ones. All of us. And I think that's why it is our second chance. But will we humans heed the warning? Can we learn and rise above? Will we use these stripes as a reminder? I hope so ... I really, really, hope so ... because I love this Earth. And I want to live a long happy life with the people on it. This truly *is* the time of the stripes. This is our second chance. To never forget what happened, and to do things right moving forward."

Richard hit stop and looked back at the screen as new comments popped up on the opened article.

"Hey," Abbie's voice called softly from the doorway. Richard turned his eyes to her and smiled. She leaned against the doorframe, arms folded.

"How's it coming along?"

"I'm just taking a break," he told her, looking at the screen, "reading the comments on the Pellan verdict."

Abbie moved up behind him and scanned the screen. "Good or bad?"

He looked around at her beautiful face, her concerned eyes, the faded stripe running down her chin and neck.

"It's all good," he said softly. "It's all good." He reached out and took her hand in his. "Are you ready for your interview, Abbie Randell? Are you ready to tell your story?"

She nodded, squeezing his hand back.

"Yeah, let's do this."

Abbie searched the aisles for the spices she was looking for, glad to be able to do this, go grocery shopping like a normal person. She'd spent the afternoon being interviewed by Richard, which had been harder than she'd thought, despite the months that had passed since the second Occurrence. But in some ways the interview had been cathartic. Now, though, she needed to take a break and set her mind to other things.

Richard had suggested dinner, and she'd agreed. After drying her tears, they'd left the apartment and headed to their local grocery store. Abbie was now a resident of New York. Victoryville was somewhere she couldn't set foot for a while. This was her home now. Richard's home had become hers.

She looked over her shoulder and saw him walking along the fresh produce aisle, basket in hand, plucking out potatoes and shallots. Things with Richard had been unexpected, and it had happened fast, but at the same time it had felt so right, so natural. Welcomed. After the madness of what had happened, they'd been by each other's side ever since.

She had watched as Magnus and Roy were taken into custody, and she watched as Richard and Dr. Pellan had voluntarily gone with the chief and soldiers. Abbie had gone with them, but Chief Blackstone had released her soon after.

Richard told her to go home and wait with Kaitlyn and Charlie. So she did.

She waited and waited until finally she received a call from him. They were being questioned by Homeland Security, but they were fine. The CDC had flooded the town and within days Abbie, Kaitlyn and Charlie had been thoroughly studied and recorded. As soon as the Victoryville border had been reopened, Kaitlyn's mother had been granted permission to come and collect her daughter and grandson and go back to their apartment. Abbie felt so happy to see the tearful reunion between them, although it cut her deep inside to know that she would never be afforded the same opportunity with her own family.

After Kaitlyn and Charlie's departure, she'd been left alone in her house with the memories of what had happened. Her broken windows were boarded up, a makeshift door was hung where her last one had been kicked in. She sat in her room and stared across the street at Josh's house, cordoned off with police tape. She pictured the bodies of Austin, Trent and Langdon lying on the kitchen floor. She pictured the bodies of the Chalmers in the parking area behind the hardware store, where now only dried bloodstains and painted outlines remained, separated from the rest of the world by more police tape.

One night, Shonda-May knocked on her door with a casserole in hand and Cassius by her side. Abbie welcomed them in and they ate dinner together. And when she finally said goodnight to them, she hugged Shonda-May so tight she wondered whether she might ever let her go. "Thank you," she'd whispered to Shonda-May. "Thank you for coming to help." Her neighbor gave her a warm smile, squeezed her hand, then left again.

Chief Blackstone had returned to question her further about what had happened across the street. She kept thinking about Trent's body and the knife she'd plunged into his back; kept thinking about her blackened fingers from when they'd fingerprinted her; kept wondering whether she would ever see Richard and Dr. Pellan again.

When the chief had left, she'd held the framed photo of her missing family to her chest as tears rolled down her face at the horrible feeling inside. At the emptiness. The loneliness. The sorrow. That night she lay on the couch and pretended that Richard lay there with her, just as he had done that one night. It felt like it was a lifetime ago.

Deputy Cann had paid her a visit to see how she was doing. She was pleased to see that the deputy's face was healed. Just like her lungs. Although the faded stripe remained on his chin, too. She wondered what his stripe had been due to, but didn't want to pry. He had a look in his eyes as he stared at her, a darkness remembered, that she understood all too well. Something that the chief, as a Clean Skin, would never quite understand, but something that she and the deputy, as Striped Ones who'd been caught up in the madness, would never forget. But she also saw relief and a slight contentment in his eyes. He'd been reunited with Claire and Lena. He had most of his family back again. But it was clear he still mourned his little boy.

A few days after Deputy Cann's visit, Richard had turned up on her doorstep. He looked tired, his unshaven face having the beginnings of a beard. She took a few moments to realize that he was actually there and she wasn't dreaming, before throwing her arms around his neck, latching onto him for dear life. He latched onto her too and they stood there in her doorway for how long, she didn't know, just holding each other tight.

"They just released me," he said when they finally let each other go.

"And you came straight here?" she'd asked.

He looked at her, then nodded, giving a half smile. "Yeah, I did."

She brought him inside and he told her what had happened, that Dr. Pellan was still in custody. She'd told him of Kaitlyn's tearful reunion with her mother, and how she was safe at home with her family. Richard had smiled. Something good had come from all of this. Kaitlyn had Charlie, and now she had her mother again.

She and Richard sat on that couch and stared at each other. They'd talked for a couple of hours, then Abbie offered him food, but he'd told her he was tired, and she'd said she was too. It was late. She asked him to stay. She took his hand and led him upstairs. He'd showered, while she waited. She offered him her bed this time, instead of the couch or the basement, wanting him to stay close now he'd returned. It seemed he felt the same way. They didn't speak, they just stared at each other as they'd crawled into her bed. They didn't sleep, not straightaway. Abbie rolled onto her side and faced him, taking his hand in hers, not wanting to let it go, as she gazed into his calm, green eyes.

"I'm glad you're okay," she'd said softly.

"And me, you," he said.

The silence sat.

"We survived," she whispered.

"We did," he nodded, raising his hand to her face, caressing her cheek with the backs of his fingers, running his thumb gently down her faded, striped chin. His hand was warm, his touch so gentle. She placed her hand over his, wanting it to stay there forever. Then she leaned in toward him, and they kissed. And that one kiss had turned into many. Slowly, their bodies had entwined and they'd shed their clothes, making love in the peaceful, yet heavy solitude that surrounded them in the empty house. And eventually, they'd fallen asleep in each other's arms.

The next day Richard was heading back to New York. He'd received clearance from Homeland Security to return to his apartment. He asked her to go with him, said he'd cleared it for her to leave as well if she wanted. She didn't hesitate. She packed her things and went. She couldn't stay in the house any longer, couldn't look at the pictures of her dead family, couldn't stare at the house of the dead Chalmers, and Richard didn't want her to.

She felt safe in her new surroundings, lying in Richard's arms every night; helping each other through the nightmares. How quickly their lives had changed. The events surrounding them had been horrible, but they'd found something in each other; a light that protected them from the darkness Victoryville had cast. Of course, Victoryville was never far from her thoughts. She knew she'd have to return one day, at the very least to pack and sell the house, but there was still a small part of her that hoped her family would one day return. That they weren't dead.

Abbie, pulling herself from her reverie, turned to peruse the spices on the supermarket shelves. She traced her fingers along the labels, seeking out the rosemary. In her periphery, she noticed a stranger staring. She turned and saw a woman in her early fifties, dark-haired with sprinkles of silver, and lines around the eyes that did not laugh. Abbie gave the woman a smile and a nod hello, but the woman did not smile back. Instead she saw the woman's stare fall to the faint stripe running down her chin and neck. A Striped One was an extremely rare sight indeed, here in New York. She saw repulsion in the woman's eyes.

Abbie dropped her smile, but didn't turn away. Instead, she stared back, as though challenging that repulsion. The woman knew who she was, knew she was that Abbie Randell who had been on the cover of papers and magazines, the one that had done those interviews on TV. The one from Victoryville. But despite all of Abbie's actions, that's not what this woman saw when she looked at her. She saw a Striped One. Someone from the Victoryville SZ. The town where the people lost control and turned into barbarians. It didn't matter that Abbie had tried to stop the violence. All this woman saw was the stripe upon her skin.

"Hey, honey!" Richard said loudly, grabbing her and planting a long, deep kiss on her mouth. He rested his forehead on hers, smiling at her as he cupped her face and caressed her faded stripe. She smiled back, then glanced over at the woman again, who was now eyeing Richard with contempt and examining his Clean Skin chin.

"Lovely evening, isn't it?" Richard beamed at the woman.

The woman scowled and brushed past them, muttering, "You ought to be ashamed."

Abbie's body tensed, but Richard soothed her, running his hands up and down her arms.

"She's not worth it," he whispered.

"They haven't learned a thing, have they?" Abbie said, shaking her head.

"No. Not everyone," Richard agreed, then kissed her forehead. "That's why we need to finish this book."

She relaxed at the sight of his calming eyes. He smiled again, leaning down to plant a kiss on her striped chin. Then he took her hand and they walked toward the store's checkout.

They began to place their items on the counter as a voice behind them cried out.

"Oh my God!"

They turned around and saw the operator at the next register, her hand covering her mouth, looking up at a TV mounted on the wall.

"It's happening again!" she cried. "Oh my God!"

There, on the TV, was a massive black spaceship hovering over a town. Abbie scanned for the Victoryville clock tower, but couldn't see it. This was somewhere else.

Another town.

She and Richard exchanged an anxious glance, as her heart started thumping overtime.

His cell phone suddenly rang, making them jump with fright.

He glanced down at his pocket cautiously, then pulled it out and answered it.

"Richard Keene," he said tentatively. A moment of silence passed before he glanced back to the TV on the wall. "Yeah, I see it . . ." He turned his eyes back to Abbie's. "Yes, she's here with me . . . What, now? Right now? . . . Can I ask why? . . . Okay." Richard ended the call and looked back at her. "That was Homeland Security. They're sending someone to pick us up."

"Us?" she asked. "Why?"

"Apparently we're experts on the phenomenon and they want our advice."

Abbie stared at him open-mouthed.

"Either that," he said, his voice laced with trepidation, "or they want to keep a close eye on us now they're back." He motioned to the TV screen and the image of the hovering spaceship.

Abbie swallowed hard.

"Come on. We gotta go," he said, taking her hand and leading her out of the store.

Acknowledgments

A big thank you to everyone who has supported me on my writing journey so far. Having launched six Aurora books at the time of this release, I appreciate my Aurora fans allowing me this indulgence to try something new. As much as I love writing the Aurora series, it's always been important to me to prove I am not a one trick pony. Also, at some point the Aurora series will end, so I'm keen to introduce readers to new work before they must say goodbye to Carrie and Harris. It's all part of my long term strategy!

Thank you to my first round beta readers, Joan, Tia, Todd and Ross—you poor things always read the roughest version of my books, but your comments help shape it. And thanks to my second round beta readers, Dave and Justin—the version you read was slightly less shabby, but still in need of some sculpting. Thanks for your feedback!

Self publishing is a lonely business sometimes, but it's made that more bearable by the one constant I've had through all my books, my editor Stephanie Smith. We've done seven books together now! Thanks for understanding what I'm trying to say in my sometimes clunky sentences! Your title really should be editor and interpreter.

Thanks to the special readers who have become part of my early review team: Carol, Shelley, Liz, and Elizabeth. I really appreciate your support and enthusiasm for my work.

To my family and friends, I pretty much say this every book, but I'll say it again: thanks for your patience and understanding, and accepting that you may not get to see me as much as you'd like to. Maybe one day I can ditch the full-time day job and be a full-time writer, eh? One can dream.

Thanks to my writer friends, namely the GMob (Amanda Pillar, Nathan M Farrugia, Steve P Vincent, Luke Preston, Dave Sinclair and Justin Woolley), for all the support and advice—and the occasional boozy nights we spend together when we're all in the same state.

Lastly, to readers of **The Time of The Stripes**, I really hope you've enjoyed this book, and if you did, I'd really appreciate it if you could leave a rating or review on the retailer site where you purchased this book and any other book review sites. It means the world and really helps to spread the word about my books.

Thanks again!

Stay up-to-date with Amanda's new releases and other book news, sign up to her newsletter:

www.amandabridgeman.com.au/signup/

www.ingramcontent.com/pod-product-compliance
Lightning Source LLC
Chambersburg PA
CBHW051209120726
47905CB00004B/1039